JUST DON'T CALL IT Love

ERIN NICHOLAS

ABOUT THE BOOK

I used to play hockey in sold-out arenas. Now my wrecked knee and I are stuck in a little bayou town that's been mad at me for a year. I need a big comeback–and ZERO drama.

So first thing, I get tackled at the airport by a sunshiny woman in yellow overalls who's thwarting my kidnapping... by her grandpas.

That's Nora Delaune—Parks & Rec director, caffeine-powered menace, and the only person in Rebel willing to give me a chance. She needs me to win games and help save the town's ice arena before it gets turned into a laser-tag nightmare.

And I... kind of like being needed by her. Even when she's producing a singing, dancing, wig-wearing ice extravaganza that is definitely not hockey.

Then my sister—the team's new owner—drops the bomb: if Nora and I "date," the town might stop hating me.
Fine. We'll fake it. As long as we don't call it love.

But between late-night practices, the sugar-addicted swamp-were-wolf mascot, otter drama, and the way Nora looks at me like I'm worth rooting for…I'm in trouble.

I came to Rebel to rebuild my career.
I just didn't expect to lose my heart doing it.

Just Don't Call It Love is a hot, hilarious, full-of-hijinks small town rom com with grumpy-sunshine, fake dating, found family energy that will make you want to buy season tickets to the wackiest hockey league ever!

To all the readers who love hockey romance…
I'm not even sorry.

"CONTENT WARNING"

Here's what you can expect from Just Don't Call It Love besides a hilarious, hockey romance full of small-town hijinks, found family fun, and a professional hockey player who is in over his head with a chaotic sunshine Parks and Rec director!

• Steamy, on-page, open-door sex scenes.
• Graphic language.
• An over-the-top story about a not-at-all-professional hockey league. Trust me, we're not taking ourselves too seriously here.
• "Bonkers Hockey" which is the product of this author's imagination with the help of some very fun expert hockey romance readers. It is absolutely untested in real life and should not be played without supervision! Possibly not even then! lol!

If any of that is something you do not want to read, close the book now and return it. No worries.

If you keep reading, I hope you love Alex and Nora's story and the time you spend in Rebel, Louisiana! Welcome to the chaos!
xo
Erin

CHAPTER 1
ALEX

HI, *Alex. Welcome to Louisiana!!!!! I don't know if you've landed yet, but do NOT get in the truck with those men claiming they're there to pick you up!!!!!!!!!!!!!*

I frown and read the message again.

I don't recognize the number, and if the message didn't start with my name, I would assume this text had been sent to the wrong number.

The plane is still taxiing to the gate, so I text my sister, letting her know I've landed, and she responds with *I've sent someone to pick you up.*

Okay, good, I'm fine.

But there might be guys in a truck trying to pick me up?

What the hell?

Once at the gate, I stand and grab my carry-on from the overhead bin and join the crowd exiting the plane.

My phone dings again.

I stop and look at the message.

They look like really nice old men, I know, but you can't trust them!!!!!!!!!!!!!

"Asshole," the guy behind me mutters as he has to step around me quickly.

"Sorry," I mumble and move to the side.

That puts me in the way of more people. I get hit in the calf by a roller bag and hear a muttered, "For fuck's sake."

I sigh. It's my first time, and I already hate flying commercial.

I always fly on chartered flights with my teammates or on private planes with family and friends, and yes, it's absolutely as nice as everyone who doesn't fly that way assumes.

But suddenly stopping while walking through an airport was asking to get plowed into. My six-three, two-hundred-and-ten-pound frame saves me from being knocked over. The average person running into me isn't going to move me. But I definitely take up space and can cause traffic flow issues.

I look around, then dodge a small pack of young women to escape to the edge of the wave of people moving through Concourse C of the Louis Armstrong New Orleans International Airport.

I frown and read the message again. I haven't seen that many exclamation marks in a text message since…ever.

Another text comes in from the unknown number. *Are you off the plane yet? Have you been to baggage claim??????*

That's also a lot of question marks.

And it reminds me I have to go pick up my bags. I've never done that.

I showed up at security this morning with my suitcase in tow and had to go back down to check it in, feeling like a dumbass. Now I'm going to have to go get it myself?

I can't believe my sister bought an entire hockey team, but she wasn't willing to fly me from Oregon to Louisiana on her husband's private plane.

I send her another quick message: *Who's picking me up?*

I start walking again, following the signs to baggage claim.

I drive my Aston Martin Roadster around Portland and out to the coast, but when Astrid said she'd send someone to take me from New Orleans to Rebel, the little dot along the bayou I'll call home for the next seven months, I agreed. I don't need to get lost in Nowhere, Louisiana.

Astrid: *His name's Leo.*

Leo. He sounds nice and normal. And there are no exclamation marks after her answer. That's good.

Astrid knows that my entire life is organized and arranged for me, from my diet to my schedule to what I wear out in public. Sure, I occasionally go out without wearing clothing from one of the brands I promote, but it's rare. And even then, I tend to wear stuff that looks like the outfits my stylist puts together for me.

Like today. I don't expect to be photographed, since no one in the sports media knows I'm here, so I dressed myself in the dark gray pants, the thick white t-shirt, white tennis shoes, and a casual gray blazer. I got some appreciative looks in the airport, so I figured I did okay.

I'm twenty-six years old and pretty much every part of my life is mapped out for me by someone else. All I have to do is concentrate on the thing my family, my *country*, has wanted from me from the time I was old enough to ice skate: playing excellent hockey.

I definitely don't like having to keep track of boarding passes and checking in my suitcase.

And yes, my personal assistant packed that suitcase for me.

Unknown number: *god, I hope you're getting these messages and aren't already in the truck!!!! Don't believe whatever they tell you!!!!*

Who is this person texting me? Who are these men? Is this person actually insinuating that I'm going to be kidnapped or something? What the hell is going on in Louisiana?

And here I am using a lot of fucking question marks too.

I get to the escalator that will take me down to the lower level, where I can already see what seems like a million people milling about, going in and out of the doors, pulling and pushing mountains of luggage. Through the large glass windows and doors, I can see lane after lane of traffic outside. Cars, taxis, trucks, vans, buses.

There is absolutely no discernible organization to what's going on. Is this how all airports are? This is an unhinged way to have millions of people traveling every day.

I scan the area below as I descend. There's a jazz band playing in the center of the large "lobby" area, and there are hundreds of people with thousands of suitcases and bags. Still, I see the three men, all wearing Portland Grays hockey jerseys, holding the WELCOME ALEX OLSEN sign immediately.

All of the exclamation marks in the texts truly had me expecting something else.

These men are easily in their seventies. They've all got gray or white hair. Well, the one wearing the bowler hat could be bald, I suppose, but these men are not going to be able to overpower me. I'm a professional athlete, for fuck's sake.

You *were* *a professional athlete. Now you're an ex-professional athlete with a fucked-up knee.*

Fine. I'm not in the best shape of my life at the moment, but I *was* a professional athlete, and I've been working on my damned knee. I'm still stronger than these three men, surely.

Unless they have chloroform or a taser or…

I look around, then drop my head and crouch slightly behind the man on the escalator in front of me. The minute we hit the bottom, I glance in their direction. They are absorbed in their own conversation and are not looking this way, so I quickly hang a left and duck behind the wall.

I text my sister again. *What does Leo look like?*

I glance to my right and see a huge silver carousel begin turning with suitcases on it. The nearest crowd of people rushes forward until they're standing right next to the circulating platform. People behind them have to push past to get their luggage and then pull the bags off without taking anyone's legs out. Some are more careful about that than others.

Is this where my bags will be? There are several carousels. How do people know where to go? Then I spot the woman who sat across the aisle from me. She's standing near the carousel next to the one that just started up. I decide to keep an eye on her even as I press back against the wall to allow people to pass, tugging their wheeled bags and carts loaded with suitcases.

I can't believe this is how people travel regularly.

Yes, of course, I realize that I lead a very privileged life.

I also realize that I am not prepared for the disorder of normal life and that this move to small-town Louisiana is going to be a tough adaptation.

At least I'll still have hockey. That will be the one constant that I can lean on. And, fortunately, it's absolutely *not* professional-level hockey. The team my sister bought is an FPHL team. It's barely a step above a beer league. I'll be in small-town-Louisiana hockey shape within two weeks.

My phone dings with another text, and I glance down to see the unknown number has upgraded to all caps along with the multitude of punctuation marks.

ARE YOU HERE???????

I sneak a peek around the corner at the three old men who are still waiting for me.

The one on the far left has short white hair. His beard is also white and hangs to the middle of his chest. He's lean and muscular, but he's only about five-eight or five-nine. He's got the sleeves of the jersey pushed up, and I can see tattoos on both forearms. His skin is tanned as if he spends all of his time outdoors. He's also wearing jeans and scuffed black boots. That guy wrestles alligators, I'd bet money on it.

The man right next to him, the one wearing the bowler hat, is a couple of inches taller and clean-shaven. He's got small, round glasses on, and he's wearing fitted black pants and black dress shoes. He's also got a cane in one hand, but he's got it propped like it's an accessory more than an actual walking aid. I'd even use the word 'dapper' to describe him, despite the jersey.

The third is the shortest and stockiest. He's got cropped gray hair and a bushy gray-and-white mustache. He's also wearing bright green cargo shorts and green boat shoes. The green doesn't exactly clash with the gray and black hockey jersey—everything goes with black and gray, right?—but wow, that green is hard to miss.

I don't think they're texting me. They appear to be arguing about something and not paying any attention to anyone else, which is fortunate for me.

I'm probably fifty years younger than they are. Surely, I can outrun them if they notice me, right?

I need to find the car Astrid sent for me.

And I need my bags.

I look around. Does someone need to check me out? Do I have to at least prove the bags I'm taking are mine? What keeps people from just walking off with any old bag? This is ridiculously hectic.

The carousel with my flight number above it gives a jerk, then a groan, then starts turning. I step in that direction, but suddenly I see a flash of yellow and hear, "Alex! Baby!"

Then a woman is launching herself at me.

So, of course, I catch her.

CHAPTER 2
NORA

WOW, he just caught me. With one arm. He just scooped it right under my ass while still holding onto the duffel bag he has over his other shoulder.

I mean, I'm glad he did. If he hadn't, I would've bounced off his broad, hard chest, and that would've been embarrassing.

Still, this whole move was poorly thought out by me, so I'm very glad Alex Olsen has impeccable athletic reflexes.

Plus, damn, he smells good.

Keeping up with my I'm-here-to-greet-my-boyfriend ruse, I press my cheek to his. "You have to come with me. They're going to take you to a cabin on the bayou and leave you there," I say near his ear.

He rears back and stares at me. "Who are?"

"The guys waiting around the corner with the big sign."

His expression goes from alarmed to *oh, you're nuts.*

He lets me go, and I slide down his body. I'm five-seven so it's not too far before my feet touch the floor, but it's a nice few inches of contact, I'm not gonna lie.

"I take it you're the one who's been texting me?"

"Yes! You got my messages? I was sure I typed in the wrong

number!" Then I think about that. I plant my hands on my hips. "Why didn't you answer me?"

"Because I don't know you. Or your number."

His gaze sweeps over me from head to toe. Then back up again. Hmmm. Tingles. I like that. That's weird. I don't usually like being ogled.

But...am I being ogled? Or is he checking for weapons? Because now I'm very aware that I'm in yellow overalls, my flower-covered Converse tennis shoes, and...my hands fly up and pull the floppy pink straw hat with the big yellow flower on the front off my head.

I didn't have time to go home and change between the text from Andi saying *L, B and W picking up *hockey stick emoji* taking him to the cabin* and me jumping in my truck and driving like a bat out of hell to get here.

I glance down and see the glob of dried mud on the brim of my hat. I look further down. Yep, there are streaks of mud on my overalls and the bare skin of my shins between the hem of the capri length pants and the tops of my shoes.

I know better than to step between Patty and Muriel when they're fighting, but I'm not the only one who left Garden Club with mud-fight remnants on them today.

So maybe he's not ogling me. Maybe that look is *what the hell is going on with this woman*?

"Who *are* you?" Alex asks when his eyes are back on mine.

I give him a bright I-promise-I'm-not-going-to-kill-you smile. "I'm Nora. Delaune."

He stares at me blankly. He's got gorgeous brown eyes. Which I already knew. I've seen dozens of photos of this man. But he's even more devastatingly good-looking up close.

"Why did you jump on me?"

"I was calling your name, but you weren't paying attention and didn't hear me."

"It's crazy in here!" he exclaims, looking around.

He's not wrong.

"Yeah. And I was afraid to yell any louder or they would've heard." I incline my head toward where Leo, Wilson, and Brewser are holding a huge sign that says WELCOME ALEX OLSEN. I'm ninety-nine percent sure they stole poster board and markers from me to make that sign. "I wanted to get your attention without them noticing."

"So you decided to jump on me?"

It was spontaneous, I'll admit. But the situation seemed to call for more than just walking up and sticking my hand out for a handshake. And I couldn't risk him doing something like running in the other direction, thinking I'm a crazy stalker fan.

Oh, I know *all* of his stats and am *thrilled* he's here, but not like *that*.

I don't want to tie him up in my basement and turn him into my sex slave.

Well, the *teeny tiny* part of my primitive brain may want the sex slave thing a little bit. But that's just because the man is gorgeous. He just exudes that *something* that makes women want to get closer to him. It's nature. Instinct. Survival of the species. Our species should definitely want more Alex Olsens in it. It's not my fault.

And yeah, it's been a while—a long while—since I did anything with anyone that was even remotely sex slavish…

No. That's not why I need Alex Olsen to get his fine ass in my truck and let me drive him to my tiny hometown.

He's here to save my town and get Harley re-elected as mayor.

And I don't need Leo, Brewser, and Wilson scaring him off before he's even out of the airport.

I smile. "We're in an airport. People are jumping into each other's arms everywhere. It helped us blend in."

He sighs. "This has to be the most chaotic place I've ever been."

It's an airport. Airports are probably in the top three most chaotic places anyone has ever been.

Out of the corner of my eye, I see a flash of neon green. I grab the front of Alex's shirt and pull him around the corner of the escalator.

It might *not* have been Brewser, but it also might have been.

"What the hell?" Alex asks as I push him up against the wall.

I think the element of surprise was the only reason I was able to move the guy. He's really big. Solid. Big hands…

I shake my head. "I can't let them see you. They'll make a big commotion."

He looks around again. "How would you be able to tell?"

I grin. He has no idea. "I'm here to give you a ride to Rebel. We just need to avoid them until we can get to town and get you settled. And make sure other people actually see you there. That way, if you disappear, lots of people will notice, and we can start searching for you right away."

He looks properly horrified. "Who are *they*?" he asks, flinging his arm in the general direction of the three men who are in *so* much trouble later.

"I'll tell you in the truck," I say. I glance toward the baggage carousel. "Grab your bag."

"You realize that getting into a truck with *you* also seems like a bad idea. I don't know you. You could just be a stalker fan. Especially with the way you jumped on me."

I tip my head. "You're *mad* about that? Okay, sorry. You're right. That was probably too much."

"I didn't say I was mad about it," he says. His gaze sweeps over me again. "It's just kind of stalker-fan-like."

I nod. "Good point."

Suddenly, he grumbles something that sounds like, "Jesus Christ," and steps around me. He heads to the baggage claim carousel, where there's now only one bag circulating. He pulls the big black garment bag up and hefts it over his shoulder.

Did he bring *suits*?

I know a bunch of his personal belongings were delivered earlier this week and are already at the apartment we've set up for him. Still this bag is surprisingly huge and unless he hangs jeans and t-shirts, he's got slacks and jackets in there.

Wow, Alex really doesn't understand small-town Louisiana.

He strides back toward me quickly.

"Okay, so—"

All of a sudden, he drops the bag and wraps a big arm around my waist, hauls me up against his body, my feet off the floor, and seals his mouth over mine.

Shocked isn't even the right word.

I have no idea what's happening.

Except that Alex Olson doesn't just look good and smell good, he tastes damned good too.

He had to have been chewing gum or something. Or do hockey gods just automatically taste like spearmint?

Doesn't matter. When he tips his head and relaxes his mouth against mine, slightly opening his lips, I do the same. Then his tongue strokes over my bottom lip and I think I sigh. Because at that point his tongue slips in along mine, and the tingles from earlier are a thousand times stronger as they race from my scalp all the way down my body to my toes.

But just as abruptly, he pulls his head back and stares at me.

I stare back. I don't know what to say. My first instinct is to start kissing him again.

He takes a deep breath and then puts me down.

"So. People in Louisiana *are* very friendly, but that's not generally how we greet strangers here," I say, smoothing down the front of my overalls. And not commenting on the dirt streak he now has on his white t-shirt.

He glances to his left. "I saw the guy in the hat come around the corner. I figured this was a good way to hide both of our faces. If he's going to recognize me, I assume he will definitely recognize you."

I take note of the fact that we are now standing with my back against the wall, and Alex's back to the rest of the airport. He is blocking me from anyone else's view, and no, I don't think anyone would be able to tell who either one of us is.

I peek around his very broad shoulder.

I see Wilson's back, yes, including one of his usual hats. He's facing away from us scanning the area.

I blow out a little breath. "Good thinking."

Alex hasn't moved back away from me, and I have to tip my head back to see his eyes.

"I guess we should just stay here until the coast is clear," he says.

No complaints from me.

"You swear you're not a crazy stalker?"

"I can prove it."

"Go," he says simply.

"I can tell you something that proves I'm here to save you from them rather than just some random fan."

He tucks his hands in his pockets. "Go," he says again.

"Do you remember the last time you were here in New Orleans? When you played the Jazz?"

"Of course. Worst night of my life. Career-ending knee injury."

I wince slightly. Yes. I'm aware of that injury. Now. We weren't that night, of course. We saw him get hit and go down and knew that he didn't return to the game. But the Grays were tight-lipped about what happened to him for three weeks afterward.

"Do you remember that you were supposed to do a meet-and-greet afterwards? With a guy who'd had a stroke? The guy was a huge fan of yours, and his friends used meeting you as an incentive for him to work hard in rehab on his rough days. His physical therapist also incorporated hockey drills into his exercise program."

Alex's brow furrows, and I find myself scanning from his thick brows, over his ridiculously long eyelashes, down his not-quite-straight nose to those lips. Damn, I really like his lips.

"Yeah, his physical therapist knew the trainer for the Jazz who knew our trainer," he says. "I remember all of that."

"Do you also remember blowing him off?"

His eyes narrow. "I remember getting really hurt and not being able to do it."

"Do you remember a little girl running up to you in the parking lot on your way from the locker room to the bus afterward and begging you to take five minutes to talk to her great-grandfather?"

I can see in his eyes that he does remember Ruth.

"Yeah."

"Do you remember telling her, 'just leave me the fuck alone, kid, it's been a long night'?"

He sighs and his eyes slide for a moment, but then he nods and opens them again. "It was not my best night."

"For her, either. You were her hero. You broke her heart. Also, her great-grandfather was that stroke survivor. You massively disappointed him. She came back and told everybody about it, and his three best friends hate you for it." I gesture in the general direction where Wilson was standing, but has now moved off, clearly searching the wider area for Alex.

"Wow," Alex says, blowing out a breath. "You 'friendly' people down here in Louisiana really know how to hold a grudge, huh?"

"We're very loyal. And a little unreasonable at times."

I noticed how his gaze goes to my mouth as well, and the tingles start up all over again.

I clear my throat. "Anyway, let's get you to Rebel. You have practice tonight, and I assume you want to see your apartment, check in with your sister, stuff like that."

"My sister is sending someone to pick me up."

"Yeah, those are the guys she sent."

"Why would my sister send guys who want to take me to a cabin and leave me there?"

"Because your sister thinks they're sweet and doesn't realize how mad they are at you. Or that Leo has a cabin on the bayou that you can only get to by boat."

Now he looks truly concerned. "Let me guess—it's surrounded by alligators?"

"There are definitely alligators out there," I confirm.

"But they would eventually come back for me?"

I laugh. "*Someone* would come for you. But that's not the first impression I want you to have of Rebel and its people. We need you. This hockey team means a lot to…all of us." I hate the way I stumble over *all of us*.

So fine, it's not the *entire* town that's excited about the team. And there are a few players who haven't fully bought in. But Alex is going to change all of that. He is a star. One of the best centers to ever play the game, he absolutely has the talent, but on top of that, he has the charm and that special something that makes people love him.

Even the little town that started a petition to ban him from the city limits when they found out he was coming to play for our hockey team. They can't control who Astrid puts on the team, but they figured if they could make it illegal for him to be anywhere in town other than the hockey arena, they wouldn't have to be around him or be nice to him.

Harley, the current Mayor, wouldn't acknowledge the petition. Even though it was on his behalf.

But that didn't help his re-election chances.

I decide not to tell Alex about the Keep Alex Olsen Out of Rebel petition.

CHAPTER 3
NORA

"OKAY," Alex says. "Take me to Rebel."

He sounds more resigned than excited, but at least he's willing to get in my truck. That's definitely the first step.

But I want him to *want* to come to Rebel. I know that might be pushing it. He was a professional hockey player for the best team in the league for the past two seasons. He was a huge part of that success until his knee injury. He was making millions. He had a great life in Portland. I've seen the interviews and read the articles.

He's downgrading to come to Louisiana.

Except, now he's going to be a part of something new and fun and *meaningful*. He's going to be a freaking hero in Rebel.

Eventually.

I have to hope that matters to him.

I look around quickly as we make our way toward the doors leading out to the parking garage. First things first—I need to keep him away from Leo, Brewser, and Wilson.

Those three men are like grandfathers to me, I would do almost anything for any of them, and they can be absolute menaces if anyone messes with someone they love.

I need to come up with a way to keep them from hazing Alex every day he's in Rebel.

I need him to *happily* live in Rebel and play hockey for our new hockey team with his whole heart. I need him to make our new league a huge success.

"We need to go upstairs and then across to the parking garage," I tell Alex. "We'll just—" My foot hits the escalator at the same time I hear someone shout.

"Alex Olsen!"

Dammit! That's Leo's voice.

"Nora? Is that you?" I hear Brewser call.

I look back and make eye contact with Brewser. They're about twenty yards away from the base of the escalator.

"Nora!" he calls.

"Nora, what are you doing?" Wilson yells.

"Crap!" I look up at Alex. "Come on!" I start walking up the escalator.

I feel Alex right behind me.

But Leo's shout has drawn the attention of more people. Alex isn't just some guy. He's a famous hockey player. Ice in Louisiana is a very rare occurrence, but there are still plenty of hockey fans here.

"Alex Olsen?"

"Is that Alex Olsen?"

"Hey! That's Alex Olsen!"

People on the escalator around us are turning. People on the descending escalator beside ours also turn to get a look. A few pull their phones out. Dammit.

"Excuse me," I say to the man on the step in front of us.

"Are you really Alex Olsen?" he asks, not moving.

"No," Alex says brusquely. "Excuse us."

"Why'd that guy say you are?"

"I look a little like him," Alex says.

He puts a big hand on my hip, still holding a duffel on his shoulder and the garment bag in his hand. He moves me slightly to the side and moves onto the step beside me, his big body pressed against mine. "*Excuse* us," he says to the man, now a few inches taller than the man who is still a step above him.

"You *are* Alex Olsen!" the man says now that Alex is closer. "What are you doing here?"

Alex sighs and puts a shoulder into the man's upper back, then with a hand on the man's shoulder, turns him so the guy is facing the side of the escalator.

"Hey!" the man protests.

"Excuse us," Alex says as he nudges me past the man, then gives the guy more pressure into the escalator railing as he passes.

"Jerk!" the guy says as Alex lets him go.

"Hey, you can tell your buddies that you scuffled with a hockey player and aren't even bruised from it," Alex says as he steps off the escalator behind me.

The man's eyes widen. "So you *are* Alex Olsen."

"Yeah."

The guy smiles, and everything seems forgiven. Especially when he lifts his phone and snaps a photo.

Alex sighs and turns to me. "How do I look?"

I frown. "What?"

"I dressed myself. I didn't think there'd be photos today. Will Lenny be mad?"

"Who's Lenny?"

"My assistant. Lenore."

"You look…" I sweep my gaze over him. Again, I ignore the dirt streak on the front of his shirt. He's fucking gorgeous. He has a big, hot, climbable body. And I both wish he'd never kissed me and really wish he would again. "Great."

He nods. "Okay. Good."

I shake my head. "Come on." I jog toward the walkway that leads to the short-term parking area.

He, of course, easily keeps up with me, even carrying his bags.

"Red truck," I say, pointing as we run into the parking garage.

I dash around the back of my truck to the driver's side. "Throw your bag on top of that wooden crate, would you?"

"Are those flowers?" he asks as he tosses the bag into the truck bed.

"Yeah. And I lost a bunch on the drive up here." The flowers had blown out of the back as I'd driven well over the speed limit and prayed for no cops.

"Alex! Nora!" Brewser yells from the doorway to the airport.

Damn, he moves fast for a guy his age. Especially one who's had two knee replacements and who's been brewing his own beer since he was fourteen.

"Get in!" I tell Alex. Then I glance over to see Leo and Wilson join Brewser. "I'm telling Bruce and Ellie on you! And you're cut off from my banana pudding for a month!"

Brewer and Wilson's eyes widen with alarm.

"Now *cher*—" Leo starts.

Yeah, they're going to regret this. "I love you! See you at home!" I call, then slam my door

Brewser has his hands on his hips, frowning, but Wilson is just shaking his head, and Leo is laughing now.

I start the truck and pull out of the parking spot, heading in the opposite direction from where the men are standing. Three minutes later, I merge into the line of cars heading toward New Orleans and blow out a relieved breath.

I concentrate on traffic for several miles. I love New Orleans and visit regularly, but I absolutely prefer the lighter traffic and slower pace around my hometown.

Finally, we cross the bridge and turn toward Rebel. I relax in my seat, then glance over and realize Alex is watching me.

"You okay?" I ask him.

"What were you doing before you came to rescue me?" He looks over his shoulder at the truck bed.

"Gardening club. We were picking wildflowers we planted earlier this summer to use in art club next week."

"You're going to have a lot fewer to work with at art club."

I look in the rearview mirror. "Dammit!"

His suitcase is keeping the flowers in one of the wooden crates, but the other is still open on top, and the flowers are being picked up and scattered by the wind.

"You sacrificed both the gardening club and the art club for me?" Alex asks.

I glance at him again. "I did."

"I appreciate it."

"You sure?" It's not like he'd been *enthusiastic* about getting in my truck.

His gaze drops to my mouth. "Yeah. I'm sure."

Damn those tingles. I focus on the road. "I'm going to drop you off with Bruce at the apartment, but I need to find out if he knew about their plan."

"Who's Bruce?"

"One of my grandfathers."

"Is he mad about the meet-and-greet and everything, too?"

I look over. "Yeah. Definitely."

Alex winces. "I feel bad about it. I don't really remember much about it, to be honest. I was in a lot of pain, the doc gave me some meds. I was pissed and worried and..." He sighs and shoves a hand through his thick, wavy dark hair. "Just not at my best."

I nod. "I know. But Harley only expected five minutes of your time. You're coming to a town where everyone is pretty generous and shows up for one another and just doesn't let their own shit get in the way."

Alex shifts on the seat, turning toward me more fully. "That night ruined my career. I only played four games this entire past season. And I didn't get my contract renewed. That's pretty bad, trust me."

I look away from the highway to meet his eyes. "Harley had a *stroke*, Alex. His impairments are permanent. He'll *never* get back to one hundred percent. And there's now a guy who's planning to take his job away from him because of it. You can at least still play hockey even if it's not at the pro level."

Alex is quiet for a long moment, then he says, "What's his job?"

"He's the mayor of our town." My heart squeezes. Harley has been a leader in our community his entire adult life. Nothing means more to him than taking care of our town and the people in it. "And now Sean Patrick, the I'm-too-good-for-this-little-hick-town asshole who couldn't wait to get away from Rebel back when he was eighteen, has moved home and is running against Harley for mayor. Worse, he's using Harley's stroke as a reason he's no longer qualified to hold the position."

Alex groans. "The guy I snubbed with the meet-and-greet is the *mayor* of the town I'm moving to?"

"Yep."

"Let me guess, he's totally adored? He's been the mayor for like ten years, and everyone thinks he's amazing? It's not just those three guys who are protective of him, right?"

I nod. "Right. Except he's been Mayor for twenty-two years."

Alex groans and tips his head back. "Of course, I fucking dissed the *beloved* mayor of the town I'm moving to."

When he puts it that way…yeah, he should be a little worried.

I'm a little worried.

"You'll be able to win them back over when you make the new team huge," I tell him with a big smile that's only half-forced.

"So, no pressure?" he says dryly.

I shrug. "You're a big shot professional player. This will be a piece of cake, don't you think?"

He sighs and sags into the seat. "I hope so."

"It *has to be*," I tell him, with more intensity than I intended. I take a breath. "This has to go well. We have to make this team the best thing that has ever happened in Rebel."

I look over to find him frowning at me.

"Seriously? That's…a lot," he says. "This is *minor* minor league hockey. Everyone gets that, right?"

I shrug. "That doesn't matter. If this season doesn't go well, people are going to question whether Harley can make good decisions for the town anymore. Sean Patrick is going to win the mayoral election, and he's going to buy the arena and turn it into an indoor fun zone."

"What's an indoor fun zone?"

I roll my eyes. "Like a climbing wall, mini golf, arcade, laser tag."

"That does sound fun."

I gasp and look at him quickly, making the truck swerve slightly. "Take that back!"

Alex holds up his hands as if surrendering. "You don't like laser tag?"

"Not instead of ice hockey and ice skating! We have a paint-ball park and *outdoor* mini golf, and arcades are dark, and people play the games by themselves on machines. We want people outside, and out in the community, and spending time *together*."

He doesn't say anything.

I glance over. "What?"

"What do you do for a living?"

"I'm the director of Parks and Rec for the town."

"Ah."

I arch a brow. "Ah?"

"You don't want Sean Patrick to encroach on what you do."

"Of course I don't! He's a pompous ass who didn't care about Rebel until he went off to the big city and realized that he could only be important in a *small* town. He's back, so he can pretend he's big shit. He's running for mayor against my grandfather now only because of the stroke and the hockey team leaving. Before this he never would have had a chance!"

"Wait, Harley, the beloved mayor is your *grandfather*?"

"Yes."

He's staring at me when I look at him again.

"Why aren't *you* mad at me for how I treated him in October?"

"I am," I say honestly. "But I need you. I need this hockey team to be successful, and you're going to be a huge part of that."

"Why is this hockey team such a big thing? Rebel really has *nothing else* going on?"

"We have a lot going on!" I protest. "We have gardening club, and art club, and walking club, and otter club, and—"

"Otter club? Like the animal?"

"Yes."

"Come on."

"*Otter club*," I emphasize. "And movie nights, and picnics, and festivals, and holiday celebrations, and camps for the kids. We have a *ton* going on." It's my entire job to be sure things are going on.

Do I go overboard sometimes? Maybe. Do I take my job *very* seriously? Absolutely. I love my hometown and I will always do whatever I can to make it a fun, inclusive, happy place. So do we have the best Parks and Rec department and programs in the entire state? Damn right.

"But hockey is super important?" Alex asks.

"Well, yeah. Surely *you* understand that." I'm chewing on my bottom lip again.

"I think hockey is the only important thing in the entire world," he admits. "But I'm biased, and my worldview is very narrow."

I look over. That was surprisingly self-deprecating.

"But I think there's more to it for you and your town," he says.

I blow out a breath. I'll tell him whatever he needs to know to get him on board. "Fine. Harley got C.W. to build the arena and was the one who got the team to come to town and…it's his first and only failure." I feel my throat tighten. "I know that sounds hyperbolic, but it's true. Harley has always done right by the town, and for this to be a failure, on top of his stroke, and losing the election…it would just be too much."

Alex is quiet for several seconds. "Who's C.W.?"

"He was Harley's son, my uncle. He passed away a few years ago. He went off and got rich and then came back and spent the money on Rebel. He owned like half the town. He left it all to my cousin, Dane. But Dane doesn't want to own half the town, and if someone would like to buy some—or all—of the properties, Dane would be thrilled." I look at Alex again. "We *have* to make this hockey team work. We need hockey and that ice arena to stay. We need the team to be a success. And Harley needs to win the election."

"Because you love Harley or because you hate Sean Patrick?"

I meet his gaze directly. "Because of the town. They need Harley." I pause, then add, "Making Sean Patrick's return home a dismal failure would just be the sprinkles on top."

"Got it."

We drive past the Welcome to Rebel sign on the edge of town and head down Main Street. We pass the main intersection, and Alex pivots quickly in his seat.

"Is that a statue of an *otter*?"

"Yeah." The twenty-foot-tall stone otter on her back legs, front paws folded, a sweet almost-smile on her face, is impossible to miss. As intended.

Alex turns back to me. "Why?"

"Trust me, you'll hear the story eventually. But otters are…a thing…here."

"Oh." He clearly isn't sure how to respond.

That's fair.

Two minutes later, I pull up at the curb in front of Alex Olsen's new address.

"Welcome home," I say, shifting into park. "Your apartment is on the second floor."

He looks at the building. "*Perks* and Rec?

I smile. "My grandpa Bruce owns it. It's right next to City Hall, where the Parks and Rec department is, where my grandpa Harley worked for twenty-eight years."

"Bruce and Harley are friends?"

"The best. Then about thirty years ago, they realized they were also in love and got married."

Alex pauses, then nods. "Got it." He turns to face me. "I think I should tell you, I'm not staying."

I frown. "What do you mean?" He *has* to stay. He just *has to*.

"I'm here for the first season. That's it. After that, I'm going back to Portland to work for the Grays. That's the deal."

Oh. Well… My surprise gives way to disappointment, but that dissolves quickly as well. Of course, he's not staying.

Alex Olsen isn't a small-town guy. He's not a minor-league hockey player. He doesn't fit in here, and there's nothing really for him here. Not long-term.

Of course, he's going to leave.

"But you're here until April."

"Yes."

Okay. That's what I *really* need. "So we're on the same page."

"We are."

I stick out my hand. "Here's to the new season."

He takes my hand, his huge palm engulfing mine. His skin is hot, even more than the weather would account for. He doesn't shake my hand and withdraw. He just holds it.

I'm aware of his size, the roughness of his skin, the solidness of even this part of his body against mine.

Damn. I don't remember the last time a guy made my mouth dry by simply touching my hand. Has it *ever* happened?

"I'll do my best to deliver what you need, Nora," he says.

Is his voice husky? Or is that just *my* brain making that sound sexy?

I swallow and pull my hand away. "You have practice soon."

"Yeah, late. Are they just waiting for me to get here?"

"Practice is at six p.m. every day."

He frowns. "Why? It might be good—"

"Because it's after work," I insert.

He blinks at me.

I smile and explain. "The other guys on the team all have real jobs. Hockey here doesn't pay like it does for you. The hockey is on the side."

He frowns as if none of that computes.

I laugh. "A job is something people do to make money when they can't convince people to pay them millions of dollars to slap a puck around on the ice."

He chuckles and whoa. The sound rolls over me like a hot, delicious vibration that I want to go on and on.

"I've heard of 'jobs'", he says.

I swallow hard and try not to shift in my seat. "Are you aware that a lot of them happen during the day and are at least eight hours long at a time?"

He gives me a horrified, clearly sarcastic look. "*Every* day?"

"Sometimes," I nod. "Though most are five days a week. It does vary which days, though, and some of them, like Beckett, who own their own businesses, work every day."

"Jesus," he says, shaking his head. "Thank god I'm good at slapping a puck around on the ice."

I laugh. "Truly. That's going to be very good for us."

"What do I do all day until six?"

"Sleep in. Work out." I shrug. "Get to know the town. If you want to volunteer, we can definitely arrange something. If you'd like a job, we can do that too."

He frowns. "I don't need the money."

I roll my eyes. "I'm aware. But jobs are also things that actually help other people. Towns and cities, communities, need the businesses in them."

He doesn't respond to that. Just continues frowning at something in front of my truck.

"You don't have to," I say. "That's not a requirement."

"It's just..." He looks at me again. "I don't know how to *do* anything. Other than hockey."

"Oh." I hadn't thought of that. But Alex has been playing hockey all his life. He didn't go to college. He came to the US as an eighteen-year-old and immediately started playing for the Grays.

He blows out a breath and opens his door. He gets out and

grabs his bags from the back, then he pokes his head back in the truck. "See you later, right?"

"It's a small town. I'm sure we'll run into each other," I say flippantly.

"For sure. At the next otter club meeting, if not before."

He smiles, and a bubbly heat swirls through my stomach. I'd love for him to come to otter club. "You don't even know what we do at otter club."

"Do I get to hang out with otters?"

"Well…yes." Kind of.

"Real live ones?"

"Yes."

"Then I'll be there."

I shake my head. "But you're a Reveler. You can't be all cute and happy with the otters."

"Why not?"

"That's the mascot for the Rascals. Your arch rivals."

He seems puzzled, which makes sense. The Rascals are also a brand-new team. I'm going to let Astrid fill him in on all the details.

"What are Revelers then? Some other cute animal I can play with?"

I laugh. "Definitely not. Your mascot is a Rougarou."

"What the hell is a Rougarou?"

"It's a swamp werewolf," I tell him, watching his rich-city-boy face carefully. Alex might be a professional athlete who has traveled all over to play hockey, but I'm getting the impression he's been in a bit of a rich-famous-hot-guy bubble. "The bottom half is human, with the head and upper body of a wolf. There's a whole mythology around them. They hunt and eat naughty children."

Yep, he looks properly horrified.

"*That's* the mascot for a small-town hockey team that you hope families will come watch? Seriously?"

I grin. "*Our* Rougarou is Rougie, and he's really cute and fluffy. My friend Andi designed him. We've even had stuffies made. He wears a Mardi Gras mask and beads and throws candy and toys to the kids. And he only eats King Cake."

"That makes it better?" Alex asks.

"Sure. We're taking a scary old fairytale and making it fun and kind."

Alex shakes his head. "I'm definitely not in Portland anymore, am I?"

I laugh. "Not even close."

"Are you going to help me navigate this?"

"Of course." I smile. "I really want you to be successful here. Anything you need."

He looks relieved. Then his gaze turns a little…hotter. His eyes once again drop to my mouth before returning to mine. "I'm going to hold you to that."

Did that sound flirtatious? Probably not. I'm making things up. "Okay."

He steps back from the truck with a smile. "See you later, Wildflower."

"Wildflower?" I ask, feeling a swirly curl of heat in my stomach again.

He glances at the back of my truck, which is filled with wildflowers. They're flung all over the truck bed from the wind as we drove, and I'm sure the highway is littered with them.

"Yeah. Wildflower."

"Oh." He's given me a nickname. I feel my cheeks heat. I'm actually *blushing*.

Wow.

I need to be careful around Alex Olsen.

We're going to be spending time together, and we need to work as a team to make everything come together with the Revelers. But I can't develop a crush. He's not staying. And he won't fit in here at all.

I've learned, the hard way, to only date men who want to make Rebel their home. For good. Like grow old here and be buried in the pretty cemetery on the hill that overlooks the town.

I do not think Alex will think the cemetery is pretty. Or that growing old in Rebel is a good plan.

So, no crush. No flirting. No fling.

Alex is here for hockey, and that's it.

My gaze slides past Alex's wide shoulder as I see movement in the big front window of Perks and Rec. I roll my eyes, sigh, and shut off the truck.

There is a crowd watching us.

"You know what? I think I'll go in with you," I say, opening my door.

Leo, Brewser, and Wilson aren't back from New Orleans yet, but plenty of the people inside the coffee shop signed that damned petition.

CHAPTER 4
ALEX

NORA DELAUNE, with her big, round brown eyes that are the color of my favorite porter, and her bright smile that says even-a-chaotic-as-fuck-airport-is-fun, who looks absolutely perfect in sunshine yellow overalls, and who tastes like spearmint and happiness and lust, needs me.

For hockey.

Of course, she does.

That's what everyone needs me for. It's what I do.

Okay, there are a few other things I'm good at that women like and come to me for—and I'd be happy to demonstrate those to Nora as well—but I'm in Louisiana, walking toward the coffee shop in Rebel, with Nora because of hockey.

And I'm *really* fucking good at hockey, so it's fine.

But I feel a low hum of annoyance just beneath the much more obvious emotions of bewilderment—swamp werewolves and a town with a "thing" for otters?—and foreboding. I mean, there are still three men wandering around who want to tie me up in an alligator-infested cabin.

It doesn't make sense that I feel *irritated* that this sunny woman looks at me and sees a hockey player who is going to fix her town's and her family's problems. I should feel heroic. Or something. Helping Nora with this aligns with my goals here, too. Astrid and I both want this team to be successful.

"How many seats does the arena have?" Declan asked.

Astrid's eyes narrowed. "Five thousand."

"And how many tickets were they selling last year on average per game?"

"Just over two thousand."

"Do you think you can improve on that?" Declan asked.

"Of course I do."

"You sell out that arena by the end of the season, and I will give you a job with the Grays."

I blinked at him, realizing that he was talking to me. "Really? I help Astrid get this going, and I can come back and work for you?"

"If you go with your sister and help make her team wildly successful, then you can come back and work for me."

I looked at Astrid. Five thousand seats. That didn't seem difficult. The Grays arena holds over seventeen thousand, and we've been selling out every game for the past five years.

"I'm in."

I feel my neck tense remembering that conversation in Declan's office just over a month ago. It had seemed like a simple plan then. But now it's real. My future in hockey *depends* on the team here in Rebel being successful.

I can't be feeling restless and itchy because Nora doesn't want anything more than hockey from me.

That's stupid.

I just met her.

So what if Nora's beautiful and her ass fit perfectly in my hands when I held her in the airport, or that I could easily kiss her for days, and listen to her rant for hours against an indoor fun zone as if the man responsible is trying to open a brothel on her hometown's main street.

She's cute when she's all worked up and outraged.

She also smiles a lot, uses *a lot* of exclamation marks and capital letters in her texts, smells like wildflowers, and her literal *job* is making sure this town has fun.

And instead of just being glad I'm here and welcoming me to town, she's convinced I'm going to save the arena and her grandfather's entire damned legacy.

"Alex, we're not renewing your contract. I'm sorry."

"What are you talking about?"

"You're not back from your injury."

"I've been working my ass off! I'm at eighty-five percent!"

"And it's been nine months. I need one hundred percent, and I don't think you're going to get there."

I was cut from the only team I've ever played for. The only team I ever wanted to play for. And not just by the owner. Declan is my fucking *brother-in-law*. Not even being kind of related to the guy and my sister's resultant ire could save me.

So, can I be the savior Nora is looking for? Maybe. Probably. But I was feeling a lot better about this Louisiana move before I found out that this barely-a-hockey league actually mattered to someone.

And I'd really rather Nora Delaune just wanted me for more kissing.

Nora pauses at the front door to the café, and I stop behind her. I look from side to side, finally really taking in my surroundings.

The pathway bisects the outdoor sitting area. On the left side of the path are light brown wooden chairs covered in thick, puffy yellow, orange, and white cushions. Between and around the chairs are wooden planters filled with brightly colored flowers in yellow, orange, pink, and white. The area is shaded by tall striped umbrellas that match the cushions and flowers. The whole area is bright and cheery.

In contrast, the area on the right side of the path is covered in dark cobblestones, and the furniture is dark gray wood with midnight blue upholstery. The center feature is a fire pit, and I swear my body starts sweating even thinking about being near a fire in the hot and humid September air. Above the entire area, small white lights are strung from wooden posts. I'm sure they give a soft glow to the area at night.

It seems clear that the two sides of the path are supposed to be day and night. Interesting.

"This is…cute," I comment.

Nora grins, and I read the words painted on the door just before she pulls it open.

Perks and Rec. Perk up from six a.m. to five p.m. Recreate five p.m. to midnight.

A bell tinkles above us as we step into the air-conditioned interior.

The inside is decorated like the outside. The room is divided right down the middle with light wood on one half and orange, yellow, and pink upholstered easy chairs, coffee tables, an enormous bookcase, and more potted flowers. There's a huge front window with a ledge, displaying a chalkboard sign that shows today's coffee, muffin, and sandwich specials. The lighter side has a counter with an enormous copper coffee machine behind a glass bakery case.

The floor on the other side of the room is covered in dark gray tile. There are long, tall tables with granite-colored tops and brushed silver barstools. The walls are painted dark blue and, similar to the outdoor area, the ceiling is strung with white lights. That side of the room also has a door that clearly rolls up, opening one entire wall that leads out onto the patio. There's a stage in the corner and a bar along the back wall.

They take the dual function of the establishment seriously.

"Hi, Nora!"

"Nora, sweetheart!"

"Nora!"

Several greetings ring out as Nora heads to the coffee counter.

"Hey, everyone!" she says with a smile, but it's not until she's at the counter that she turns and finds that I haven't followed her across the room.

I'm still at the door, frozen by the fact that every single person in the coffee shop is suddenly staring at me. Now dead silent.

But hell, I'm used to being stared at. I lift a hand. "Hey, everyone, I'm Alex."

"Oh, they know who you are," a woman says.

I focus on her. She's sitting on one of three stools at the coffee counter. She's beautiful. Long blond hair, probably in her early thirties. She's dressed in white shorts, a hot pink tank top, and pink sandals. She somehow looks casual and classy at the same time.

She lifts a coffee cup and takes a sip. "We've been waiting for you."

For some reason, that doesn't sound like a good thing.

Suddenly, Nora is beside me again, tugging me toward the counter. "Alex, this is my friend, Anderson. Andi, this is Alex."

"Hi," Andi says. Her smile seems genuine.

"Hi."

"So the apartment is—" Nora starts.

The sound of glass hitting the floor interrupts her.

Nora whirls around as my attention is jerked to the girl who has just walked out of the kitchen. And dropped a glass. A thick blue concoction is now oozing all over the floor. Blueberry smoothie, if I had to guess.

"Ruth!" Nora gasps. "Are you okay?"

"Oh my God," the girl says, staring at me.

I recognize her immediately.

This is the girl who chased me down in the parking lot almost a year ago. Who wanted me to talk to her grandfather. Nora's grandfather. The girl who is—was—a huge fan of mine who I disappointed that night.

Well, hell.

A man comes out through the swinging door behind her and nearly plows her over.

"Ruth, what the hell?" the man exclaims.

"Alex," the girl says.

That's all she says. But the man's eyes find me immediately. "Oh. Great," he says flatly.

Where the young girl looks like someone just slapped her, he looks like someone just told him his dog is ugly. She looks shocked. He looks offended.

Awesome.

"That's a little dramatic, don't you think?" Nora asks.

The man just shrugs.

"Alex, this is my grandfather, Bruce. Your…landlord." Nora winces as she says it.

Terrific. Not only am I living in the town of the man I dismissed after his stroke and promised to meet and greet, but his three best friends are out to teach me a lesson, and now his husband is my landlord. Awesome.

And I kind of want to date his granddaughter.

Well, not *date* her. Spend time with her. And kiss her again.

I think Bruce should *not* know that.

I force a smile. "Hi, Bruce."

He just makes a grunting sound.

"And this is Ruth," Nora says, gesturing toward the young girl.

"Hi, Ruth."

Ruth's eyes get even wider. "Hi," she breathes.

I abandon my luggage for a moment and step forward, offering my hand. "I know I was a big jerk the last time we met. I'm really sorry about that."

Her eyes widen, and I'm afraid she's not breathing. She steps forward, extending her arm, and takes my hand. The sound of crunching glass makes her look down.

"Here, I've got this." A very pretty brunette suddenly rounds the counter and takes the two plates from Bruce's hands.

"You don't have to do that, Everly," Bruce grumps.

"It's no problem." She smiles at me and steps out into the restaurant, delivering the plates to a table near the bookcase.

"And I've got this." Andi slides off her stool and goes behind the counter to begin picking up the broken glass.

Ruth pulls her hand away from mine. "Oh my gosh, I'll do that, Andi."

"No, honey, that's okay. You help welcome Alex."

Ruth's gaze bounces back up to me, then to Nora. "Oh! I can do that." She looks around, seems to realize we have an audience, then looks toward the counter. Her eyes widen. "Grandpa! You have to put the jars away!"

"Why?" Bruce asks.

"Because that's—" Ruth looks at me again, her cheeks red now. "Mean."

I frown and look toward the counter, too. What's she talking about?

Nora steps in front of me. "You know what? I just realized that I should show you around *town*. Give you a little tour. Get you something to eat." Nora grabs my arm and turns me toward the door.

"Don't they have food here?" I ask. Obviously, they do. People are eating all around us.

"Before he sees the apartment?" Ruth asks.

"Other food," Nora says to me. "Yes," she answers Ruth. "Right now."

"But I can..." Then I see the jars.

There are two mason jars sitting next to the register. The front of one jar has a pink sticky note that reads "Alex Olsen." The green sticky note on the other says, "Brussels Sprouts".

What?

I can't quite read the sign behind them, because Nora is in the way. I lean to the side, but she moves to block my view. I shake my head, put my hands on her waist, and lift her, depositing her to the side.

The sign says, *Which is Worse?*

My eyebrows climb.

The Alex Olsen jar is nearly overflowing with dollar bills, while the Brussels sprouts jar has maybe four bucks in it.

"What is—"

Nora grabs my arm again and tugs harder this time, leading me to the door.

I'm mildly amused by this, so I let her.

"Ruth, can you take Alex's bag up to the apartment?" Nora asks over her shoulder. "He'll be back after practice."

"Sure!" Ruth says happily.

"See everyone later!" Nora calls cheerily to, I assume, the entire shop.

"Bye, honey!"

"Bye, Nora!"

The door closes behind us, but Nora doesn't slow down until we're beside her truck. She opens the passenger door and only then releases her hold on my arm.

"Nora."

She takes a deep breath and looks up at me. "Yeah?"

"What the hell is going on?"

"Um…"

Both of our phones ding with texts at the same time.

She pulls hers from her back pocket, so I slide mine out as well.

"It's my sister," I say.

Nora nods. "Me too." She looks up. "Your sister, I mean."

"She wants to see me," I say. "Right now."

"Me too."

"So are you going to tell me why there's a straw poll going on in your grandpa's coffee shop-slash-bar in which I'm losing to Brussels sprouts?" I ask.

She sighs. "It's not just Leo, and Wilson, and Brewser who are upset with you."

"No?"

"No. The whole town, well…hates you."

CHAPTER 5
ALEX

REBEL, Louisiana, hates me.

Awesome.

"They'll get over it," Nora says as she drives toward the hockey arena.

"You think so?" I ask.

I don't like knowing that the town hates me. I'm actually surprised by how much I don't like that.

"Of course. Once they get to know you."

Well, that's nice. Once they know me as a person, they'll see I'm a good guy.

"Once the team is doing well and they see how good that is for the town, and once they're having fun watching you play," she continues.

Right. Once I'm playing hockey. Doing the hockey thing. People will like me as a hockey player. Of course.

But that's a few weeks away yet. I'm going to have to put up with being second to Brussels sprouts for a few *weeks*? Who knows what other vegetables they'll put ahead of me. Broccoli? *Beets*?

And right downstairs in the coffee shop I have to walk through to get to and from my apartment.

Wonderful.

"You've got to be kidding me," Nora says as we pull into the circular drive in front of the hockey arena.

It's nowhere near the size of the Grays' arena, but it's clearly new-ish. There's a lot of glass, big signage, a large parking lot, and an electronic advertising board declaring the arena the home of the Rebel Revelers and Rebel Rascals.

"What's—" But I see what caught her eye a second later.

There's a protest going on.

"I swear to God…" Nora mutters. She jams the truck into park and shuts it off. She's out of the truck and stomping toward the five people holding posterboards that say, "Go Home Alex Olsen", "Alex Olsen Can Puck Off", one with a number fourteen —my number with the Grays—circled in red with a line through it, and one that says "No Justice, No Peace" which I assume is a leftover from another protest, and one that I don't read fast enough. They all scramble to hide the signs behind their backs or stuff them behind the bushes along the sidewalk when they see Nora coming up the sidewalk.

"Nora!" One woman with bright white hair, wearing a pale green tee with a variety of flowers on the front, loose green pants, and a wide-brimmed straw hat, hurries forward. Everyone else tries to act nonchalant. "Hi, honey. What are you doing here?"

"Really, Patty? A protest?" Nora asks, planting her hands on her hips.

"What do you mean? We're out here checking out the murals Andi finished yesterday," Patty says. "They look fantastic."

I come to stand next to Nora. Patty looks up at me with a smile.

A purely fake smile.

"I can see the signs!" Nora says, exasperated, gesturing toward the bushes. "George!" she calls. "I can see the signs!"

The man who is fighting to get his sign tucked fully behind the bush stops, sighs, and turns with a sheepish smile. "Hi, Nora."

"If you're so upset you're willing to protest, why are you trying to hide it now?" she asks.

"Well, obviously we didn't want *you* to see the signs," another woman says, walking up to stand next to Patty. "We just wanted Alex to see them." She's in blue jeans, a bright orange shirt that says *Dirty Hoe Gardening Club* with a sketch of a hoe, and muddy white tennis shoes. She's also got a grass-green colored bandana wrapped around her equally white hair.

I'm going to assume these ladies were with Nora at Garden Club earlier.

"Muriel!" Nora says. "This is so rude!"

"Yeah. We're protesting *against* him. That's the point." She shakes her head. "But you're way too sweet to protest. Do you ever even write bad reviews or email a company when they send you a broken item in the mail?"

Nora doesn't say anything.

"Nora, you really need to complain and get a replacement or a refund," another woman says, joining the group. "You don't just let it go, do you?"

"I'm sure she does," Muriel says. "Do you remember when Sandra gave Nora food poisoning with her chicken casserole? Nora never said a word and asked Sandra for the recipe in front of everyone in the coffee shop!"

"That was four years ago!" Nora exclaims. "And she didn't *mean* to give me food poisoning. And anyway, we can't *prove* it was from the casserole."

"Three other people were also puking their guts out that same night and they all ate that casserole," Muriel says. "That's proof. But *you* defended her."

"Because she didn't mean to do any harm!"

"But when a company sends you something that gets broken, even if they don't mean for it to happen, they should replace it or refund you, honey," the other woman says.

"She's right," George agrees. "Next time you let us know and we'll help you write the email."

"I like calling better," Patty says.

"But with email, you get the interaction, and whatever they promise, in writing," George says.

Patty nods. "Good point."

"Who are we emailing?" the other man with the group asks, now coming forward so he can hear better.

"The company that sent Nora a broken…" Patty looks at Nora. "What was it that got broken?"

Nora throws her hands up. "Nothing! It's a hypothetical that didn't actually happen, and we are *way* off topic. You all are out here *protesting* against the newest hockey player! We need to welcome Alex to town and make him feel at home!"

"He was rude to Harley!" the woman who isn't Patty or Muriel says.

"And he was hurt that night and under immense pressure, facing the end of his career!" Nora says. "He didn't mean to upset Harley!"

Muriel looks up at me. "See what I mean? She'll give everyone the benefit of the doubt. She's too nice for her own good."

This entire conversation has gone way off the rails, but it's clear that Nora is very well-liked and I have to agree, she seems sweet. Even when she's exasperated.

I can't help but smile. "She did save me from a kidnapping earlier."

Muriel nods. "That's how we found out we should come out here to protest. The boys called and said they lost you in the airport."

I assume 'the boys' are Leo, Brewser, and Wilson.

Nora sighs. "Everyone, this very nice man, who is moving his whole life clear across the country to *help us*, is Alex Olsen. Please say hello."

"Hello, Alex," Muriel says.

"Hi, nice to meet you." I suppose that's what I should say.

"For the record," George says, moving in next to Muriel and

extending his hand, "I'm here because Patty and Muriel needed a ride. I look forward to seeing you play."

"Noted," I say, shaking his hand. "Thanks." I'm just going to assume George's sign was the "No Justice, No Peace" and that he grabbed it reluctantly at the last second.

"Oh my God," Nora says, rolling her eyes. "You all need to go home. And take those signs out of the bushes and *throw them away.*"

"Okay, sweetheart," Patty says.

"Sure, sure," Muriel agrees. "And we'll see you at walking club tomorrow morning."

"Of course." Nora then proceeds to hug each of them before they grab their signs and head for their cars.

"So…wow," I say.

"I'm so sorry." She grimaces.

"I'm going to write a very strongly worded email to the Parks and Rec department about the Protest Club," I tell her.

That finally gets a smile. "Yes, do that." She glances in their direction. "I have to admit, they did pretty good on the signs with such little notice."

"You don't think they had them made and were just waiting for a chance to use them?" I tease.

Her smile dies though and she groans.

Oh, damn, I didn't think that was actually a possibility.

"Let's go see what Astrid wants," I suggest. Maybe my sister can take Nora's mind off of the less-than-warm welcome Rebel has given me so far.

"Yes. Let's."

Nora leads me into the building and to the elevators that take us up to the top floor where the offices are located.

"Alex!" My sister bolts out of her white leather office chair from behind her white wooden desk and launches herself into my arms as we walk into her office.

"Hey, sis." I catch her around the waist and hug her tightly.

It's so nice to have a familiar face here. I hadn't realized how much I needed that until this moment, and I give her an extra-long squeeze.

Astrid and I don't look much like siblings. Her petite gymnast's frame next to my big hockey-player body has been commented on in the sports media several times. Our older sister, Linnea, and I also took after our dad with our dark hair and eyes, while Astrid is the spitting image of our blond, blue-eyed mother.

But despite our physical differences, Astrid and I have a lot in common. Besides blood and a family tree, we were both raised to be world-class athletes from a very young age and were sent to the US to fulfill the dreams of not just our family, but our entire country.

We're both dual citizens of the US and Cara, the tiny island nation at the southernmost end of the Faroe Islands. Until Astrid and I landed on the world stage, most people couldn't have found us on a map, and even now, it's mostly the sporting communities that know that Cara is an independent country with its own ruling royal family. But we've succeeded in bringing recognition to our country, and we've made our family proud.

"I'm so glad you're here," she says, beaming up at me as I set her back on the floor.

"That makes one person in this town," I say dryly.

She actually grimaces, and I know that she knows how the town feels about me. Great.

Astrid leans around me. "Hi, Nora."

"Hi, Astrid."

Astrid doesn't even blink at Nora's overalls or the mud streaks. No one in the coffee shop did either. I wonder how often Nora walks around messy and tousled.

"Come on in." Astrid takes my hand and tugs me further into her office toward the little sitting area across from her desk. She sinks down onto the couch and kicks her heels off, tucking one foot under her butt.

Nora takes a seat in one of the bright yellow chairs that sit perpendicular to the sofa. Her overalls nearly disappear against the upholstery.

I blink as the full picture hits me.

Astrid's white pantsuit, silky and no doubt expensive, makes the *purple* velvet couch even more striking. Because it's *really* purple.

I look around the office, taking in more details.

"How long have you been here again?"

"A couple of weeks." Astrid drapes her arms along the curved back of the purple velvet settee. Which stands out even more on top of the furry green rug at her feet. "Do you like it?"

The rest of the office is white with shiny gold accents on the wall sconces, knobs on the cupboards and desk drawers, and upholstery embellishments.

"It looks like Mardi Gras threw up in here," I tell her, sinking into the other armchair across the coffee table from Nora.

It's surprisingly comfortable. Or maybe not that surprising. My sister has great taste, and it's clear she spared no expense here, despite the color palette.

Astrid nods happily. "These are the colors of the Revelers," she says, running her hands along the back of the couch lovingly. "I love it. And Declan would hate it. Everything in his penthouse is gray or black."

I think about the last time I saw my sister.

It was also in an office.

Declan's.

"COME WITH ME TO LOUISIANA."

I turned quickly as my sister strode into Declan's office.

"Are you going on vacation?"

She stopped in front of Declan's desk and propped her hip against it. "I'm moving there."

I turned to face her more fully. "Excuse me?"

"I bought a hockey team. I could use an All-Star Center. You're a huge name in hockey. And if Declan doesn't see it, I'm happy to capitalize on his loss."

I gaped at her. "What do you mean you bought a hockey team? In Louisiana?" I looked at Declan.

He looked… amused. He sat back in his chair and linked his hands, resting them on his stomach.

"You did it," he said to Astrid. He didn't seem shocked.

She finally looked at her husband and lifted her chin. "Yes. I told you I would."

"You seriously bought the Jazz?" I asked.

I didn't know what exactly was going on between my sister and her husband, except that Declan's grandfather arranged their marriage with our grandfather. And that they seem to have a lot in common. They're both stupidly good-looking, incredibly successful at whatever they do, and frustratingly stubborn. They also seem unable to stand one another.

So yeah, the idea of my sister buying an opposing team tracked.

But Astrid shook her head. "Not the Jazz. A much smaller team. It's in a town that had an FPHL team until the end of this past season. The owners pulled out. The town still wants hockey, but they need a new owner. They came to Declan with the idea." She looked across the wide stretch of Declan's desk. "But of course Declan would never do something like that. Hockey has to be perfect. The highest level to be worth anything. Heaven forbid anybody have any fun or do something just for the love of the game."

Her tone was biting, and I knew her ire was obviously targeted at the billionaire across the desk, but I felt a jab in my chest at her words.

I love hockey, but I also take it very seriously. I don't remember the last time I played hockey just for fun or the love of the game. It's serious stuff. It's statistics and standings and money and fame and glory.

"FPHL," I repeated. "That's not even the minor leagues. That's like a step up from a beer league."

Astrid nodded. "And it's a little tiny town in Louisiana where there's no food delivery, nothing is open past ten—except the bar on the weekends—they wear denim and work boots and call people honey and darlin' a lot. And they love hockey just for the sake of hockey. I get to build it from the ground up. With the help of the town and the fans. Which is how it should be. And they have a lot of ideas." She met my gaze. "Come with me. You'll be able to learn everything about managing a team. It's not at Declan's level, but it'll be hands-on. It's everything from working with the players to interacting with the town, the press, and the fans. We're deciding on mascots and what to serve at the concession stands. We're hiring all of the staff, from social media managers to janitors. You'll literally be able to touch every single part of what goes into making a hockey team work."

I looked over Declan. "She has a point."

He arched a brow. "Your sister is a very smart woman."

Wow, a blatant compliment. I glanced at Astrid. Her cheeks were pink, but she wasn't smiling, and she said nothing.

"If I go with Astrid and learn about everything from the ground up, that would be a very good, interesting experience."

Declan nodded. "It would."

"You know that Alex and I are very used to getting our way and being extremely successful," Astrid said. "Obviously, this is going to be amazing."

"Not to mention expensive," Declan said, though he didn't seem upset.

I guessed my sister used some of his money to buy this hockey team. She does fine, but there's no way she's got hockey-team-owner money.

She shrugged. "You're the one who told me that I didn't have to worry about money."

Declan simply inclined his head in acknowledgement.

• • •

AND NOW I'M in Louisiana, about an hour and a half away from my first practice as a swamp werewolf. For fuck's sake. I focus on my sister in *her* office. "Declan *would* hate it?" I ask. "He hasn't seen it?"

Astrid laughs. "No. And I don't expect him to."

"Really?"

"Declan O'Grady is *not* coming to small-town Louisiana." She frowns, studying the way the velvet moves as she brushes over it. "Declan likes things very neat and polished and perfect. Things here are way too messy for him."

"Yes. We're going to talk about your husband and the fact that you're here in part to annoy him," I tell her, leaning forward to rest my forearms on my thighs.

"We are not talking about that," Astrid says. "We're talking about what we're going to do about the ticket sales here."

"What's going on?" Nora asks, sitting forward.

I realize from their body language that they're very comfortable with one another.

"I had three hundred season tickets sold as of this morning," Astrid says.

"Only three *hundred*?" I ask, my attention effectively torn from Nora and the cute way her hair flips up at the ends just below her jawline.

"Well, two hundred ninety-three," she clarifies. "But I had five hundred and sixty-five before they found out you were coming to play here. And since you got to town, I've lost thirty more."

I sit forward. "What? You're *losing* ticket sales because of me?" I scowl. "Do you mean you've lost more in the past *thirty minutes* since I got here?"

Astrid shrugs. "They don't like you here."

"I'm aware." I turn my gaze on Nora.

She's chewing on her bottom lip.

She still looks really fucking cute.

"Your *grandfather's friends* don't like me," I say. "And they're not making a secret of it, at all."

"I know." She looks really sorry, actually.

"Can you talk to them?"

"I have."

I huff out a breath. "Am I still at risk for being kidnapped?"

"Maybe? Probably not. But I can't be one-hundred percent sure."

Astrid looks from Nora to me, then back. "What?"

"Leo, Brewser, and Wilson were going to take him out to Leo's cabin and dump him off. To scare him a little. Punish him for how he treated Harley," Nora explains.

"I would have noticed he was missing," Astrid says.

"Yes. But you wouldn't have been able to find him. And even if you *did* find out where he was, you couldn't have gotten to him. You would need an airboat, hip waders, and a very good knowledge of the bayou. Which, I'm just guessing, you don't have."

I can tell Nora's trying not to smile.

She thinks this is funny?

"The *cops* probably have all of that, though, right?" Astrid asks.

But then I really look at my sister, and I think she's also trying not to smile.

Nora nods. "Yes, except for the very good knowledge of the bayou. I mean they do have some knowledge, but it's a very wild, winding place. They simply can't know it as well as those guys do."

"So he would have just been stranded out there until they decided to go get him?" Astrid asks. "Is there food? Water?"

"They probably would have left some food and water. Though nothing perishable, of course. Nothing that would attract critters."

"Define critters," Astrid says. "Like raccoons?"

"More like nutria. And gators, of course."

Astrid nods. "Of course."

"And nothing that would need to be cooked. Since there's only a generator for power and I would guess they don't have it hooked up. Or that Alex would know how to hook it up."

"So he'd also be in the dark," Astrid says.

"Yes."

"Wow. That really would be a pretty great way to make him think about what he did and regret it."

My sister looks at me. I meet her gaze with both brows up. "You enjoying yourself?"

"Picturing the guy who travels with his own pillow and who complains if the hotel thermostat doesn't work perfectly in a cabin with beef jerky and no power? Yeah, a little," she says with a grin.

"Okay, Mrs. Pot, look who's calling the kettle black."

Nora giggles and I have an urge to reach over and pull her into my lap for some reason.

"I would have come to get you," she says. "As soon as I realized what happened."

"*You* have an airboat, hip waders, and great knowledge of the bayou?" I ask.

"I do," she says with a grin. "At least, I know where to get an airboat. But I have the other things."

I want to see her in hip waders. I really do. What the fuck is happening to me?

"Anyway," Astrid says. "We need to figure out a way to help the town get over their grudge against you."

"Give me a minute. I just got here," I say.

"As charming as you are, I think it might take more than a minute," she says. "And we don't have a lot of time. We can't keep losing ticket sales. We need to be *gaining* every day. I could just fire you, I suppose. That would probably get me huge points and would solve the problem."

I frown. "That's not an option." Jesus, what would I do then? Even if this is small-town, minor-league hockey, at least it's *hockey*.

"That's not good," Nora says. "We need him."

Fuck, I like having Nora on my side. Even if it's just because of hockey, I like the idea that she's choosing having me here over… not. Or leaving me in a dark, critter-infested cabin. I shudder.

"The people in town are mad at him, but there's a lot of potential for him to pull in hockey fans from a much bigger radius," Nora says.

Astrid waves her hand. "I know. And I knew about the town's feelings toward you before today. If I was going to fire you, I would have done it before you got on a plane."

I'm relieved to hear that she's already thought about and discarded the idea of me leaving.

"So, should we let everyone know he's only here temporarily?" she asks Nora. "Would that help?"

But Nora shakes her head quickly. "No. Finding out that he's not fully committed won't be good."

"I am fully committed. While I'm here," I say firmly.

She looks at me. "Good. I believe you. But this town is very… loyal. We have deep roots. We commit *long term*, here. They'll see that as another mark against you, trust me."

I sigh. It's a full season. That's not short-term. Not in my mind. But in a town that elects mayors for twenty-two years straight, I guess they don't think quite the same way.

"This is exactly why we need Nora's help," Astrid says with a huge smile at Nora. "She knows this town and everyone in Rebel *loves* Nora." She glances at me. "Once people get over not liking him, they'll realize he's a great guy. We just need to give them a reason to give him a second chance."

Nora nods. "Exactly. A way to get them over their preconceived notion."

"Right," Astrid agrees.

"So…how do we do that?" Nora asks.

"I was hoping you'd have an idea," Astrid says. "Since you know them all so well."

Nora and Astrid both turn to look at me. To *study* me. As if trying to figure out a complicated equation.

"Maybe we can play up the idea of coming to games to cheer *against* him," Nora suggests. "They'll at least buy tickets then?"

Astrid laughs. "Okay, that's one idea."

"No," I say firmly. "I don't want to play in front of a crowd that's rooting for me to *lose*."

"You play in front of crowds like that all the time," Nora points out. "The opposing teams always want you to lose."

"They want my *team* to lose. They want their team to win. But it's not personal. Not really. And at least *some* of the crowd is on my side any given night." I shift on my seat uncomfortably. "I can't have the whole town where I live hating me. I can't do that for seven months."

What can I say? I'm used to being adored. That's not a bad thing. Why would someone *not* want that? I like being admired and being someone people want to be around.

"Okay," Nora says. "I wasn't serious about that. I don't want people coming out for the wrong reasons either. I want this to be fun, positive, and uplifting. I don't want it to be about retribution."

"So what can we do?" Astrid asks. "Public apology? You two having breakfast together? Alex going to gardening club? We need ticket sales now. Yesterday, actually. I want over half of those seats sold in the pre-season.

That's not enough. It needs to be something that will work faster.

I sit forward, resting my elbows on my thighs. "We need something bigger. Something that will make people quickly and easily believe I'm a great guy and that they should like me right now."

"Agreed," Nora says.

"Should I donate money to something?" I ask.

She shakes her head. "They'll see through that."

"Breakfast with Harley?" I ask.

"That would help," she says. "But again, it's not big enough. Harley will forgive you. He's a total sweetheart. He's not the problem."

"Breakfast with the three musketeers?" I ask. "Leo, Wilson, and Brewser?"

Nora's eyes go wide. "No. We can't risk that. Not yet."

Good. I was nervous about that one. "You could come along," I suggest. "Have your hip waders ready to go."

She laughs.

"I don't know, going on an airboat ride with you sounds fun," I say, stupidly.

She grins. "We can arrange that *without* the kidnapping in the middle."

I chuckle.

"I've got it," Astrid says.

We both look at her.

My sister looks triumphant. "I have the perfect solution."

"Awesome," I say. "What?"

"You're going to date."

There's a beat of silence. Nora and I look at each other. My heart kicks hard against my ribs. Then I look back at my sister. "What?"

Astrid nods. "You're going to be Nora's boyfriend."

Nora's mouth drops open. But she doesn't make a sound.

That…makes sense.

I like it. A lot.

I look at Nora again. She looks shocked. But her cheeks are pink.

"That's *crazy*," she says.

"No, it's perfect," Astrid says. "If *you* like him enough to date him, they'll all realize that not only do you forgive him, but he must be a great guy."

Nora starts shaking her head. "That's…"

"The perfect way to make this hockey team work," I interject. "It's the fastest, easiest way to get the town to give me a chance. You know it's true. You're everybody's favorite girl next door. If *you* love me, *everyone* will love me," I say, repeating my sister's words.

Nora shakes her head more emphatically. "You can't say it like *that*."

"Like what?"

"The...lo—love part," she says, stumbling over the L word. She takes a deep breath. "If you want to pretend that we're dating..." She takes a breath, then blows it out. Then nods. "Okay, fine. That does make some sense. You're probably right—" She grimaces slightly when she says that. "If I like you, they'll all give you a second chance."

"And if I'm romancing you, being sweet to you, treating you like a princess, they'll *love* me," I say, this idea suddenly seeming like the most brilliant thing I've ever heard.

"What does *that* entail exactly?" she asks, looking like dating me might involve eating cockroaches or something.

"Dating me? It means hanging out with me *a lot*, and..."

Well...shit. What the hell does dating me entail?

Dammit. That's a good question. In the past, it meant going to dinner, or clubs, maybe a concert, and sex. And yeah...that's about it.

While I'll happily take Nora anywhere she wants to go and will *happily* spend hours between the sheets with her—and my certainty there is strong considering I've only known her for a couple of hours—I also want to hold her hand while we walk down Main Street. Or something. I frown. Why do I want to do that? I've never walked down a Main Street, or any other street, holding anyone's hand. I'm clearly filling in shit I've seen on TV. What do people in real small towns do on dates?

Otter club. I almost laugh. I don't think otter club is designed as a date night activity, but...yeah, I'm going to find out what the hell otter club is. For sure.

"And?" she asks, now looking amused by how long it's taking me to answer the question.

"And whatever you want," I say. That's got to be a good answer.

Her expression turns sly. "*Whatever* I want?"

That might sound playful or sexy from another woman. From Nora Delaune, in Rebel, Louisiana, it sounds a little ominous.

Still, I nod. "Sure. *But*," I add. "It also involves holding hands." I guess I just really want to hold this woman's hand. "And kissing." I definitely want to do more of that. "And…" *Don't say sex*, I tell myself. "Sitting really close to me whenever we're together."

She laughs. *Laughs.* "Okay."

Okay. That's all she says. Just okay. Well, that was easy. Maybe I should have said sex.

She takes a breath. "But…"

I brace myself.

"When you leave, they'll be upset. You need to know that. They'll hate you again."

I don't like that. But I suppose it makes some sense. This woman is everyone's favorite. If they're pissed at me for ducking out of a meet-and-greet with Harley, they'll *definitely* be mad if I "break up" with Nora.

I nod. "I get it." I don't like it, but there's not really another option. I need them to like me *now*. Once I'm back in Portland, when I'm not walking into that coffee shop every damned morning, it won't matter as much.

"They'll be upset for me, and for themselves, once they really start liking you. So, all along, we say this is a *casual* dating relationship. We don't let them get too invested. And we do *not* call it love." She shakes her head. "Especially with Ruth and Harley. They were huge fans before…everything. And they'll be thrilled to have a reason to cheer for you again. We can't let them think this is serious and that you're going to be sticking around and really becoming…"

"A part of the family?" I supply.

She nods. "Yeah. I don't want them to get their hopes up about this being something real."

Something in me wants to reject the fact that this wouldn't be real. But she's right. It's temporary, if nothing else.

"So in April, we'll say I have to go back to Portland and—"

"That will be enough," she interjects.

She's not meeting my gaze now.

"Are you okay?" I take a step toward her.

She nods. "It's just…they know I'm not leaving Rebel. When you get a chance to work for the Grays, everyone will know it means we have to break up." She shrugs, looking at my chin instead of directly at me. "It's happened before."

This is the first time I've seen Nora look anything less than bright and shiny. I don't like it.

"We could tell them—" I start.

"You'll leave, we'll break up," she interrupts. "That's just how it will be. We don't have to tell them anything."

Well, that seems simple enough. I get to hang out with and kiss Nora Delaune a bunch for the next seven months, then leave to work for the Grays, with everyone here disappointed but understanding.

"Great. So this is casual," I say.

She nods. "Yep. When people ask us, we say we're just having fun."

"People won't mind me just messing around with their favorite girl?"

Now she looks at me. Her pupils dilate, and I hope it's because she's thinking of all the ways she wants me to mess around with her. I certainly am.

"If I'm happy, they'll be happy," she says simply.

"Then I guess I'll have to try hard to make you happy."

Something flickers in her eyes, but she reiterates, "In public. When other people are watching. But *we* know it's fake. And I really think that as you get involved with the team and show the town how much fun all of this is going to be, they will like you for that. For hockey."

That jabs me in the chest. I have spent my life being liked because of hockey. I'm used to that. It's my comfort zone. I should want that. It's far easier than dating everyone's favorite person. There are a million ways I could screw this up. I don't screw up hockey.

Still, I say, "Oh, Nora, I'm going to date the *hell* out of you."

CHAPTER 6
NORA

"NORA!"

"Hi, honey!

"Hey, Nora!"

"Hi, sweetheart!"

I smile and greet everyone as I make my way from the door to the coffee counter at Perks and Rec.

Whenever I walk in here, everyone acts like it's been weeks since they've seen me, and it always makes me smile. Truth is, I was here for breakfast just this morning. As I am every single morning. And, of course, my stop by with Alex this afternoon.

I would've been here earlier this evening for dinner if I hadn't made a quick side trip to New Orleans that put me behind a couple of hours on my schedule.

But now all of the wildflowers are in the community center, laid out to dry so the art club can use them, I finished up the rest of my to-do list—at least for today—and I finally showered and cleaned up.

I glance surreptitiously toward the stairs leading to Alex's apartment as I slide up onto the stool between two of my best friends at the counter.

I know he's not there. He's still at practice. Still, I am hoping to run into him because, as much as I never worry about how I look, it's been bugging the crap out of me that he met me, and agreed to be my boyfriend—my *fake* boyfriend—when I was in overalls with mud all over me and stems and petals in my hair.

I'm now wearing a blue sundress that hits me just above the knees and features wide straps that crisscross over my shoulder blades. I'm in tennis shoes again, but these are white…and clean. And then at the last minute, I also added a bracelet and necklace set. They are tiny blue and white flowers linked together by their stems.

I've considered taking them off about twelve times since I got in the car. It's silly. Just because he called me wildflower…

Fuck. It *is* ridiculous and really obvious, and I should definitely take them off.

I'm overcompensating for mud and leaves.

"You look really nice," Andi says.

She gives me a knowing grin.

Yeah, if Alex doesn't notice, my two best friends will.

"That dress makes your legs and boobs look great," Everly agrees from my opposite side.

Gee, it's almost like they saved the stool between them for me so they could accost me from the sides.

"You never wear necklaces," Thea, my cousin and Ruth's mom, says. "That one is so cute."

And now if I take the necklace off, it will be even more obvious.

I can't let them think I like Alex.

Except I need to tell them that I'm dating him.

Fake dating him.

I should like him enough for that, shouldn't I?

I can like him as the guy who's going to make all of my plans a huge success. Who is going to save the hockey team. Who's going to help make Harley the mayor one more time.

But I can't like Alex more than that.

Alex is leaving.

I don't date guys who aren't from Rebel. Or guys who are from Rebel but plan to leave. Or guys who come to Rebel but don't intend to stay.

Well, I don't date those guys *anymore*.

I've done all of those things with bad results, so I'm not doing that again, and these two know that.

Alex Olsen is the epitome of *do not get involved with him*. He's not only planning to leave, but he already knows that, unlike my last boyfriend. Hunter really did think he was going to stay. He wanted to make it work. I think.

But even Hunter, born and raised in Houston, fit in here better than Alex Olsen will.

"Thank you. Have you two been here all day?"

"On and off since you and the hockey player showed up," Andi says.

"The *cute* hockey player," Everly adds.

They're both self-employed, so I should have known they'd take time off for this.

"You met him already?" Thea asks.

"Yep," Everly says. "Did I mention he's very cute?"

I roll my eyes. "You already knew he was cute. It's not like we've never seen photos or seen him play hockey."

"He's cuter in person, and when he feels awkward. You know how much I love when men are uncomfortable." Andi lifts her iced tea and sips from the straw.

"You do look nice. Is there an event tonight?" Jesse Parsons asks, interrupting as she lays cash and her receipt down next to the register on top of the pile of receipts and money already there.

I sigh and slide off my stool again, rounding the counter and opening the register to add all of the bills. There's no sense in trying to ring everything up and make it all balance. I'm just grateful that Bruce's accountant, AJ, has to deal with him and his year-end receipts, and I don't. They've known each other since grade school, like everyone else here, and AJ knows exactly what to expect from Bruce and his "paperwork."

Bruce hasn't ended up in jail yet, so I'm going to assume it's fine that people just round their bills up or down to the nearest dollar and leave the money lying around if Bruce is too busy in the kitchen to collect it. Which he always is.

Could he hire help? Sure. Does he sometimes during the summer when the high school kids are out of school? Sure. But he also lets them off work for everything from a shopping trip with friends to "it's a great fishin' day!". So it's just easier for everyone to assume there is no extra help, get their own soda, tea, and water refills, gather up their dishes and take them into the kitchen when they're finished with their meals, and pay on the honor system.

"No event," I say, feeling my cheeks get pink.

"Oh, good," Jesse says. "We're supposed to play cards with Greg and Donna. Though obviously, we'd all come to whatever you had going on."

"I know. I appreciate that," I tell her sincerely.

Jesse, her husband Brad, and Greg and Donna are regulars at all of my Parks and Rec events. Movie nights, sand volleyball tournaments, craft fairs, and a multitude of clubs. They even come to the Turtle Derby—yes, it includes turtle races, but also a costume contest, and a lettuce eating contest—the Pumpkin Parade where everyone who has grown pumpkins or other gourds gets to show them off to the town, and the Future Chart Toppers music concert, where the kids in town ages five and under play "instruments" including homemade maracas, xylophones that are glasses filled with water, and yes, of course, drums.

That last one is a true test of people's support and dedication, but we always have great attendance.

"You just don't wear dresses unless it's a Parks and Rec event," Jesse goes on. Then her eyes widen. "Do you have a date?"

Suddenly, the entire café quiets and turns toward us.

Thea actually chokes on a laugh and a drink of soda, and Andi smirks.

Everly leans in with mock interest. "Yes, Nora, why *are* you wearing a dress?"

"I just threw it on," I say with a shrug. "Didn't really look at what I was grabbing. It's so hot today, and I spent the day all dirty. Just wanted something besides overalls."

Andi's grin is wide, and Everly looks positively delighted.

"So your day was *hot* and *dirty*," Ev says. "Tell us more."

"Muriel and Patty," I say. I give the room a smile. "Need I say more?"

There's laughter and nodding, and people start to turn away as they realize there's no gossip about my love life forthcoming.

Jesse is smiling. "Muriel and Patty got into it?"

"At gardening club," I say. "There was mud."

She chuckles. "Say no more." She gives me a fond smile. "You look lovely, though. My nephew in Shreveport is still single. If you want to—"

"Thanks," I cut in. "But I'm good. You know I want someone who will live *here*."

She does know that. Everyone knows that. And they support me in that. Everyone wants me to stay here, too. It's not my ego talking when I say that I help this town run.

So when you're 'dating' Alex they're all going to assume he's staying and then when he leaves they'll hate him all over again.

That bugs me. Not just misleading everyone about Alex's commitment to the town, but the idea of them being upset for me —again—and hating a guy who is truly only here to help us out.

"Of course. He's in real estate. I think we could convince him," Jesse says.

But it's a risk. He's not from here. He doesn't love this town like I do.

I shut my thoughts down as they start to spin. Good lord, it doesn't matter. I'm not going to date Jesse's nephew.

"Thanks, Jesse. I'll…let you know?"

She looks thrilled with even that much. "Of course."

She heads out the door, and I blow out a breath.

"You've got to quit giving people false hope that you're going to marry into their families," Everly says, clearly amused as she lifts her glass of lemonade.

"Seriously, you know Jesse is going to go tell Donna that you're considering a date with her nephew, and Donna will get all worked up and will invite her six nephews to town for something, and you'll have to meet them along with Becky and LeAnn's nephews. Between the two of them, I think they have like ten," Andi says. "There will be an absolute harem of men for you." She gets a sly smile on her face. "Maybe that's what you should do. Have like eight boyfriends. Surely, they can rotate who's out of town at any one time, and the rest can take care of you while he's gone. You won't even notice one or two missing."

"Stop it," I say, laughing. I push the register drawer shut. "You make it sound like everyone wants to marry me off."

"They do!" Andi, Thea, and Everly say in unison.

We all laugh.

"You're the most eligible bachelorette in the parish!" Everly says.

"And you're number two," Andi tells her. She lifts her tea again. "If you want to avoid all of that, you need to let me coach you in bitter-eccentric-witchy-divorcee vibes."

Andi is gorgeous and intimidating as hell. She's four years older than me and seven years older than Everly. She feels like an older sister in many ways. Mostly in her advice about men and romance. Which is to not fall for any romance bullshit and not believe anything any man says.

She's been divorced for two years since her husband cheated with a mutual friend. She's not actually a witch but is definitely bitter. She's also an artist, teaches art classes, and does anything "artsy" the Parks and Rec department needs, including designing the new hockey teams' mascots.

She has also decided to let all of her suppressed artistic flair—suppressed by her asshole ex—spill all over her house, the only place she's ever lived alone and called her own. The house is a little cabin down by the bayou. It's hard to get to, and she doesn't like having visitors. She never invites anyone but me, Sutton, and Everly out there, and in public talks about curses and hexes. She's going for a 'swamp witch' reputation. I'm not sure it's working, but I do know that *no one* has tried to set her up, and she's ecstatic about that.

Everly, on the other hand, is sweet, funny, and beautiful. She does landscaping for a living and is responsible for all of the beautiful public spaces in town—we work closely together—and people definitely love her. Would everyone who wants me to marry their nephews be just as thrilled to have Everly in their family? Absolutely.

"You know I'm into the witchy stuff," Everly tells her. "Totally into potions."

She's actually into plants and flowers and how they can be made into perfumes and teas. But sure, we can call them 'potions'.

"You'd be a good witch," Andi says. "And I don't mean that as a compliment. You'd be a good witch, versus a bad one."

Everly laughs. "Well, I'll come live in your cabin with you and balance out your evil impulses."

"Nope," Andi says. "Love you, but that house and those impulses are *all* mine. And Merlin's."

Merlin is her cat. He's, of course, black. He's also nothing but a big floof who seeks out and gets comfortable on the nearest lap, no matter who it belongs to. He's the goofiest, sweetest animal I know. And considering Andi is painting her 'swamp witch house' mostly pink, I think asking Merlin to be a scary witch cat is just confusing him.

Not that anyone in town knows her lair is pink and other pastel colors. She has a long, winding lane up to the front of the house, so even the postman and other delivery people don't know what the house looks like.

I brace my hands on the counter and lean in. "I have to tell you something about Alex," I say in a hushed voice.

"And we're back to the hot and dirty part of the day," Andi says.

Everly laughs, but I shake my head. "No. Not like that. Gardening club and then a mad dash to the airport. Dirty and sweaty from work and panic."

"But you're worried about him," Andi says.

"Of course I'm worried about him. I don't want him scared off! We need him. I went to the airport to save him from being kidnapped!"

Andi nods. "Okay. Well, yeah, he seemed awkward stepping into a café full of people who don't really want him here."

"Yes, and he's not supposed to know that," I say with a frown, straightening. Obviously, Leo, Brewser, and Wilson didn't give a great first impression, but I thought the rest of the town would behave.

I should have known better.

"It was Bruce's fault," Everly says, pointing towards the cash register.

I know she's pointing at today's straw poll.

"That was here when Alex showed up?" Thea asks.

"Yes," I say.

"Oh my God," Thea mutters.

Our grandpa Bruce has been doing these polls every day for as long as I can remember. People vote by putting a dollar into the mason jar that's labeled with the answer they agree with. Of course, he combines all of the money when he donates it at the end of the month, but it's a fun way to collect the money.

Usually, it's things like best sundae topping or worst place to get an itch while giving a public speech. And yes, sometimes the answers are inappropriate.

But today is the first time Alex Olsen's name has shown up in the polls.

Which reminds me... I want to scold my grandfather. I spin toward the kitchen door. "Bruce!"

Ruth pops out from behind the swinging door, her eyes wide. I hope we're not going to have to have another talk about child labor laws. "Where is Grandpa?" I ask.

"He's up to his armpits in barbecue sauce," she reports.

Whatever. I step forward and push the door open. "Seriously?" I demand of my grandfather.

Harley is my grandfather by blood. He was married to my grandmother, and they had my mom, my aunt Bebe, and my uncles, C.W. and Ben. I never knew my grandma. She died before I was born. And Harley and Bruce, best friends while my grandparents were married, realized they were more than friends after Bruce helped my grandpa regroup. Bruce and Harley have been married all my life, so Bruce is my grandpa as much as Harley is. In fact, they're both more like fathers, having raised me after my mom left.

"I didn't put all those dollar bills in the Alex jar," he says.

He's hardly up to his armpits in barbecue sauce. He's stirring a big pot, and it smells like barbecue for sure—deliciously so—but still, he can step away.

"You put the jars there. You labeled them," I say, planting my hands on my hips, and propping the door open with one foot. "You have to stop being mean. You need to be welcoming. Kind. Friendly. Helpful. We *need* him."

"I don't like him," Bruce says curtly.

"Why not?" I personally thought Alex was very…likeable.

Then again, Bruce hadn't kissed Alex and realized just how likable the man's mouth was.

"What do we know about him? He's a spoiled, rich, professional athlete who has probably always gotten his way and couldn't even take his time to talk with a guy who has been a fan since his first day in the league, who had a major medical event."

I blow out a breath. "I know. But the only thing we need to know is the professional athlete thing. We need him for hockey. Period."

"I know things about him!" Ruth says. "He likes Fruity Pebbles but only eats them in the off-season. He takes his training *very* seriously. He gives money to the hospital where his sister had surgery and rehab after her accident. He does lots of meet-and-greets! He got hurt the night that Harley and I were there."

I blink at her. She knows what kind of cereal Alex likes? I knew she was a fan, but…wow. I look at Bruce. "He sounds like a nice guy."

"He is!" Ruth insists.

"He was a shit to you and to your great-grandpa," Bruce says.

"Yeah, and he was having a really bad night, and he said sorry to me. He was nice today."

Ruth is a big-hearted, happy kid who loves hockey, baking cookies, and the sci-fi channel. Not necessarily in that order.

Okay, actually exactly in that order.

Bruce, on the other hand, is big-hearted but does *not* just automatically like everyone. He's not Harley. But he knows how to get along. How to schmooze. How to fake it. He's a politician's spouse. He's lived in Rebel all his life, though, so he doesn't have to do that much here. He can't erase sixty-four years of not getting along with certain people or the things he said forty years ago. Or twenty. Or two.

Thankfully, those people vote for Harley because they've known *him* for seventy-six years.

People also keep coming to Perks and Rec because Bruce is a hell of a cook, his coffee is the best in town, and the rest of the people in the building are people they like and get along with.

I love Bruce dearly, but how he and my happy, sunshine-y, sweet grandpa Harley fell in love is something I sometimes wonder about.

But then I sigh. Bruce is acting like this toward Alex because he's protective of Harley. He doesn't like Alex because Alex snubbed Harley. Bruce has been especially surly ever since Harley's stroke reminded him that Harley isn't invincible. And that scared the shit out of Bruce.

So when Harley's big chance to meet his favorite player came up and was then a huge disappointment, Bruce took that personally.

I get it.

I hated Alex Olsen that night, too. And for a long time after that.

I still wouldn't be a fan if he weren't the answer to all my problems.

"And you forgive him?" I ask Ruth. I raise my voice slightly. I'm standing with the swinging door propped open so the whole café can hear me. I'd hate for anyone to strain something trying to eavesdrop.

"For sure!" she says exuberantly.

"That's great." I give her a smile. "I'm proud of you." I want them all to hear this. Everyone in here is a regular. No doubt some of those dollar bills in the Alex Olsen jar are theirs. They also need to spread the word to those who aren't here.

I turn to address the whole café. As expected, everyone is watching and listening. "Alex is new to town, new to small-town life. He told me he was really sorry about how he treated Harley and Ruth, and I believe him. We need to give him a chance." I get heads nodding in unison, and I give them a big smile. "Thank you."

Then I lower my voice and say to Bruce, "We need the hockey team to do well for the election."

Bruce's shoulders slump slightly. "I know."

Bruce doesn't want Harley to run again. He thinks Harley should retire. But Harley doesn't want to end his tenure on the heels of the stroke. He doesn't want that to be the reason. He wants to prove that he can still do the job and then go out on top. On his own terms. Not because his body gave out and betrayed him.

I'm going to do whatever I can to make that happen for him.

"We need the team to be successful, so everyone sees that Harley's idea for hockey in Rebel was a great idea and he's still able to lead," I reiterate. I know Ruth, Thea, Everly, and Andi are all still listening. They're part of our inner circle and definitely need to be on board.

"But this new hockey thing is your idea, sweetheart," Bruce says.

"No." I shake my head. "Harley's helped with it a ton."

Bruce gives me an affectionate smile. "Yes, he has. A lot of people have. But it was *your* idea to make it something new and fresh."

I wave my hand. "It doesn't matter whose idea is whose. We've all worked on it, and Harley has been integral."

Bruce's look is I'm-not-buying-it, but he nods. "Whatever you say."

Okay, fine—the overall idea of making hockey more fun, more participatory for those watching, and more of an event than just a game was mine. But I've had help with the details for sure. I didn't know the rules well enough to know how to bend and twist them. I didn't know what was possible and what wasn't until I got Harley involved. And Ruth. And Leo. And Astrid Olsen.

"We just have to beat Sean Patrick," I insist. "Whatever it takes. We can't let the newbies take over."

Sean Patrick isn't *new* to Rebel. He grew up here. Graduated from school here. His parents and grandparents still live here. But he left. For nine years. Didn't come home for anything other than holidays and even missed a few of those.

Now he's back. But he's part of the new part of town. The north part of town where the chain stores, and restaurants, and hotels are going in. Where they're building new apartments. Where there's a fancy coffee shop and two new bars that compete with Perks and Rec.

The 'newbies' are the people who have moved to Rebel and have expanded the town in ways that have taken away from the quirky, homey charm that those of us who are truly *from* here love and want to protect.

Has it helped the local economy? Sure. Whatever. It's allowed us to add on to the school, bring in more teachers and new programs, and I do have more people coming to some of the Parks and Rec events. But I also have things showing up in the suggestion box and my emails about things like bringing in bands from New Orleans, hot yoga—as if otter yoga in the park isn't enough—and Mommy and Me activities. I don't think I can swing concerts like that, and people who don't like otters are highly suspicious. But I do like the Mommy and Me idea, dammit.

It's just that new people don't have the heart or loyalty to the town like those of us who have always been here, and it's hard to trust that they'll really invest and stick around.

So things have become divided between the old school—those of us who live in the older part of town, hang out and frequent the downtown businesses, and love the traditions—and the newbies who like the chain restaurants, don't care that they haven't known the woman doing their hair ever since the terrible incident with cutting their own bangs in fourth grade, and don't want everyone in the coffee shop to call out "Hi, sweetheart!" when they walk in.

Weirdos.

"We won't let them take over," Bruce assures me. "We'll win the election."

It's one thing for them to want a big, fancy, automated car wash instead of Dean Kitch and his sons washing their cars, but to think about one of "them" becoming mayor makes me shudder.

"Then we have to keep Alex Olsen happy," I say firmly. "He needs to love it here. He needs to lead this hockey league. He needs to sell out that damned arena."

Bruce nods. "Okay. But…"

I sigh. "But what?"

"He needs to be genuine." He points his barbecue-covered spoon at me. "He needs to be a part of the town. He needs to try to fit in."

I nod. "It will just take a little time."

"Yeah, well, we don't have a lot of that," Bruce says, going back to stirring.

No. No, we don't.

I turn back to my friends. "I need to tell you something," I say, letting the kitchen door swing shut behind me.

I need to tell them what is going on with me and Alex. We can't let the town find out we're faking our relationship, but I also can't let my best friends think this is real. And I need to tell them before they see us together. They'll hear about that within about ten minutes of my smiling at him.

I lean my forearms onto the counter across from where Everly, Thea, and Andi are sitting. Ruth has gone back into the kitchen with Bruce. I glance around to be sure no one else is close.

"Alex and I are dating. Pretending to. So that the town will give him a second chance and focus on hockey and the Revelers instead of making him miserable for what happened with Harley."

They let that sink in.

Thea nods. "That makes sense."

"It does?" I ask.

"Sure. Everyone loves you. If you love him, they'll all love him."

I groan. "It's not *love*."

"You know what I mean."

Everly grins. "Good for you jumping on *that* opportunity."

I smile. That's Everly. She's always telling me that I should go out with *someone* for no other reason than to scratch a few horny itches. "It was Astrid's idea."

"You didn't fight it too hard, I hope," Everly says. "You're a smart girl. Take a good deal when you see it."

Did I fight it at all? I think I said something about it being crazy, but I really mostly remember my thoughts spinning and my body feeling really hot and thinking about how I would probably get to kiss him again.

I should not be this hung up on that one spontaneous kiss at the airport that wasn't even a real kiss. I should deny that this is anything other than a PR stunt. There will be no itch-scratching or enjoyment.

But my brain instantly rejects that.

Why can't I enjoy hanging out with Alex?

And I don't like the word stunt. It's a PR *tactic*. I'm not trying to fool anyone into thinking Alex is something he's not. I do actually like Alex, and he's going to be great for the team, and I think once people give him a chance, they'll think he's a good guy. So this is just a way to cut through the noise and make people shut up and *listen* to him. Get to know him. Want to come buy a ticket and watch some hockey. I'm not asking them for much. And I'm *not* tricking them into anything.

Plus, this will be good for Alex. His sister is here, but otherwise he's alone in Rebel. I can be his personal welcoming committee.

Why that makes my stomach flip, and my cheeks heat, I'm not going to get into.

"You sure that's a good idea?" Andi asks.

Andi is the most practical of all of us. She definitely no longer believes in true love. Not since her ex-husband cheated on her after emotionally and financially abusing her for five years. And she definitely doesn't trust instalove, which is what this would have to be between Alex and me.

"I'm just getting to know him and helping him transition to living here and playing for this team. It's pretty different for him. And in the process, we'll actually be essentially dating. And if that helps the town give him a second chance, all the better."

Yeah, that sounds good.

"Just be careful. I don't want you to get your heart broken."

I shake my head. "It's not serious. It's not even *real*. He's already told me that he's going back to Portland at the end of the season."

"Good," Andi says.

Yeah, these women know how I feel about leaving.

I'm staying in Rebel. This is home. This is family. I have no intention of going anywhere, and I won't be seriously dating anyone who doesn't feel the same.

"But you might as well enjoy him while he's here," Everly says. "If you know what I mean."

I laugh. Of course, I know what she means. Even without her wiggling her eyebrows.

"I can't argue with that," Thea says.

I laugh at my cousin's response. That is definitely not something she would have said before Josh. She was a single mom who was pretty determined to stay single. He broke down a lot of walls when he came into her life at Christmastime almost a year ago now.

"Yeah, have you seen him, Thea?" Everly asks.

"Just photos."

"Even hotter in person. Huuuuuge hands."

He does have huge hands. And now I'm flushed again, thinking about how he caught me at the airport when I threw myself into his arms. And how those hands felt on my face and in my hair when he kissed me.

That was all a show too but… wow.

Yeah, maybe being *careful* is good advice.

"*Anyway,*" I say. "If you hear anything about us, just know it's part of the plan."

"Sure." Everly winks.

"The end of the season is seven months away," Thea says.

"Yes." Is she going to say just enjoy that man's hot mouth and big hands for seven months? What's the harm?

"That's seven months of not getting set up with anyone's nephews, sons, or grandsons," Thea says. She lifts her soda glass. "Enjoy the vacation."

Okay, that's not a bad perk either.

"And the start of the season is only a couple of weeks away, right?" Everly asks.

"Yeah."

We don't have much time at all.

"You better get *on* that then," Everly says with a grin.

I laugh. But yeah…

I guess I'll have to date the hell out of Alex, too.

CHAPTER 7
ALEX

THE LOCKER ROOM IS EMPTY. I'm surprised. Shouldn't the other guys be here changing? Am I late? I check the clock. No. I managed to get myself here on time.

The empty locker room is freaking me out, though.

For one, it's much smaller and plainer than the locker rooms I'm used to, and it only serves to drive home the point that I'm in a much lesser league, and yet I'm still way out of my comfort zone here.

The arena is very nice. It's only a few years old, and they had a huge budget. It's just small. Really small. It seats a third of the number of people the Grays' stadium can seat.

The ceilings are lower, the hallways narrower, there are fewer windows, and there's less…shine. There are fewer fancy embellishments, less glitz.

None of that matters, of course. It just makes me feel a little claustrophobic. Or something.

For another, I realize that most of my socializing, conversation, time off the ice with my teammates happens in the locker room. Being in here alone is very odd.

I head for an empty locker—there are several—and toss my

duffel onto the floor. I drop onto the bench and stare into the empty space.

I think I'm nervous. Holy shit. I've never been nervous about hockey before.

I've been revved up for a game for sure. I've felt adrenaline, anticipation, an I-want-this-one-to-go-well excitement, of course. But I've never been nervous about a *practice*. I can play hockey in my sleep. Everything about it is practically instinct at this point.

But I don't think it's the hockey, exactly, that I'm jittery about.

I've never started with a new team before. Not since I came to play for the Grays at age nineteen, and that almost doesn't count. Declan recruited me. Everyone was excited to have me come. I was a hot shot, at the top of my game, and better than anyone else anyone was recruiting. And I was too young to know that I shouldn't have been that cocky. But the next several years did nothing to quell that confidence. I never gave anyone reason to believe I was anything less than the best.

But that was before the injury. Before I realized I'm not invincible. Before other people surpassed me. Before people started talking about me in the past tense.

Now I am not only starting with a new group of players, I'm definitely not at one-hundred percent. I'm not the star I once was. And I'm starting over in a place that doesn't want me.

Nora does.

That thought echoes through my head and settles in my chest.

Yeah, she fucking does. Nora wants me here. She *needs* me. She said so herself.

That makes me shove up from the bench and start dressing for practice. Fuck these nerves. I'm going out to play hockey in podunk Louisiana for a team that has a swamp wolf as a mascot for fuck's sake. I'm fine.

Several minutes later, I make my way out of the locker room and down the hallway toward the ice. As I near the rink, I finally hear voices. At least I'm not going to be alone on the ice.

But now I'm faced with another first. Feeling strange about being the last to arrive to a party. That has never bothered me before. I don't mind making an entrance.

Man, fuck feeling anxious. I hate it.

You're Alex fucking Olsen. You're a professional hockey star. You won the Cup last year.

They pay you millions of dollars to slap a puck around on the ice.

I grin to myself as Nora's words come back to me. But she's not wrong.

And Nora wants you here so much she dropped everything and sped to New Orleans to save you from the Old Man Posse.

I take a deep breath and skate out onto the ice with a big smile.

Several bodies turn in my direction, and one guy calls, "Hey! Alex is here!"

That causes everyone else to turn toward me as I skate up.

I give the group a grin. "Hey…everybody." There are two women in the group. "I'm Alex."

The guy who called out extends his hand. "We know." His grin is large and genuine. "I'm Beckett. Beckett Moore. Welcome."

Gratefully, I take his hand. "Hey, nice to meet you."

I recognize him from the laminated page Nora gave me. He's the left-winger for my team, the Revelers.

There was a page for each player on each team. There are two teams. My sister has a *league,* not just a hockey team.

"Well, the Revelers need someone to play against," she'd said when I'd looked confused.

I mean…yeah. But why not play against other FPHL teams?

But then Nora had distracted me—her biggest talent, it seems —by handing me a binder.

"Everything you need to know is in here," she'd said with her pretty smile and those big brown eyes shining.

All I could think was, *she's your girlfriend now.*

No, my brain doesn't put "fake" in front of girlfriend. I'm just all in on this dating Nora Delaune thing, it seems.

Which made her handing me a *binder* of things I need to know about my new team and flipping to the first section full of laminated pages, one for each player on the Revelers and the Rascals, and saying, "You can study up on everyone before practice" not really register until she'd left Astrid's office and the little cloud of wildflower scented air and I-get-to-kiss-her-again thoughts cleared.

So, I'd gone through the pages.

All twenty-four players. Each team has only twelve players, significantly fewer than a typical pro team. Each of these teams has a mix of ages, hockey backgrounds, and each has one woman, which is cool. Ingrid Archer is the left wing for the Revelers, and Quinn Trahan is the center for the Rascals.

"We're thrilled to have you," Beckett says.

"Thanks. Sorry, I'm a little late."

My nerves quiet a little, and I take in details. Like the fact that they are not actually practicing yet. Which I guess is a good thing. I didn't miss anything. But no one seems actually dressed for hockey practice. They've all got skates on, but there are no pads, no shin guards, no helmets. There aren't even sticks or pucks anywhere. They all look like they just showed up for a day of ice-skating.

Now I feel like a dumbass, and I'm not sure why. Other than the fact that I am clearly dressed for practice in full gear with a hockey stick in hand.

Are they hazing me? Possible. And that would be fair. They've all been together since I don't even know when. Some of them have been playing together as teammates from the previous FPHL team. I am sure they've been practicing together all summer.

"So yeah, I know I'm late to join and catch up with everything. And most of you probably know about my injury. But I can assure you, I've been working out, and working hard on coming back. I promise I'm bringing my full game and will work as hard as everyone else," I say.

Someone snorts, and I turn toward the dark-haired, muscled, tattooed man.

I recognize him right away. This is Lawson Landry. He played in the big leagues for a couple of years. He was cut from his team —something that almost never happens—after he beat the absolute shit out of one of his own teammates at a bar one night. I knew about that without reading his binder page. Everyone in hockey knew about that. He sent a teammate to the hospital. But the page had told me that his extended family is from this area and that he'd come back here to be close to them after his career imploded.

"Your fifty percent is better than anyone's one-hundred percent down here. Nobody's worried about that," Lawson says.

"Hey," someone grumbles.

"Real nice, Landry," someone else says.

"Hey, he's not the only Landry," a big man with a full beard and long hair says, grinning. "Call him Outlaw so we don't get mixed up."

Outlaw was the nickname Lawson picked up during his relatively short stint with the pros and, according to stories, was accurate. The fact that he didn't even last a full season with the Dallas Dragons makes me think most were.

"Oh sure, Zeke," someone else says. "You and Lawson are *so* much alike."

The big man laughs. "Just don't want to risk it." He claps Lawson—his cousin, I guess?—on the shoulder.

Lawson rolls his eyes.

"We appreciate what you're saying, Alex," Beckett jumps in, shooting Lawson a frown. "But yeah, none of us are worried about you catching up."

"Well, it seems I missed practice," I say, looking around the group.

"Oh, you thought you were coming to *hockey* practice?" Zeke asks.

I nod. "Well, yeah."

"Nah, this is a dance lesson," Beckett says with a grin.

My brows arch. "A dance lesson?" My gaze drops to his feet. "On skates?"

"It's a choreography rehearsal," Lawson says.

"That's what I said." Beckett shrugs.

"It's not dance class," Lawson says, turning toward Beckett. "We also have a couple of fights *choreographed*. A couple of you have choreography for how you come onto the ice. There's intermission stuff."

Beckett also turns to face Lawson more fully. "It's all set to music. Like a dance."

"Does your sister know that you're referring to her choreography as dancing?"

Beckett frowns. "How about you don't worry about my sister?"

"Well," I jump in as the tension between the men climbs quickly. "Clearly, I'm here at the wrong time. Sorry to interrupt."

Lawson looks back to me. "They didn't tell you?"

"Tell me what?" I ask. Trepidation slithers down my spine. Fuck, I don't like trepidation either.

Lawson's scowl eases, almost as if he's now entertained. "This *is* what you're here for."

I shake my head. "No one said anything about choreography or...dancing." I shake my head harder as they all start to smile. "I don't dance."

Someone chuckles. "Oh, you think you're here for real hockey."

Beckett shakes his head. "This is real hockey. It's just got... embellishments." He grins at me. "It's fun. Seriously."

The trepidation definitely grows. What are they talking about? "Embellishments?" I don't want to know. I'm not sure how I know that, but I do.

Beckett nods, and he actually seems enthusiastic about it. "Yeah. It's hockey. I swear. There's just a little more to it. More *fun* to it."

"Oh yeah, you're gonna love it," Lawson says, sarcasm dripping. "A professional hockey player who's given his life to the game and made it his career is totally going to think doing skits and playing with fan-voted rules is a *great* idea."

Skits? Fan-voted rules?

What the fuck…

"You've got the worst attitude," Beckett says, turning back to Lawson. "What's wrong with having a good time? Making it more fan-friendly? Wanting people to be involved?"

"We're not all working on 'branding ourselves'," Lawson says, making air quotes with his fingers. "As the feel-good, good-time hockey goofball, so that some team will pick us up because our social media following is huge. Some of us actually want to play serious hockey."

"I take having fun and interacting with the fans seriously," Beckett says, moving closer to Lawson. "There's nothing wrong with that. Marketing and PR are a part of professional sports, and social media is a serious part of professional sports. Everyone knows that. If I can put butts in the seats, that will matter."

"Uh huh. Well, some people make it based on skill and talent." Lawson glides closer to Beckett. Everyone else parts to let the men face off.

But I note that Zeke and a couple of other guys stay close. Within arm's length at least. Which makes me wonder how often these two have gotten into it.

That doesn't bode well for the team.

Astrid and Nora didn't mention dancing and skits, and they didn't tell me that I've got two teammates who clearly are polar opposites—the dark cloud and the sunshine—who let their differences spill onto the ice.

"And some people make a name because they've got a huge fucking chip on their shoulders and can't control their temper and end up in the headlines when they get *cut*, rather than because of anything positive," Beckett says, nearly on top of Lawson now. He's got the other man by a couple of inches, but Lawson is wider and more muscular and was one of the toughest defenders in the league when he played.

I move in. "Okay, guys."

They don't care about me—or anyone else—right now, though.

"You don't know anything about me getting cut, Moore," Lawson says through clenched teeth. "Back off."

"No one's making you stay here. You could leave if you hate it so much," Beckett tells him.

"Guys—" I start again, moving in so I can step between them if anyone lunges.

But just then a shrill whistle splits the air.

"Okay! Let's go!"

I turn to find a gorgeous, petite brunette skating toward us.

She's in leggings, a cropped sweatshirt that falls off one shoulder, and she's got a whistle around her neck.

I glance back to find Beckett and Lawson with several feet between them, both looking at the woman, and stoically not at one another.

She comes to a stop in front of me. She has to tip her head back to look up at me. She can't be more than five-five.

"Hi! You must be Alex!"

"Yeah, hi."

"I'm Sutton. I'm the choreographer."

I look back at the team. If this is a hazing prank, they're really going all in.

But my gut is telling me that's not what this is.

Dammit.

"Nice to meet you. I should warn you, not only can I not dance, I had no idea there would be choreography involved with...this."

She casts a glance at the group behind me. "I've heard all of that before," she assures me. "It will be okay. When you can't dance or lip sync very well, it actually makes it even better. Provided you can laugh at yourself."

My brows arch. "Lip sync?"

"Yeah, it's too hard to get mic-ed up and some people..." She glances behind me again with an exasperated look. "Seem to think they're not good singers and don't believe me that people would like that even more."

My sister has some explaining to do.

"Can I ask *why* we're doing choreography and lip syncing?" I ask. "I know I'm late to get here and should maybe know all of this, but someone needs to catch me up."

"Nora didn't tell you?" Sutton asks.

Nora. Just hearing her name makes my pulse beat harder. Damn.

"*Nora* should have told me? Not Astrid?"

Sutton laughs. "Well, Nora sold Astrid on it, so she'd be the best one."

Interesting. "Neither of them told me anything." Nora was a little busy dodging kidnappers. And telling me about Rougarou. And completely enchanting me.

But seems there were a few additional details I could have used...

"Can you give me the short version, and I'll ask Nora about it later?"

I will *definitely* be asking Nora about this later.

"Well, there's this baseball team in Georgia that does something like this with baseball. They play the game, but it's mixed with choreography, different rules, fan involvement, and just fun."

I frown. "The ones that dress in all yellow? They're a minor league team or something, right?"

"Yes, the yellow ones. They're not even minor league. They're in their own league."

Oh...no...

That team is wildly popular and all over social media, that's true. But it's definitely not straightforward, "real" baseball. It's over the top and chaotic.

Does it look like fun? Sure. I guess. If you're into rambunctious shows that look a little like sporting events.

"Can you…" I clear my throat and glance over my shoulder. "Fill me in on these new rules and things?"

Sutton smiles. "Oh, you'll have a binder. Nora will get that to you."

The binder.

I sigh. I clearly should have looked through it more thoroughly.

"Yeah, bring it to the Rec," Beckett says, clapping me on the shoulder. "We'll go over it with you."

"Bring my binder to the Rec?" I repeat. Do I need to go buy highlighters at the bookstore too? "Where's the Rec?"

"Below your new apartment." Beckett grins. "It's the bar half of Perks and Rec."

Right.

I blow out a breath. "Great." The bar where they vote that they hate me more than the most disgusting vegetable on the planet.

"But for now," Sutton says, addressing the group. "You all need to line up. We *are* getting this choreography right today and yes, we *are* keeping the song from *Princess and the Frog*. It's not up for debate."

Beckett elbows me as Sutton skates to the center of the ice, and everyone starts moving into position. "That's a movie set in New Orleans and on the bayou."

"I've heard of it." Though I'm not sure how I've heard of it.

"I've got a solo." He grins.

Of course he does.

I nod. "It's a cartoon, right? Frogs and a big alligator?"

"Yep." He chuckles. "Just let Sutton know if you want a solo, too. She's had to bribe and threaten everyone except me, Zeke, and Josh."

"I'm good."

He laughs and skates off to get into position at the front of the group.

I hang back and wait for instructions on where to go.

But I have a bad feeling that I might end up at the front eventually. Because that's where the star, the *leader*, the big name should be, right? Even on a dancing, lip-syncing hockey team.

I groan internally.

Astrid owes me an explanation and a fucking raise.

I don't even know what she's paying me.

"You can just hang out and watch for a little bit," Sutton calls to me. "I'll work you in, for sure, but let's give you an idea about what we're doing. Then we'll probably need a couple of one-on-one sessions to get you caught up."

I give her a thumbs up.

The music starts, and everyone starts moving.

And Jesus Christ.

Beckett's actually pretty good. He's hamming it up anyway.

Josh isn't bad. Zeke's into it. Ingrid is actually quite good.

Everyone else... well, half of them look like hockey players who are trying to dance on ice. Meaning, they look ridiculous, but at least they're upright and they're moving in unison. The other half look like people who can probably skate forward and can *maybe* change direction without falling, but I'm not sure they can skate *and* hit a puck at the same time because they sure as hell can't skate, turn, and move their arms at the same time.

Wow. This is so bad it's...yeah, it's entertaining.

I catch myself grinning.

But Nora owes me, too. She should have told me about this. She knows who I am, where I'm coming from. She should have *warned* me. She should have known this is a huge departure from what I do on the ice.

As Zeke turns the wrong way and bumps into Lawson, sending the other man onto his ass, cursing loudly, and knocking over another man, who knocks over another man like burly dominos, I'm torn between laughing and heading straight back to the airport for the first flight back to Portland.

I don't need hockey. I could be a...

Nothing comes to mind. I have no other skills. I'm stuck here.

Nora's definitely in trouble for keeping this from me.

How should I make her make it up to me?

I feel a little kick in my chest.

Hmmm… that could be fun.

And it's not lost on me that every time my thoughts start to get anything less than happy and optimistic, the thought of Nora picks me right back up.

CHAPTER 8
ALEX

I APPROACH the front of Perks and Rec and wonder if there's a back entrance I'll be able to use to get to and from my apartment. Going in and out of the front door of the coffee shop-slash-bar where most of the town gathers, seemingly all day long, will ensure my life is front and center for everyone.

How will you get Nora in and out, you mean.

Yeah, especially because everyone greets the woman like a long-lost friend every time she sets foot inside the shop.

But for now, I go in through the front door, tinkly bell over my head and all.

Sure enough, everyone turns to see who just arrived.

And I definitely don't get the warm, "Alex!" greeting welcoming me in.

It's about twenty after eight and I'm sweaty and annoyed from hockey practice. The team is coming over to the bar after everyone cleans up, so I need to head upstairs to shower before they arrive.

At least I don't have to go far to meet them.

And I don't need to worry about driving home after a beer or two.

I spot Ruth sitting at the coffee bar working on what looks like homework. I'm so relieved to have a friendly face that I bee-line for the girl.

"Hey, Ruth!" I give her my best smile, trying to hide the exasperation I've been feeling since…well, since I got on the plane this morning.

"Hi!" Her smile is big and wide. "How was your first practice?"

Easily the most bonkers thing I've ever done. "Great. Everyone was really nice," I say. That much is true. The team seems great.

"Oh, good." She hops off the stool. "I'm supposed to tell Grandpa when you're here. He'll take you up to the apartment."

"Great."

She starts for the kitchen. "Could you, uh, help show me around?" I ask.

Do I feel like I need my twelve-year-old fan to buffer between me and my gruff landlord? Yes. One thousand percent.

"Sure!" she says enthusiastically. She pushes the kitchen door open. "Grandpa! He's here!"

"Fine. Just a minute," comes his brusque reply.

She looks back at me. "There's only one apartment up there. And it's small. You wouldn't have any trouble finding things. But it's probably really different from where you live. I saw pictures of your apartment in Portland in *Hockey Hunks* magazine."

Her cheeks flame red, and I rush to cover her embarrassment. "Oh, they did a great article. They made my place look really cool." I rack my brain for something, someway, I can relate to a twelve-year-old girl. The only thing I know we have in common is hockey and Nora. "Which room did you like the best?" I'd love to ask her all about Nora, but that would probably come off creepy.

I can talk about my apartment easily enough. So, the kid looks at *Hockey Hunks* magazine online. A lot of dudes do, too, actually.

It's called *Hockey Hunks*, and yeah, they take a bunch of photos of us, and sure, some of them are shirtless, but they also do in-depth stories. They highlight where we live and our favorite restaurants, movies and books we like, giving a behind-the-scenes look at our lives. At least that's the idea. Their goal is to appeal to a demographic they think might be less into stats and offensive strategy and more into the players as men. But my experience is that women know just as much about the game as men, and men are just as into what our apartments look like, what cars we drive, and how we like to spend our free time as women are.

"Your living room," Ruth answers without even pausing to think. "You don't cook, and you don't seem to spend much time in the other rooms. But you hang out a lot in your living room. Plus, you have that really great view. Of course, you're not gonna have a really great view here. But you probably won't be here a lot either. The town is going to want to get to know you, and there are a lot of activities for you to attend." She's a chatterbox now.

And she's observant. She's completely right about my apartment. I don't spend a lot of time in any of the rooms other than the living room. That's where I kick back and watch TV and movies, play games, and entertain. Sure, my bedroom gets some use… But I don't expect a girl this age to really think about that.

Now her cousin Nora, on the other hand, may be a different story.

I'd like Nora to do more than think about my bedroom, though.

"Well, come on then," Bruce says, coming through the swinging door. He sets a hand on the back of Ruth's neck and steers her around the edge of the counter.

He doesn't ask if she wants to come with us, and I wonder if he wants a third person to dispel some awkwardness between us, too.

In the corner of the restaurant, behind a tall potted tree that is, no shit, growing lemons, there's a pink and orange curtain-covered doorway, and beyond the curtain is a staircase.

I follow them up the fourteen steps to the second floor.

Bruce opens the door on the landing, and it swings in with a groan.

He steps in first, and Ruth follows. I have to duck slightly to avoid hitting the doorframe with my forehead.

Bruce crosses to a lamp and clicks it on. "This is yours while you're here," Bruce says, walking into the middle of the apartment, which is also the middle of the living room. "One of the hockey players from last year's team lived here. Most of the other guys stayed in town, so there aren't too many places open. But if you can find something better that you like more, feel free to go."

I arch my brows. Warm welcome, this is not.

"My sister seems to think this is the perfect place for me," I tell him. I notice my bags sitting at the end of the hallway that I assume leads to the bedroom and bath. "Have you met Astrid?"

Bruce stands with his feet shoulder-width apart, his hands tucked into the back pockets of his jeans. The bright orange T-shirt he wears reads Perks and Rec, and has a coffee cup leaning against a beer mug on the front. He's taller than the other three men that wanted to do me harm, and he seems a little younger. He's maybe in his mid- to late sixties, rather than mid-seventies. He's also got a rounder stomach, a broader chest, has a very neatly trimmed beard, and looks at me with an air of disdain that I have rarely experienced.

The three men at the airport seemed mischievous. This man looks like I tracked pig shit into his mansion, and I'm not even qualified to clean it up.

"I have met your sister," Bruce tells me. "She seems used to getting her way."

I chuckle. "That's an understatement."

"So you're going to stay here because she tells you to?"

I shrug. "I'm going to stay here because it has a bed and a shower, and that's really all I need while I'm in town."

He looks around, then back to me with an eyebrow. "For what it's worth, I saw the photos of your Portland apartment, too. Are you sure about that?"

I look around too. I've never seen this many flowers in one

place in my life. The apartment's decor can best be described as Grandma-core.

The floors are hardwood, but clearly old and not refinished. The draperies at the window are lacy. The walls are covered in floral wallpaper with bold burgundy, gold, and greens. The side tables are mismatched, and each holds a lamp. One is a round porcelain lamp covered in flowers with a plain white shade. The other has a brass base, and the shade is the flowered part. Glass with bright red flowers that, again, don't match anything else.

The couch in between is an oversized, lumpy, floral-upholstered piece—this time featuring pink and blue flowers. There is a blue armchair, a scarred coffee table on a braided, multi-colored rug, and a television that easily weighs fifty pounds sitting on a very rickety stand. There's a ceiling fan, turning lazily overhead, and an air conditioning unit in the window, humming and rattling intermittently.

To my left is a half wall that divides the living room from the kitchen. From what I can see, there are more flowered curtains on the window over the sink.

I smile. Someone either did it intentionally or honestly did not care *at all* and just threw furniture into this room haphazardly. There's no in between.

There's got to be a flowered comforter or a quilt on the bed, and a wooden side table that was new sometime in the sixties, and if there's not an armoire, I'm going to be very disappointed.

"All of this furniture was donated by people in town," Bruce says. "So treat it well."

I give a soft snort. This furniture has seen some stuff. I don't think I can do anything to it that hasn't been done.

He frowns. "And be careful what you say about it down in the café."

"I would never disparage the furniture down in the café," I tell him.

"Miss Dora says this is the most comfortable couch in town," Ruth says, crossing to the piece and plopping down in the center cushion. She bounces up and down. "She says her husband took hundreds of naps on this couch."

"Is that right?" I ask, eyeing the couch. I do like a good nap now and then.

"Yep, took his very last one right there," Bruce says.

I look at him quickly. "Do you mean…he died there?"

Ruth nods. "Miss Dora said she didn't know he was dead for hours because he always slept here."

I take a step back from the couch without thinking. I have a sofa a guy died on. A guy was *dead* on that sofa. Terrific.

"Was that recent? In this room?" I ask.

Bruce shakes his head. "She had it in her living room for a couple of years before she donated it to us."

I look at Ruth. "How do ghosts work? Do they stay with the furniture, or do they stay in the room where they die?"

She giggles. And doesn't answer me.

That isn't reassuring in the least.

"The refrigerator won't be telling you the weather, or giving you the headline news, or making you different shapes of ice," Bruce says. "There're a couple of ice trays up in the freezer, and if you come to the café before eight, you can get all the weather and headline news in person."

He really did read that article from *Hockey Hunks*. Yes, my fridge in Portland does all of those things. But I can live without all of that for seven months.

Probably.

"Washer and dryer are downstairs, back of the kitchen. You'll have to share with the café."

Now *that* makes me pause.

I'm going to have to do laundry.

I don't do that in Portland. The same woman who cleans my apartment and cooks for me three nights a week also does my laundry and handles my dry cleaning. And yes, we had a housekeeper and cook when I was growing up. No one taught me to do things like laundry, and it's never been an issue.

That's not really my *fault*. It's just a thing. Like people who are never taught to ice skate can't play ice hockey. It's not a mark against their character.

But I'm not going to say that to Bruce. He probably read that in the article and is just waiting for me to react.

I nod. "Sure. Great. No problem."

Bruce rolls his eyes but turns on his heel and starts for the door. "I'm downstairs if you need anything. I'll let you run a tab for meals, but only up to a hundred bucks before you pay it off."

I wonder if a one-hundred-dollar tab is extending me a favor or if that's like half or a third of what he lets everybody else do.

Ruth hangs back as Bruce stomps down the stairs. I can hear every step.

"Is the apartment really okay?" she asks.

"Sure. It's fine."

"I know it's not as nice as what you have in Portland. I know how much you like your shower."

Jesus. I probably said that in that article, too. I love my fucking shower. But I've stayed in hotels without rainfall shower heads and multiple heads in the wall. That's been fine. It's seven months. I can definitely survive seven months without a fancy-schmancy showerhead.

Probably.

"Okay, so you read that article in *Hockey Hunks*," I start.

"Oh, yeah. And I've read a ton of other articles too," she gushes.

That could be really helpful to me right now as embarrassing as some of that might be. "Great. So you know that I'm not very good at anything but playing hockey."

She shakes her head. "I'm sure that's not true."

"Well, thanks. Let's put it this way, I don't do a lot of laundry."

She nods. "You have to focus on your career. And there's a lot of training. And promo and stuff.

I like this kid. I was a dick to her, and she's still defending me. To me. "Yeah. And I am pretty spoiled, if I'm honest."

She grins at that.

"Do you happen to know how to use the washer and dryer downstairs?"

Her whole face brightens. "I *totally* know how. Do you want me to do your laundry for you?"

She says that as if she's eager for me to hire her.

I frown. "No. Absolutely not. No, I was kind of hoping that you could teach me to do it, though."

She smiles as if this amuses her. "Totally. And you can ask Bruce stuff. I mean, he might kind of frown a lot. But eventually, he'll come around. Everybody was a big fan of yours before…"

I wince. Right, *before* I was an asshole to everyone's favorite person. "Everybody?"

"Well, half of town."

"There was already half that didn't like me? Before…?"

"The newer part of town doesn't really care about hockey. They probably didn't *hate* you," she says as if trying to comfort me. "But they won't be excited you're here because if you make the hockey team great, then Sean Patrick can't buy the arena."

"But half *did* like me?"

"Oh, for sure! The half that hangs out downtown and lives around here. The ones you'll see all the time!" she says enthusiastically. "They're all really good friends of my grandpa Harley's. Like Brewser and Wilson. They were the lawyer and doctor in town back when there was just one of each."

I straighten. "Was Brewser the lawyer or doctor?"

"The doctor. Wilson was a lawyer. Before they retired. They grew up here, and everyone from here used them at one time. Those guys have always been around here. Lots of people are like that here. So they're really close to my family, and they were big fans of yours because Harley and Leo were big fans of yours."

"Have I lost them forever?" I ask her.

She shakes her head. "I don't think so. Especially because you're going to help this hockey team be great."

Right. No pressure at all.

And I probably shouldn't care too much about this tiny town and its people that I don't even know. Especially when I'm not going to be here for long. A lot of my teammates would tell me that I'm already overthinking this. I'm going to come and play hockey, to the best of my ability. But that's what I always do. It's not fully on me if this team fails or succeeds.

Probably.

CHAPTER 9
NORA

YOU NEED *to start dating me tonight. Right now. I'm at Perks and Rec…I guess the Rec part?… with the team.*

My stomach does a very obvious swoopy-flippy thing when I read the message from Alex.

I'd waited around, stalling over my dinner with the girls, but they all eventually had to get going, and even though I was there until well after eight, Alex hadn't shown up.

I knew eventually he would. His apartment was upstairs, after all, but I'd finally walked over to City Hall to get some work done.

Now he was texting me. To come date him at the bar.

Well, if he insists.

"Nora!"

"Hi, honey!"

"Hi, Nora!"

I smile and greet everyone calling out to me as I cross the coffee shop. I wave at my cousin Violet, who is behind the bar.

I find Alex immediately upon stepping from the coffee shop into the bar.

He's sitting at a long table with the rest of the hockey players.

And he's scowling. Darkly.

Great.

The players' table is just inside the arched doorway that separates the two sides of Perks and Rec. He's sitting with Beckett, Josh, Lawson, Quinn, and Wes. He has the binder full of rules and activity ideas open in front of him. They've got mugs and glasses in varying states of emptiness. I appreciate them all coming out with him and text Violet that I'm covering the tab.

It's already covered, she responds.

By who?

Astrid.

Ah. That makes sense. I give her another wave across the room to let her know I got the message.

I should have expected that. Just like I should've expected Alex's scowls once he opened the binder.

Alex Olsen is a professional hockey player. A very, very good professional hockey player.

Revelers hockey is going to be a huge change for him.

If I had to choose the people I wanted taking him through the rules and set up, Lawson Landry would not be at the table. Lawson thinks this is all ridiculous.

I would have fired him from the team if he weren't so damned good. And to be honest, his bad boy reputation might just pull some people in to watch him. If nothing else to see if he'll lose his shit on the ice. Or maybe to see the big, tattooed grump performing "Shake It Off" after he gets a penalty. Either way, he promises some entertainment.

And maybe not Quinn. I love Quinn Trahan. She's great. She's been a tomboy as long as I've known her and is actually a hell of a hockey player. But she's not as good at the goofy stuff. She's shy and very awkward unless she's got a ball or a stick in her hand. That's a long-running joke with her best friend, my cousin Jasper, in fact. Quinn has never had a boyfriend, so he thinks it's even funnier that she handles "balls and sticks" so well. Jasper is basically a thirteen-year-old boy in a twenty-five-year-old man's body.

But Josh is a very good sport, and since he's gotten together with Thea, he feels even more invested in the things that make Harley and this town happy.

Wes, the Revelers goalie, is also a nice guy and has embraced what we're trying to do with the new league.

And then there's Beckett Moore. My favorite person on the team, most days, truly. Beckett might be hamming it up and enthusiastically learning every step, donning every costume, and even bringing us additional big, fun ideas in order to personally gain followers on social media and grab the attention of a professional team, but he is the loudest advocate for this new kind of hockey. It's perfect for him. Beckett is like a ray of sunshine, always smiling, laughing, and having a good time.

And thank God, he and Sutton moved home a few years ago. Not only is Beckett's attitude huge for this project, but his sister has turned into a great friend. She's a dancer and figure skater, too, so not only does she teach dance lessons—everything from ballet and tap to little kids to ballroom dancing for our senior citizens—for my Parks and Rec department, but she's also taken on the role of choreographer for the hockey team.

I approach the table, avoiding Alex's attention for a moment since he's scowling at Beckett.

I need to "start dating him". But what should I do? Go up to him and rub my hand up his arm? Kiss his cheek? Just pull a stool close and sit pressed up against his side? All of those are appealing. But suddenly, the prospect of launching our relationship here in public *right now* makes it feel really real. And I'm not sure how to do this. Or if I'm ready. Not for the town's interest and questions, but for *Alex*. He specifically said this would involve spending a lot of time together, hand-holding, kissing, and sitting close.

That means I'm going to be perpetually horny for the next seven months. I'll admit it.

Am I ready for *that*?

"Say that again," he demands.

"There are still three periods, like in regular hockey, but in the first period, every goal counts for one point. In period two, goals count for two points, and in period three, goals count for three points," Beckett says.

"No." Alex shakes his head. "That's ridiculous. Scores could be like fifty to twenty."

"Exactly," Beckett says with a grin. "Fun, right?"

Alex just growls.

And my stomach and girl parts have evidently not gotten the memo about this all being just for show and to be careful because they definitely respond to that gruff, masculine sound.

My gaze is immediately drawn to his big hands and thick fingers splayed over the binder pages.

A shiver goes through my body.

It's just to make him more popular in town. You're not going to get to feel those hands anywhere important.

Disappointment jabs me. Which is *really* stupid.

"This also says that the last minute of period one and period three everything that even touches the net counts as a point." He looks up at Beckett accusingly. "The puck doesn't even have to go in the net?"

"Nope. Super exciting. Fans love big scores."

I can see Alex's jaw clench.

"What else?" he asks, looking at everyone around the table. "I'll read this later. Give me the highlights. What are the absolute craziest rules in here?"

"Fans get to vote on what happens when you get a penalty," Quinn says.

Yeah, I agree that one's a little wild.

"What does that mean?" Alex asks.

"There are two options each time there's a penalty," Quinn explains. "The fans get to vote on what happens. For instance, there might be a song the players have to sing, or maybe the player has to play for a minute with a tiny stick."

"What the hell is a tiny stick?" Alex interrupts.

"A smaller than average stick. It's shorter and thinner," Wes helps.

"What else?" Alex asks, clearly not really wanting to know.

"There are actually a few other things," Quinn says, her voice hesitant now.

"It's not Quinn's decision," Lawson says, frowning at Alex. "If you don't like it, talk to your sister or Nora."

I appreciate Lawson defending Quinn, but not so much blaming me.

Even though it's my fault.

And I think Alex is very aware of that.

I can't see Alex's full expression, but I can imagine it's dark and scary.

"There's *a lot* of shit you're not going to like," Lawson says.

"Tell me some of it," Alex says.

"Fans get input on who does the face-off. They can decide if they think the refs got a call wrong. They can change the rules in the last third of—"

"The rules are going to change *during the game*?" Alex asks.

Based on the way Quinn's eyes widen, Alex must be shooting daggers. I need to step in. Not as his fake girlfriend, but as the ambassador for the new hockey style. This is not Quinn's fault. I know, for a fact, my friend would rather play straightforward hockey as well.

"Hi, everybody."

They all turn toward me, and there are multiple looks of relief. Quinn immediately spins on her stool and slides to the floor. "Oh, hi. Now that you're here to handle this, I've gotta go."

I grin at her and lean over to give her a quick hug.

Quinn doesn't initiate hugging, but she always accepts it from her girlfriends. "Thanks for helping welcome Alex."

She glances at him. "We're glad he's here."

I meet Alex's gaze over her shoulder. He's watching me intently. "I am too."

Lawson also climbs off his stool. "I'm out of here, too, boss. You've got this." It's not a question. He's turning Alex over to me.

I'm okay with that.

We have some fake dating to kick off, after all.

I nod. "Sure. I can finish filling Alex in." I look at Wes. "Unless you want to stay?"

He shakes his head quickly, as does Josh.

Josh gives me a wink. "I can't wait to get home and hear how excited Ruth is that Alex is in town."

Alex looks at him. "Wait, you're Ruth's dad?"

"Her mom is my girlfriend. Hoping to be stepdad eventually," Josh says.

My chest warms as I take in Josh's smile. His whole face changes when he talks about Thea and Ruth.

I glance at Alex and note that he looks sheepish now. "So you're probably not my biggest fan. Thanks for being so good at practice and with this whole thing," he says, circling his finger to indicate the binder and the conversation that happened at the table.

Josh nods. "I wasn't. Ruth was definitely disappointed. But I don't think it's all bad for her to see someone she admires go through a tough time and then come out on the other side a little humbled and be willing and able to make an apology."

Alex looks surprised. "I did. I met Ruth earlier. She seems great."

Josh smiles proudly. "She is. Her mom's done a fantastic job."

"I am really sorry I was a dick to her," Alex says.

Josh extends his hand. "Just don't let it happen again."

Alex takes his hand and pumps it once. "Promise."

I know Alex won't directly be an asshole to Ruth. This town would literally run him out of the city if he did that. But if Ruth thinks that we're dating, when we break up, Ruth is going to be disappointed.

All the more reason to make sure everyone knows this is *casual* and we're mostly just friends.

It's also important for *me* to remember all of those things. Because if I show even a glimmer of heartbreak, Ruth will notice, and it will bother her.

"You staying?" I ask Beckett, taking the stool that Josh just vacated.

Beckett looks from me to Alex, then back to me. "You think you can sell him on this all by yourself?"

I look at Alex. "I'm not sure. I know a lot of the stuff we're going to try with the hockey team is going to be different for him. I might have to try to sell him on more than just hockey while he's here."

There. Just a tiny hint of something else. Beckett Moore will absolutely pick up on that and run with it.

Beckett's huge grin tells me I nailed that. He rotates on his stool and climbs off. "Then I think you definitely have this handled and don't need me at all," he says. He glances toward the door, and his eyes light up. "Actually, I see someone I need to speak to very badly."

I glance over and see Andi and Everly coming through the door.

My friends didn't mention they were on their way back to the bar.

Probably because they weren't until someone texted that the team was here, which they knew meant I would be too. With my new "boyfriend" for the first time.

Alex looks over as well. "I kind of met them this morning, too. Is one of them your girlfriend?" he asks Beckett.

"The gorgeous blonde," Beckett says.

I laugh. Beckett has an enormous, obvious, everyone-knows-it and he knows everyone knows it crush on Andi.

Andi does not feel the same way.

"Really?" Alex asks.

"No," I say. "But I think Beckett has a rejection kink or something."

Beckett laughs. "Just an eternal optimist."

He starts in Andi's direction. I see Everly grin and Andi roll her eyes when they see him coming.

"Has everyone in this town pretty much lived here all their lives?" Alex asks as he closes the binder.

"You don't want to talk about the hockey team anymore?"

"Is all of the information in the binder?" he asks, his tone resigned. "All the crazy rules, the big ideas? Things like fans getting to vote on fucking everything?"

"Yeah. Pretty much. Keep in mind that the rules will be evolving. There are probably some we haven't even thought of yet."

He closes his eyes and groans.

I like that sound too much too.

Do not like that sound. You should not like his sexy groans and growls.

"This isn't just regular hockey with some singing and dancing thrown in, Wildflower."

"I know."

His eyes open, and he pins me with an intent stare. "You are asking me to play a game according to rules that are going to be made up as we go along. Rules that are going to be changed week to week."

"Yes. Fan engagement is the main priority."

"That sounds chaotic as fuck."

"Hockey is already pretty chaotic, isn't it?" I ask with a laugh. "All these guys skating in all different directions all the time. The puck shooting up and down the rink. Guys scrambling to get to it. Never know where it's going to go."

He sits up straighter and frowns at me as if I just said the most offensive thing he's ever heard.

"Hockey might seem chaotic from the outside, but it's absolutely not. Everyone has a position to play. Things proceed according to a strategy and rules. Certain things happen for certain reasons. When you hit the puck in certain ways, it responds in a fairly predictable manner. Sure, sometimes things happen that you don't expect, but you know what to do when they happen. And everyone understands that."

I think about that as I study him.

"Okay, I'll accept that."

He nods.

"So, yes, this is going to be a little chaotic."

He sighs.

I smile.

"Why didn't you tell me that this isn't real hockey?"

I lift a shoulder. I have to make this seem like it's fine. Like *he'll* be fine. Because he will be. I hope. "It's real hockey. There are just some…extra things."

"You can *not* call this hockey, Wildflower."

I can't help it. I kind of like him frustrated. I think things in Alex Olsen's life have always gone pretty smoothly. Maybe this will be good for him. "You act like we're asking you to play a totally different sport. It's hockey. There are just some new rules and a few songs thrown in. And, honestly, I think it's going to be big."

"Hockey's already big. Why can't we just play regular hockey?"

"People can drive to New Orleans for regular hockey. To get them to stay here, we have to give them something different. To get people to *come here*, to actually drive in from other places— which we do need because we need a bigger crowd than we can get depending just on Rebel itself—then we need something really fun and unique."

"Sutton said it's like that baseball team from Georgia."

I sit forward. "Yes! Have you watched them play? I've watched every interview with the owner of that league and read his books. He set out to create a game that people simply *had to* pay attention to. He wanted to give them something that was fun the entire time."

"Hockey is *way* more fun than baseball already," Alex protests. "It's often rated as one of the most exciting sports to watch."

I laugh. "You're not biased at all, of course."

"I am. Completely," he admits. "But still…it's faster paced. That's just a fact. There's more happening. Constant motion. Possession changes all the time."

"I love hockey," I remind him. "That doesn't mean it can't be *more* fun."

"You really think fans want to see the players out there *dancing* and lip syncing in stupid hats?"

"I think fans are going to love this," I say with a nod.

He sighs and slumps over the table. "Sutton didn't pull out the wigs for the *Princess and the Frog* song, but there were cowboy hats for "Friends in Low Places,"" he says.

I grin. "I love that song from *Princess and the Frog*."

"Of course you do," he mutters. "And, apparently, when "Hard to Say I'm Sorry" plays during a penalty, there will be wigs and giant sunglasses."

I nod. "I love that."

"There was also swaying. And kicking."

I grin. "Amazing."

"I don't sing and dance. I play hockey."

"And that's what you're going to do here. You might have to do a few other little things. But there are plenty of guys to do the big stuff. Beckett wants to be the goofball front man anyway."

His eyes narrow. "You don't seem too bothered by me being bothered."

I prop my chin on my hand. "Should I be?"

He leans in. "Shouldn't my *girlfriend* care when I'm upset?"

God, he smells good. He must have showered at the arena, because *surely* he would have commented on the apartment upstairs if he'd seen it.

And he's so *warm*. The air around me and between us seems to heat ten degrees.

"That's a good point. I probably should," I agree.

"You should probably make me glad to be here *in spite of* bonkers hockey," he says.

Hot tingles race over my body.

"And how would I do that?"

"I only have fifty-eight ideas," he says.

I laugh.

His eyes heat. "So how are we going to let everyone know we're dating? Should we make some kind of announcement?"

"Oh, we're not going to need to do that," I say.

"No?"

I lean in, wrap both arms around his neck, and say, "Trust me. It's going to be all over town in about twenty minutes."

Then I kiss him.

CHAPTER 10
ALEX

THE MATTRESS on the bed in my new apartment is too short. I am also too tall for the showerhead in the shower. The water pressure sucks, and it takes forever to heat up. It's also cramped. But instead of being upset about it, all I can think is that it would be very difficult to fit Nora in here with me. Which makes me wonder about the shower at her place. And her bed. And the fact that I am going to find out about both of those things.

I understand that we are pretending to be in a relationship. But we are actually going to date. I'm going to take her out. We're going to get to know each other. Which also means that I'm going to get to touch her, be very in her personal space, and kiss her some more. Now that I've had a taste, there's no way I could resist it anyway, and it's absolutely imperative that we make it seem real. If Nora is the key to making this town like me, and this town liking me is the key to making the team successful for Astrid, Nora, and me, then I'm going to have to kiss Nora. A lot.

Darn.

I'm grinning as I towel off my hair.

Her kissing me in the bar last night did exactly what she said it would. Everyone noticed, people immediately started asking us what was going on, confirming that we were a couple. One woman, I think her name was Jesse, was very disappointed and said one of her nephews was also going to be disappointed.

Good.

Nora Delaune is now taken. At least for the time being.

We had no further time alone together. There was no more kissing. I even had to say goodnight to her in front of an audience. Nora having a boyfriend is big news, and this town clearly has no understanding of privacy and boundaries, but while I would have liked to take the kiss further—a lot further—Nora obviously did it to get exactly the reaction we got.

So the plan is in motion.

I'm still going to be kissing her a lot more in the future. And I think she knows it. And I don't think she's upset about it.

I also don't think there's very much fake about her liking me or agreeing to spend time with me. Maybe the motivation is a little unconventional. And we both already know how this ends. But that's a good thing. Nobody's hopes get up, nobody's making long-term plans, and nobody's upset when in April, I kiss her goodbye at the airport, get on a plane, and head back to Portland. And then don't call her.

I frown at myself in the mirror.

It would be silly to call her. You're not gonna have a long-distance relationship with the small-town sweetheart in Louisiana, I tell my reflection. *That's ridiculous.*

You'll be working for the Grays. You'll be busy, traveling, back in your penthouse apartment.

That shower in Portland is definitely big enough for the two of you.

Would Nora come visit me in Portland?

As out of my element as I feel here in Rebel, I can't imagine Nora in Portland.

She hosts a thing called Otter Club.

I don't even know if there are otters in Portland.

I grab my phone from the counter, and look that up.

Huh, there are otters in Portland.

I look back to my reflection. *Nora Delaune is not going to visit you in Portland. You can't have a long-distance relationship with a small-town girl from Louisiana.*

I haven't even taken her out on one date yet.

I blow out a breath, push all of those stupid thoughts out of my head, and get ready for my day.

Which proves difficult, considering I'm not sure what I'll be doing today.

I don't have practice till six tonight.

I guess I'll explore the town.

That'll probably shave about thirty minutes off my day.

As I descend the steps, the scents of cinnamon, sugar, coffee, and vanilla grow stronger, and I take deep breaths.

Living above a coffee shop and café is not going to be all bad.

I decide to head to the kitchen first to ask Bruce if it's okay if I replace the bed and the showerhead. And the TV. It's way too small, and if my teammates have jobs that are going to keep them busy all day, I am probably going to be watching TV more than I'm used to.

I may need to get a hobby.

I'm looking up furniture stores in New Orleans when I realize that the sound around me has changed.

I look up. And once again, every pair of eyes in the establishment—there are many since we're right at breakfast time—is trained on me.

I give them all a smile and lift my hand. "Morning."

"Good morning," a chipper voice greets.

One voice. Singular.

I meet Everly's gaze. She's sitting at the counter with a plate in front of her, remnants of eggs, bacon, and toast obvious. She is lifting a coffee cup to her smiling lips. She's dressed in dark green shorts and a khaki-colored tank top. Her hair is pulled back, and she has sunglasses propped on top of her head.

"Hi, Everly."

"How did you sleep?"

"Okay, I need a new bed." I glance around. "Have you seen Bruce? I need to ask him about it."

She points toward the kitchen, but then says, "Just get it. It's easier to get forgiven than get permission from Bruce. And he'll laugh. He moved that shorter bed up there on purpose."

I sigh. "He did?"

"Yeah, Shane, the guy who lived up there before you, was also a hockey player. Not as tall as you, but definitely too big for the bed that Bruce's got up there."

I realize everyone's listening in, so I grin. "Well, he got me."

"He'll be thrilled that it bugged you, but admire that you just took care of it instead of whining about it," she advises me.

I nod. "I'll be sure to get an extra heavy one that makes it hard to move out."

She grins. "There you go."

"What are you up to today?" I ask.

"Work," she says simply.

"What do you do?"

"Landscaping and lawn care."

"Really?"

"Yep, I own the business," she says proudly. "Quinn works for me. And a few other guys. Have you ever used a riding mower?"

I grin at her. "What do you think?"

She laughs. "I'm going to guess you had gardeners growing up."

"You would be right."

"And in Portland, you live downtown in a high-rise with very little grass around. And you think the grass that is there always magically just stays the same length."

"I do live downtown in a high-rise. There is some grass. I guess I've just never given it a lot of thought."

She sips from her cup. "Yeah, I'm not going to offer you a job."

"I didn't realize that was a possibility," I say with a chuckle.

Two older men shuffle up to the register and lay money down. One a ten and two ones, the other three fives. Then they each give me a frown and tuck a dollar bill into one of the jars next to the register.

They move toward the door.

I lean around to look at the front of the jars. The sign says, "What is worse?" again today, but the front of one jar says, "Biting into a chocolate chip cookie to find out the chocolate chips are raisins", and the other says, "Alex Olsen".

My jar is winning again. And those two men just tucked money into my jar.

I blow out a breath. "Having gardeners growing up isn't helping me."

Everly laughs. "Definitely not."

"Tell us something about yourself. Help us get to know you," a voice calls out.

I turn toward the room. They need to get to know me. Okay, well, I guess that makes sense. "I have the best faceoff win percent in the league."

There's a long silence.

"A faceoff is—" I start.

Then suddenly… I get booed.

Fucking booed.

The woman who starts it is sitting at a table in the center of the room. She's wearing a bright multicolored shirt, lime-green pants, and a purple hat. I recognize her. She was carrying a picket sign at the arena. It's Muriel.

But several people join in, including her sister, Patty, who is sitting to her left, dressed in a much more muted outfit of lavender and white.

My eyes widen. The only times I've been booed, it's by opposing teams' fans, and I fucking earned that. They boo me because I'm amazing and I'm going to kick their team's asses.

I've definitely never been booed in a coffee shop.

A few more people get up from their tables and come to the register. I back up. Then I realize what I did and brace myself.

But all they do is lay money next to the register and then tuck dollar bills into the jar with my name on the front.

Come on. Biting into a cookie and expecting a chocolate chip but getting a raisin is bullshit. There is no one here who thinks that's worse than me?

I pull out my wallet and take out a ten-dollar bill. I step forward and tuck it into the jar about the raisins.

Everly snorts.

"You'll be happy to know that all of this money gets collected and taken to the same place at the end of the week."

"And where is that?"

"The library for new books, after school clubs, and supplies for the Parks and Rec department." She gives me a knowing grin.

"Isn't the Parks and Rec department supported by the city? Taxes and stuff?"

"Sure. That's why it's always underfunded. And Nora has... grand ideas. Her grandpa Bruce enables her." Everly grins. "Well, the rest of the town too, since they always put money in the jars no matter what's on the front. I guess it's kind of in lieu of tips. Which Bruce does *not* earn."

"This." I gesture between the jars. "Is rude."

She nods and finishes off her coffee. "Very."

"Can I sit next to you while I eat?"

But she's already sliding off her stool and pulling money from her front pocket. Cash like everyone else. She unfolds a ten and leans over to add it to the stack of money next to the register. "Sorry. I have to get to work."

"Is that seriously how everyone pays their bills here?"

She nods. "We all know how much everything costs. A lot of us get the same things over and over. But nobody would ever want to stiff Bruce. This is the cost plus tip."

"And you just pile it up next to the register? No one's ever going to swipe it? Or walk out and forget to pay?"

Her eyes round with horror. "No one would ever steal from

Bruce or stiff him. And if someone saw someone do that, that person wouldn't get more than two steps outside the door."

"Where is Bruce?"

"Back in the kitchen. Just lean in the door and tell him what you want." She points to the swinging door leading to the back.

"I might need to get some cereal and a toaster in my apartment," I mutter. I'm not sure I want Bruce cooking my food now that I think about it. At least until I win him over by romancing his granddaughter.

"Oh, you don't have anything to worry about. You treat Nora like the princess everyone here thinks she is, and you are going to be golden. Bruce will make you things off menu. And trust me, he's an amazing cook. You're going to miss breakfast here when you leave."

Treat Nora like the princess everyone thinks she is. For some reason, I don't think that's going to be difficult.

"So I'm going to be okay?"

Everly grins. "Well, I didn't say that. You're going to have to treat Nora like the princess everyone thinks she is," she repeats.

"Is that a high bar?"

"Nora could tell everyone that the sky is green, farts smell like candy, and eating mud will reverse the aging process, and they would all happily nod and go right along with it."

"She's a cult leader?"

Everly laughs. "She sure could be. Fortunately for us, she's also smart, down to earth, and loves everyone right back."

Suddenly, I realize that I may have gotten myself in over my head.

"So I need to talk Nora into having breakfast with me every day."

Everly pats me on the shoulder on her way to the door. "You could do that. Or you could go have breakfast at that table by the window."

I turn and find a table by the window occupied by one older gentleman who is nursing a cup of coffee and reading a book.

"Yeah?"

Everly nods. "Trust me."

Then she steps behind the counter, leans in the door, and calls, "Hey, Bruce, we need a ham and cheese omelet and cheesy grits out here!"

"Fine!" comes the surly answer.

Everly lets the door swing shut and gives me a wink. "Have a good day, Alex."

I take a deep breath and start toward the table by the window. "Hi. Would you mind if I join you?"

The man looks up and smiles at me. "Hi, Alex. Sure, sit down."

I take the seat across from him, feeling immediately at ease. I extend my hand across the table. "Thanks."

He takes my hand. "It's nice to meet you. My name is Harley."

Surprise ripples through me. "Harley. You're Nora's grandfather."

His face lights up. "I am. And you're her new boyfriend, from what I hear."

I think I might be blushing. Fuck. I nod. "I couldn't resist asking her out."

He smiles. "I understand completely. And you're brave."

"Brave? Nora seems sweet," I say with a grin.

He laughs. "She is. That's why this whole town is protective of her, and you now have a town full of people who are going to want to be sure you treat her right."

"So those jars will get even more stuffed full if I don't take her on amazing dates?"

Harley chuckles. "Oh, way worse consequences than that."

I try to smile, but even though he laughed, I have a feeling that is a completely serious promise. And I'm not sure Harley is the one who will be carrying out those consequences.

And since nothing has been simple and straightforward since the very first text from Nora, I should have expected that even taking her out on a few dates would come with a side of oh-you-might-die-from-this.

I sit back in my chair and take a deep breath. "I am really sorry I didn't meet with you last October. I understand that we had a meet-and-greet scheduled, and I screwed it up."

Harley slides a bookmark into his book, closing it and setting it on the table. "We did. But you were having a bad night."

I nod. "I was. Maybe the worst I've ever had."

"I've had a few of those in my time. I accept your apology. And I'm glad to see that you've recovered."

"Thank you. But I haven't. I can't seem to get over this final hump."

Harley reaches for his coffee cup. I study him closely. I am definitely no expert in strokes, but I don't see anything obvious about Harley that tells me he has any impairment.

"I know how that feels," he tells me. "It's absolutely devastating when your body betrays you."

I feel a stab of recognition. He does understand. Better than most people. Maybe even in a way that *I* don't fully understand. What he went through was life-threatening. And as Nora reminded me in the truck on the way here, he'll never be one hundred percent.

"I'm glad to see how far you've come as well," I say. "I know next to nothing about strokes, but you look damn good."

He smiles. "I'm guessing you know a little something about putting on a façade as well."

Again, that feeling of being seen hits me hard right between the eyes. "Yeah. I sure do."

He looks around the place, then back to me. "Tomorrow when they ask you to share something about yourself, make it something about you as a person, not hockey."

"Pretty much everything about me is hockey," I say. "And that's why I'm here."

"Dig deep," he says. "Or fake it." He smiles. "They want to know you as a person."

"I'm a hockey player," I say with a shrug. "There's not much else."

"Everyone here has a label like that. Bill is an electrician. Mary is a teacher," he says. "But there's more. Tell us things you like. Things you don't like. Places you've been. Places you wish you could go. A joke or story that makes you laugh. Just something about *you*, Alex."

I nod. I have some time to think about it. Maybe I can come up with something.

"So, I have something you can definitely help me with," I say.

"Shoot."

"Where should I take Nora on our first date?"

"Oh." He smiles. "She'll love anything you come up with."

"Really?" That seems way too easy.

"Certainly. You'll find that Nora always appreciates other people and whatever efforts they go to. If someone does something for *her*, she loves it, no matter what it is, simply because they did it for her. That's all it takes."

I frown. "But…I don't want her to be *grateful*. I want her to have a really wonderful time."

"She will," Harley says with a nod. "At least as far as you'll ever know."

My eyes widen. "So…" This isn't helpful at all. "I can't mess this up? No matter what?"

"Well, not with Nora, no," he says.

I lean in. "You're saying that Nora will love whatever I do, and even if she has a great time, other people will still judge it, and me."

Harley lifts his coffee cup with a smile. He seems like such a happy, friendly guy.

"Pretty much," he says.

I slump in my chair.

I maybe should have just stuck with hockey after all.

CHAPTER 11
ALEX

THERE ARE two areas of my life where I'm always confident. Two things I've been doing for a *very* long time, two things I've been praised for over and over. And they are the two things that have made me actually feel jittery since coming to Rebel, Louisiana.

Hockey.

And romancing women.

Bonkers hockey has me in my head thinking about feeling like a dumbass on the ice for the first time in…ever.

And I'm actually feeling my nerves jumping as I pull into the short driveway outside of Nora's tiny bungalow for our date.

What the *fuck* is this?

I've been taking women out socially for longer than I've had an official driver's license. Before that, I had a driver. Yeah, yeah, I grew up as a rich kid. Not my fault.

And it never occurred to me to be nervous about dating. I was popular, what can I say? Girls, then women, wanted to go out with me. I never had to worry about having a date to any event I wanted to attend, and to several I didn't want to attend. I've dated models, actresses, and singers. Women who are more famous than I am. Women who have to duck more paparazzi than

I do. I've never minded the cameras or gossip columns or attention.

But as I sit in the ten-year-old blue pickup that sounds like it left its muffler several blocks back—one of the many ways my sister is amusing herself, I'm sure—outside of the house that would fit inside my penthouse three times, I'm nervous.

Nora is different. She's not going out with me because she wants to. She's going out with me...to help me. I shove a hand through my hair. Yeah, that's new.

Yes, it's also helping the hockey team, and that's going to help her grandfather, which will make her happy. But all of that put together simply means that she's going out with me tonight for a whole lot of reasons other than actually wanting to date me.

And the attention we're going to get is this entire town judging if I'm good enough for her. The sporting world, and the world that's made my past dates and girlfriends celebrities, has no idea I'm even here, so there won't be cameras and reporters.

The "paparazzi" here worships otters and has known Nora since she was in diapers and doesn't love her because she sells lipstick and lingerie or movie and tour tickets, but because she's...Nora.

And they have duct tape, airboats, and remote cabins, and aren't afraid to use them.

I study the house that is painted lavender with bright yellow trim, steps, porch railing, and front door.

Of course, it has a bright yellow front door.

I think I would've been disappointed if this house were white with typical colored shutters and front door.

Okay, no matter what else is going on around us, I'm going to make tonight fun for this woman.

She makes everything fun for other people. That is literally her entire job description. I studied brochures and their website today during my downtime. There are so fucking many events, clubs, and activities in this town. Entertaining people is seemingly all she does every day.

So tonight, instead of concentrating on the fact that I am trying to win an entire town over, keep from getting kidnapped, and help an old man get reelected mayor for the four hundredth time, I'm going to concentrate on Nora. The woman who makes me feel warm and happy without effort. And, apparently, does that for everyone else, as well.

I'm going to treat her like a fucking princess. Period. That's the whole plan.

I get out of the truck and head toward her front door. It strikes me that I'm not sure I've ever gone up to a date's front door. Not like this. Not without cameras watching, or PR people staging it, or long corridors and private elevators involved.

This is just a normal front walk, a normal front porch—scratch that, this is a very tiny front porch—and a normal front door.

Except for the bright yellow paint.

I lift my hand to knock, but the door swings open before I can.

And there she is.

Nora is standing in the doorway, wearing a pretty pale blue sundress with straps that cross her tan shoulders and leave her arms bare. The bodice hugs her breasts and torso deliciously, the skirt falling straight from her waist to just above her knees. Her tan legs and the still warm weather, despite it being late September, mean she doesn't need leggings, and she's wearing strappy sandals.

Her toenails are painted, also pale blue.

I'm surprised by that, though I'm not sure why. I've certainly seen my share of pedicured feet. But her fingernails are cut short and unpolished, and I know this woman walks barefoot in sand and dirt. I don't know how I know that, but it just fits.

There's also a pink flower painted onto the nail of each big toe.

"Did you paint your toenails for me, Wildflower?"

Probably a dumb first thing to say.

Her cheeks get a little pink, but she smiles as she looks at her feet. "I did." She steps onto the porch and turns to pull her door shut, but doesn't lock it.

I start to say something, then realize no one is going to break in and steal anything from this woman. Everyone loves her. Besides, if they do take something from her, they're going to have old men hunting them down and taking them to remote cabins surrounded by bayou, snakes, and alligators.

"I painted them myself, though—well, except for the flowers. Ruth did those." She lifts one foot and turns it side to side, studying it. Then she looks up at me. "I didn't go to the salon or anything, so don't get cocky."

I grin anyway. "How often do you paint your toenails?" I ask as we walk to my truck.

"As often as I wear dresses and sandals. So hardly ever."

I shake my head as I open the door. "Still feeling cocky."

She laughs. "I know who your last girlfriend was. I painted them because Ruth insisted. She had Ingrid's number half dialed when I made the compromise. But I figured it wasn't worth more effort. Your last girlfriend had an entire team to get her ready. I can't begin to compete with that."

At the moment, I can't remember the name of my last girlfriend. Not even what color hair she had. But I'm mesmerized by the fact that Nora has three different browns, a reddish hue, and a dark gold in hers.

"Are you insinuating that you're my *new* girlfriend?" I ask.

She blinks rapidly. "No. *No.*" She nervously tucks her hair behind her ear. "I shouldn't have said it like that. I mean, the last woman you dated. I know who you're used to going out with."

I reach up and capture her wrist, stalling her fumbling fingers. "You painting your toenails yourself, even under duress, is sexier than anything any of the other women have ever done. For them that was all second nature. None of them did it for me. They did it for the photographers we were going to encounter on a night out. Or because they were paid to by the polish company. Or just out of habit. And not that you should do it for me, but it's cute. I like the blue. And the flower. A lot."

Her cheeks are even pinker now, but she smiles. "Don't look at them too closely. They're kind of messy. I'm not good at nail painting."

Suddenly, I want to get very close to her toes. Close enough to see just how far out of the lines she painted.

"I promise if I get that close to your toes, I won't care about messy paint. And neither will you."

Now her cheeks are very red, and I am very satisfied. I grasp her waist in both hands and lift her up onto the truck seat before she can protest. I shut the door and round the front of my truck. I am feeling instantly better about the date. Yes, I have a lot to prove in this town. Yes, the date has to go well. Yes, everyone in this town will care if Nora has a good time and will judge me harshly if not.

But now I don't care about any of that. I only care about her and showing her a good time. *I* will judge me harshly if not.

I can play hockey that will put butts in the seats in that arena, and I can date the hell out of this woman.

"You're wearing a suit," she says as I slide in behind the wheel.

I start the truck and wince as the engine grumbles, clearly protesting being forced to turn over and actually run.

I wish I was taking her out to dinner in New Orleans in one of my cars. I would've probably picked the Rolls-Royce Ghost. It has a gorgeous leather interior and is an incredibly smooth ride. Very classy for date night. But my Aston Martin Vanquish is also very sweet for nights out in the city.

"Yes. We're going somewhere really nice."

I slipped into my suit and took a deep breath tonight. I feel great in this suit. I don't have a tie on, and the crewneck knit shirt underneath keeps it looking casually sophisticated, but the tailored pants and jacket and the Italian leather shoes are impeccable.

"How nice?" she asks as I turn down the street that will lead out to the highway while avoiding Main Street. The last thing I need is everyone looking out the front window of Perks and Rec and watching us go.

"Really nice. Italian. It has fantastic reviews and looks gorgeous inside. It's on the edge of the French Quarter. It's called the Italian Barrel. Have you been there?"

Her eyes widen. "No." She looks down and smooths her dress over her lap. "I'm not dressed for a place like that, Alex. Can we go somewhere else?"

I look over, scanning her from perky head to cute blue toes. "You look absolutely gorgeous, Nora. You're dressed perfectly."

"I'm not." She laughs. "This dress is very casual. I can wear it to church, and a few places for dinner in New Orleans, but certainly not white tablecloth restaurants. It's four years old."

I reach over and snag her hand, threading our fingers together. "You look amazing. You have absolutely nothing to worry about."

She takes a deep breath and blows it out. "How many forks are there going to be?"

I chuckle. "What?"

"I know fancy restaurants use lots of different forks. That's not the kind of place I'm used to. At Bruce's we keep the same fork from salad to dessert."

I shoot her a smile. "Probably one for salad, another for the entree, and another for dessert. But it will be obvious which is which. I promise we'll get through it." I look over at her again. "Tonight it's just about spending time together. I just want to treat you. Please don't worry."

I didn't think about any of this. Yes, I thought about taking her somewhere nicer than she's used to. Nicer than Bruce's. Nicer than a place that would serve her fried catfish and gumbo. But I hadn't thought about whether she'd be comfortable or not. She seems so easy going and is clearly beloved by all kinds of people so she seems comfortable in various situations and settings.

But she *will be* comfortable. I'll be sure of it. Five-star dining is simply about learning. I've always known about the different forks and how to place my napkin and multiple courses. It was simply how I was raised. My mother loves elaborate feasts and dining is always an event. But I've been around plenty of teammates who come from simpler backgrounds who needed to learn. It's fun to teach people about different cuisines and give them new experiences. Just like I had to learn about frozen pizza and that chicken wings should never be eaten with utensils. No one should feel strange or uncomfortable when it comes to new foods or about eating in new places.

She doesn't pull her hand away and I enjoy the feel of her hand in mine. "So I've now met your grandfathers, cousins, friends...what about your parents? How will they feel about us dating? Will I meet them?" I ask as we turn onto the highway.

"Oh."

Her quiet, one word answer pulls my eyes from the road to her. She's staring out the windshield with a slight frown.

"Nora?"

She looks at me. "I haven't been asked about my parents in so long..." She gives me a little smile. "Everyone knows all about them in Rebel, so no one talks about them. And the guys I've dated knew the story. I honestly haven't actually told anyone... this...in..." She frowns again. "I was trying to figure out if I've ever actually told anyone."

I shift on the seat. Dammit. Clearly this isn't a 'you can have dinner with us on Sunday' situation. What did I stir up here?

"You've always dated guys from Rebel?" I ask, distracted by that piece of information as much as whatever this story about her parents is.

"Yes. Well, two of the three. The other was here for a while before we went out so he must have asked someone else." She pauses. "Or maybe he didn't care." She says that last part almost thoughtfully, as if that's just occurring to her.

She dated a guy who didn't care about her parents? What?

"You've only dated three men?" I'm aware I'm getting off track but I'm definitely interested in this too.

She nods. "Yeah. They were all long-term and pretty serious though."

I don't respond to that, focusing on the road.

I decide to repair my reputation in this town and pick the woman who is basically everyone's granddaughter and who only gets involved in long-term serious relationships? *Great job, Olsen. Really great.*

"So, um, anyway, my mom isn't around and I never knew my dad."

That jerks my attention away from pondering if my luck is really truly horrible…or really amazing despite myself.

"Oh," I answer stupidly, looking at her.

She shrugs. "My mom got pregnant with me during her first semester of college. It was just a fling. They dated but it wasn't serious and he was relieved when she told him she didn't want to get married or anything. So, he was off the hook and I've never met him. She didn't even have any photos of him. I think his first name was Carter. Or Conner. Something like that."

She isn't even sure of her father's first name? But she truly doesn't seem bothered by this.

"Bruce and Harley were married by then. My grandma, Harley's wife, died of cancer when my mom was ten. Bruce was always around anyway and then Harley and Bruce got married three years later. Bruce helped raise my mom and my aunt Bebe." Nora is watching the road again. "My mom is super smart. She wanted to be a doctor. An oncologist, because of her mom. So, she finished her freshman year in Georgia, had me that summer, then went back to school and I stayed with Bruce and Harley."

I frown. Her mom left her with her grandfathers?

"Then she got into medical school in California. Then got her choice of residencies and picked Los Angeles and she ended up staying there." Nora looks back at me now. "She's done amazing research and work in new surgeries for cancer. And she met her husband there. They have two boys."

She's quiet for several long moments, so I finally ask, "So you have a step-dad and half-siblings?"

"Yes."

"But they live in California and you live here?"

"Yes. My mom is more like an…aunt, I guess. And the boys are like distant cousins. I've only met them a handful of times. When she comes back to Louisiana to visit, which is maybe once a year, they're often busy with school or sports or other things. I've only met my step-dad three or four times.

"I know my aunt Bebe, Thea's mom, a lot better. She's more like a mom to me. She was there with Bruce and Harley when I was sick, she came to school programs, celebrated birthdays and holidays. And Thea is like a sister. Harley and Bruce are basically my dads. The whole town has helped raise me. This is my family and home. She's…not." Nora shrugs. "It's weird, I know. Especially for a guy like you. I know you're close to your mom and dad and your sisters."

She seems fine. She really does. She's never really known her mom. But I still want to hug her.

"I am close to them," I agree. "But I also live in a different country from one of my sisters and from my parents," I remind her. "And I have since I was eighteen."

"But you know them well. And you grew up with them. Bonded with them. And you go home to visit and they come here."

She's clearly read about me. Or Ruth has filled her in.

I nod. "Yeah."

"Anyway, that's why I'm so attached to Rebel," she says. "Why the people mean so much to me. They're literally my family. They've always been there for me. They took care of me when my mom…couldn't. So I take care of them now."

I think about that. She says her mom *couldn't* take care of her, but is that true? Maybe. It's possible her mom wasn't equipped to be a young, single mom. But maybe she just *wouldn't*. She had other plans. Dreams. And Harley and Bruce helped those happen.

They also took care of and loved Nora. It seems everyone turned out great.

Nora definitely takes care of them right back. Her job is literally making the whole town happy. Entertaining them. Keeping them together as a community.

Does she worry what would happen if she didn't do that? If people didn't come together for community activities and celebrations? Does she feel like she's keeping her family together?

"Is that why you only date guys from Rebel?"

"Yeah. I mean, one wasn't from Rebel, but I really thought he was going to stay. I intend to stay there, so there's no point dating anyone who doesn't want that." She sighs. "But, honestly, I think I'm over it."

I glance over again. Dammit, having a conversation where I can't look at her as much as I want to is frustrating. "Over it? Over wanting to stay in Rebel?"

"No," she says quickly. "I think I'm over dating."

I laugh. "Come on." She's young, beautiful, full of life, clearly loves having a lot of people in her life. No way is she going to stay single.

"I'm serious. I've been in three pretty serious relationships and my one must-have is staying in Rebel. Pretty simple. But none of them have worked out."

"Why not?" I'm truly curious. Obviously, there *are* men who want to live in Rebel.

She shrugs. "The ones I fall for just don't want to settle down in that little town. I mean, Sean Patrick grew up in Rebel."

I hate that guy. My hand flexes on the steering wheel.

"He should have known and loved it as much as I did," she goes on. "We dated for three years. But when we graduated, he wanted to get out, go on to bigger and better things. Broke my heart."

"But he's back," I point out. "And he wants to stay now, right?"

It's not that I want her with him, but I have no say in that. I'm fucking leaving too. My chest feels tight for some stupid reason.

"Yes, but it's different now. He went to college in North Carolina and ended up staying there, trying to 'make it'," she says, making air quotes with her fingers. "Then realized that was harder than he thought it would be. Now he's back where being popular is easier for him, but he's trying to change things in Rebel, and I hate that. I want someone who loves it the way it is."

Right. Of course. This is very clear—I'm not her type.

"The other was a guy who moved to town and *he* even thought he was going to stay," she tells me. "We got serious. But then, after a couple of years, he got restless. Bored, I guess. Realized the small town life wasn't as charming as he thought it would be. So he left."

Small town life isn't for everyone. That's not a character flaw. But maybe wanting to be a big shot in a big city where there are endless amenities like twenty-four-seven food delivery and people to hire to do things for you is…okay, not a *character flaw* exactly, but also not that admirable.

Yes, I'm a big shot in a big city. Definitely not her type.

"And the third guy was part of a tech company that relocated their headquarters and all their employees to Rebel," she goes on. "They got a big tax break because they brought people to town which helped our local economy and they were able to give their employees a quieter, more affordable lifestyle. They invested in building houses, a couple of restaurants, even some things like a spa salon and a golf course. They seemed so excited, but it only lasted two years. Their employees didn't fit in at all and didn't like it here long-term, so they moved the company back to Tennessee. Including my boyfriend who was a Vice-President. It was a mess."

Yeah, I'm…just like all of those guys.

I left my home country for bigger and better things. Just like Sean Patrick did. I'm here in Rebel now to help build something, but I don't fit in. At least, unlike the second guy, I already know that Rebel is not going to be a long-term thing for me. But I'm sure Nora sees pieces of all of her boyfriends in me pretty clearly.

"Wow," I finally say.

"Yeah, not dating seems like a good choice."

I shake my head. "You're going to have to get *really* good at saying no." I glance over. "I imagine you'll be asked out a lot no matter what."

She smiles. "A lot of people in town try to set me up with guys they know."

That doesn't surprise me a bit.

We arrive at the restaurant a few minutes later. Driving through the French Quarter is not for the faint of heart, but my GPS is, thankfully, very helpful and we find parking on the street just a block from the restaurant. The evening is pleasant so the walk is easy and we arrive exactly on time for our reservation.

Nora is smoothing the front of her dress again as we approach the tall wooden french doors in the old stone building on the corner.

I grab her hand, again entwining our fingers. I love the feel of her hand in mine. Her skin is soft but she has a few calluses on her palm which is a surprise. But this woman is always busy with her hands and clearly isn't shy about getting into the dirt—or probably paint, drywall paste, or otter dung—if needed. She was covered in mud from picking flowers when I met her, after all.

"Relax," I tell her. "You look beautiful."

She smiles up at me. "Thank you."

I usher her through the door into the restaurant.

It's small, maybe twenty white linen tablecloth covered tables in total, with a light wood bar to our right and multiple tall, thin windows all along the wall to our left.

There are softly lit sconces spaced out along the brick walls and each table has a center glimmering candle giving the room a golden glow. The floor is polished wood, the ceiling soars high overhead, and the air is filled with a tantalizing combination of Italian spices.

"Oh my gosh, this is gorgeous," Nora says in a hushed voice, looking around.

"Welcome," the hostess greets us warmly.

I give her my name and she escorts us to one of the small tables near a window.

A server arrives within a minute, bringing water, a bread basket, and menus. He also sets the wine list in the center of the table. "I'll return soon," he promises.

Nora is still looking around, taking in all the details of the restaurant. It's just getting dark outside and the lanterns on the poles along the street come on. A car drives by, followed by a horse-drawn carriage. There are people sitting at tiny bistro tables along the sidewalk, laughing and talking.

She turns her gaze back to mine, a smile on her lips. "This place is so *pretty*. And oh my *God*, it smells good," she says enthusiastically, looking down at the menu.

"I'm so glad you like it." I point to the silverware next to her empty wine glass. "And only two forks."

She laughs. "I feel better already."

Fuck, she's beautiful. And I love her laugh. And I love bringing her to a place like this. I love that things like tablecloths and extra forks are an adventure for her.

I've never dated a woman who would have been so obviously enchanted by a restaurant, and I find myself wondering what Nora would think about a chartered flight to the Amalfi Coast in Italy where we could have truly authentic Italian food.

Maybe she *shouldn't* date. None of the guys in Rebel are going to take her to Italy. Or even rack their brains trying to figure out the next best way to make her look like she does right now.

I actually have no idea if that's true, but *that* should be her standard. Not if he wants to settle down in Rebel, but if his primary goal in life is making her eyes light up with pleasure.

What about Cara? I'll bet she'd love Cara. I could take her there.

I could. Easily. Tomorrow.

My home country is a gorgeous, remote island. It's not tropical, for sure. It's windswept. The rocky soil, climate, and year-round cool-ish temperatures keep us from being able to even grow many trees. But we have amazing blue water on all sides, gorgeous cliffs, and incredible waterfalls.

And great people who truly feel that I'm a hero.

I, along with Astrid, put our country on the map. Before Astrid became an Olympic contender and I joined the Grays, no one outside of our country and a few students in class in Ireland and Denmark—the two countries that settled the island and still have friendly diplomatic ties to us—had even heard of the independent island at the southern end of the Danish-governed Faroe Islands.

Now nearly everyone in the sports world at least knows what and where Cara is.

I do really love it there. There are definitely no jars filled with money contending I'm worse than Brussels sprouts or raisin cookies or stubbing your toe on the end of the bed first thing in the morning or whatever the fuck else Bruce is going to come up with.

"Good evening. I'm Enzo," a man dressed in a white dress shirt, burgundy tie, and black pants says. "I will have the pleasure of serving you tonight."

"Hello, Enzo," Nora says. "We're so happy to be here tonight."

He smiles, clearly charmed by her reaction. "Can I start you with some wine? Or answer any questions about the menu?"

"Do you like wine?" I ask Nora.

She shakes her head. "I'm more about lattes and mixed cocktails."

I chuckle and say to Enzo, "I'd like a Barolo. And maybe something sweeter and lighter for you?" I ask Nora. "A moscato?"

She lifts a shoulder. "I trust you."

Oh, I like that too. She means with the wine, but I like even that much. I want to treat her. I want to spoil her. I want to show her so many delicious, extravagant things and if she'll let me lead the way, we can have a lot of fun.

I nod at the server, "Let's do that and we'll start with the small cheese plate."

"Excellent," he agrees.

"What is your favorite dish here?" Nora asks him. "I'm sure it's all amazing."

He smiles and gives a single nod. "It is. I like several dishes, but the pumpkin ravioli is truly amazing."

She sighs happily, looking down at the menu. "That sounds so good."

He gives me a smile that clearly says, *she's lovely* and I can only nod.

"I want one of everything," she says. "And every appetizer and dessert..." She trails off, her head coming up, her eyes wide. "Alex."

"What?"

She leans in. "That cheese plate you ordered is *sixty-nine dollars*," she hisses.

I chuckle. "It's not. That's the large plate. We're getting the small."

She looks down again, but then says, "That one's still *thirty-six.*"

I grin. Yes, spoiling this woman will be fun. I'm running a tab at Bruce's with the one-hundred-dollar limit, but now that I've checked out his menu more carefully, it's going to take me a while to hit that limit.

The food is simple and inexpensive. It's also delicious. But I could eat three meals there for thirty-six dollars and still get change back.

"The cheese will be worth it," I tell her.

"Thirty-six-dollar *cheese*?" she asks.

I laugh. "They'll bring crackers too."

She shakes her head. "Bruce is going to roll his eyes so hard he'll get a headache."

"Nora." I wait until she looks up at me. "Get whatever you

want. And I mean that. Get two things if you want to try them. We can take the extras with us and let Bruce try them too."

She starts to respond, I'm sure with a protest, but I reach out and hook her index finger with mine. "Please," I say. "I can absolutely afford it, and I want to treat you. Seeing how much you're already enjoying this makes me happy."

She opens her mouth, then shuts it. A few emotions flit over her face and I *have* to know what she's thinking.

I wiggle her finger with mine. "What?"

"I was just..." She shakes her head. "It's silly."

"So what? What were you thinking just now?"

"Just that..." She swallows. "I know what you mean. When you said that watching me enjoy this makes you happy. That's how I feel about all the events and things I put together. I love watching other people try new things or do something that makes them really happy. And I realized that...I haven't had someone do that for me in a long time." She bites her bottom lip, then continues. "It's not that I *need* that. I enjoy the events and clubs I organize too, but it *is* fun having someone else have the knowledge and all the details put together and I can just enjoy it." She shakes her head. "I know it's just dinner. I know that sounds silly."

Someone has sucked a bunch of oxygen out of this room.

Nora can even be delighted by a meal.

She puts together festivals and events and clubs for other people all the time. She's working to bring an entirely new form of hockey—one that most people, including the players, don't really understand—to the town to entertain everyone. She wants people to have fun and be delighted.

And all it takes to light her up is to shell out a stupid amount of money for cheese.

Jesus. She's...unexpected. And I want to spend all my time figuring out other ways to make her eyes brighten and her smile widen.

I pull in some of the remaining air and say, "Nora, I think

that's the best thing I've heard in a *very* long time and it makes me want to buy you four grande cheese plates."

She laughs. "I like cheese. *A lot.* But that's probably overkill. I really might let you buy me two desserts, though."

Fuck, I'll buy this whole damned restaurant.

Enzo returns with our wines, and the cheese plate, and Nora's eyes widen and yes, light up, when she sees the beautiful presentation of the variety of cheese, crackers, honey, grapes, and dried cherries and apricots.

My chest warms even as a knot tightens much lower in my gut.

I want her.

And I've known her for two days.

CHAPTER 12
ALEX

WE PLACE our orders for entrees, Nora going with Enzo's recommendation of the ravioli, and then we're alone with our cheese.

She dives right in with enthusiasm I love. She also moans and gasps about the different flavors and combinations, and I'm shifting on my chair within minutes.

"So what about *your* parents?" she asks after she's tried every type of cheese once.

"What do you mean?"

"I know I won't meet them—wait, unless they'll come to one of your games with the Revelers?" she asks. "But what will they think about us dating?"

"Oh." Well, hell. How do I tell her that I didn't intend to tell my family much about my time in Louisiana without hurting her feelings? I think I have to just tell her. "I wasn't really intending to talk to my parents much about my time in Rebel."

She pauses with a piece of cheese to her mouth. "Oh."

In all of the articles about me, and Astrid for that matter, our family has been painted as being very close. And it's true that our parents have been supportive, both verbally and financially, of us pursuing our sporting dreams. But my sisters and I are the tight family unit, less so our parents.

"They don't come to many of my games. They watch them on TV. Sometimes. The king of our country—well, our past king, who just stepped down from the throne—had a major satellite system put in so that everyone could follow Astrid and me when we came to the States."

"It must've been a big deal for your little country," Nora says. She wipes her hands on her napkin. "I've read up on your country. It is really small, right? So you and Astrid are big stars."

I nod. "We are."

I study her for a moment. She is extremely close to her family, the entire town she's from, but not her mother and father. Maybe she'll understand what I'm about to tell her. I never talk about this stuff with girlfriends, but there's something about Nora that is so warm and accepting that I find myself wanting to tell her.

"My sister Linnea, the oldest one, was supposed to marry the prince. The one who's king now."

Nora's eyes widen slightly with interest and surprise. It's definitely an unusual story.

"But Torin married Abigail."

I nod. "Right. He fell in love, and he and Linnea agreed that he should marry Abi instead."

"Abigail is my cousin," Nora says. "She's like a second cousin or something. But yeah, I know all about her and the prince, now king."

Damn. That's right. Abigail's last name was Landry. She was from Autre.

What a small fucking world.

"But Torin almost married *your sister*?" Nora shakes her head. "That's wild."

"Our grandfathers set up the arranged marriage a long time ago." I roll my eyes. "Actually, if I go way back to the beginning, Linnea was supposed to marry Declan since he's the oldest of the O'Grady grandsons."

Nora blinks. "Declan. Your sister Astrid's husband?"

"Yep. Linnea and Declan were promised to each other when they were toddlers."

"Whoa. That still happens?"

"I don't think so. Not anywhere but Cara. And this was a long time ago." I start smiling. I haven't told this story in a long time. Nora is also grinning. I have to remember that she is from a town with people who are also a little…unique.

"Anyway, long story—okay, several long stories—Linnea ended up falling in love with one of the prince's bodyguards."

"Go on. *Please*," Nora tells me, plucking another piece of cheese off the plate.

I relax and lean in as well. See? She's so easy to talk to. Accepting of even the craziest things I could say. "Okay, so my sister Linnea was betrothed since before she can even remember. She grew up thinking she was going to be queen and that she had no choice in the matter. Because her entire life was mapped out for her, and she was weighed down by expectations from our family, the royal family, and really the entire country, she wanted Astrid and me to have more options. Every option possible. She realized that us leaving Cara and making our own money and having our own names would open up opportunities and would give us a lot of power."

Nora is chewing her cheese, her eyes glued on my face.

"So she became our agent. She found training facilities for both of us, pushed us, gave us all the emotional support and financial backing we could need. I mean, our families were fine with all of it, too. Linnea was—is—a great saleswoman, explaining to our families and the king how we could bring fame and honor to the country." I pause. "And money. Our parents were very interested in that."

Nora reaches without looking for a piece of fruit. "But that comes with a lot of pressure for you too."

I shrug. "It didn't feel like that. Hockey was easy for me. And I was basically told from a very young age that that's all I had to do. Just focus on hockey. Everything else would work out then." I take a breath. "But for Astrid, it was different. Some of the "opportunities" that were offered to her were more sleazy."

Nora frowns. "Of course."

"And then she got hurt." I swallow. "And that changed things. She wasn't going to be a gold medal Olympian. The doors that would have opened with that medal were suddenly shut. Without warning. And with no plan B."

"But she made a plan B," Nora says. "She documented her rehab. She became huge on social media. She wrote a couple of books. She does public speaking."

I nod. "She's incredible. She's probably more famous and has more opportunities now, honestly. She was able to widen her sphere of influence outside of gymnastics."

Nora's expression softens. "Is this why you feel like you don't know how to do anything else? Because your focus has always been hockey? Because your family told you that's all that mattered?"

"Because I *don't* know how to do anything else. Hockey has literally been the only thing in my life."

Enzo arrives with our entrées, and we spend a few minutes adding Parmesan cheese and cracked black pepper, as well as adjusting an amazing-smelling bread basket in the middle of the table, declining further wine, but having our ice waters topped off.

I watch as Nora leans over her plate and inhales deeply of the aromas coming from the pumpkin ravioli and the savory sauce. She pulls the napkin away from the bread. "Oh my God," she mutters softly, obviously enthralled by the look and smell of the bread as well.

She takes a piece, butters it, then looks up at me. "Keep going."

I chuckle and choose bread for myself, but I do continue telling my story. "Astrid and my success bolstered my parents' name, and I guess power in the country. They were not only the parents of the future queen, but now they were the parents of two huge sports stars who were making our country famous." I pause. "It's really always been about status with my parents. They don't really care about hockey or gymnastics. When Astrid got hurt, they were worried for her health, of course, but they were so relieved when she made something out of that. They didn't care she wasn't doing gymnastics anymore. They just cared she was still a well-known name and could monetize that."

"Oh, Alex," Nora says, frowning.

It is what it is. "They won't care what kind of hockey I'm playing here. They won't care if I'm singing and dancing. What they'll care about is that I'm not getting paid the way I did in Portland and that I can't get endorsement deals from it, and that I won't get interviewed or my face on the front of magazines."

Nora has taken a bite of her ravioli and now takes a moment to chew, as she watches me. I try to take a bite and chew as well, but I don't really taste my penne alla arrabbiata despite the spicy sausage that's been added.

After she swallows, she says, "You had a setback in your professional career, the thing that they think is so important, the thing they've been proud of, and now, instead of returning to the Grays, or moving into coaching or something, you're stuck in a tiny town in Louisiana, playing bonkers hockey. So you don't want to go into detail about it. You want to wait to really get into what you're doing next until you get back to Portland."

Well… "Yes."

Nora nods and takes another bite of her ravioli; she chews and swallows. "I get it. I mean, if all they cared about was your big pro hockey career, this would seem like a step back."

Yes, it would. And it did to me. But now, sitting across the table from this woman, only two days in, hearing her say it that way, just accepting the situation and my parents with their flawed, superficial approach to what Astrid and I do, makes me feel defensive of bonkers hockey.

"It's nothing for any of us to be embarrassed about," I say with a slight frown.

"I agree. I mean it's not going to win you any trophies…" She pauses. "I mean, I guess we could come up with a trophy and some way of winning it. We should put out a poll—"

I chuckle. "Focus, Nora."

She grins at me, and I feel the tension that had grabbed my shoulders, neck, and the back of my head ease.

"Anyway, it's not going to get you on the major TV networks or interviews in *Hockey Hunks*, but you are going to make a whole bunch of people happy, and make money for my town, and save my grandfather's political career. So, it's not without any goals and good outcomes."

I'm not going to tell her that my parents won't give a crap about her grandfather's political career. I suspect she knows that. And my parents would absolutely sit in the stands completely confused and very judgmental about everything from the mascot to that mascot throwing beads and toys to the children to the fact that there is a very good possibility that at some point I'm going to have to put on a foam Joker's hat and dance to a Lady Gaga song.

The jury is still out on whether I'm going to be able to handle the lip syncing, too.

"It is possible, however, that my sister Linnea and her husband would come."

Nora perks up at that. "Is her husband still good friends with the prince?"

"He is. But that prince is now the king."

"Is it possible that the king might come?"

I groan. I hadn't thought of that, but yes, there is a chance that Torin would come watch me play bonkers hockey. "I'm sure he'll be too busy," I say.

Nora points her fork at me. "So that's a yes, if he finds out about it."

"He's got a whole country to run."

I chuckle when she says, "Does the palace have an email address?"

"I'm sure it does not." It totally does.

"So that's also a yes."

I chuckle again and realize that I have never enjoyed a date conversation this much. Even though it was about my parents.

I've also never told another date about my parents and their feelings about my hockey career.

That either says amazing things about Nora or really pathetic things about me.

Of course, it could be a little bit of both.

We spend the rest of the dinner chatting casually about my home country, my siblings, their very interesting husbands, and their husbands' friends. Declan is friends with Rebel's very own hometown billionaire, her cousin, Dane.

Nora tells me about how Dane inherited all of his father's businesses—a little over half the town of Rebel—but that he doesn't want any of them. But he also can't get rid of them because no one in town can afford to buy them and he has just enough of a heart to not sell them to anyone outside of Rebel.

When it's time for dessert, Nora first tries to tell me she's too full for any, then agrees to a scoop of gelato. I, of course, have Enzo bring one of everything.

She laughingly protests, but does take a bite or two of each thing before Enzo boxes them up for us to take back to Rebel with us.

"Will Bruce think you've been cheating on him and his café?" I asked as I re-pocket my wallet and grab the to-go bag, then pull out Nora's chair and help her to her feet.

"Maybe. But then I'll have him try the tiramisu, and he'll forget all about it."

I'm grinning again—or still? Have I stopped?—as I escort her to the door.

"Do you want to walk around for a little bit?" she asks. "I

haven't been down to the quarter at night in a long time. I love to just walk and people-watch."

"Of course. I am up for anything." Mostly prolonging my time with Nora.

We start down the sidewalk toward the French Quarter since we are right on the edge. She slips her hand into mine, seemingly naturally, and my chest expands.

Damn. What is it about this woman?

We walk for about three blocks without speaking.

This area is mostly businesses that are closed at this time of night. It seems all of the businesses in the quarter have apartments above them, so lights are glowing in many of the windows and a few people are out on balconies, but it's clear that most of the music and noise is coming from a few blocks away.

We start past the French Market. It's closed for the evening, but the multi-block outdoor market, which sells everything from local produce to fresh-baked goods to handmade jewelry to antiques, will be open tomorrow morning at nine.

"You know, we were actually hoping that you *would* do some interviews about the Revelers," Nora says.

I look down at her. "What kind of interviews?"

"You're a big name in hockey. You were hurt and left the team you've played for for your whole career, and you took off for Cara for a few months. Surely people—fans and the sports media—are wondering what you're up to."

Ah, she's thinking I'll do interviews with the hockey world. "And you think they'll want to know about the Revelers and bonkers hockey?" I ask lightly.

That's why you're in Rebel. You're there to play hockey. You're important to her because you're a hockey star. You can't be butt hurt because she wants you for hockey. Everyone wants you for hockey.

"I don't know." She looks up at me. "Do you? I guess, I'd *hoped* they would? It's definitely a story that a star hockey player is now playing a new kind of hockey in small-town Louisiana."

"And that would draw attention to this new league," I say.

"Right."

I don't think she's aware of it, but she starts walking with a little bounce.

"If people are intrigued, maybe they come to Rebel for a game. Then we can hook them with our crawfish boil and the beads and the Zambonis decorated like Mardi Gras floats and the fan involvement. And maybe they decide to stay over Friday night and see more of the town on Saturday."

I'm distracted for a moment. "The Zambonis are going to be decorated like Mardi Gras floats?" I only have a vague idea of what that even means, but I have an image of a huge 3-D court jester head and a million balloons and people on the float dressed in masks and feathers and lots and lots of sequins.

"Yes!" she says enthusiastically. "And each week two new businesses get to sponsor and decorate the "float" however they want to. Just like the real parade floats. And they'll choose what prizes get thrown out to the crowd. Of course, we'll need people walking through the stands doing the throws, since they won't be able to really do them from the ice. Unless..." She pauses, both talking and walking for a moment. "They might be able to throw a few things over the glass right in front."

"That sounds..." Chaotic as hell. But I don't say that. "Fun," is what I go with instead.

She beams up at me. "Thanks. I think so too."

"And then you hope that people will stay at the bed and breakfast and eat at Perks and Rec and shop at the other shops," I say. I get it. That makes sense and is completely something someone like Nora, who doesn't just love the town but also works for the town, would think of. Hell, it's something her grandfather, the *mayor*, would be all over.

"Exactly." She looks excited and is clearly completely oblivious to the fact that I'm feeling stupidly stung by this.

I'm fucking here for hockey. If I weren't a hockey player, I would probably never set foot in Louisiana. *Maybe* for Mardi Gras once or twice. But I wouldn't even know that Rebel, Louisiana, or Perks and Rec, or Nora Delaune exist.

And I'm a fucking hockey star. I'm hurt, fine, but I still have a name synonymous with hockey. Would the hockey media and fans be interested in the story of the big star hanging out in small-town Louisiana and singing and dancing on the ice?

Yeah. Fucking probably.

This just makes sense from Nora's point of view.

Probably from Astrid's, too. My sister is a bestselling author and speaker. She knows about marketing and what it takes to draw in crowds. She might have even realized that Nora was the best one to talk me into this.

I have a soft spot for Nora, and I'm guessing that's obvious to my sister.

We're getting closer to Jackson Square. There are more people on the sidewalks and the sound of music and conversation gets louder.

"I love this area," Nora says, definitely bouncing as she walks now.

We get to the corner of Decatur and St. Anne. The Cathedral is to our right, and Cafe Du Monde is to our left. There are people everywhere.

I look at Nora and see her face bright and happy as she takes in the people, the horse-drawn carriages waiting along the curb for passengers, the one-man band in front of Cafe Du Monde, his music case open for donations, and the street performers and artists dotted along the wrought iron fence that surrounds Jackson Square.

She turns us toward the Cathedral, and we walk until we get to the front steps, where a full jazz band is performing.

There's a magician a few yards away, entertaining a small crowd, and four tarot card readers set up at tables along the wide mall area in front of the church.

Nora stops, watching a magician raptly. She sways slightly to the music, and I can't resist slipping my arm around her waist and pulling her closer to my body. I love having her close to me. She has to tip her head back to meet my gaze and smile up at me. She slips her arm around my waist as well. To anyone passing by, we are clearly a couple.

"You know," I say. "We should probably practice."

"Practice what?"

My gaze drops to her mouth, then returns to her eyes. "If we're dating, we need to act like a couple. We should practice when no one we know is watching, get over the bumps and awkward spots, so that when we're around people who know us better—especially you—they won't think that we're acting strange."

Her brows arch, and the corner of her mouth tips up. "You think I'm going to act strange if you're close to me in front of people I know?"

"Well, we should make sure you don't."

I turn to face her more fully and drag one hand up her arm, over her bare shoulder to the back of her neck, and into her hair.

I tip her head back, and she murmurs, "I guess that's a good point," as I brush my lips over her.

She tastes like cappuccino and chocolate. A perfect, decadent combination.

Too bad I didn't have more wine at dinner that I could blame on the warm, fuzzy feeling in my head and the desire to do stupid, dangerous things with her. Like fall in love.

But I'm completely sober.

Or at least I am not drunk on alcohol.

When she sighs, her warm breath against my lips, I realize I'm drunk on *her*.

I drop our bag of dessert and cup her head with both hands, pressing my lips more fully to hers, then teasing my tongue along her lower lip when she sighs again.

Fuck. Kissing her is as good as the samples I got at the airport and in the coffee shop promised.

Better.

And I want more.

CHAPTER 13
NORA

IT'S NOT like I'm surprised that Alex is a good kisser. He's a very talented man in many ways and, much like hockey, I am sure he's had lots of practice in this area.

Still, with both hands holding my face, his hot mouth covering mine, his big body seeming to surround me with his heat and just him being *him*, I'm overwhelmed.

I arch closer and find my hands fisting the front of his shirt. I'm just trying to stay upright.

Not that he'd let me fall.

Somehow, I know that.

And that seems like an outlandish thought to have after knowing the guy only two days.

The jazz band finishes their song with a loud trumpet flourish, and people applaud, the sounds breaking through my swirling emotions, including confusion and a big dose of *oh crap*.

Alex lifts his head and stares down at me. I am certain he notices the fact that I am practically panting.

"How about beignets?" he asks.

It takes me a second to compute what he's saying.

I glance toward Café Du Monde just across the square.

"Oh, Bruce would definitely have a problem with me eating anyone else's beignets. His are amazing. You'll have to try them."

Alex drags his thumb across my lower lip and my pussy clenches. I just barely resist flicking my tongue out against his skin.

"Then tell me another way that I can convince you to stay here in the city a little longer."

"Why do you want to keep me in the city longer? We live in the same town."

"So it can get very late and I can suggest that we need to stay over."

My smile grows. Even though falling for Alex is a *very* bad idea, I do like the idea that he wants me too.

He shakes his head. "I want to take you to a gorgeous, very expensive hotel, and get the biggest, nicest suite they have, and make sure you have a spa appointment, and order lots of room service, and buy you new clothes for tomorrow, and basically spoil the hell out of you for tonight. Or maybe for the weekend. Or the month."

I almost can't breathe.

I want that. So much. God, the spa treatment and room service alone. But *with Alex*? Yes, please.

Like hockey and kissing, I'm guessing Alex Olsen has had lots of practice with women in bedrooms, and I'm sure he's *amazing.*

I'd really love to find out.

But that would be a *really, really* bad idea.

I step back. "Neither of us can stay in New Orleans for a month. We have a lot to do in Rebel."

"So how about tonight?"

Yes, absolutely, take me there now.

"I..." Shouldn't even tell him how much I want to, should I? That's a bad idea if I'm going to be adamant about *not* doing it. And what if he decides to kiss me again? He could convince me that my worries can be dealt with tomorrow. "...can't." I shake my head. "There is no way I can sleep with you, Alex."

He steps closer. "Am I misreading our chemistry? Tell me, and I'll back off."

I believe him. I feel completely safe with Alex. And god *no*, he's not misreading anything. "No. It's not that. I *want to*. I just can't." I laugh lightly. "I *shouldn't*. And it's been a really long time. And it'll probably be a really long time to come. What with the no dating and all."

God, it's been a *really* long time. And the last few times weren't great. And it will be a really long time before it happens again. My trust has been shot. Men can tell me they're staying, that they're in it for the long-haul but I don't know if I can believe anyone anymore. And if they're not staying, if it's not going to lead to something more, then why risk getting my heart involved?

I realize I'm rambling and my thoughts are wandering. I clear my throat. "The thing is, you're leaving. And I like you. And if I sleep with you, I will get even more attached and when you leave, it will be even harder. I already don't deal well with people leaving me and Rebel."

He doesn't say anything right away and I think that, maybe, he looks surprised. I'm sure he's surprised that someone is turning him down for sex. But that's not what this feels like.

"You think you're going to be *attached* to me?" he asks.

How is that hard to believe? "Yes. I think we're going to be friends. I think we already are."

"I mean, I know that you probably think the hockey team will miss me. But hopefully everything will be well-established by the time I go back to Portland. The people will be coming for the fun and the team will be playing well together so you'll be selling plenty of tickets and won't need me anymore."

I'm not sure what's going on here. "I hope all of that's true. But I'm not talking about missing you on the hockey team. I'm talking about the fact that we're going to spend the next seven months working together, getting to know each other. I'll miss *you*."

"Oh."

He looks like he's trying to solve a complicated calculus equation in his head.

"Don't you miss people in Portland?" I ask. He seems confused about the concept of missing someone.

"Well, Astrid. But she's here. I miss my family. But that's normal. And I go back to see them."

"Don't you miss any teammates?"

"Yes. I guess so." He shakes his head. "It's been kind of a whirlwind since I got here so I haven't really thought about it. And I've got a new team. New people to play with so I guess I thought maybe they'd fill in those gaps."

"Well, I'm sure your teammates in Portland miss you."

He frowns. "I haven't been playing for several months. I've been hurt since last October."

"Yes, I know they've adjusted to not having you on the ice with them." He winces slightly when I say that. "But I mean you as a person."

He doesn't respond to that. Does Alex Olsen actually think that no one cares about him other than when he's in skates?

I really can't sleep with him. Because regardless of what he understands about missing humans as people and friends, *I* definitely understand it. I get attached. I know it has to do with my mother basically giving me up when I was an infant and moving on with her life and then starting another family without me. And to me, that's okay. That is a normal reaction to having a mother who had bigger and better things to do.

But I do get attached, and I do like having lots of people to love. And being loved by lots of people. And I'm well aware it is why I am so co-dependent on my hometown. It is full of people who love me.

I suddenly want to show Alex Olsen what it's like to have *friends* who he is not related to and who do not suit up for hockey games with him.

"Maybe we could—"

"Hey, are you Alex Olsen?"

I'm cut off from suggesting we find a jazz club or somewhere else to spend some time by three boys in their late teens.

Alex turns toward the boys. "I am."

The boys all brighten.

"No way. We're huge fans!" the one wearing jeans and a blue hooded sweatshirt exclaims.

"I can't believe you're just here!" the one wearing the plain white T-shirt and black athletic shorts tells Alex.

"I told you it was him!" the third says. He looks almost exactly like the one in the blue hoodie and I assume they're brothers.

"Just here having dinner and enjoying the night," Alex says.

"We are here on vacation with our parents," the youngest one says. "I can't believe we just ran into a huge hockey star out here walking around."

"You're hockey fans?" Alex asks, his stance relaxing and his smile growing warmer.

"Yeah, of course. We've watched you play a ton," blue hoodie tells him.

"I appreciate that," Alex says. "Are you having fun here in New Orleans?"

"Yeah. It's pretty cool. Seeing people just out playing music on the streets is pretty awesome," the one in the T-shirt says, gesturing toward the jazz band that is getting ready to start a new song.

"What are your names?" Alex asks.

"I'm Matt," the one in the hoodie says.

Alex extends his hand for a handshake. "Nice to meet you, Matt."

The boy looks amazed as he takes Alex's hand.

"I'm Austin," the one in the white T-shirt says, extending his hand and taking Alex's.

"Hi, Austin," Alex says, his smile genuine.

"My name is Alex," the youngest one says, sticking his hand out with a big grin. "Cool name, right?"

Alex chuckles and takes his hand too. "The best. Any of you boys *play* hockey?"

They all do and tell Alex they're from Wisconsin and were so bummed when Alex got hurt, and how cool it is to meet him.

"I appreciate that," Alex says. "It's been tough. So do you guys have anything you want me to sign?"

Their jaws all drop, and they look at one another. "I don't really have anything," Matt says. "We didn't expect to run into any celebrities."

I rummage in my bag and pull out a four-by-six bright green index card, a cardboard coaster from Perks and Rec—it's only got a tiny coffee stain on it—and a package of playing cards. I pull a Joker out—we almost never need jokers. I hand the three items to Alex along with a black Sharpie. "Here you go."

He looks at the odd collection of items, then at my bag, and gives me a grin. "Thanks." He holds them up to the boys. "How's this? Something pretty unique. Nobody else will have my signature on any of these things."

The boys excitedly agree, and Alex signs his name along with the date and *Jackson Square, New Orleans* at the bottom. That all barely fits on the Joker playing card, but I suspect that the younger Alex will treasure that playing card for years.

"I can't wait to watch you play again," Austin tells Alex as he hands me the pen back. "When do you think that will be?"

"Uh, thanks." Alex hesitates, then glances at me. "As a matter of fact, I am going to be playing for a small team down here in Louisiana this season."

The boys' eyes go wide. "No kidding?" Matt asks.

"No kidding. They're doing something new in a little town near here. It's really unique and pretty fun. It's not professional hockey. It's…well, you'll have to see."

"Where can we watch it?" Matt asks.

"You would really want to?"

"Sure, why not? Hockey's fun no matter what."

"Really?"

"Oh, yeah," the younger Alex says. "Our uncle Derek is old, he's like forty-something, and he plays hockey with a bunch of his buddies. We go watch them sometimes. They're hilarious. They cuss and give each other shit. One time they had a bet going on how long the goalie could go before saying the word 'fuck'. Then every time he said it, he had to buy another pizza after the game."

The boys are all laughing at the memory, and Alex chuckles. I can feel my grin. Our hockey will be like that, only *way* more fun.

"Hockey is hockey," Matt says. "It's always good. Pro hockey is great, but hockey can always be fun to watch, especially if someone's playing that you really like and know."

"We used to have to go watch Alex play," Austin says, nudging his little brother. "His team was *terrible*, but we just found ways to make that fun. We had a special scoring system that we kept track of. Every shot on goal Alex took, he got a point. Every assist was two. If he got a takeaway, he got three. Goals were four. The points rolled over game to game. Every five points, he got a treat at the store, and every ten points, he got to choose something at home. Like where we all went to dinner, or what chore he wanted to trade with one of us, or what movie we'd watch on movie night."

Alex is listening intently. He nods. "That's very cool of you, as brothers. You made it fun for him and gave him an incentive to work on his game, even if it was a little frustrating at times with the whole team."

"Keeping track of his stats and coming up with things he could get for his points made watching it more fun for us too," Matt says.

"I like that a lot. Good job," Alex tells them.

The boys all beam proudly.

"I'll tell you what, you keep looking up the Revelers." He spells Revelers for them. "I don't know when stuff will start showing up online, but it's coming. You keep watch, then you tell all your friends that they need to watch us too."

The boys nod eagerly. "Okay! Sure, of course."

"I've got another idea," Alex says. "I'm going to put together some game day baskets. T-shirts, snacks, swag. You guys email our office—when it gets up online—and I'll send you one of the first. Then you can put together a watch party. You post about that online—photos of you and your family and friends watching us play—and tag me so I can check it out, okay? I'll send you some signed Revelers stuff, too. When we get it."

He glances at me again with a questioning look.

I'm staring at him stupidly.

That's all an amazing idea. My mind is spinning with ideas for the baskets and to-do lists, like getting an organization email for this, and what hashtags we should use and encourage others to use.

"Nora?" Alex asks.

"Yeah?"

"We'll have merch I can sign for these guys, right?"

I shake myself out of my Alex-Olsen-is-amazing daze and my planning haze. "Yes! Yes, definitely."

"Great." He grins at the boys. "Then be sure to stay in touch, okay? Just mention your names and Jackson Square, and I'll remember you."

The boys have so many stars in their eyes, I'm not sure they can actually see Alex.

"Definitely!" Matt gushes.

"Can't wait!" young Alex says.

Then Alex asks, "Would you guys want some photos right now? Wait, do you guys have social media?"

Matt laughs. "Of course."

"Okay, let's get some photos tonight for you to post."

Matt, Austin, and Alex all pull their phones out, quickly swiping to open the camera apps.

"Okay, I want one with each of you and then all four of us together," Alex says.

The boys take individual photos of each other, but when it

comes time for all four of them to be in the photo with Alex, I step forward. "Here, I've got it."

Adult Alex pulls his phone out of his pocket. "Get a few with mine too."

I do, my chest feeling warm as I focus on the four hockey lovers in the frame. The boys are radiant. Alex looks proud and actually excited.

I haven't seen that expression on him yet.

Alex needed this. He's not getting this in Rebel right now, and I'm frustrated with my hometown. Alex is used to being a star. He's used to being recognized like this when he's out and about in Portland. He's used to people wanting to talk to him and get photos with him. He has a signature that people treasure. Hell, his signature has probably sold for a few thousand dollars. Maybe more.

Then he moves to a small town in Louisiana to help save our hockey team, and they all treat him like he's Public Enemy number one.

But even though Alex claims that all he knows how to do is play hockey, I can see that's not entirely true. Sure, he likes the attention from these three boys, but he's making them feel pretty great too.

"Now one with the two of us." Alex is holding his arm toward me.

"What do you mean?"

He grabs my wrist and pulls me up against his body, wrapping his arm around me again.

"Take a photo of me and Nora and include it when you post the other photos tonight," he tells the boys.

The boys lift their phones and snap photos of Alex grinning at them and me looking up at him with a few obvious stars in my eyes too, I'm sure.

"How should we caption this one?" Austin asks.

"Alex and his girlfriend, Nora," Alex says.

Their eyes widen, but they quickly type it in.

Finally, with all of that finished, Alex says, "Okay, guys, it was really nice to meet you."

"Oh my God, it was great to meet you," Matt says.

"Thanks. Be sure you keep an eye out for the Revelers."

The boys promise to, and go running across the square to rejoin their parents.

"That was really great," I say, watching them disappear in the crowd.

"It was." He retrieves our bag of dessert, then links his fingers with mine as we start walking back across the square.

"I mean *you* were great with them." He'd made those boys' nights. Maybe their trip to New Orleans. There's plenty about this city that excites visitors, but those boys are of an age that meeting a professional athlete they admire probably outweighs any museum, jazz band, or even spooky ghost tour.

He looks in the direction they disappeared. "Thanks. They were…" He shrugs. "That was just really nice to run into some fans."

"That must happen a lot in Portland." That won't happen much here, I realize. Even without Rebel being particularly unwelcoming, most of the New Orleans hockey fans will be fans of the local team, I'm sure.

So, we've not only taken him away from his really nice penthouse—yes, Ruth showed me the photos in *Hockey Hunks*—and his really nice cars—yes, those were in that article too and are a far cry from the truck that Astrid procured for him. We've also taken him away from his fan base. A guy who thinks all he's good at is hockey at a time when his pro hockey career has been derailed because of an injury and a long, ultimately not fully productive rehab. I found that part out with some online searching of my own. I couldn't help it. It's not every day a girl has a date with a guy she can get an entire background on via her phone. Oh, sure, you can get arrest reports, but while those are definitely important to find ahead of time, even those don't tell the *whole* story. Not like the plethora of information, photos, quotes, and stats I found on Alexander D. Olsen, number fourteen, the six-foot-three-inch, two-hundred-and-ten pound center for the Portland Grays.

"I do," Alex says of being spotted out and about by fans in Portland.

"Do you like that or not?"

He hesitates as if he's not sure how he should answer. He looks at me. "I like it. Kind of a lot."

I smile. "That's a good thing then."

He goes on. "I know that sounds like I just like having my ego stroked, and that's not bad, but it's really just that I like knowing people like what I do. Since that's my whole life, what I give all my time and attention to, it would suck if I'd put all these years and all this work in and no one gave a shit, you know?"

"It's your *whole* life?" I repeat.

"Pretty much. It's my job, so my days are spent in workouts and practice. Even what I eat is chosen to make me the best hockey player I can be. Even when I'm out and about socially, I'm still Alex Olsen Number Fourteen. Which has gotten me endorsement deals. Which also fills my time—commercial shoots, being spotted out wearing things or doing things for the brands, and just being me, so they want me to represent their brand. All of that has to do with me being a hockey player."

I frown as I realize this feels weirdly familiar. "What about when you're with your friends or family? Just at home relaxing?"

"When I'm with my family, it's a little less...obvious. But we still talk hockey. And my friends are all in the hockey world."

"What about your girlfriends?"

He looks at me with an eyebrow up. "The women I've dated are women I never would have even met, not to mention gotten their numbers, if I wasn't a hockey star. And they *really* like the things that come with hockey. The parties, the other famous people they can rub elbows with, the money."

I frown. I suddenly hate all of his exes and not just because *they* got to have naked Alex time. Yes, that too—definitely—but also because they were only with him because he's a hockey player.

Then it hits me.

You're with him because he's a hockey player.

Oh.

Damn.

I would have never met him if he wasn't a hockey player. I wouldn't have agreed to "date" him if I didn't need him to be a *popular* hockey player in Rebel. I do need him because he's a star hockey player...

Dammit.

I'm using him for his hockey-star-ness, too.

I meet his gaze. I don't want to use him for that. But it's inescapable. The Revelers need to be great, and I know Alex can make them that.

But I can also make his time in Rebel about more than hockey. I can be his friend and not just another woman who sees him as a hockey player who can do things for her with his star power.

"You told those boys I'm your girlfriend."

"Right. That's what we're doing, right?"

"For *Rebel*. So they're nicer to you. And we're just...spending time together. I'm not your *girlfriend*."

He shrugs. "I don't mind if other people know we're dating. And—" He looks down at me. "You *are* my girlfriend while I'm here, right? You're not dating anyone else. I'm not dating anyone else. Isn't that what that means?"

I think about that. "But..."

"What?"

"I just told you I'm not going to sleep with you."

He stops walking, and I'm forced to stop too. He frowns at me. "So what?"

"I don't know... I just..." I look around, then step closer. "That's kind of the difference between friends and girlfriends.

Girlfriends are friends you get naked with. Otherwise, they're just… a friend who's a girl."

His gaze roams over my face as he thinks about that. "I'm not sure I would have called any of the women I've gotten naked with friends."

My eyebrows arch. I hate them even more. But also…that's on him too. "Wow. That's really kind of sad."

"Everyone had a good time. I promise."

I roll my eyes. "Well, I hate to break it to you, but you're going to have to get to know me. Talk about things that aren't naked-time related or hockey-related. Do things that aren't naked-time or hockey-time."

He's watching me with a faintly amused look. "Give me an example. And please say otter club."

I grin. I really might have to take him to otter club one time. "Movie night in the park." I have to be there anyway, so he might as well join us. In fact, he definitely *should* join us.

"That sounds like you're asking me on a date, Wildflower."

My heart does a little stutter-step with his use of the nickname. I nod. "Kind of. The town will think so. But for us, it's friend time. Like the time I spent with Everly, Andi, and Sutton. Since that time won't lead to naked time."

"*Every* time you spent with your boyfriends led to naked time?" he asks.

Okay, that's a fair point. "No. I guess…it's just that *we're* not together tonight because we met and liked each other and then wanted to spend time together…" I trail off. That doesn't sound quite right. It's true, but if I'd met Alex and had a conversation at a coffee shop, for instance, I think I would have wanted to spend more time with him. I try again. "We're not spending time together because we want to sleep together…" I trail off. Okay, that's not technically true either. We *want to*. We're just not *going to*. I take a breath. "We're spending time together because we want…" I trail off again, still not sure how to really define all of this.

"Because we want other people to like me," he fills in.

I don't like how that sounds. I frown. "I guess. But I do like you. And tonight has been fun."

Something flickers in his eyes. "I can promise you, Nora, that I very much like spending time with you, regardless of the naked-less status of our relationship. And I'm sure that even if I wasn't trying to get people to like me and buy hockey tickets, I would still want to spend time with you."

That's so…dammit, is that romantic? Or is it just nice? Is it a thing a friend would say?

Andi or Everly or Sutton might say that to me, but they wouldn't mention our naked-less relationship status. Nor would they have that low gruffness in their voice or the heat in their eyes.

And I wouldn't have the very vivid memory of how it felt to have them kissing me imprinted on my brain, or be obsessed with how their big hands felt on my face, or be unable to stop staring at their shoulders in the suit they're wearing.

It definitely feels strange to think of Alex Olsen as just a friend.

But I can not make him more than that. Not for real.

"But regardless of what *we* know, those kids are going to put the photos and captions on social media," I finally say.

"I know."

"But you told me that you weren't going to make a big deal out of being here in Louisiana or what's going on with your parents. Now you have those kids talking about the Revelers and posting on social media, and you talked about letting them watch the team. How are they going to do that?"

He shrugs. "Astrid and I can make that happen. We'll get someone to film the games, and we can stream them online somehow. It really just takes money. And a few connections. We've got both. Astrid will love the idea."

I'm so not used to having people with resources who can just make any wild and fun idea happen.

I like it.

"You were right," Alex says. "Fans and the media are going to be interested in the Revelers. And they're very much going to be interested in who I'm dating. I told you that the town would like our romance better than all the hockey stuff. I'm thinking we widen the net of interest. Get people talking."

"The hockey fans are *definitely* going to care more about the game and this new league than *me*," I say.

He grins. "Let's find out. Either way, if we want to put butts in the seats and sell tickets and stir up interest in what we're doing down here, then we might as well *really* stir up interest."

My heart does a somersault. I'm going to ignore the idea of my name and face being splashed across the internet by the sports media. "So you're going to be public about this? The Revelers? The singing and dancing?"

"It's still hockey," he says. "Like Matt and Austin and Alex said, hockey is hockey on some level. Did you see how Alex was looking at his brothers when they were describing how they made his season with the horrible hockey team fun?"

I shake my head. I'd been watching this Alex.

"He was so crazy about his brothers and what they did. It wasn't *really* about hockey." Alex shakes his head. "It was about them being involved and those brothers all coming together like that. Hockey was just the way they showed their brother that they supported and loved him."

My heart pounds harder in my chest.

Alex shakes his head. "I don't know. There was just something about that that made me think that if the Revelers can bring Rebel together to have some fun and be together and can show people that Harley is the best choice for mayor because he cares about them enough to go all out and over-the-top…being a part of that could be cool."

Oh…crap.

Not sleeping with this guy is going to be *very* difficult. Because I really want to hug him. And hugging him will remind me of how good it feels to be up against him and how great he smells and how big his hands are. And that will make me want to kiss him and kissing him definitely makes it difficult to remember that I shouldn't take my clothes off.

"You know," I say softly. "I totally get what you said earlier about loving having hockey fans come up to you."

"Yeah?"

I nod. "Putting together events and clubs and fun stuff for the town is all *I* do. It's what I spend my time and energy on. Even when I'm not in the office, I'm thinking of things or getting supplies ready or making phone calls. And it's really amazing when people come up and tell me how much they enjoyed something or how a town tradition has meant a lot to their family or how they've had something I planned on their calendar for weeks or even months."

He gives me a smile that warms me from my chest to my toes. "You do get it. You work hard, put yourself out there, and it's awesome when people care about that."

I nod. "It is."

"So we'll do this thing. This bonkers hockey is going to be amazing."

"Thanks, Alex," I say sincerely.

"This is why I'm here, right? To bring people into that arena. It's what I do. It's what I'm good at."

I squeeze his hand. "Right."

But I will admit as we walk away from Jackson Square to his truck and then head back to Rebel, I feel a tickle of unease.

Yes, this is why Alex is here. His name, his stardom, are also supposed to help us.

But I can't shake the feeling that I want this to be more than that.

I want to help the hot, famous, hugely talented, multimillionaire pro-athlete.

And I also want to do a whole bunch of things *to* him. Inappropriate, dirty, will-definitely-ruin-me-for-other-men-and-break-my-heart-when-he-leaves things.

Which is why, when he pulls into my driveway and puts his truck in park and turns to me and says, "I had a great time tonight," I look at him for a long moment, then lean over and press a kiss to his lips and say, "I really do love spending non-naked time with you."

And then I get my ass out of the truck and head inside *alone*.

CHAPTER 14
ALEX

NOT GETTING Nora Delaune naked is something I'm going to regret forever. I just know that. I have never been on a date like the one last night, and I want to go on fifty-seven more with her. Even knowing that I'm not going to get her naked at the end of the night.

That doesn't mean I don't want to.

I really want to. More than I did at the beginning of the night, and I really wanted to at the beginning of the night.

Still, she's my girlfriend.

She seems to think that she's just a friend, and I heard all of her explanations last night, but I've been thinking about it. Her. Last night.

I can't remember the last time I thought about a date for hours after it ended and then woke up in the morning thinking about it. Especially without the woman next to me in bed.

I grin and reach for my phone on the spindly bedside table. I shake my head at the crocheted doily thing it's resting on and the lamp that has birds and flowers and tree branches carved into the base.

I text her: *I think there's a problem with your theory about just being my friend who's a girl.*

She answers within just a couple of minutes, and I wonder what she's doing. It's only seven a.m.. I'm shocked I'm awake considering the time difference between Portland and Louisiana, but I feel pretty good.

Nora: *Oh? Tell me more.*

Me: *I understand what you're saying about not getting naked and that does make it different, but we're going to be kissing. And touching. Acting besotted with one another. That's a weird gray area at least.*

Nora: *Besotted? Wow, I didn't peg you for a guy who would use the word besotted.*

Me: *Don't distract from the topic. If I'm kissing you—which I will be—and touching you—which I will be—and staring at you as if you are the best thing since the caveman decided to hit something across the ice with a stick—which I will be—then I think you're still my girlfriend.*

Nora: *Do you really think the caveman played hockey?*

Me: *Stop distracting.*

I realize I'm grinning like an idiot all by myself in bed with a quilt that was, no doubt, hand-made covering me. I would ask more about it, like who made it and if the pieces of the quilt have special meanings, but I'm afraid that someone might've died under it or on top of it and I really don't want to know that.

It took me four hours to fall asleep under it the first night just thinking that might be the case.

Nora: **laugh crying face* Sorry, I just can't get the image of cavemen batting rocks around on frozen ponds with tree branches and being like 'omg this is so awesome!' out of my head.*

Me: *When you could be distracted by me kissing you?*

Nora: *LOL! Fine. You might have a point. Let me think about the definition. Maybe we can come up with a new term.*

Me: *Don't waste your time. We're just gonna call you my girlfriend. My very sexually frustrated girlfriend.*

Nora: *I'm the one who's going to be sexually frustrated?*

Me: *I didn't say you were going to be the only one. But yes.*

Nora: *Being near you is going to be so difficult that I'll be constantly fighting the urge to get naked?*

Me: *I think you already know the answer to that, Wildflower.*

She doesn't respond and I get out of bed with a huge grin.

I shower and don't even have the urge to take care of myself. I am definitely turned on by her and could certainly conjure some delightfully dirty fantasies, but I don't need to. It's interesting. I feel good just thinking about being with her and a little bit of morning text teasing.

I'm not saying that's always going to be enough, but I'm definitely feeling content as I head downstairs, breathing deeply of the buttery, cinnamon and sugar scented air.

Living above a café that makes bacon and bakes fresh pastries every morning is not going to be a hardship, that's for sure.

I step out from behind the multicolored curtain and the conversation and clinking of silverware against plates immediately ceases.

Oh boy.

"Morning, everyone," I greet.

"A fancy dinner in New Orleans? Really?" someone asks.

I focus on the owner of the voice and realize that it is one of my would-be kidnappers.

Studying Brewser this morning in his pink plaid shorts, pink polo shirt, and sandals with pink socks, it's still hard for me to believe that he was the town doctor.

I realize that I am stereotyping, but every doctor I've ever seen has either been in a white coat or khakis and a polo. I've certainly had my share of visits with the team doctors, but none of them have been wearing shorts and sandals.

"We had an amazing time last night," I say carefully.

I'm not surprised that everyone in the café, probably the entire town, knows about my date with Nora last night. That's the point after all, right? They're supposed to think that we're dating. That Nora has chosen to spend time with me. That she fucking likes me.

And she does.

She definitely does.

It's almost ridiculous how much I like that.

"Well, I'm sure she told you she had a good time," the man I now know is Wilson, the town lawyer—or ex-lawyer?—says. "She's a very positive and kind person."

I lift a brow. "So, she would've told me she had a good time no matter what?" I ask. I want to call bullshit on that. We had a good time last night. Because I took her somewhere new. Because I spoiled her a little. Because it was *us*.

"I'm sure she really did have a nice time. That's not really the question," Brewser says.

I nod.

"But you've probably taken dozens of women to dinner," he adds.

I don't know about dozens. Then again I'm not going to do the math.

"You should've done something special for Nora. She's special. Dates with her should be unique."

"Define unique," I say.

He shakes his head. "That's something you're going to have to figure out for yourself."

I blow out a breath. These people are confusing, not helpful.

My gaze lands on the jars next to the register and I sigh. Now the front of the jars simply have a drawing of a thumbs up and a thumbs down. The sign behind them reads *Alex's date with Nora in New Orleans.*

Now they're voting on my dates? While the dollar bills in the two jars are more even than the Brussels sprouts question, the thumbs-down jar is clearly still winning over those who feel I did a good job.

Obviously, this is going to be a regular thing. And I can't avoid this café. It's basically the first floor of my house.

Did I say that living above a café had its perks?

The cons are starting to outweigh the pros.

"Well, Nora invited me to movie night," I tell them. There, see? She wants to spend more time with me.

"Movie night here in Rebel? Down at the park?" Beckett asks.

I focus on the fact that the friendly, easy-going hockey player is sitting at the counter next to his sister. Sutton gives me a friendly smile.

"Hi," I greet.

"Thought maybe you could use some reinforcements this morning. Friendly faces," he says.

I nod and glance over the room full of people who are still listening in on everything as if we're all having one giant conversation together. "I appreciate that."

"I think the dinner at the Italian Barrel sounds really nice," Sutton says, lifting her voice. "It's a super fancy, expensive restaurant."

"With a sixty-nine dollar cheese plate," I say for some reason.

There are gasps around the room.

"I can give you three kinds of cheese for four-ninety-nine," Bruce says, coming through the swinging door.

How could he have heard all of that from back in the kitchen?

I sigh. "Is that right?"

"Yep, all shredded up together in one package."

Laughter ripples around the restaurant.

"Yes, movie night here in the park," I say to Beckett, deciding to ignore Bruce.

He nods and lifts his cup. "Well, that will be good."

"That's straightforward, right? Movie night. What do people do? You spread out blankets on the grass? Bring lawn chairs? Who knows Nora's favorite movie candy?"

"Oh, you're not gonna have to worry about that," a woman sitting near the bakery case tells me.

"I wouldn't really call movie night at the park straightforward," Sutton says, lifting a sausage link on her fork to her mouth. "It's probably not what you're thinking."

Why does that not surprise me? "How so?" I ask.

"Honestly, you should just go," Beckett says. "I think that will explain a lot about making dates with Nora unique."

Why do I feel nervous all of a sudden? "You can't even help me prepare?"

Beckett chuckles. "Nope. Just go."

Sutton nods. She's grinning. "It's definitely very Nora."

That also doesn't surprise me. But I don't have even a guess what that means.

Still, there is a tiny surge of anticipation behind the nerves. Whatever this all means, Nora will be there. I'm sure I'll enjoy myself. And it's a public forum, with the woman I'm supposedly dating. That means I will definitely need to kiss her.

I look out over the room. "Great, I can't wait. How many of you will be there?"

Hands shoot up all over the room. Wow.

"Great."

"Tell us something about yourself," a woman says. She is sitting at the table near the window where Harley was sitting yesterday. He's there again today, and the third of my kidnappers is sitting with him. By the process of elimination, this is Leo.

Okay, I'm getting another chance at this. "Anything specific?" I ask.

"Just something interesting," she says. She's got her long gray hair in two braids and is wearing a blue-and-green plaid shirt with jeans.

Everyone turns from looking at her to looking back at me as if they're watching a tennis match. "But you don't even like me."

"We're mad at you," Leo says. "That's not the same thing as not liking you."

"We don't know you well enough to not like you," Bruce says. "Yet."

Okay, I think quickly. "I had the most hat tricks in the league last season."

"Boo!"

I think the first *boo* comes from Brewser this time, but several people join in again.

Great.

"We don't need to know about hockey," someone calls.

"We can look all the hockey stuff up," someone else adds.

"Yeah, I already knew that," a guy near the bookcase says.

I guess that's true. "Okay, I am from a small island nation called Cara. It's the island south of the Faroe Islands—"

"*Boo!*"

The boo-ing is louder and even more people join in this time.

I hold my hands up in surrender. "That's not about hockey."

"We all know about that. From the article," the guy by the bookcase calls.

"The article?"

"Ruth passed around the Hockey Hunks issue about you," Beckett says helpfully.

I look around. "But…you all don't *like* me."

They all laugh.

Right. They're just mad at me.

Fine, so they all know all about my apartment and my cars and the clothes that I endorse and my favorite snack foods and a ton of other trivial details. I think quickly for something that was not included in that interview or really in any of the others that I have done over the years and that these people could easily look up. What is something they would consider a good share?

These people are truly bananas.

Bananas.

Bananas. A thought hits me, and I give them all a grin. "Okay, here's something I've never said in an interview. Or in public. Or maybe out loud to another person." I hesitate. Maybe this is a bad idea.

"Okay, come on then," Brewser says.

"Unless it's sexual. Do *not* share something sexual in here," Bruce says, pointing a thick index finger at me.

"I have very strong feelings about bananas," I tell them.

The room gets even quieter. They all stop eating and drinking and stare at me.

Okay, I'm going all in. "I *love* bananas. I truly consider them the perfect food. They're delicious, nutritious, come in their own wrapper, and are good any time of the day. But," I add as people start nodding their agreement. "I hate when they are turned into other things. People put bananas with peanut butter, chocolate, and other fruit in smoothies and stuff. And I *hate* that." I take a breath and keep going because it sounds crazy and, honestly, that fits right in here. "Bananas are perfect as they are. They do not need to be blended up into smoothies, added to sandwiches, dipped in chocolate, with ice cream—seriously, banana splits are the *worst*—or turned into bread. I don't like banana flavored candies or syrups. A banana is good only when it is just a banana."

I stop and take another deep breath.

Then brace myself.

There is a long moment of silence.

Then another.

Then another.

I finally look at Beckett. He's staring at me with a huge grin. He looks delighted by my banana outburst.

Sutton has a hand over her mouth.

Everyone else is just staring.

But then the woman at the table with Leo and Harley starts clapping. "Love a man of conviction," she says.

My eyes widen.

A few people clap with her, but mostly people laugh and start talking and finally Bruce comes past and claps me on the shoulder. "Well, that will end things between you and Nora for sure." He moves past me.

I look at Beckett. He scoops a big bite of cereal into his mouth.

"What did I just do?" I ask.

Sutton looks from me to her brother and back. "Um…Nora makes amazing banana pudding. She's known for it."

"You'll try Nora's pudding though, won't you?" a woman says. She's come up to pay her breakfast tab. She lays a few bills next to the register.

Banana *pudding*. What the actual fuck? "Uh, no, probably not," I say honestly.

She frowns, then holds up a dollar bill before stuffing it in the thumbs down jar.

I sigh.

Bananas. All of 'em. Seriously.

CHAPTER 15
NORA

ASTRID: *Negative twelve season tickets at six-thirty a.m.*

I frown. What? Twelve more people cancelled their season tickets *this* morning? What happened?

Astrid: *But plus eight at eight twenty a.m.*

What the hell is going on?

Beckett: *This kind of green?*

Nora: *No, lime green.*

Beckett: *This is lime green.*

I send him a photo of a lime green square.

He sends me a photo of a lime.

I laugh. Okay, fair enough. *I need balloons the color I just sent you.*

Astrid: *Negative two at eight forty a.m.*

I sigh. For fuck's sake.

Beckett: *So neon green.*

Nora: *Okay, neon green. Yes.*

He sends me a photo of a balloon he's holding that is the correct color.

Nora: *Yes. That one. I need one hundred. And a helium canister. Maybe two.*

Yes, two would be good. My helium canister is nearly out and I can never have too much back-up helium.

Astrid: *Positive eight at nine a.m.*

Nora: *So we're plus two today?*

Astrid: *Yes. *eye roll emoji**

Beckett: *How about this for the 'aqua' balloons?*

He sends another photo.

Nora: *Perfect.*

He already got the purple ones I need.

Beckett: *Heading to the candy store next.*

Nora: *Thank you!*

I love Beckett's delivery service. The whole town does. He not only does specialized shopping like this, he also does grocery shopping, will pick up catering orders from restaurants, will pick up and deliver furniture, hardware, appliances, lumber, even people. He takes many of our seniors to and from medical appointments, or even just to shop. There's very little he can't or won't pick up or drop off between Rebel and any of the cities within about a ninety-miles radius, including New Orleans.

We, of course, have the usual services like Fed Ex and UPS, along with the postal service. We also have ride-share services within the town, and many of our restaurants, including Perks and Rec, provide delivery services, but Beckett's services fill a gap. He'll pick up the specialized drill someone *has to have* today to finish a repair job, but that would cost them time away from their work site to get themselves, and that would take at least a couple of days to get through one of the other services. He'll take Miss Susan to her neurology appointment in New Orleans and take detailed notes of what the doctor says for her daughter, Lori, so that Lori doesn't have to take time off from her teaching job. Miss Susan likes going with Beckett better anyway, because he doesn't need to get back to get the kids from daycare and will take her through the drive-through daiquiri place and then for a walk along the riverfront before heading home.

I also love that Beckett's services are income-based. Some

people don't pay anything to have him pick up special items for them. Those who are able pay him a very reasonable fee. I know all of this is possible because my cousin Dane, everybody's favorite billionaire, subsidizes the service.

No matter how much Dane complains about his father leaving him with all of these businesses he can't get rid of and the dependency of this little town that he never asked for, Dane constantly uses his father's riches to help the town, even when he's doing it in secret.

"Emergency movie night committee reporting for duty!" I hear Everly call as the outer door to the Parks and Rec office opens.

"Get in here. I've been dying for you guys to get here," Sutton says.

"Do you know more about The Date?" Everly asks.

"I know more about Alex Olsen," Sutton says.

"Oh, *yes*," Andi says.

I'm up and out of my desk chair immediately.

I walk to the outer office as Andi, Everly, and Sutton start setting up our usual lunch potluck.

Everly is in her standard shorts and tank that she wears when she's doing lawn care. I know this morning she was up at the park making sure everything is trimmed and neat for movie night.

She takes the lid off the bowl of the salad she brought. She always contributes a salad of some kind. Sometimes it's a lettuce salad with tons of ingredients, sometimes it's a fruit salad, sometimes pasta, but it's always amazing.

"This is a rosemary and sundried tomato bread," Andi says as she unwraps a round, crusty loaf of bread. "I'm not sure of it." She's wearing loose flowy silk pants in a light blue that matches the sleeveless silky top. I can't tell where she's been—could have been yoga or coffee or shopping. All I do know is that she isn't covered in paint or clay, so she didn't come straight from either of her art studios.

"I'm sure it's delicious as always," Sutton tells her.

Sutton has been here in the office with me. Besides being the dance teacher for several classes, and now the hockey team's choreographer, she's also the Parks and Rec department's receptionist and my assistant. She's wearing her typical sundress with sandals, her hair in a French braid.

I cross to the refrigerator and pull out the peach and mango iced tea I made last night. This is not a brand-new addition to our potlucks, but I added honey to it so we'll see if it's sweet enough for Sutton, our sweet-tea aficionado.

We don't plan who's bringing what. Everly is in charge of salads, Andi always makes us bread, Sutton brings the sandwich fillings, and I'm in charge of drinks.

We fell into these assignments a long time ago. Everly loves her fruits and veggies, Sutton is used to cooking and always has a fridge full of meat and sandwich fixings because of Beckett, and Andi has been trying out this cottage-core lifestyle since her husband left. She mostly hates it, but, for some reason, has fallen in love with baking bread.

We all just know what we're supposed to bring to our lunch potlucks and somehow it always magically works together.

"I've got crab salad today," Sutton says, also going to the fridge for her container. She's made this before, and it's always delicious.

I carry the glass pitcher to the table where we spread out our lunch offerings.

We start making our sandwiches and dishing up salad as I say, "What is this about Alex?"

Sutton grins across the table at me. "I was at the Rec this morning for breakfast."

I stop with my spoonful of quinoa, cucumber, tomato, and feta salad, positioned above my plate. "Oh?"

"I thought maybe Alex could use a friendly face. Beckett, too." She slides a glance at Andi. "He's sweet like that."

Andi doesn't respond. She completely ignores the comment about Beckett entirely.

"Did he?" I ask. "Need a friendly face?"

I texted Sutton, Everly, Andi, and Quinn that our date last night was great. I told them where we went, that we had a wonderful time, and that I was home safely. I'd also informed my grandpas about where we were going as soon as I knew, and then when I got home. Nothing more or less.

"He did," Sutton confirmed. "The straw poll was about if the date was good or bad."

"What? How could they vote on that?" I demand, dumping salad onto my plate with a frown.

"They knew you went out to a fancy dinner in New Orleans," Sutton said. "There were several people who thought that was a poor choice on his part."

"The date was amazing," I insist, choosing a piece of bread from the basket Andi also supplied. Along with her new aesthetic, she's collecting things like baskets, and quirky mugs, plates, and bowls to replace the perfectly matched and incredibly expensive sets of silver and china she shared with her ex.

"How could that be a poor choice?" Everly asks. "I mean, it's pretty safe, actually."

Sutton nods. "I think that's the problem. Several people think it's boring and that it didn't take much thought or planning on his part."

I tip my head back and groan at the ceiling. "This was discussed at Perks and Rec this morning?"

"Yep," Sutton confirms.

"That explains the texts from Astrid about the ticket sales going up and down," I say.

"Season ticket sales are fluctuating based on your date with Alex last night?" Andi asks.

"I guess so." I love this town. I really do. But they're a lot. "Clearly Alex was wrong."

"About what?" Sutton asks.

"He thought the town would love us dating and that would bring butts to the seats. We've only increased by *four* season tickets with last night's date." I take a deep breath and turn toward my friends. "So now it's time for the town to learn more about the hockey team."

We take our plates to the table near the window, and I pull my phone out. I text Astrid.

Nora: *I think we need to open practice up to the public. Show them what we're doing live. They can even start giving us ideas for rules and penalties and fun stuff.*

Astrid: *You think the team is ready?*

I lift my head. "Sutton, what do you think about having a scrimmage with the team tomorrow night and inviting the public in to watch? We could explain what we want from fan involvement and maybe have them even give suggestions in real-time?"

She thinks about it, then shrugs. "They'll have to get used to changing things up without a lot of warning. We're only three weeks away from the first game."

"Exactly," I say. "So we should do it, right? We can tell everyone that now that Alex is here, we want them to come in and see what we've got planned."

"Sure. I mean, they've still got some work to do on the chore-ography, but maybe this would be a good incentive. A dress rehearsal always makes things feel more real."

I reply to Astrid: *Maybe not 100% but they could use the push.*

Astrid: *Let's do it. I'll tell the team tomorrow is a scrimmage so to dress appropriately.*

"So there was a thumbs up jar and a thumbs down jar," Sutton was telling Andi and Everly. "The thumbs down jar had more money in it for sure."

"Shouldn't *I* be the one saying if the date was good or not?" I ask my friends.

We really do have business to discuss. I need to make sure the final arrangements are in place for the pre-game festivities in three weeks. I need to make sure concessions are fully stocked—a nearly impossible feat since I don't know how many people are going to show up, especially if ticket sales are going to jump up and down literally hour to hour. And we've got movie night tonight.

"Everyone knows you're going to say you had a good time," Everly tells me, biting into her sandwich. "You always want people to feel good about things they do for you."

"Well, yeah," I agree. "It was a *super* nice restaurant in the Quarter."

"Heard the cheese was sixty-nine dollars," Sutton comments.

I look at her. "Where did you hear that?"

"Alex."

I set my spoon down. "Alex was there *while* everyone was discussing the date?"

"Oh, yeah." She grins as she takes a bite of salad.

"So he knows they were downvoting his date?" Andi asks. She laughs and shakes her head. "Poor guy. He's definitely going to need friendly faces at breakfast."

I sigh. "This is *not* helping! He has to like it here! And they have to like him!"

"Okay," Everly says. "I get that."

"But you have to admit that date wasn't really your thing," Sutton says. "You're a leftovers on the back porch while you watch the sunset girl, not a white tablecloth girl. He was trying to show off. The town saw right through that."

I think about that and feel a little pain in my chest. I don't know if I would have labeled it as showing off, but it was clear that Alex had been much more comfortable in the setting we were in last night than he probably was at Perks and Rec this morning.

Our lives are so different. And the people in my life, and the places I love here in Rebel, all around him, are constant reminders of that to him.

"Well, I didn't hate the white tablecloths," I say honestly. "But it was the company that I enjoyed. He's a good guy. And we have a chance to show everyone that he can fit in here too. That's what this movie night is about."

"So the emergency is that you changed to a new movie,"

Sutton says, getting up for a second helping of salad. "Why the change?"

Of course, these three are on the text message and email list that I send out Parks and Recreation information to. When I decided to change the movie for tonight at the very last minute, I had to notify everyone. Interestingly, no one had asked why. Or pushed back. I assume everyone is just taking this in stride.

"Because this movie is Alex's favorite. I wanted it to be something familiar to him, so he'd feel comfortable."

Everly stops mid-chew. "You changed the movie for movie night to Alex's favorite?"

I nod.

Her eyes narrow. "Wait a second."

"What?"

"You *actually* like him."

"I…" I frown.

I do. I told him that I was at risk of getting attached. But I need to be careful. Not just because I don't want the heartbreak, but I don't want the people who care about me to be upset either. I don't want my grandpas or Ruth or Thea getting attached to Alex thinking he and I are more than we are. I don't want these girls thinking Alex is more to me than he can be.

"He needs to feel comfortable here," I say for what feels like the hundredth time. "He needs to feel accepted and happy. We want him to play well and do a great job promoting what we're doing here with the hockey team. If he feels like everyone is against him and they don't like him or want him here, it's going to be hard for him to smile and be happy in interviews and to ham it up on the ice."

Everly chews her bite of salad, then shakes her head. "But you *like* him."

I sigh. "Fine. I like him."

"So…what else happened last night?" Everly asks, leaning in with a smile.

"Nothing."

"More than dinner," she says, pointing her fork at me. "I can tell."

I look at her in surprise. "You can not."

"I can. You are so easy to read, Nora. You like him, and you did not just eat dinner and come home."

"We walked through the Quarter."

"And what else?"

I blow out a breath. "Fine. He kissed me."

Andi sets her fork down. "Wow. Already?"

"Well, it wasn't the first time." I'm fighting a smile now. Alex makes me feel like smiling. That's… complicated. But impossible to deny.

"They kissed at the Rec the first day he was in town," Sutton says. "After practice."

I nod.

"What?" Andi demands. "The guy's been in town for what? Two days?"

"But we kissed at the airport the first time," I tell them, suddenly enjoying their disbelief.

"*What?*" they all three say at once.

I tell them about how he kissed me to hide from Leo, Wilson, and Brewser.

"So what *else* did you do last night?" Everly presses. "Since you clearly like kissing him?"

I can't help the little giggle that escapes. I should *not* feel giggly about this guy. "Nothing. I swear. He did *offer* a really fancy hotel suite…" I say.

"*That* is not your style, but I love it," Sutton says.

"Smart guy," Andi comments. "It's not like he can take you to his place here…right above your grandpa's kitchen."

"Or her place," Everly says. "Everyone in town would notice his truck parked there overnight."

"We did *not* go to a hotel room," I interject.

They all turn to me in unison.

"Why not?" Andi asks.

"I'm not going to sleep with him!" I exclaim. I get up with my empty plate and carry it to the wastebasket.

"Why not?" Everly echoes Andi.

I turn back with a laugh. "Because this is all for the team. It's not serious."

"You *like* him for real," Everly says. "And you like kissing him. Why not let it go further?"

Sutton nods. "It started for the team, but why can't it be more?"

It sounds reasonable, but are they forgetting that he's leaving?

I frown. "I can't get involved with him *knowing* it's temporary."

"I know that you've been hurt by guys in the past when they've left," she agrees. "But that's because that was a surprise. You got into a relationship with them, thinking it was going to be long-term and *here*. What hurt was them upending your plans and leaving you when you thought you were building something lasting."

"Well…" I frown again. "Yeah."

"But with Alex, that's not the situation. You already know he's leaving. So why can't you just enjoy him while he's here? Go out? Have fun? Have amazing sex with the hottest guy you've ever dated? The one that makes you smile like I haven't seen you smile in…maybe ever?" she asks.

My hands fly to my face.

Everly is now nodding. "She makes a good point."

"He *is* easily the hottest guy you've dated," Sutton says.

"Does he make me smile like that?" I ask.

"Oh, absolutely," Sutton says.

"You didn't know that?" Everly asks.

My heart is now beating double-time.

Could I just go to a fancy hotel with Alex?

Could I just go to *any* bedroom with Alex?

Why not?

Suddenly, I can't think of a good reason.

I can feel heat sliding through my veins like I've just taken a shot of my great-uncle Leo's moonshine. It's sharp at first and makes me suck in a breath, but then the warmth spreads and I feel a relaxed *ooh, this is nice* rolling along behind it.

"You all are bad influences," I tell my three friends.

"I think you mispronounced 'thank you very much'," Andi says, lifting her drink in a toast.

CHAPTER 16
ALEX

I DO PREFER to pick up my dates, but when the woman I'm spending the evening with is in charge of the event, I have to agree to meet her there.

The park in Rebel is half a block wide and six blocks long. It's bordered on one side by Main Street and on the other by Otter Avenue. Magnolia trees line the sidewalks along the edges, and one end of the park has a huge gazebo, while the other end has a small amphitheater.

The soft grass is broken up by park benches and flower beds and crisscrossed with cement paths.

Movie night is set up near the amphitheater end of the park, and I shouldn't be surprised to see it is colorful and over-the-top. I immediately notice the purple, blue, and lime-green balloon frame around the gigantic sheet stretched between two wooden poles, which will act as the screen. Then I take in the twenty-foot-long table that is draped in a purple plastic tablecloth and covered with treats, including the multitude of popcorn toppings and add-ins at the end of the table near the popcorn machine.

The lawn in front of the screen is dotted with lawn chairs and blankets, and there are already easily thirty people sitting and standing around chatting and snacking. But there are just as many people still walking toward the area with me.

It takes me ten seconds to figure out what movie we're watching tonight.

I smile, pleasantly surprised. I love this movie.

Not that anyone here knows that. In any interview where I am ever asked, I say my favorite movie is *The Dark Knight*, the Batman movie. And I do like that one a lot. It also seems like the kind of tough, adult-guy movie I should claim as my favorite.

If I'm completely honest, however, *Monsters, Inc.* is absolutely my favorite, and I find myself smiling even more widely as I search for Nora in the crowd.

As soon as I spot her, laughing at something someone has said as she ties a character balloon to the framed area where people can get their photos taken next to full-size cutouts of the monsters, I realize that I have been anticipating seeing her all day.

I head straight for her.

"Oh my gosh, hi, "she greets, her smile brightening when she sees me.

I don't give her any warning or ask for permission. I wrap my arms around her in a big hug and kiss the top of her head. I'm her fucking boyfriend. She's lucky that that's all I do to her in front of all these people.

She looks up at me, surprise in her eyes.

"Hey, Wildflower. This is impressive."

Her surprise disappears and excitement replaces it. "Do you like it?"

"Of course. I was expecting a simple movie projector and a few lawn chairs. This is a whole production." I give her a little eye roll. "But of course it is. You don't do anything small."

"It's some balloons and snacks," she laughs. "It's not like it's a red-carpet premiere in Hollywood."

"They should completely put you in charge of movie premieres in Hollywood," I tell her. "People will talk about them for weeks after."

"Thank you," she says sincerely. "I love when people talk about something I put together long after the fact."

I believe her. And I also believe that it happens on a regular basis.

"Come check out the snacks," she says excitedly, pulling me toward the table.

In addition to the buttered popcorn that people can add everything to from cheddar cheese flavored powder to mix-ins like M & M's and pretzels, there are also lime green popcorn balls with a single eye-ball on the front, sugar cookies in various monster shapes and colors, and what would essentially amount to a charcuterie board, but the meat, cheese, olives, and fruits have been added to little wooden skewers.

"What are those bright blue balls?" I ask.

They are stuck on the skewers with pieces of ham and salami, large green olives, and cherry tomatoes.

"Those are herbed cream cheese balls," she says. "Dyed blue for Sully." She grins as she names one of the main monsters in the movie.

"Monster balls?" I ask, grabbing one.

She laughs. "Not like *that*."

"Good. Because they'd have to be *way* bigger."

She swats my arm. "Alex! It's a kids' movie!"

I look around. "And there is a surprisingly large number of adults here."

She shrugs. "We do a different person's favorite each time, and since most of the attendees are adults, often they're R-rated, so it's not necessarily kid-friendly. We leave it up to the parents and sometimes kids come if it's a kid movie, though." She looks around. "This one was kind of last-minute, though. I just sent the movie name out late last night so it's possible a lot of families didn't have time to watch."

"Wait," I say. "Time to watch what?"

But she's already heading toward the movie screen.

I follow simply because she's the entire reason I'm here and I don't know where she's set us up to sit.

Nora picks up a wireless microphone.

"Hey, everyone!" she greets.

The crowd choruses a "Hi, Nora!" back to her as people head for their seats.

"Anyone want to guess whose favorite movie this is?" she asks.

I look around. I'm curious who else loves *Monsters, Inc.*

No one raises their hand or speaks up, which is odd. I don't think this town has a single person in it who wouldn't speak up to share information about themselves. Or anyone else.

"Yours?" someone asks Nora.

I look at Nora in surprise. Do we have the same favorite movie?

"How long have you been doing movie nights?" I ask her.

She frowns. "I don't know. Three years?" She looks back at the group. "I do like the movie, but no, it's not my favorite," she says with a smile.

So no, we don't share the same favorite.

But the group doesn't already know her favorite movie? Haven't they all watched it together here with themed decorations and snacks? In *three years,* they haven't gotten around to *Nora's* favorite?

I look out at the crowd. "How often do you do this?"

"What?" she asks. I'm obviously distracting her. "Monthly." She turns to the group again. "Any other guesses? It will surprise you, I think!"

Okay, so if every single person here gets a chance at their favorite and it's only monthly, that's thirty-six movies. There are fifty people here. I suppose it's possible they haven't gotten to Nora's. But she runs the whole damned thing and hasn't been able to watch *her* favorite?

"What's your favorite movie?" I ask her.

She shakes her head as if to tell me *not now*. "It's Alex!" she announces to the group.

Oh…wait, what?

The crowd gives a collective surprised "aw" sound, and there's light applause.

We're watching *Monsters, Inc.* because of *me*?

I stare at Nora. "How did you know that?"

She looks smug. "I know you tell interviews that your favorite movie is *The Dark Knight*."

I do. And she says this right into the microphone so the whole group is included.

"Right," I say. "Because that's a fantastic film." It is. Great acting, great cinematography, great themes.

"Sure," she agrees. "But your *real* favorite is *Monsters, Inc.*"

I narrow my eyes. There is not even a handful of people who know that. I know who told her. "You asked my sister, and she blabbed?"

Nora grins. "Yep."

I sigh. Well… *Monsters, Inc.* is great. I look out at the crowd. The group looks pleased. No one's judging me. I assumed sports fans and sports magazine writers want to hear that a big, tough hockey player likes dark action films with lots of crashing and blowing up. But this group… they're all grinning at me, not in a 'that's so funny that you like a cartoon movie', but in a 'how delightful' way.

"How many times have you seen it?" Nora asks into the mic, then she tips it toward me so everyone can hear my answer.

"What?"

"How many times? Usually, people see their favorites more than once, and typically, you pick up extra things when you watch it again and again."

"Uh…" I scrub the back of my neck. Do I admit the real number? Looking out at the lawn chairs and blankets, all I see are people who are watching me with open, interested expressions.

And she's right. You don't watch a favorite just once. "Probably a dozen times."

Nora looks thrilled by that answer. Okay then, I could probably tell her it's more like twenty.

"Who's your favorite character?" she asks.

Again, I'm tempted to lie. Or fib, at least, because of course I do like the two main monster characters. But I give Nora the truth. "Boo. The little girl."

She's clearly surprised. "Really? Why?"

"I think because I'd like to be her," I say, a little uncomfortable. Okay, a lot uncomfortable. "She's vulnerable and the bad guys are out to get her, but this big monster does whatever he has to to protect her. And his friend steps up to help because he's a good friend. She just has to trust them. I like that idea. Just being able to be yourself, trust someone, and be taken care of."

As soon as those words leave my mouth, my eyes widen. Oh… damn. That was a lot. I've never said that to anyone about that movie. I don't think I've ever really thought it. I've never thought about who my favorite character was specifically.

But Nora looks like she wants to hug me.

And maybe take her clothes off and let me more-than-hug her.

And I like that a lot, so I'm not sorry for baring my stupid mushy soul there for a second.

"And what do you like about the movie overall, Alex?" Nora asks. "What makes it your favorite?"

I wasn't prepared for all of these questions about a movie I haven't watched lately. I'm not sure…. Yes, I am.

"It's funny," I say simply. "Billy Crystal and John Goodman are the voices of the two main characters, and they're both fantastic."

Nora watches me, clearly waiting for more.

I shrug. "It's a fun movie. Puts me in a good mood."

There's another long pause.

Someone in the group says, "It *is* funny. I like the way the two main characters, Mike and Sully, are such opposites but clearly care about each other and support one another. They're good friends."

I nod. I like that too. "You've seen it?" I ask the guy who is sitting with two women and another man.

"Well…yeah," he says, as if that's obvious.

Okay, fair enough. It's an older movie. Maybe he's got grand-kids. It's not at all an *obscure* film.

"Anything else?" Nora asks me.

I start to shake my head, but I look at the group again. They're all watching me. I had no idea that we were going to watch a movie *because* it was my favorite, but Nora specifically asked Astrid for a suggestion.

Many of these people have been in the diner when I've been there, and I remember how they all want to get to know me. Not about me as a hockey player, even though that's why I'm in Rebel. They want facts about me as a person.

So I say, "I like the movie because to me it seems it's about the idea that there's often more to people than what you see on the surface. That just because we've been told something about a person, or a group of people, if you look deeper, you'll find out that we have more in common than we have differences."

Now Nora beams at me.

Yeah, she wanted a real answer. Well, I gave her one. That's truly how I feel about the movie.

"I love that," she says.

"Oh, I see that," a woman off to the left says. "Like the idea that the monsters are supposed to be scary, but we immediately see them just going to work, and that they have families and friends, co-worker drama, paperwork, and all kinds of really normal things we can all relate to."

"And they're only scary because it's their job. When they're not working, they're just like us. They have all the same emotions and experiences we do," someone says.

"And of course there's the message of laughter being stronger than the screams," someone else says. "That happiness is stronger than fear. That's such a great message."

I've lean toward Nora. "Are they spoiling it?"

"What do you mean?"

"All of this discussion before we watch the movie might spoil it for the people who haven't seen it."

"But they've all seen it."

I frown. "You're going to make them watch a movie they've already seen? They're going to be so bored."

"If they already saw it, they didn't have to watch again."

"What?" I ask.

"What?" she asks in return, seeming puzzled.

We just stare at each other for a second.

"I had an imaginary friend when I was a kid," the man near the front says.

Muriel is sitting next to him and says, "Sully wasn't Boo's imaginary friend. He was the monster in her closet."

"But there aren't really monsters," the guy says.

"In the movie there were. But they weren't monsters like we're used to thinking of them," another man says.

"So you think those monsters were real?" the first man says. "In the movie?"

The guy he's talking to shifts on his lawn chair to look at him more fully. "You don't?"

"I just assumed it was all part of the kid's imagination."

"But there were multiple kids," Muriel says.

"There were?"

I look at Nora. She's got the microphone cradled to her chest, and she's watching the group talk with a smile on her face.

"Did you believe in monsters as a kid?" a man to our right asks the people around him.

At least, I think that's who he asks. He's not talking to the group, who is still debating if the monsters in the movie were real or in the little girl's head, or imaginary for everyone in some existential commentary on how we let our fears become too big and real sometimes.

"I did," a woman with bright red curls says. "I was *sure* that werewolves and vampires were real."

"Are vampires monsters?" Patty asks.

"How are they *not* monsters?" the redhead asks.

"Well, they look like humans, right?" Patty asks. "And aren't they human before they get turned? I think of monsters like the ones in the movie. They're always monsters. Not something else that turns into something."

"Werewolves are human before they turn into werewolves, right?" someone else asks.

"I think so. Do they get bit too? Like vampires?"

"Yes. And like zombies."

"What about Godzilla and King Kong?" someone new asks. "Are they monsters?"

"Well, obviously," Muriel replies.

"Why obviously? What makes a monster a monster? Because Godzilla is a gigantic dinosaur or something, right? And King Kong is a gigantic gorilla. Is something a monster just because it's *big*?"

"Monster trucks are really big," a man further back says.

"So the word monster just means big?" Patty asks. "Don't they also have to be scary?"

"Yes!" a few people chorus.

"For sure," a woman says. "I have a gigantic dog, but he's the biggest marshmallow ever. Definitely not scary, and not a monster!"

Several people laugh.

"Movies with dogs in them are always the best," someone off to the left and back says.

There's a lot of nodding.

I feel my eyebrows arching.

But I can't stop watching Nora.

She's glowing.

She fucking loves this. She's clearly in her element.

I bet she looks the same way at Garden Club, and Otter Club.

I can't wait to see her at hockey.

I can't. I want her smiling like that while she watches us—me—play. No, I want her even more excited. I want her yelling and cheering and…laughing and singing along.

If I'm going to fucking sing and dance, I want to look to the stands and see Nora singing and shaking it with me.

"But the little girl calls Sully *kitty*," someone calls out. "She doesn't think he's a dog!"

People laugh.

"That's true!"

"He should have been a dog," the first guy says. "Movies with dogs are always the best."

"I don't think Old Yeller was!" someone shouts.

More laughter and some groans.

I finally can't stay quiet as I look out over the group. They're moving about, returning to the snack table, everyone just calling out pieces of conversation, some smaller groups are having their own conversations the rest of us can't hear.

I step closer to Nora. "Have they *all* seen the movie?" I ask.

She looks up at me. "Of course. They watched it before they got here."

I frown, thinking that over. "They watched the movie *before* movie night?"

"Yes, how else would they be able to discuss it?"

"You intended to just discuss it?" I ask, stupidly.

"Yes. With all the conversation everyone always wants to have, it takes us forever to get through a movie when we're stopping and starting it as we go—"

"You stop and start it as people want to *talk* during the movie?" I ask.

"Well, no. Not anymore. We did that the first two times, but then I realized it was better to just let them talk. That was the fun part."

I blink at her. "The fun part of *movie night* was the *talking*?"

"Of course. Anyone can watch a movie. By themselves, in groups, with one other person. But if you want to discuss it, you need a group that has all seen it. So we all watch the movie ahead of time and then get together to talk about it."

I look over my shoulder at the screen. "But…the screen."

"Sometimes we play a clip or something if someone wants to rewatch a certain thing for the sake of the discussion or to make a point," she says. "But we couldn't get the movie working on Bill's laptop tonight. So that's just decoration."

She grins, truly unbothered.

"This sounds like a book club but with movies," I say.

She nods. "Yeah, it's a lot like book club."

"Why don't you just have a book club?"

"We do have a book club."

Of course they do.

"*All Dogs Go to Heaven* is definitely the best," someone is yelling from the back.

"*Turner and Hooch*!" someone else calls.

"*Marley and Me*!"

"I had a cat named Marley once," a man says. "Smartest cat I ever met."

"I love cats, but I have birds now, and I'm telling you, they are *so* smart," a woman behind him says.

"Birds really are smart," Muriel says. "Did you know, if you feed crows, they'll bring you gifts as a thank you? Like beads and rocks and stuff."

"Oh! I had a raven that did that once!" someone says excitedly.

"Well, obviously, I feed *my* birds," the woman who started this says. "I wouldn't not feed them!"

"No one said you didn't feed your birds, Natalie!" Muriel says.

"Why did you bring up wild birds? We were talking about pets!"

"I had a chinchilla once. Very cool pet."

I've lost track of who is saying what. Things are being called out from all over the collection of chairs and blankets in front of the "movie screen" that is now truly just a white sheet between two wooden poles.

"Do they talk?"

"The chinchillas?"

"No, the birds!"

"I don't think crows talk."

"I mean Natalie's birds!"

I'm watching this with wide eyes. What the actual fuck is happening? "They're talking about birds now," I tell Nora, unnecessarily.

"Yep." She nods happily. "And chinchillas."

"You're losing control."

"Control of what?"

"The...movie night."

"Am I?" She turns to face me.

No one is paying attention to us anymore.

"Aren't you?" I ask. "They're not watching a movie, they're not talking about the movie, they're not talking about any movies at all."

"Do you want to talk about the movie some more?" she asks, handing the mic to me. "Go ahead. They'd love to hear from you."

I quickly put up a hand. "No. I didn't mean that."

"Then why do you care what they're talking about?"

"It's just...it's movie night."

She laughs. "Well, that's what brought everyone here," she agrees.

I shake my head. "You can't honestly think *I'm* wrong for showing up here on *movie night* expecting to sit in the dark, watch a *movie*, and make out with you."

Her smile changes. Now it's got a mischievous edge. "Is that what you were planning?"

I lean closer. "Of course."

"Well, that's not how this works."

"I shouldn't be surprised that even movie night isn't what I expect it to be with you, should I?" I ask, realizing it even as I say it.

Nothing about being in Rebel has been as expected, and about ninety percent of that has to do with this woman.

"I guess I could have explained it to you. But I didn't want to spoil the surprise," she says.

"What surprise?"

"The surprise of it being your favorite movie tonight."

"Oh, yeah…that is a surprise. Why did you want it to be *my* favorite movie?"

"Because the town wants to get to know you, and someone's favorite movie says a lot about them," she says. "I send out the name of the movie ahead of time, and everyone watches it on their own time, and then we get together to talk about it. Or whatever else comes up."

Obviously. I look out at the crowd in the park. "This is…chaotic."

"It's not. Not really. Not if you understand what's going on." She pauses. "It's like hockey."

I laugh. "How so?"

"It's like you said at Perks and Rec the other night. On the surface, it might look chaotic, but when you're in it, you see that it's working just the way it's supposed to."

I did say that. And that is true of hockey. The game is fast-paced with lots of moving parts, and it can look like a bunch of guys skating around, constantly chasing a puck, but there's offensive and defensive strategy, and when seasoned players hit that puck, they know what to expect.

"Movie night is supposed to devolve into talk about birds?"

"It's not *devolving!*" she protests, looking a little offended. "Yes, if our goal was to sit here and quietly watch a movie, then sure, what's happening now would seem like the event is falling apart. But our goal is to just all be together and have a good time." She looks at the group gathered and smiles. "Mission accomplished."

"That's it?" I ask. "Just get together and have fun?"

She nods. "It's always about community and enjoyment and including everyone and making the town better. Sometimes the conduit for that is a movie, sometimes it's gardening, sometimes it's otters."

"That's…"

"Not what you expected."

"Right."

She gives me a thoughtful look. "I get it. Your perception of something's success and worth really depends on why you're doing it. Like, if you're at a hockey game to score a lot of points and have amazing statistics and get a win, when things go off the rails it will feel very different to you than it will for me who comes to that same game, sits in the stands, has a great time with my family and friends no matter the final score."

"We're talking about the Revelers now?" I ask. "You're saying movie night and hockey games where the team sings, and dances are the same thing?"

She shakes her head. "Yes, and no. I'm talking about you and me more broadly. Your goal for your career was hockey—playing, scoring, winning. Then you got hurt and couldn't do those things anymore. You were used to having all of that govern your life, and then it was suddenly gone. Then you come here and have a chance to play again, but the goal isn't the same. Because *my* goal is to bring people together and give them a good time.

"I took hockey and made it even *more* entertaining for the people *watching*. Because that's always my goal. But it changes the game for you. It's not what you expected. It's not straightforward. It's not just about the points on the board or even the rules as you know them. I can understand why that would feel really chaotic and out of your control."

I frown. Dammit. She hit the nail directly on the head.

But she's not apologizing. Or saying she's going to change things.

I don't feel panic or resentment, though. Nora is in charge. It might be a constant string of what-the-hell-is-happening events while I'm here, but if she's leading the way, at least it will be done with heart.

I look around the park. *This* is life in Rebel. This is life in Nora Delaune's orbit.

If I'm going to stay here for any length of time—in this town or where this woman's energy can reach me—then I'm going to have to accept that.

"You never feel out of control because you just embrace the chaos?" I ask her. "I mean, you *create* chaos. Does that help you feel more in control somehow?"

I need to know this. Maybe I can learn something here that will make things feel less tumultuous when I leave Rebel. Because, honestly, while I'm here, I have no chance of escaping the mayhem. I'll just have to hold on and let Nora drive this bus.

"I wouldn't say I embrace chaos," she says. "I just always keep my goal in mind."

"Having fun."

She lifts a shoulder. "Enjoying the moment. Being present in the right now. Making the moment the best it can be for the people around me. That keeps things simple. Sure, things might get a little loud or tumultuous around me, but if I focus on what I really want, then it keeps me clear. If I go to bed at the end of the day and can think of one person whose day was better because of me, then I succeeded and the rest is just noise."

I study her. It sounds very simplistic and idealistic, but I don't think Nora is naïve. She knows bad things happen. She just tries to be one of the good things that happen to people.

And she actually *enjoys* the things she does for others. Including Not Really Movie Night and Definitely Not Really Hockey. I can only imagine what Not Actually Otter Club actually is.

She's just so fucking *cute* when she's putting together a plan and then watching it go off the rails.

She reminds me of a kid setting up dominoes just to knock

them over. Or a cat gracefully walking across a table, weaving and stepping carefully, only to get to that one full glass…that she tips right off the edge.

Sure, it might all be planned to happen that way, but it still results in a mess.

Jesus. How can I be so attracted to someone who not only doesn't get bothered over chaos, but often causes it?

But I am.

It's more than physical attraction. Something that pulls me closer as a voice in my head whispers, *What if you let her mess up your life a little? Would that really be so bad?*

Looking at all of these people tonight, thinking about all of the people I've met here, all of the people who interact with Nora on a regular basis—my sister included—is there a single one who feels like she's actually messing anything up?

I almost laugh out loud at that thought.

No. Nora makes people happy.

With intention.

Even bypassing her own favorite movie to make everyone else who shows up here feel like what they enjoy matters to her.

I don't know if I *should* let her mess up my life a little while I'm here, but I'm not sure I can avoid it.

CHAPTER 17
NORA

ALEX OLSEN IS SURPRISING. I probably should have explained movie night to him more clearly. Or at all. It's just that we've been doing it this way for so long, I don't always remember that it's odd to have a movie night and not watch the movie together.

Still, he's mostly just rolling with it. Oh, sure, he's *commenting* on it. To me. I think he can't not point out to me how *I* keep surprising him. Because I don't think he knows if he hates it, or if he doesn't really mind it, or if just maybe he kind of likes it.

I can't help but smile. I don't think Alex is used to being out of his comfort zone. I think his comfort zone is huge, and I think a lot of people have spent a lot of time, and maybe even money, keeping it *very* comfortable.

But I like him off-balance.

Yes, he was clearly in his element at the Italian Barrel the other night, and he's sexy when he's confident and in control.

But he's sweet and…something else…when he's befuddled.

He's…real.

That's what it is. I like confident Alex, for sure, but I like this real side of him. Not the professional hockey player who knows he's a star. Not the guy in the magazine. Not even the guy who knows all about sixty-nine-dollar cheese plates.

I like the real guy who has no idea what grits are—I heard about that from the breakfast crowd, of course—the guy who has adamant opinions about bananas—Sutton told me about that pronouncement—and the guy whose favorite movie is a cartoon about monsters.

I've watched him play hockey. He's amazing. Watching him was fun before I knew him—before I *kissed* him—and I think now it would, well, probably turn me on. But I'm *really* looking forward to him playing with a big foam cowboy hat on his head to a Shania Twain song. And I *know* that's going to turn me on.

But I also loved the look on his face when he first arrived for movie night and saw the decorations and food and realized what movie we were discussing.

I wanted to delight him, and it worked.

I love delighting people. I love making people smile and make that little gasp of surprised pleasure. But with Alex it was even better.

I'm in trouble.

I'm *trying* not to like him too much, and here I am feeling like Miss Freaking America because I made the big, cocky hockey player light up over a movie.

That we didn't even watch.

"Chinchillas are *not* related to otters!" Henry Bordelon says loudly. "Otters are not rodents! They are mustelids! Shame on all of you for not knowing that!"

"We *do* know that, Henry Bordelon! Don't you start acting like you're so smart!" Caroline Robertson snaps.

"Well, then you would *know* they're not related! Chinchillas are rodents!" Henry says.

"Maybe that's the part they didn't know," Jake Clairborne offers.

"Then they should stay quiet," Henry says with a frown.

"They do look a little alike," Jake's girlfriend, Madison, says.

"They most certainly do *not*," Henry says, clearly affronted by the suggestion.

"Okay, I think movie night is over," I say to Alex.

"You just call it at some point?"

I grin. "Yep. You know, when things start to go off the rails."

He snorts.

And then Muriel officially wraps things up for me. She chucks a popcorn ball at her sister. The ball bounces off Patty's shoulder and hits Niles Cooper on the cheek.

"Muriel!" at least four people say all at once.

"Time to go," Henry declares, standing and folding his chair.

Caroline and Natalie follow suit, and soon everyone is gathering their blankets and chairs and heading for the snack table to grab leftovers to take home.

They call out their thanks to me and their goodbyes to each other as they go and within five minutes the area is ninety-nine percent cleared out.

"So what now?" Alex asks. "Want to have a drink? Take a walk? Have hot sex at…"

I wait for a moment, amused. Yeah, we can't go back to his place, considering someone in my family is there manning the kitchen and bar, and my grandfather will be there to start the breakfast shift at five a.m..

"The back of my pickup?" he finally asks.

I laugh. "I haven't had an offer like that in years."

He moves closer. "Did you take your panties off in some lucky guy's pickup, Wildflower?"

"Of course," I say. "But that was before I knew there were places that sold sixty-nine-dollar cheese plates, that there were people who paid for sixty-nine-dollar cheese plates."

He looks amused, and turned on, and a little exasperated all at once. "Is that your way of saying that yes, you would like to go to the Windsor Court Hotel in New Orleans with me?"

"I definitely want to," I admit.

He starts to pull his phone from his pocket, and I realize that he really will call and book us a room. I laugh and reach out, grabbing his forearm. "I can't. I have to clean all of this up, and I have curvy girls' yoga in the morning, and then a busy day."

He stops, frowns, then looks toward the tables. "You have to clean all of this up?"

I drop my hold on his arm. "Of course."

"Who set it up?"

"I did."

"You're not a curvy girl," he says.

I blink, following his conversation jump, and say, "I lead the class."

"You *lead* an early yoga class the morning after a late-night movie club thing?"

"Yes."

"What are your work hours?" he asks. "When's your day off? We'll go then."

"I don't really have set hours or a day off. I just take time… whenever." I don't really take time off. I don't like to sit around. Unless I'm at silent book club or I'm sitting to do a craft project or something.

"Then take time tomorrow," he says, but his eyes are narrowed and he's studying me intently.

I feel like I'm being tested.

"I can't."

"Is your schedule full of activities that you invented, scheduled, and run completely by yourself?"

I drop my gaze to the collar of his Henley. "Sutton will help me with some of it."

"Uh huh." He reaches out and tips my chin up, making me look at him. "You do it all."

That's not a question.

"I love it," I say with conviction.

"I don't doubt that. But no one, I mean *no one*—and I don't even know everyone in this town—expects you to work twenty-four-seven."

"I…" I wet my lips. "It doesn't feel like work."

"Okay. But it still is."

"But what would I do with time off?" I ask. "I'd be at the park, or the library, or Perks and Rec, or doing crafts anyway. Why not just make it something other people can do too?"

For a second, his expression softens, and I feel his thumb slide over my cheek.

Then the look in his eyes turns sly as his mouth tips up on one side and he drags his thumb over my lower lip. "How about I give you some things to do with your time off that other people are *not* invited to?"

I want to suck on his thumb. I resist, but my stomach has hot ribbons swirling through it now.

"You'll ruin me for after you leave," I say softly, voicing that very real fear.

He takes a deep breath, then says, "Fuck, I hope so."

I swallow and take a step back. "That's a bad idea."

I still want to do it.

My friends pointed out that I won't be *heartbroken* after he leaves because I know it's coming.

But I could become addicted to…things…that I can't have again after he's gone.

"Is it any consolation that I'm worried about being ruined by you, too?" he asks.

I feel my eyes widen and my heart thump hard.

Yes, actually, that is some consolation.

"We shouldn't do that to each other," I say.

He nods. "Maybe not. But I really, really want to."

Yeah, same.

"Nora! The tables are in your truck!"

I jerk out of the little daze Alex put me in and look toward Henry and Wilson. Wilson gives me a thumbs up from beside my truck, where it's parked at the curb.

"Thank you!" I call. I look up at Alex. "See? They help. I just need to take down all the balloons and the screen and carry any boxes of leftover treats to the truck." I glance toward where the snack tables were. There's only one box, which means most of the snacks got taken. Awesome. "And load up the popcorn machine. I'll clean it at the office. So, I won't be too long. Don't worry about my late hours."

"I'm still going to."

I don't say anything to that or protest when he begins taking down the balloons from around the screen as I unfasten the sheet from the wooden poles.

I like that he's thinking about me. He doesn't need to *worry*, but I like being on his mind.

Once he's back in Portland, that won't be the case, so I'll enjoy it for now.

It's not like my family and friends don't sometimes worry about me.

I frown as I start to fold the sheet. Actually, I'm not sure they do *worry*. What would they worry about? I don't do anything dangerous. I don't go anywhere dangerous. The people I spend time with are people I've known—and my family has known—for years, if not their entire lives. Hell, my grandfathers know the grandparents of most of my friends.

I'm healthy. I do a very public job where they all see me every single day. I've had some emotional ups and downs—who hasn't —but I'm generally a happy, positive person.

There's simply no reason for people to worry.

"Let me," Alex says, nudging me out of the way as I start to pull the first of the wooden poles out of the ground

"I can do it." I've done it dozens of times.

"I know," he says simply. Then picks me up, sets me to the side, and pulls the pole out of the ground.

I simply start laughing.

He looks over. "What?"

"People don't tell you no very often, do they?"

"A few do, but I don't listen." He pauses. "Generally."

I watch as he pulls the other pole from the ground, then turns to face me with them both.

"There's someone you *do* listen to?"

"Well, Declan O'Grady told me that no, I can't play for the Grays anymore," he says wryly. "I guess I listened to that one."

"That probably doesn't really count," I say. "You didn't listen, you just didn't have another option."

"Good. I hate being soft." He gives me that sexy-cute half-smile again.

I grin. "You'd rather be hard?"

"Since I met you, I don't remember being any other way."

I giggle and roll my eyes. I saw that coming and I let it happen.

Because I really like flirting with Alex Olsen.

We carry everything to my truck, and with Alex's help, it only takes one trip.

"Thanks," I say.

"Give me a ride home?" he asks. "It's right next door to your office."

"Of course."

It's a ridiculous four blocks from here. I had to drive from my office at City Hall because of all the stuff I had to bring, but I can see City Hall and the roof of Perks and Rec—and Alex's apartment—from here.

But I want to extend my time with him.

Even though it's a bad idea, I know it.

Sure, I could sleep with him, enjoy it for seven months, and not be heartbroken when he leaves because I know better than to make plans beyond that. And I probably will. Sleep with him and enjoy it, that is.

But spending time with him, talking and laughing and flirting and *liking* him, is where it gets more difficult to believe that my heart will be totally intact when this is over.

We make the short drive, and without a word, Alex helps carry all the stuff from my truck up to my office.

I twist the knob and push the door open.

"You don't lock this door?" he asks, following me in.

I hit the light switch just inside the door. "No. City Hall is locked up, but I don't lock this one."

"Why not?"

"Why would I?"

"So people can't take your stuff," he says, as if that's obvious.

"If someone needs markers or posterboard or a confetti canon, they'd come ask and I'd say yes anyway," I say with a shrug, carrying the snacks to the countertop near the fridge.

"What about your computers and other expensive equipment?"

I point toward the closet where the poles and sheet are stored. He heads in that direction, and I start unpacking the treats.

"I guess I just don't think anyone would do that," I say when we meet in the main outer office area.

"You're very trusting."

"I am," I agree. "I haven't been given a reason not to trust people in this situation."

"But with your heart…that's a different story."

My eyes widen, but I nod. "For sure."

"With men. And your mom."

I nod again.

"Got it."

"What have you got?" I ask, stepping toward him.

"That you believe the best of people until they screw up."

"Oh. Yeah, that's true."

"And I'm fucked."

I frown. "What do you mean?"

"I messed up already. With Harley. And Ruth."

Oh.

He did.

Dammit.

How did I forget that?

Did I forget that?

Of course not. But… I like him anyway.

But do you trust him?

Strangely, I know the answer right away.

I do. I trust Alex. I trust the things he's told me, and the way he looks at me.

He likes me. He wants me. He's out of his element here, but he trusts me. Like the little girl did with Sully, the big monster, in *Monsters, Inc.* She just went with it, trusting that Sully would take care of her, lead the way, keep her safe.

Am I Alex's Sully?

Do I want to be?

That's hilarious but…I like it.

I know he's waiting for an answer, and there is something in his expression that makes me think this really matters.

"Yeah, that did happen with Harley and Ruth," I say, acknowledging the situation. "But I still trust you. I guess you're an exception to some of my rules."

"On the surface, I would say it's because I didn't do anything directly to you, but I know you now," he says. "I think doing something to someone you love is even worse."

I'm glad he knows this about me. "That's true."

He steps closer again and now lifts his hand to cup my cheek. "Who takes care of you, Nora?"

"What do you mean? Everyone."

"Do they? Or do they let you take care of them and that makes you happy, so it feels like they're taking care of you?"

I stare at him. I've never had anyone ask me that before. "It's true that taking care of the people of this town makes me happy," I admit.

"I know. And I'm so glad you have that. But you know you don't have to keep paying them back, right?"

"I don't know what that means." But I think I do.

"You take care of them because they took care of you. Your mom left you here. This town raised you. You're grateful."

"Of course, I am. They gave me an amazing life. Tons of love.

Wonderful memories. I am safe, secure, loved, and taken care of here."

"But you don't have to keep paying them back for all of that," he repeats. "They would still love you if there were fewer clubs. If you took a day or two off." He pauses then says, "If you left."

I step back. "What are you talking about?"

"You don't want to leave this town. I understand your life is here. All the people you love. But do you want to stay or are you afraid of leaving?"

My heart is pounding now, and I'm not sure why. "I've never had a better reason to leave than I have for staying," I say honestly.

He watches me for a long moment. Then he nods. "Okay."

I don't move. My heart is still racing, and I don't want him to stop touching me, but I feel like he's seeing things no one else sees when he looks at me.

This makes no sense. He just got here two days ago. He doesn't know this town. This town confuses him. It makes him shake his head and roll his eyes. But now he's asking me if I'm here because I'm afraid to leave. Why? Why does he care if I stay?

My heart gives an extra hard thump in my chest.

He's leaving. Is he wondering about what I might be open to when that time comes?

I take a deep breath. I have to *stop* those kinds of thoughts. All of the other guys have left Rebel, and I've chosen to stay. It's the reason my relationships haven't lasted anyway. And Alex knows this. So he shouldn't be asking me these things. I cannot let my heart get involved here.

Then he does something that makes me think simply *uh-oh.*

He cups my face in both hands, says, "Fuck, I like you so much," and kisses me.

CHAPTER 18
NORA

I LEAN INTO HIM, suddenly *needing* to have my body against his as fully as possible.

His tongue is demanding, and I moan as I open for him to taste me completely, hungrily. He walks me back as he kisses me, and just as my knees feel like they're melting, he lifts me up onto Sutton's desk.

I part my knees and he steps close. He's too tall to press the part of him against the part of me that I *really* want to be against, but I still rub against him like a cat against a pillar of catnip.

He runs his hands up my arms, resting one heavy palm on either side of my neck, making me feel held captive and at his mercy.

And I love every second of it.

Heat swirls through my body, pooling heavy and thick in my lower stomach, making my pussy ache.

I so want to press against him. No, *grind* against him.

I wiggle, shrugging out of the light flannel I'm wearing, leaving me in only a black tank top.

"Alex," I breathe as I squirm on the desk, moving back, thinking I'll pull him down on top of me, where I can get his full weight against me. "I—"

Suddenly, there's a loud clatter, and I jump, pulling away.

We both look at where Sutton's pen holder hit the floor and pens scattered across the floor. She has a round woven rug under her desk, but the plastic cylinder hit, bounced, and clattered against the linoleum, throwing pens everywhere.

"Oops," Alex says.

I look up at him.

God, he's cute.

And I really want to kiss him some more.

I just can't do it here.

I push him back and scoot off the desk, kneeling to gather the pens. As I stand with the intact pen holder and set it on her desk again I say, "Sorry. I can't make a mess on Sutton's desk."

He groans and steps close, cupping my face again. "Fuck, I want to make a mess of you."

My eyes widen as sparks snap along my nerve endings. "That sounds really dirty."

"Good. That's exactly how I meant it."

I grip the front of his shirt and pull him down, kissing him this time.

He lifts his head several delicious moments later, but not nearly long enough. I don't think I'll ever get enough of this man's mouth.

"Do you trust me?" he asks.

I nod. "Yes."

"Will you trust me to do something for you without expecting anything in return?" he asks.

"I don't—"

"Wildflower," he says, his voice husky and chiding. "You do things for people all day long every single day. You trust that they care about you, but you still feel this need to do things for them. I'm asking you to trust that I want to do something for you, and I don't want anything in return. In fact, if you try to do anything for me, I'll be upset and think it means that you *don't* trust me."

"Wha...?" I stop and wet my lips. "What do you want to do?"

"If you trust me, you'll let me just show you."

So that's the real question. Do I trust him enough for this? To do something without telling me what it is beforehand? And then to not feel obligated to repay him or somehow even things up?

"Wildflower," he says, his voice coaxing, tempting. "Let me do this."

I say the only thing I can. "Okay."

Alex makes a little groaning noise that almost sounds like relief. Then he kisses me again. "Where's *your* desk?" Alex asks against my mouth.

"In there," I say, breathless. I motion toward my office.

He sweeps me up and starts for my doorway.

Wow, I love when he picks me up. The muscles, the hard chest, the warm body, the *you're mine* feeling. We could do just this, and I'd be really happy.

Except, I think I have an idea of what's going to happen, and *that's* going to make me really happy too.

I know it's not going to help my infatuation. But I don't tell him no.

He pauses just across the threshold. "I'm gonna need some light."

I reach over and flip the switch. I had Mark, the maintenance guy for City Hall, set it up so the wall switch would turn on the lamp on my desk instead of the overhead lights. I much prefer soft yellow light to fluorescent light.

But as the room lights up, Alex doesn't move. He just stares.

My desk is enormous, taking up about half of my office. To be fair, the office isn't huge. But it's also full of boxes. There's a walkway between the boxes and my desk and the doorway—Colton, the fire chief, insists on that, of course—but there's not a lot of extra space.

But I *need* those boxes in here. They are full of T-shirts, plastic tumblers, totes, caps, glossy *Welcome to Rebel* pamphlets, pens, and, in a couple, frisbees.

I never know when I might need one of those things.

"You don't have storage here at City Hall?" he finally asks.

"Of course we do," I say. "We just don't have *enough* storage."

"Ah."

"And…I need this stuff closer."

"Uh huh."

I know it looks like a mess. There are notebooks, books, folders, and catalogs stacked everywhere on my desk. And the lamp is…big. And…ornate.

It's a smaller version of the Julia the otter statue from Main Street. The lamp shade is a colorful patchwork of purple, yellow, and green, and Julia is about a foot and a half tall, wearing Mardi Gras beads and a mask, and holding a plate of beignets. It also plays "Mardi Gras Mambo" by The Hawketts when I press a button on the back.

George Barbin, who fixes lamps, clocks, and small appliances, made it for me just because and I fucking love it.

There are also sticky notes everywhere, a million pens, three or four coffee mugs, and several binders.

In other words, there's no room for me to sit *on* my desk.

I can't even sit *at* my desk unless I remove those two binders from my chair.

I definitely can't *lie* on my desk. Which is what I'm hoping Alex was thinking.

"You're going to tell me that this only *looks* chaotic, but everything is actually exactly where it should be, right?" he asks.

I laugh. "Right."

He looks down at me. "Well, I suppose it's a good thing I'm pretty talented at thinking on my feet and pivoting."

He swings me to the ground at the front of my desk, then turns me so I'm facing it.

"Hands on the desk. Somewhere," he says.

I smile as I push a few things to the side and flatten my palms on the surface of my desk.

Alex moves in behind me, somehow fitting between me and the box of, I think, plastic water bottles.

He puts his hot mouth against the side of my neck. "There's a lot going on in this office, but I want you to think of me when you walk in here tomorrow."

I have no doubt I'll think about him far more often than just tomorrow.

I already do.

"Just tomorrow?" I tease.

"You want more than that, Wildflower? I can make *quite* the impression."

I swallow before answering a simple, "Yes."

He makes a low groaning sound and sucks lightly on my neck. "Have I mentioned that I really fucking like you?"

I smile even as I think my whole body is melting. "Yeah, you have. But I like hearing it."

He presses close, his body fully against mine, his hands on my hips. "This is not how I envisioned it, but I should be getting used to things not being what I expect them to be with you," he says roughly against my ear.

I take a shaky breath. "What did you envision?"

"You really want to know?"

I nod my head.

"Are you sure?" His big hand glides back and forth over my stomach, fingers splayed wide.

"Yes," I say.

"What if it's really dirty?"

I know he can hear the breathiness in my tone when I say, "Then I especially want to hear it."

He reaches up and grasps my chin, turning my head so that he can kiss me. It's still deep and sweet, but now there is a hunger and intensity that wasn't there before.

When he pulls away, he practically growls, "I wanted to lift you up on your desk, strip you down, spread you out, and make you come on my tongue."

Okay, then. He really is going to tell me exactly what he was thinking, dirty and all.

I feel my pussy clench. "That might be the one thing that could be effective in getting me to clean my desk and be more organized," I tell him.

There's a brief pause, and I think I surprised him. Then he chuckles, the sound rumbling against my back where his chest is pressed. "Orgasms as an office organizational technique. I am willing to discuss this method."

"I'm also tempted to just throw it all on the floor," I admit.

He growls, and it's not a lusty sound this time. "That actually makes my head hurt," he says. "The idea of all of this on the floor, and then you just continuing with your work, picking things out of the piles off the floor rather than sorting it and putting it back in any kind of order."

His hands are resting on my hips now, and we're both fully clothed, but our bodies are pressed against one another, and we're talking about oral sex, so this still feels intimate. Which makes the fact that I'm laughing seem odd. But I like it.

"I would do that," I admit.

"Oh, I know. Which is the only reason that I'm going to keep you standing right here." He squeezes my hips. "But I'm going to make this good too."

Without thinking, I press my ass back against him. I can feel his erection against my lower back. "I guess this would work."

He presses into me, his hand gliding around to my lower stomach again. "Oh yes, Wildflower, it would. But that's not what we're doing tonight."

A stab of disappointment jabs my chest. "No?"

"You told me we weren't going to sleep together."

I did say that. Dammit.

"I've had some revelations between then and now," I tell him.

His hand presses into my stomach, bringing me back against him more firmly. Then his hand glides lower so he's cupping me through my jeans.

"Have you now?" he asks. "Such as?"

"Um." I have to think about what he asked me. "Well, that I really want to anyway," I say. "For one thing."

He softly grinds the heel of his hand against my clit, and I gasp. Fuck that feels good. I grasp his wrist, not to stop him, but to keep him *right there.*

"And also," I continue, before I lose my words. "We've been really upfront. I know you're leaving in April. I'll just keep that in mind and not start planning a wedding."

His hand pauses, the grinding stopping.

Which is intensely disappointing.

I grip his wrist, grinding into his hand myself. "I was joking, Alex. Don't stop."

"Sorry, I got distracted by the images of otters as ring bearers," he says.

And here I am with a very hot hockey player's hand against my clit, laughing. "That would be cute. If they behaved. Which they would not."

"They'd run off with the rings?"

"One hundred percent guaranteed."

"That is not statue-worthy behavior," he says.

Or something like that. I'm not paying full attention as his hand is grinding against me again.

"No, it is not. But may—"

I lose my words as his other hand slides up and cups my breast.

The amount of heat and tingling his hands are causing, even through my clothes, is intense, and I completely lose my train of thought.

"But what?" he asks, humor evident in his tone.

"I have no idea," I say, my head dropping forward as I lean harder on the desk to keep from crumpling. "Is there any chance that you would put your hands *under* my clothes?"

He makes a deep growling noise in the back of his throat and says, "Fuck, Wildflower."

"I'm going to take that as a yes," I tell him, quickly unbuttoning and unzipping my jeans, then pulling my tank out of my jeans where I had it tucked. Now there's plenty of room for his big, hot hands.

He's not shy about the invitation. But he seems determined to continue playing with me. His thumb and index finger tease my nipple through the silk bra cup now. The hand between my legs slides up and then into my jeans, his thick middle finger sliding over my clit with the thin barrier of my panties keeping him from touching me fully.

"Oh God, Alex," I say as the heat rushes from his fingers throughout my body.

"Fuck, I love hearing my name from those pretty lips," he says. "Let me make you come like this."

I nod enthusiastically.

"Hands back on the desk, Wildflower," he orders.

I slap my palms flat. Anything to make sure he keeps going.

"But more," I beg.

"More?" he asks, pressing against my clit, a little more firmly and circling faster. "Like this?"

"Yes. But no panties."

I worry he's going to tease me a little longer, but I nearly melt when his hands are suddenly at the waistband of my jeans and he's tugging them and my panties to my knees.

I recover from my surprise quickly enough to reach up and pull my bra down, freeing my breasts. I need this man's hands directly on me wherever I can get them.

"Oh yes," he praises gruffly as he runs his hand over my bare butt cheek. "God, you're pretty everywhere."

I giggle. It's my *butt*.

He gives me a light smack. "It *will* look even prettier nice and pink from my palm, Wildflower. Don't be laughing at me."

God. I moan. And I should be embarrassed that the threat of a spanking makes me moan, but I'm not.

"You like that?" he asks, running his hand over my ass and

pressing close. "Oh, girl, you are going to get me addicted for sure."

I push into him. "*Alex.*" The idea of him not being able to get enough of *me* is as arousing as his hands on me.

Then he slides his hand over my hip to my now-bare stomach and I amend that thought to *almost*. Because nothing is as good as his hands on me.

But *then* he puts his mouth against my neck where it curves into my shoulder and says, "Give me a little preview of what it will be like to have you riding my face, Wildflower," as he slides his thick, slightly rough middle finger over my clit while squeezing my nipple while biting down gently on my neck.

Fuck. His hands, his mouth, his teeth, his tongue as it licks over the spot…

I can't breathe. My eyes slide shut, I lean into him, and reach back, looping my arm around his neck to hold myself up.

"Yes, I've got you," he says gruffly, circling my clit, then sliding his finger into me.

I whimper.

"Fuck, you're hot and wet."

I just nod.

"Oh, yeah, Wildflower, you are goddamned perfect." He twists his hand, adding a finger to my pussy and then pressing into my clit with his thumb.

I try to spread my legs further, wanting him deeper and harder, but my jeans restrict me.

"You want to be wide open for me, don't you?" he asks.

I nod against his chest.

"Don't worry, I'll get you there just like this," he promises, his fingers moving faster, hitting *that spot* that toys can rarely get to.

"But you'll need to spread these pretty thighs nice and wide to straddle my face," he murmurs.

My pussy clenches.

He clearly feels it. "That's right. And then to take my cock you'll need to be *very* open."

"Oh, *God*." My pussy grips his fingers as if *pleading* for more.

"We'll have to be sure to get you really hot, and wet, and stretched out first."

I tighten my grip on him, feeling at risk of sliding down his body into a puddle at his feet.

"But don't worry, I'll do whatever it takes to have the pleasure of fucking this tight, perfect pussy deep and hard."

And that's all it takes. I clamp down on his fingers tightly as my orgasm explodes low and deep, flooding me with heat and endorphins that have me thinking things like *yes, sir, whatever you want, just never stop making me feel like this.*

"That's my girl," he praises in my ear, his fingers moving slower as I come down from that glorious peak. "You are perfect."

Uh, *he's* the one with perfect fingers and dirty talk, but okay. If he's that fond of my pussy, I'll take it because I want him back there *soon*.

I drop my hold on his neck and start to turn. He moves his hand, lifting his fingers to his mouth.

I watch, ripples of pleasure still pulsing through my pelvis as I watch him suck his fingers clean.

"You smell and taste like flowers too," he says.

I pull my bra and shirt back into place, then slide my panties and jeans up. "I *taste* like flowers?" I ask with a smile.

"You're right. If flowers tasted like this, it would be a main dish on every man's plate every night."

I laugh.

Right after the best orgasm, even including my self-induced ones, in a *very* long time—maybe ever—I'm laughing.

"So that was…"

"Amazing? Your new nightly ritual? The best thing you've ever done in this office?" he supplies helpfully when I trail off.

I grin. "I was going to say surprising."

He quirks a brow. "You're surprised I'm good at that? You just wait for—"

"No!" I say quickly, laughing again. "Surprising that *that* was what you wanted to do for me." My eyes drop to his fly and the very prominent bulge there.

"Wildflower," he says, crowding close, my butt bumping against the edge of my desk. "I've wanted to do that since the New Orleans airport."

My eyes widen. "Come on."

"On some level, since minute one," he says, nodding.

Oh. That's…going to be very hard to forget.

"You really don't want anything in return, though?" I ask, looking at his fly again. "I know what I said about not sleeping together but…"

I'm already at risk here. I could fall for him. But I think knowing he's leaving will make the difference between sad and heartbroken. Sad, I can handle. Probably.

He tips my chin up so our eyes meet. "All you have to do is say the word and I'm in any bed, backseat, sleeping bag, park bench…wherever… you'll have me," he says. "Any time except for tonight." He leans in and kisses me. "I want you to know that sometimes people, some people anyway, really do just want *you* to feel good because you're awesome and deserve that. This isn't about me."

He leans back, gives me a wicked grin, and sucks on his middle finger again. "Though this is not *entirely* without perks for me."

I laugh.

Then he grows more serious and leans in to pin me with an intense look. "Making you come apart like that was fucking hotter than hell and so damned satisfying. Thank you."

"Thank *me*?" I ask. "Seriously? Thank—"

He puts the pads of his fingers over my mouth. "No," he says firmly. "No thanking me. That wasn't a favor. You *ever* need an orgasm, you just call. I'm your guy. Got it?"

I nod, my lips moving against his hand. He pulls it back. "Okay."

Then he looks around the office, and then out to the main area. "You done here?"

"I am."

"Then I'll walk you out to your truck."

He does. He even kisses me before opening my door and giving me a hand up. And it doesn't even occur to me that he might have done it because there are people on the sidewalk who might see.

It felt right. Natural. And like we both wanted it. Nothing fake about it at all.

CHAPTER 19
ALEX

I DON'T THINK I ever appreciated just how great I would feel the morning after giving a woman an orgasm without having one of my own.

I do, however, realize that this incredibly good mood has a lot to do with the woman I gave that orgasm to.

Nora Delaune has turned my world upside down. I thought it was my knee injury. I was wrong. Knee injuries make sense. The injury itself, the surgery and rehab after, even the fact that Declan couldn't renew my contract all makes sense objectively. Nora Delaune and her life in this town is unlike anything I've experienced before, and my reaction to all of that doesn't make sense at all.

I shouldn't like it. I definitely shouldn't want more and more of it.

But fuck, I do.

I head to Perks and Rec with an extra bounce in my step this morning.

I know better what to expect now as I brush aside the curtain that separates my staircase from the coffee shop.

I am pleasantly surprised by the multitude of "good morning,

Alex!" greetings I receive, and I give everyone my best celebrity hockey player grin and say, "good morning, everyone."

Lawson is seated at the counter, and I notice Zeke Landry sitting at the table near the window with his grandfather. There are two other men with them that I haven't met or seen before.

I appreciate my teammates showing up for me again.

I take the seat next to Lawson. "Who are the guys with Zeke? The guy looks just like him. I'm gonna guess a brother?"

Lawson nods. "Twin brother. Zander. Cop in Autre. The other guy is Knox. Family friend, and mayor of Autre."

"Wow, heavy hitters in here today," I say cheerfully.

Law gives me a *what's with you* look, but says, "It's a big deal they're here. Zander and Knox usually have coffee over in Bad."

I haven't been to the little town between here and Autre, but I've heard of it.

"They changed up their routine this morning for you," Law says.

"What? For me?"

"Zeke's told them about the straw polls going on here. They think it's hilarious."

I wouldn't use the word *hilarious*, but speaking of those polls…

I check out the mason jars next to the register this morning.

I sit up a little straighter.

They're rating my date with Nora again. Movie night.

And the thumbs up jar is nearly overflowing.

"Fuck yeah," I say.

"Movie night was good?"

I look at Lawson. "Have you ever been?"

He shakes his head.

"Movie night was bonkers," I say.

He cracks a rare smile. "You still must've done something right."

I settle back onto my stool and bite back my first hockey-locker-room response to that. *Fuck yeah I did okay.* "We had a really good time."

"Well, good job."

I look around, but don't see any of Nora's girlfriends. Bruce comes through the swinging doors from the kitchen.

"Morning," he greets. "What are you eating?"

"A number fourteen," I tell him. I have no idea what the number fourteen is, but all the food here is good so I can basically close my eyes and point at the menu and be happy with whatever I get.

When he returns from delivering the plates he was carrying I ask, "I assume you know Nora's favorite coffee drink?"

Bruce lifts a brow. "Why?"

"Thought I'd take her and Sutton coffee on my way to work out."

"Do you know how to make an iced chai latte with cherry cold foam?"

I shake my head. "Um, no. No idea at all." I'm not even completely sure what cold foam is.

Bruce shrugs. "Then I guess you're out of luck."

"You don't know how to make that?"

"Nope."

I look at the gigantic, clearly expensive coffee machine with multiple levers, knobs, and buttons behind him. "So what's that thing do?"

Bruce looks over at it. "Not really sure. When people want frou-frou fancy drinks that don't involve me pouring out of that," he says, pointing to the basic round glass coffee pot sitting on the hot plate, "they do it themselves."

"People just come in here and use your coffee machine to make what they want?"

"Yep."

"What if they want some mixed drink in the bar you don't usually serve?" I ask with a laugh.

"There too. But they'd better wash their glass. There are no to-go cups over there." He hits the swinging door with his hand and disappears into the kitchen.

I shake my head. "Bonkers," I say under my breath.

"I've got you," Law says, putting his heavy boots on the floor and stretching up.

"You know how to make an iced chai latte with cherry cold foam?"

"Yup. And I know that Sutton likes raspberry white chocolate mochas."

I watch him move behind the counter and start turning knobs and making the machine hiss and rumble.

Lawson Landry can make fancy coffee drinks. I didn't see that coming.

But that gives me an idea.

I pivot on my stool to face the room. "Does anyone want to know another personal fact about me?"

Everyone quiets down and looks over.

"So I'm not much of a coffee drinker, mostly because I try to avoid a lot of caffeine," I say.

There's some grumbling and eye rolling at that.

Yeah, that's not the first time I've been judged for not being a coffee drinker. It's a cult. And no one can convince me otherwise.

"But," I go on. "This place in Portland does have a coffee drink that I really like. I don't have it very often and the first time I ordered it on a dare. When I've ordered it a couple of other places I've gotten some really funny looks, but it's delicious."

Everyone continues to watch me until Muriel finally calls out, "Well? None of us are gonna live forever and some of us have less time than others."

I grin at her. "Avocado coffee."

That's met by silence followed by a couple of grimaces.

"I know," I say. "But avocados are really good for you. And what you do with this is you blend a fresh avocado with ice *and*," I say when more faces look appalled. "Sweetened condensed milk."

Now I see some curious looks.

Yeah, it's pretty hard to believe something isn't better with sweetened condensed milk added.

"Then you pour espresso into that and drizzle chocolate syrup on top. It is thick and rich, and I'm telling you, delicious."

"Have you ever convinced anyone else to drink that with you?" Leo asks.

"One time," I say.

"And it was a woman, right?" Leo asks.

"As a matter of fact, it was. None of the hockey players have been willing to try it."

He nods.

Patty pipes up. "I promise you that woman did not drink that because she thought it sounded good. And if you weren't cute and a hockey player, she wouldn't have drunk it either."

I laugh along with the rest of the room, but feel pretty proud of myself. That was a fact I have not shared with any interviewers and this group seems pleased with yet another personal yet also I'm-a-little-weird fact.

Bruce comes out of the kitchen with something wrapped in aluminum foil at the same time Lawson carries over two tall paper coffee cups with lids. One says *Nora* on the side, the other has *Sutton* written on the side.

"Thanks, Law. How much?"

"I'd just lay down a twenty," Lawson says. "Especially since Bruce is standing right here."

"You're one of the smart ones," Bruce says, handing the foil-wrapped package to me.

"What's this?" I ask.

"We don't have a fourteen on the menu," Bruce says. "It only goes up to twelve."

I chuckle. Because of course, instead of telling me that, he just made something up. Still I know whatever is inside is going to be great. "Thanks. I'll make it thirty."

Bruce just nods, but I swear I see the hint of a smile as he turns away. I dig into my pocket for my wallet as Lawson does the same. We both lay bills on the small pile next to the register.

"Thanks for your help this morning," I tell him.

"It seems like maybe you're getting to the point where you don't need as much," he says.

I glance around the restaurant. "Yeah, maybe."

"Well, I gotta get to the shop. I'll see you tonight at the scrimmage."

I pause. "Scrimmage?"

"Didn't Nora tell you?"

I like to think that Nora was a little distracted last night. "No. But I love scrimmages. This will be great, especially since we haven't really played together."

We've done a lot of drills and, of course, dance practice, but we haven't *played*.

"I agree," Law says. "See you later."

I watch him throw his leg over the seat of his motorcycle and take off down the street. He's an interesting guy. Pretty quiet, stays to himself until Beckett pokes him. And he's an intense player. I can tell all of this crazy hockey stuff rubs him the wrong way, but I also get the sense that it's more than just the unconventional hockey rules. I'm hoping that over time we'll get to know each other better and maybe I'll get a look inside his head.

I head around the corner and up the front steps of City Hall. I realize that I am excited to see Nora. That's not new, but it's starting to become a habit now and I wonder how I should really be feeling about that.

We are going to sleep together. I know she keeps saying we're not and she has good reasons for it. Which means I'm always going to be prepared to stop if she says that's what she wants. But last night was hot as hell and I just want more.

I want to give *her* more. That's different.

I love when the women I'm with have a good time. That's always been true. But I don't think I've ever been as consumed by making a woman lose her mind as I was Nora.

She gives so much of herself all the time. She's constantly thinking about other people and how to make them happy. Taking her out of that headspace and making her fully focus on her own pleasure, on what *she* wanted and needed, was the most delightful challenge.

And fuck, the satisfaction I felt after meeting that challenge was incredible.

I've felt a lot of satisfaction in my life. Lots of scores, lots of wins, lots of accolades. But damn, I could easily become obsessed with making Nora Delaune be completely in a moment with me, and be all about *her*.

Which is probably why when I find the Parks and Rec department dark and empty— but the door unlocked, of course—I am stupidly disappointed.

I know that most of Nora's job happens outside of this office so I shouldn't be surprised, but I had hoped to surprise her with her favorite coffee. And steal a kiss.

That's going to be impossible to do once you're back in Portland.

Yeah, yeah, this is short term. Still I've got seven months of Nora kisses and smiles and orgasms and, yes, fun craziness.

At least I can leave a sticky note. I don't even attempt to find a blank piece of paper or pen in Nora's office. The stacked boxes and piles of "work" still give me a little clench of anxiety when I look at it, but that spot on her desk where she braced her hands while I fingered her is perfect. It's right beside the strangest lamp I've ever seen, but it's so Nora and this town that I smile looking at it.

And maybe get a little hard.

Shaking my head, I pull a bright pink sticky note off the top of the perfectly organized stack on Sutton's desk and borrow one of the pens that Nora and I accidentally sent tumbling to the floor last night.

Thinking of you.

I refrain from mentioning where I'd like to put cherry cold foam on *her* and sign it simply -*A*. If I wasn't leaving it on Sutton's desk, I'd be flirtier and dirtier. But I can't leave the cup on Nora's desk. She might not find it until sometime in March.

I stick the note to Sutton's desk, and set Nora's drink on top of it. I place Sutton's drink beside it and leave the office before I decide to do something stupid like just wait for Nora to get back.

That could be anywhere from five minutes to five hours from now. I don't have a set schedule, which is still taking a lot of getting used to, but I can't just sit around in Nora's office. Instead, I head for the arena and the training room there. If we're scrimmaging tonight, I don't want to work out too hard, but I want to get at least a few sets on the weight machines and a short run done.

As I reach to pull the door to the training room open, it swings out and Thea Chabert steps out, chatting with a teenage boy.

"Oh, Alex. Hey," she greets.

"Hi, Thea."

"Alex, this is Ethan."

I extend my hand. "Hi, Ethan. Nice to meet you."

"Oh, hi." He gives me a wide-eyed smile. "You too. Big fan."

"Thanks."

"We were just doing some workouts on the ice," Thea says. "Ethan had an ACL surgery about ten months ago."

Thea's the town's physical therapist, which in my experience and opinion means that no matter how sweet she seems, she's a hardass underneath. "I know way too much about that and the rehab. Sorry, man."

"Thanks. It's sucked."

"Yeah," I agree. There's not much else to say. If he's that far out from surgery and into his rehab, there's nothing I can really say to encourage him. I'm only a little ahead of him and it still sucks.

"I'm coming to the scrimmage tonight," Ethan says, brightening.

"You are?" I ask. I look at Thea.

"Me too," she says.

"I didn't realize it was open, or is Josh just getting you in?" I ask.

"Josh is working tonight," she says. "He won't be there."

"He's missing the scrimmage?" I frown.

She laughs. "Yeah. He'll be saving lives and shit."

Right. Josh is a firefighter and paramedic. That's more important than hockey any day of the week. It still hasn't fully sunk in for me that all these guys, and girls, have other jobs. Hockey is not their number one priority. Hell, for most of them it's not even number two or three. Beckett and Lawson might be the only ones who put hockey up there with their jobs, businesses they own. But they're also single and don't have kids or big families in town to take up time and energy.

"Of course," I say about Josh. "We'll miss him."

And it won't be as effective a scrimmage without the entire team, but I leave that part out because Thea, and probably Josh, don't care about that.

"See you later," she says as they step out of the building and I head inside.

"Yeah, later. Bye, Ethan," I add. "Keep up the hard work."

"Of course!"

Yeah, of course. What choice does he have? We either work our knees and get better or…we deal with not being able to do all the things we've always dreamed of doing.

Unless, of course, those dreams change.

CHAPTER 20
ALEX

TWO HOURS LATER, I get a text from Nora that says, *Wow, an orgasm and a latte? This fake dating thing is awesome.*

Four hours later, I get a text from my sister that says, *Plus eighty-eight ticket sales!*

Six hours later, I get another text from Astrid that says, *Plus one hundred and four ticket sales! And there is a bag of avocados here for you??*

That's followed by a text from Nora that is just a series of emoji faces with party hats on their heads, blowing party horns.

I just smile. And shake my head.

They're sending me avocados.

Seven hours later, Astrid sends, *Holy crap! Three hundred new season tickets sold! You two are amazing!*

Seven hours and fifteen minutes later, a major sports podcaster texts, *Hey man! It's been a while! Can we set something up? I'd love to talk about what you're doing in Louisiana.*

Seven hours and seventeen minutes later, Sutton texts, *Hey, that big podcast guy Greg Whatever-His-Name-Is said he's going to text you when I reached out about the Revelers!*

Seven and a half hours later Declan O'Grady texts, *Sounds like things are going well. Tell your sister to pick up my calls and stop only texting like we're in high school.*

I only answer Greg Simon, the podcaster.

I don't think the others need an answer. Except maybe Declan. But yikes, I'm not getting in the middle of those two. Anything I would text Nora would end up dirty and distracting, and I'm trying not to show up at her office, drag her into the storeroom that is considerably less crowded than her office, and replay last night.

And ten hours and forty-two minutes later, I'm standing just off the ice, frustrated, confused, amazed, and…frustrated listening to Nora address the crowd who showed up for the first scrimmage between the Revelers and the Rascals.

My head has been spinning, and my chest has been tight with this exasperation for an hour.

Ever since I skated onto the ice and realized that we were going to be scrimmaging in front of nearly five hundred people who were dressed up, with signs, jerseys, and hats—Astrid and Nora have already managed to get jerseys and other merch?—as if this is a game, not a practice. There are even concessions, though they are less elaborate than they will be once the season officially kicks off.

Still, this has the feel of an actual game, and I have been off kilter from minute one.

Minute one of *many* minutes.

The first period took forty-two fucking minutes.

Because there is a lot more than just hockey happening.

And sure, I knew that. Bonkers hockey has been a part of this deal all along. But this is bonkers hockey in real time with an audience, refs, an opposing team, the whole thing.

And it is so much worse than I'd expected.

Sutton and Nora gave us a quick run-down before we came out on the ice.

For the first five minutes of play, it seemed like regular, *normal* hockey.

Then there was a penalty called.

The two players were given a choice of how they wanted to "serve" their penalty. They could either sit together, wearing a huge T-shirt that went over both of their heads and allowed each of them to stick one arm out, for two minutes in the penalty box, or they could lip sync the first verse and chorus of "You've Got A Friend In Me", from, of course, *Toy Story*.

The guys turned to the crowd and, using applause, let the fans vote. The crowd chose the lip sync.

And they pulled it off perfectly. Everyone loved it.

My headache started around the time three guys from each team joined them on the ice, swaying with their arms around each other, behind the lip-syncers.

Later in the period, the ref made a call that the crowd hated. Nora agreed to show the replay and let the fans decide. When it was determined the call was wrong, the ref, Tanner, had to wear a dunce cap for the next two minutes of play.

And then we got to the last minute of that first period.

There was a buzzer, and Nora and Sutton tossed twenty pucks onto the ice at once.

Every puck in the net still counted as a point, and we were torn between defending our net and trying to put as many of the extra pucks into the Rascals' net.

In other words, it was chaos.

Now we're preparing for the second period, and Nora is center ice, with that fucking microphone, explaining what will be added in this new period of the game.

And she looks fucking adorable in a pair of bright purple overalls and purple skates.

And even as she literally makes my head pound by heaping more craziness onto this 'game', I still want to peel those overalls off of her and lick her from head to toe.

Maybe after painting her body with cherry cold foam.

"So now," Nora says, her grin bright, the spotlight shining on her like she's a rockstar, "We've got even more fun."

I rub a hand over my forehead.

"But we want *you* to be part of it," she says to the crowd. "We want to know what you think players should do for penalties, we're going to let the teams celebrate after they score four points—oh, in this second period, goals are worth two points!" she adds.

The crowd cheers.

I sigh.

"And we want *you* to choose each team's celebration song. And finally, you get to pick what happens in the last minute of play! Turn your attention to the big screen for the options!"

She points to the big screen that hangs over center ice.

Then she has everyone pull out their phones and reveals the new app they've created, where people can vote for all of this shit right from their seats. No applause necessary.

Oh, and they can definitely buy tickets, gift tickets, and put together packages that include tickets, merch, concession vouchers, and local hotel stays.

They can also share photos and videos they take during the games, message the team, check out behind-the-scenes content, and order merchandise for both the Revelers and the Rascals from the app.

Nora and Astrid have clearly been working on all of this for a long time. They've thought of everything. It's impressive. If you want intense fan engagement and in-the-minute audience participation *during* the games.

But who the hell wants that?

The "there's no such thing as too much" owner of the team and the "everything has to be a good time" PR director—which is, let's face it, what Nora is for the team—that's who.

And judging by the cheering and excitement buzzing in the air, the few hundred people in here tonight.

A few minutes later, we skate out onto the ice, prepared for which song we'll be performing after we score two goals. We also know that if we get a penalty we'll have to answer three trivia questions at center ice—but not if the trivia is about hockey, or otters, or something completely unrelated to anything going on here (and that would be my bet)—and that the last minute of play will involve us trying to hit colored wiffle balls into the nets with our hockey sticks. Of course, there will be forty wiffle balls bouncing around on the ice, and the Revelers can only score with the purple ones while the Rascals' balls are green.

Because why not?

My headache is worse, I'm wound tight and completely distracted, even during the first six minutes of play that are completely normal.

Then Beckett scores our second goal, and I actually groan in disappointment. Because now I have to dance to "I Gotta Feelin'". Of course, *after* they play a few seconds of "Simply the Best", by Tina Turner—the part about being simply the best, better than all the rest—Beckett's choice for what's to be played every time he scores.

It's not even the most fitting one.

Zeke Landry's "Ice, Ice Baby" is maybe obvious, but it made me, and everyone else, laugh.

But Ingrid's might be the best. "Immortals" by Fall Out Boy really fits our left winger.

I told Sutton to pick one for me. I heard it for the first time tonight in the first period when I scored. "Don't Stop Me Now" by Queen. I gave her my stamp of approval, and she said that growing up with Beckett means she knows all about how to pump up cocky men.

But I thank God, literally, that Beckett loves being out front and actually has a good singing voice. *Thank you, lord, for this funny, outgoing goofball.* Beckett is already happily taking the mic from Nora and skates to mid-ice.

As we start, looking like lumbering jackasses going through dance steps on skates, I look at Nora. She's front row, right by the glass, of course, across the ice from the benches. Ruth is beside her, phone up, recording every second, I'm sure.

But I can't look away from Nora.

She has that same look on her face she did at movie night. A mix of delight and affection. The look that I wanted to keep there. The look that made something shift in my chest that had nothing to do with how attracted I am to her physically. Or maybe it made my physical attraction to her even stronger. I just know that seeing her watching this now, looking like that, I suddenly don't hate this as much.

And then I don't pull my gaze from her fast enough to execute the twirl—I'm supposed to fucking twirl—and my skates tangle, I lurch into Ingrid, who weighs half what I do, and send her sprawling to the ice. Lawson trips over her skate and starts to fall, grabs our goalie, Wes's, arm, and, surprised, and with only one skate on the ground because he's doing some kick-thing, Wes goes down with Lawson instead of holding him up.

It all happens in the matter of a second.

I just stand there, stupidly staring.

The music stops.

The place is totally quiet.

I look at Nora. She's staring at me with her mouth open.

So I say the first thing to come to mind.

"Oops."

There's another beat of silence.

Then Nora bursts out laughing.

So does the rest of the crowd.

And just like that, it's all fine. The team helps Ingrid, Law, and Wes up. Law rolls his eyes at me. Wes shakes his head but grins. Ingrid rubs her ass, then grins and skates off.

And somehow, we make it through the second period.

I fucking *hate* the wiffle ball thing. Obviously.

But finally it's over.

Between the second and third, Nora spends more time on the ice with her mic, talking to the fans.

Then the mascots show up.

Rougie the Rougarou and Rascal the Otter weren't there at the start.

It's just a damned scrimmage.

But clearly between the start and now, Nora, or Nora and Astrid, or maybe just Astrid…no, Nora was definitely involved… decided the mascots needed to be here, so they've skated, done a dance of their own, and are now up in the stands with the fans.

And they're pulling options out of a hat for the third period.

Literally.

Nora has a gigantic fedora , and she's apparently got picks for things like what the final three minutes—*three* minutes? Good lord all this extra shit is already making every period take twice as long—of the game will look like, what the goalies have to do, how the mascots will be involved—kill me now—and what the losers of the game will do at the end.

Options include something with the Zamboni that I didn't fully understand (because I wasn't paying attention), serenading the audience, and something else with the mascots that I didn't catch.

I'm far more focused on the fact that we have a cool app to use for voting, but we're pulling stuff out of a hat, the scoreboard isn't working, and no one seems to know what exactly the score is, and that I can't believe I didn't hit one fucking wiffle ball into the goal.

The third period starts, whether I want it to or not, and I pray for ten minutes of straightforward hockey.

I don't get it.

But it's not because of a random dance number, too many points, or a bad call.

It's because all of a sudden Lawson and Beckett are brawling on our end of the ice.

What the *fuck*?

By the time I get to them, Lawson has Beckett pinned against the glass and his face pressed against Beckett's.

"Knock it off, Moore!" Lawson yells. "I'm not putting up with this shit!"

Beckett shoves against him, but Lawson has a few pounds on him and doesn't move much.

"Get off me, asshole!" Beckett swings his arm, smacking it against the side of Lawson's helmet.

"Stop being a cocky little shit!"

"Stop acting like you're better than everyone!"

"Take something seriously for one fucking minute!" Lawson lets up and then slams Beckett into the wall again.

"Why can't you *ever* not be a prick?" Beckett fumes, shoving Lawson back.

"Okay, *enough*!" I bellow, pulling Lawson off of Beckett.

All four refs are around us, along with our entire team. Wes grabs Lawson when he tries to go for Beckett again, and Teddy and Ingrid both move in front of Beckett to keep him back.

"What the fuck is going on?" I demand, a hand on each of their chests.

"I'm fucking sick of his attitude," Beckett says.

"*My* attitude?" Lawson says. "Jesus, at least I'm here for hockey and not as some publicity stunt."

"This is not the time for this! Jesus!" I shove at them both.

"So what do we do if the players fighting are on the same team?" Tanner asks the other referees.

I shake my head and look over to where Nora is sitting.

Well, now standing. Everyone is on their feet.

She looks worried though. Upset even.

I don't fucking like that.

These two jackasses upset Nora on this night when things were going so well *for her* and making her happy.

This is bonkers hockey. It makes no sense. It's constantly changing. There's no set rules.

But everyone is having a great time. At least they were.

"Come on," I say to Beckett and Lawson.

"What?" Beckett asks.

"Where?" Lawson asks.

"Center ice. There's got to be a penalty for this, right?" I grab them both by the back collar of their jerseys and skate to the middle of the rink.

The spotlight finds me. "Well," I say to the crowd. "I guess as the captain of the Revelers—"

"You're the captain?" Beckett asks.

"I am now," I tell him dryly.

There's light laughter all around.

"As the captain," I say again, addressing the crowd. "It's kind of a me problem when two players on *my* team go at it, I guess." I look from Lawson to Beckett. "So I suppose I'm the one who needs to do something about it."

They both look at me with curiosity. Not fear or intimidation, which I should probably be offended by, but interest and mild amusement.

I sigh.

"Can I borrow your mic, Nora?" I ask.

Her eyes widen, and she looks, thank God, delighted again.

She's behind the glass, but right by her first row seat is a door that leads onto the ice. She skates out, handing me the mic.

"What are you doing?" she asks softly.

"Trying to remember the real goal here tonight," I tell her.

Her smile tells me this is the right call.

I clear my throat.

And start singing.

I'm not sure I know all the words to "Lean On Me," but hopefully I only need to get through the first little verse and the chorus.

Not only did she not expect me to sing, but I can tell she didn't expect me to have a really good voice. Yeah, I can fucking sing. I don't do it much, but, what can I say? I'm a talented guy.

As I croon "to" Beckett and Lawson about leaning on me during their "tough times", her smile gets brighter and brighter, and her eyes actually sparkle.

Both Beckett and Lawson are laughing by the time I'm done, the entire crowd cheers loudly, and Nora whispers, "That was really hot," when I hand the mic back to her.

I still hate the rest of the third period.

But maybe not as much as I did before.

CHAPTER 21
NORA

"YOU KNOW every single woman there tonight now wants him, right?" Sutton asks.

I look at her. "But…"

Dammit. Yeah. Alex was pretty great tonight. He's good-looking, incredibly athletic, and then tonight he not only allowed himself to be goofy, he did it with this grumpy, put-upon air that made it even funnier.

And then he sang.

The guy shouldn't be good at *everything* he does.

"What about Beckett?" I ask.

She rolls her eyes. "Everyone already thought Beckett was cute and funny. And they've seen him play before. Alex is new."

"New does get more attention," Andi agrees. "And Beckett is an attention whore. He's a goofball. That's not everyone's type."

It's not *her* type. That's what she means.

Though I think she protests too much. I'm just not brave enough to call her on her shit. Yet.

My friends are sitting at the coffee counter while I load a tray with plates for the hockey guys who've congregated around a table in the bar.

"He's not *always* a goofball," Sutton defends her brother. "He takes things seriously when he needs to."

"But for him, hockey is about the videos and likes online," Andi says, popping a fry into her mouth.

"Well…" Sutton can't really argue that.

I know that Beckett wanting to be popular with hockey fans and make a name for himself as a good-time player to watch has to do with more than just being famous, but I can't tell Beckett and Sutton's story. That's up to them. Though I'm surprised Sutton hasn't told Andi. Maybe it's because she wants Beckett to tell Andi if and when he wants her to know.

Beckett's crush on Andi is obvious, and he makes no secret of it, but it is a little hard to know how serious he is about wanting to really get to *know* her. He might just want to sleep with her. Or he might just want to flirt. He may simply consider her a challenge since most other women tend to swoon for him pretty easily.

"Okay, what about Lawson?" I ask. "He's hot and broody."

Andi nods and looks at Sutton. "He sure is. Don't you think, Sutton?"

Something in her tone makes me look at our younger friend, too. She's blushing.

"Is something going on with you and—"

"No!" Sutton says quickly.

"But she'd like it to," Andi says.

"What?" I ask.

"No," Sutton repeats. "I do think he's attractive. But he's…"

"A total bad boy," Andi says. "Probably *a lot* to handle. Very experienced. Very—"

"The one guy my brother can't stand," Sutton breaks in.

Andi frowns. "You can't let Beckett get in the way if you like him."

"I have no idea if I like him," Sutton says, shaking her head. "I don't really know him. He's hot. That's what I know."

But she's not making eye contact with us.

"*Nothing* has happened?" I press. Then a terrible thought

occurs. "He hasn't done or said anything that made you uncomfortable, has he?"

Now Sutton looks up quickly. "*No*. Definitely not." She presses her lips together. "I feel totally safe around him," she adds. "There've been a couple of times it's just been the two of us before or after practice, and I don't feel uncomfortable at all. There's just…" She leans in.

So do Andi and I.

"Chemistry," she says softly. "But, like Andi said, he's got a *vibe* that tells me he's way out of my league and—" She sighs. "The Beckett thing." She sits back. "So, no, nothing has happened and nothing will."

"That's bullshit," Andi says, biting another fry in half. "This shouldn't be about your brother at all."

Sutton opens her mouth, but Andi continues, "*But—*"

Sutton closes her mouth again.

"I don't have a brother I'm super close to like you guys are, and I'm talking about sex, not love. If you're thinking about something besides letting that tattooed, broody hockey player try to break your headboard, then don't listen to me."

Sutton reaches over and grabs two of Andi's French fries. "Deal," she says. "I won't listen to you."

I laugh. "Well, then everyone can just lust after Lawson and *not* Alex."

Sutton doesn't look *thrilled* about that idea, but she doesn't say anything.

The door to the shop opens, and I look over, my heart tripping when Alex strides inside.

He clearly showered at the arena. His hair is slightly damp, and he's got different clothes on.

There are numerous greetings called out as people notice him. He returns them absently as he looks around.

Then our eyes meet, and he seems to relax.

I give him a smile, and his lips curl up, though the smile looks a little tight. Or tired.

I point toward the bar, and he nods, heading for the table with his teammates rather than straight up to his apartment.

Everyone else in the place is boisterous and happy and talking about the scrimmage, and personally, I'm feeling great.

Opening the scrimmage up to the fans was a great call, and Astrid has already gushed to me about how much she loved it. I've had numerous people approach me and tell me how they're looking forward to the season now, and a local radio station in New Orleans wants to do an interview with me, Astrid, and whichever of the hockey players we can get. I think it should probably be Beckett. But of course, the station dropped Alex's name too.

No matter how enthusiastic and online Beckett is, Alex is our big star name.

I'm right behind him with the tray of food for the table.

Even though he readily came to the table with the rest of the players, he's frowning and is clearly not in a sociable mood.

I should not find it funny that he's grumpy about this scrimmage. But what can I say? I like pushing Alex out of his comfort zone. I have a feeling I know the *real* Alex and I like that. A lot.

When he's reacting to unexpected circumstances, he's honest and authentic. He doesn't have time to rehearse lines or put on a façade. I'm not sure he does those things in Portland. I don't think he needs to do those things in Portland. When he's there, in that bubble, things go according to a plan he knows and understands, and it doesn't require prepared lines or fake expressions, because nothing throws him off-kilter.

And even though I shouldn't think about what we're doing as a relationship, there's a little voice at the back of my mind that wonders how well the other women he's dated have known him.

When he's in his perfectly arranged world where everything goes his way, does anyone ever see him unsure, or vulnerable, or anything other than fully in control? When he simply follows a carefully laid out plan, does *he* ever think about emotions other than satisfaction, pride, and cockiness?

The scrimmage was amazing. Everyone loved it. He was fantastic.

But he's going to complain about it. Because he was *not* comfortable.

I smile. His grumpiness doesn't intimidate me. And if he'll let me, I can make him feel a lot better about everything.

I set my tray down as Zeke says, "Hell yeah, sounds awesome. Let's do that."

I start passing out plates of pie.

Beckett notices me and says, "We're brainstorming more ideas. Like, what if the Zamboni came out just randomly at some point and drove around while we try to dodge it? Whichever team manages to pass the puck around it the most times before it exits gets a bonus point. What do you think?"

"Love it," I tell him honestly. I also love that they're over here talking about more things to add to the games. "Just email both Sutton and me whatever you guys come up with. We are very happy to have any and all of your ideas."

"That's fucking dangerous," Lawson protests. "We can't be skating around the damned Zamboni."

Beckett nods, but he looks thoughtful. "Yeah. Okay. What if we get a fake mini-Zamboni with pedals? And one of the mascots rides it around?" He looks at Lawson. "Would that be safe enough for you?"

Lawson doesn't even reply. He does, however, give Beckett a you're-an-idiot look.

"What about some different face-offs?" Josh asks, possibly jumping in to keep Beckett and Lawson from coming to blows. "Like we do rock, paper, scissors one time?" He grins. "Or we have a dance off and the fans vote and whoever wins gets the puck."

I laugh. "Absolutely."

I glance at Alex. He's rubbing the middle of his forehead. That makes me laugh.

"Can we turn the lights off? Or change the color of the lights?" Teddy asks.

I prop the tray on my hip. "Probably. I promise that Astrid, Sutton, and I will try to make anything work. Why?"

"What if we did light up pucks? Like flashing disco light pucks? Or glow in the dark?" Teddy asks. "We could do different lights around the ice so it's not totally dark and—"

"Or black lights!" Ingrid says. "Like when they do glow-in-the-dark bowling."

I nod and start to reply, but Wes chimes in, "We also have a huge budget. It's pretty great being owned by a billionaire who seems intent on making things totally over the top."

I catch Alex's eye now. "Astrid definitely likes over the top," I agree. "And she's broken her piggy bank wide open."

Alex rolls his eyes. "Her husband's piggy bank," he mutters.

I would love more backstory about Astrid and her newfound fortune and sudden ownership of this team. And her very hot, very rich husband. Who continues to live in Portland.

But I know the most important things: she's definitely enthusiastic, and I don't doubt her authenticity and commitment to the Revelers and Rascals.

"Are you open to ideas about what to do between periods? Like with the fans?" Quinn asks.

"Of course," I tell them. "Listen, we haven't brought a lot of this to you guys because you're all busy, and we know that this hockey thing is part-time. But we want you guys to love this. Sincerely. If you love it, everybody else will love it even more. You all were amazing tonight. The way you had fun with it, the enthusiasm you showed. Thank you so much."

"It was a good time," Wes says. "And I'm looking forward to work tomorrow. I'm guessing we're all gonna hear a lot from people out in the community, our families, and stuff."

That actually gives me a thrill. "I hope so. Tell them all they can send in ideas, too. This isn't just my show."

"You're so good at it, though," Ingrid says. "I mean, we've

been working on all of this stuff for a while now. I think we all understood the basic concept. But bringing it all together tonight, and actually performing, really made it real."

"Playing," Alex interjects.

Everybody looks at him.

"What?" Ingrid asks.

"We were *playing* hockey tonight. Not performing."

She waves her hand. "Tomato tomah-toh. But really, it was more of a performance, don't you think?"

Alex looks at me, and I can tell he's thinking, *yes, it was, and it's all your fault.*

I just grin at him.

"So you're all fine with it?" he asks, looking directly at Lawson. "Nobody's frustrated? We don't need to talk about anything that went wrong? Anything that was confusing or *chaotic*?"

Of course, he uses his favorite word.

Everyone shakes their heads, and Zeke sets his fork down, his plate clean.

He starts to dig for his wallet, but I stop him. "It's all on the house."

Zeke gives me a smile. "You don't have to do that."

"It's not like you're all making millions playing here. I think we can throw in pie once in a while."

"But we *could* make a lot more," Beckett says. "If this catches on, we could get sponsorships and all kinds of stuff. When we fill up that arena, money is gonna be pouring in."

Alex sighs but doesn't say anything. I don't say anything either, but I want to say, "Damn right."

"Do you want something to eat?" I ask him.

"Sure. Just… bring me something. Anything."

I love that answer. I actually have a surprise for him. "Okay, I'll be right back."

I gather up the used dishes and head into the kitchen. I have stored my surprise in the refrigerator, planning to give it to him before he goes up to his apartment. I grab it, unwrap it, and grab a spoon.

Back at the table, I set it down in front of him.

"Oh, *man*," Beckett moans when he sees it.

"I didn't know that was an option!" Teddy protests.

"It wasn't," I say with a wink. "This is just for Alex."

Teddy slumps on his stool. "Damn my love for dick. I don't think I can do the things to you that got Alex that pudding."

Everyone laughs.

Except Alex. When I look at him again, he's staring at the bowl in front of him with a pained expression. When he looks up and meets my gaze, he tries to cover his horror, but I see it.

I frown. "It's banana pudding."

He nods. "I figured."

"Wait, you don't like banana pudding?"

"I don't… I've never had it."

I narrow my eyes and look at Beckett. "Someone told me you're crazy about bananas."

Beckett gives me a mischievous smile.

Oh, no.

"I love bananas," Alex says. "But I don't like banana…things."

"Banana *things*?" I repeat.

"Things made with bananas. Like banana pudding."

I look at Beckett, a hand on my hip. "I wonder if this person knew that."

Alex also looks at Beckett. "I think that person did. And I'm guessing that person really likes your banana pudding and was hoping to snag it when I didn't want it."

"He does, as a matter of fact," I say, my eyes on Beckett as I push the bowl toward Teddy. "Everyone does."

"Oh well, if you insist. I mean, if you're not going to eat it," Teddy says to Alex, grabbing the bowl and cradling it against his chest. "Well, I gotta go. See you all tomorrow." And then he's off his stool and out of the shop before anyone can stop him.

Before *Beckett* can stop him.

"That was cruel," Beckett says, staring after Teddy.

"Yes, it was," I say, smacking his arm. I look at Alex. "I'm sorry. I was led to believe that my pudding would be the perfect treat after your first scrimmage."

"It's...fine," Alex says. He looks very uncomfortable suddenly.

"Okay, then I gotta get outta here too," Zeke says. "There are rules at my house for how long any single adult has to be alone with our twins. Letting them outnumber you is never a good idea."

Everyone chuckles and starts to move to leave as well. The plates all have only crumbs left, and Beckett is even closing his notes app on his phone.

"You're leaving too?" Alex asks.

Beckett stretches to his feet. "Got work early, man. Actually, I was gonna ask you if you've got anything big going on tomorrow."

Alex shakes his head. "No. What do you have in mind?"

"I need to head into New Orleans and pick up a new stove for someone. I could use an extra hand."

"I could do that," Alex says.

"Great. I'll meet you down here for breakfast."

Everyone heads out, stopping here and there to chat with people on the way to the door.

Leaving just Alex and me.

"Let me get you something else," I say, turning away.

"Wildflower."

That name always makes my stomach flip. I turn back. "Yeah?"

He looks like he wants to say something important, but he just says, "Thanks."

"Be right back."

When I get back to the table with a club sandwich, he's hunched over his phone, frowning as he types.

"Everything okay?" I ask as I set the plate down and take the stool to his right.

"My emails and texts are blowing up."

I press my lips together, so my grin isn't too bright when he looks up. "About the scrimmage?"

"Yeah. Apparently, Ruth got some really good video. A couple of players from the Grays who follow me saw the tag, checked it out, and shared it."

My stomach flips with excitement, but I still tamp it down. Then I frown. I don't want to tamp down my excitement about things with Alex. "That's so great," I say with enthusiasm.

He lifts a brow. "Tonight was a mess."

I shake my head. "Tonight was a fantastic first effort. Are there things to smooth out? Sure. But then not being smooth and polished is part of the fun."

He sighs, then opens his mouth, but before he can respond, I say, "I know you don't agree with that. But everyone loved seeing you out there, Alex."

"Because I looked like an idiot?"

"You didn't."

"I'm a professional hockey player. I shouldn't be tripping and missing shots with wiffle balls." He shakes his head. "I shouldn't be *taking* shots with *wiffle balls.*"

"Everyone knows that you are an incredible hockey player. That's not what this is about. They loved seeing you doing something different. They loved seeing you be goofy and have fun."

"I didn't have fun."

"Liar."

"I don't like it when I don't know what to expect."

"I thought you said you were getting used to that around here."

"Getting used to it and liking it are two different things."

I prop my elbow on the table and lean my chin onto my hand. "You know, just because you've always done hockey, and love it more than anything, and think it's all you're good at, doesn't mean that that can't change and you can't be good at something else."

"So you admit that wasn't hockey we were playing tonight."

I grin, even though I know it's going to irritate him further. "What you were doing tonight was making a bunch of people happy and entertaining them."

He studies me for a long moment. A very long moment. "It made you happy," he finally says.

I nod. "Very."

"I'm sorry," Alex says.

"For what?"

"I was a bad sport tonight."

"You really don't understand, do you?"

"Understand what?"

"How great it is to see someone like you do something like tonight. You're a famous, rich, incredibly talented hockey player, Alex. There is nothing you can't do in a pair of ice skates with a hockey stick. It's fun to see someone like you be able to let go of that polished persona and have fun. Do some things that are definitely outside of your comfort zone. Let yourself not be perfect. It gives other people permission to let go of the idea that they have to be perfect and can never just enjoy the things they are most dedicated to." I shrug. "Everyone has goals and dreams. Everyone's working for something. And everyone wants to be great at something. But you can't just work and drive all the time."

"You can," he says.

"But then, when something out of your control happens, like a natural disaster, a financial hardship, or, I don't know, a major injury that changes what you're able to do—", I say, giving him a pointed look. "Then it's harder to pivot. Because it was work. It was something you did because you *had to*. It's important to also *love* what you're working for, to laugh and have fun with it, too. That makes it easier to remember why it matters when things are tough."

"But I didn't have a good time tonight," he mutters. It lacks conviction, though.

"I don't believe you. Not completely."

He frowns at me. "I do not like being uncomfortable. I do not like feeling like I don't know what's going on or what to expect. I like when things go according to a plan. Nothing about tonight went according to any plan."

"That's not true. My plan was—"

"Let me clarify," Alex interjects. "*Your* plan was to put us on the ice and deal with things as they came along, just try things out willy-nilly, and put on an exhibition. So yes, it went according to your plan."

He's not *wrong*. "And like we talked about at movie night, success depends on what your goal is," I remind him.

"And I didn't even know how to have a goal because I didn't know what was going to happen tonight. I mean, I don't think the point of any of this is actually to win the game, is it?"

"No."

"I don't know how to play hockey like that, Nora. I know how to score points and win games. What was the final score anyway?"

I laugh. "We honestly don't know. We kind of stopped keeping track." But I say quickly. "I promise that won't happen again. Tonight was also an experiment. To see what things worked and what things didn't. Obviously, our score-keeping tonight didn't work."

"As far as I'm concerned, none of it worked."

I shake my head. "But it *all* worked because everyone had a good time."

He blows out a breath and rises. "I think this is just where we're going to agree to disagree."

I feel my heart drop. I really thought I could bring him around.

I shouldn't be surprised, but I'm a little disappointed. I'd thought he would have more fun with this tonight. I thought once he was out there, he would see the point and understand it. But I can't force this on him. I can't force him to enjoy something. He's either going to or he's not.

"Well, at least it's only 'til April," I quip, trying to lighten the moment.

Instead, I feel a lead ball settle in my stomach.

My words make him stop. He studies me, frowns slightly, then nods. "I guess that's true."

I watch him head for the stairs, but as he brushes aside the curtain that covers the doorway, he looks back. He looks a little regretful. I'm not sure about what, but I'm hoping maybe it's that he didn't kiss me goodnight. After all, he's my pretend boyfriend. I want more of those not-at-all pretend kisses, dammit.

CHAPTER 22
NORA

IT'S NEARLY midnight when I hear the knocking on my door.

I still have the lamp on my bedside table on. I haven't been able to fall asleep, and I've been reading over the email that Beckett has already sent with new ideas for future games.

I've also scrolled social media and seen that it's not just Alex's buddies who are talking about the Revelers and the Rascals. Sports media has picked up on it, and while the conversation is hardly viral, there are rumblings of how interesting and fun things in southern Louisiana sound.

I grin. Earthquakes often start with rumblings.

I throw my covers back and head downstairs in my pajamas. Whoever it is is likely a very close friend or relative and has seen me in pajamas before.

But when I open the door, I realize that this person hasn't.

He's seen me half-naked in my office, though.

"I realized I don't like the idea of other men eating your banana pudding." He holds up the bowl that Teddy took home with him.

"You went over to Teddy's and got it back?"

He nods. "And then I took it home and tried it."

"Oh. And now you're bringing it to me because I need to discard it? Since no one else can have it?"

He hands me the bowl. "I ate all of it. It's fucking delicious. And I can't fucking believe that you have made me like something with bananas that's not a banana. But then I realized that, *of course*, you did. Because you've turned everything else upside down. Why not bananas?"

The bowl is indeed empty. I have no idea what to do with this information. "You seem upset."

He crowds close, stepping me back into my house, then closing my door behind him and locking it. "Wildflower, I think upset is a pretty good way to describe how I have felt since I've met you."

I open my mouth to respond to that because *hey*, but he puts a finger over my lips.

"But not upset in the angry way. Upset in the confused and befuddled and riled up and my world is all messed up way. And yeah, I don't love that. Because I haven't had that in my life. Ever. I pay people very good money to make my life the opposite of that. But the minute I met you, there has been chaos and things swirling around me and my life going off the rails and nothing happening according to any kind of plan and…" He drops his hand and blows out a breath. "I have never wanted anyone more than I want you. All of you. All the time. I can't get enough of you."

I swallow hard, my heart pounding, my entire body hot and tingling.

"Oh," I say. Brilliantly. Then I take a breath and say, "Well, we'd better go upstairs then."

He sags, almost as if in relief. He steps in close again, and I realize I'm backed up against the wall. He leans in, resting his forearm on the wall over my head, caging me in.

"There are two things that I am very good at," he says. "Two areas, I *never* have to question things. Two places I am fully and completely in control. Hockey. And fucking. And you have managed to twist and turn hockey so much that I barely recognize it. Which means there's now only one thing that I know for sure I am really good at and where I can be totally in control. And you're going to let me be in control of this, aren't you, Wildflower?"

Well, what can I say here? Do I want this man to ravish me? Yes. Yes, I do.

"My bedroom is the second door on the right."

Alex makes a low, growling noise that makes my pussy clench, then he bends and throws me over his shoulder and starts up the stairs.

Fuck, yes. More of this. All the time.

Am I going to be ruined in April? Yep. Do I care? Not one bit.

When we get to my room, he strides in without hesitation, kicks my door shut behind us, stops next to the bed, and lets me slide down his body.

He doesn't give me a centimeter of space. He cups my face with both hands and lowers his mouth until it's hovering just over mine and says, "I'm going to *own you* tonight."

Then he gives me a very good idea of just what he means by that.

His tongue is possessive, tasting every inch of my mouth. His hand tightens at the back of my head, making it impossible for me to move away from his onslaught. As if I would.

I arch closer, my body needing to be closer to his.

One big hand drops to my ass and squeezes. I feel a lick of heat across my clit as my pussy clenches.

Oh, God. I've never been this hot and wound tight just from kissing.

All at once, he pulls his mouth away. I whimper. I want his mouth *on* me at all times. It doesn't have to be just on my mouth, but I want that hot, knowing, greedy mouth on my body somewhere.

"There are three positions I *must* have you in," he tells me as he reaches behind his head to grasp his shirt and tug it over his head. "Spread out under me, thighs as wide as they can go, hands and knees, and you on top taking me deep."

His voice is a little gruff, maybe, but he says it like he's telling me his top three choices from the movie selection on the TV.

On the other hand, hearing those words and the images they elicit make my entire body go hot and start throbbing.

The soft yellow light from my bedside lamp allows me to see the cocky grin he gives me when he says, "Then you can pick what you want."

"That's very agreeable of you," I say.

Alex Olsen's rock-hard, perfectly sculpted abs are less than a foot away.

My eyes travel up from the trail of dark hair that disappears behind the waistband of his jeans. His chest is perfect. I want to bite his shoulders. I want to lick his throat. I want to sit on his face.

That's the position I pick.

I lift my gaze to his.

He has one eyebrow up. "You have an idea?" he asks, reading me somehow.

I nod.

"Tell me." It's a command, not a question.

"I want to sit on your face," I say bluntly.

"Jesus Christ, yes," he practically growls. He grasps me by the waist and tosses me back onto the bed. He steps close to the mattress. "But I'm going to make you come at least once first so I can lap up all of that sweetness while you're up there."

"Oh my God," I breathe out before I can stop it. Lust shudders through me.

He braces one hand on the mattress by my hip and runs his other hot hand up under my ass. "I intend to hear a lot more of *that.*"

I have no doubt he will.

He grasps the waistband of my shorts and panties underneath and tugs.

I lift my ass so he can pull both down my legs, reaching to help on the other side. Together, we strip me from the waist down.

He lifts them to his nose, inhaling deeply. "Flowers," he says. He tosses them on the floor. "Fucking addictive."

He stops, studying me for a moment. I can only imagine how I look. Nothing is exposed, yet. But my shirt is bunched just below the point of being scandalous. I'm sure my hair is a mess from his fingers. My cheeks are probably flushed.

"Fucking hell, Wildflower," he says, stepping forward. "I could stay here for days."

Yes, I want Alex Olsen in my bed for days. Only getting up for water and food occasionally. I don't want him to get dressed. I don't want him more than a room away. I don't want either of us to talk to another human for at least forty-eight hours.

I almost gasp at all of those tumbling thoughts.

Who am I suddenly?

Not leave the house? Not talk to anyone else?

What would even happen to my family? My town?

I have never even spent *hours*, plural, on sex. Not ever.

But for Alex, I'd even consider calling in sick. I *never* call in sick. I'm a good girl. Highly responsible. The town sweetheart. The one who plans the farmer's market, and street fairs, and the—

"Fuck, you're pretty."

Every other thought flies out of my head as Alex sinks to his knees at the foot of the bed.

He reaches up, slides his hands under my ass, and pulls me to the end of the mattress until I am right on the edge.

"Prettier than any flower," he tells me, staring at my pussy.

He leans in and kisses my inner thigh. Then he drags his tongue from that spot to the outer edge of my pussy.

"Prettier than even the all-pink flowers."

I feel like laughing. He's comparing my pussy to *flowers*. And I swear if he calls my labia 'petals' I'm going to lose it—and maybe cringe—but I can't laugh, or caution him, because he licks up one side, over the top, not quite touching my clit, then down the other.

I gasp, and everything in me clenches. I feel my stomach suck in, my thighs tense, and my pussy tighten around nothing.

"Addictive," he murmurs, before moving his hands forward, his thumbs resting on either side of my pussy. Then he spreads me open.

I have never felt this exposed. I've never *been* this exposed. But I don't feel vulnerable or embarrassed or awkward.

It's absolutely Alex's low growl and the, "Jesus Christ, so fucking perfect," that helps with all of that.

I feel like I have the power here. He's on his knees, he sounds like *he's* a little overwhelmed. That's ridiculous, of course, but he's really doing this right.

You're never going to stop thinking about him at this rate.

Yeah, and he's only looking at me. Well, okay, there's a little touching going on too, but seriously he hasn't even—

He licks me before I can complete that thought.

"Alex!"

"More of that," he says. "A lot fucking more of you calling out my name." Then he licks again. A long, firm stroke of his tongue over my pussy, ending with a swirl at my clit.

He lifts his head and blows. The warm air hitting my most sensitive tissues makes me arch closer to his mouth, even as I tip my head back and close my eyes.

"Oh, *God.*"

He licks again, this time sucking on my clit slightly when he gets there.

My thighs shake slightly. He feels it because he slides his hands down to the backs of my thighs, spreading me wider, letting my thighs rest on the mattress.

He leans back, taking in the sight of me spread out.

"Fuck *yes*," he says roughly. "I'm going to take you just like this first."

My eyes widen. The guy doesn't mince words.

"Okay," I say softly.

His eyes come to mine. He gives me a half grin. "But it's gonna be a bit."

"But…why?" I'm really okay with it being now. Like right *now*.

"Because I don't even have you completely naked. I haven't made you come yet. I've barely gotten my hands on you."

Much to my regret, he rocks back on his heels and stretches upright.

"But you can do all of that. Later. After," I protest.

His grin grows. "I like seeing you a little desperate."

"I… well…I…" Am I desperate? My gaze drops to the massive bulge behind his fly.

Yes. Yes, I am.

"But you're going to be so much more so soon," he says, stepping close. His gaze settles between my legs again.

I'm still spread open and naked from the waist down. I can only imagine how wanton I look.

A shiver of pleasure goes through me as I note the heat in his eyes and the way his jaw tightens as he looks down at me as if he's barely containing himself.

I love this feeling. It's powerful, feeling sexy like this.

And knowing that I don't need to worry about Alex. He's not going to be intimidated by what it means to be with me like this. Not like the men I'm used to. The guys in Rebel. The guys who know I'm the town sweetheart and have not just two grandfathers looking out for me but have an entire village—literally—of people invested in what happens to me. Including my dating life.

"Show me those pretty tits," Alex says. "I want a taste before you play with them while I eat you to your first orgasm."

Yeah, um, Alex isn't worried about who I am or who in Rebel might have an opinion about this. Or him. Or anything.

I slide my loose, silky shirt over my head and toss it.

He blows a breath out and shakes his head. "Fucking pretty as hell." He leans in, bracing a hand beside me, his other hand going to my chest and pressing me back onto the mattress.

He looms over me. "You *are* going to remember tonight."

I wet my lips and nod. "I know."

He lowers his head and licks his hot tongue over one nipple. I arch closer, wanting so much more. "Alex," I moan.

"That's right. Use my name." He moves to the other side, licking with a firm stroke, then sucking.

Heat streaks through me, settling in my pussy, my clit throbbing with the need for friction and pressure. My hands go to his shoulders, and I run them down over his arms, feeling the muscles bunching and relaxing as he holds himself up with his left arm and cups my breast with the right. He squeezes, kneads, toys with the nipple between his thumb and first finger. He rolls it, pinches, and plucks, and I desperately want to squeeze my thighs together to try to relieve the aching there. His big body is between my thighs though, preventing me from moving them together. So I lift up, seeking contact with his hard body instead. Anything. I just need pressure against my clit.

"Greedy girl," he mutters against my right breast as I rub against him. He drags his teeth lightly over my nipple.

"Yes," I say, practically panting. "Please."

"Please, what?"

"I need more."

"More what?"

"More of *you*."

He sucks hard on my nipple while pinching the other one.

I cry out. And rub shamelessly against the fly of his jeans. The rough fabric against my clit is torture and relief at the same time.

"Are you getting the front of my jeans wet, Wildflower?" he asks, lifting his head.

Maybe. I don't even care. No one has ever talked to me like this, talking about my body so graphically, calling out my wetness, and my neediness, and being so blatant about looking at me, tasting me, touching me.

I fucking love it.

I grab his ass, holding him against me as I rub against him even more brazenly.

"Fuck, that's hot," he tells me. "You want to make yourself come?" He grinds into me slightly. "Take what you need, pretty girl."

I do the hip circle again, rubbing my clit against the denim and the big, very hard ridge behind the denim.

"It's… not enough," I tell him, but still rubbing anyway.

"What do you need?"

"Fingers."

He pauses, then I swear I see a glint in his eyes. "Yes." He shifts back, holding himself up away from me. "Do it."

I pause. I have nothing to grind against now, and it takes me a second to realize he means…

"*Your* fingers," I correct.

He shakes his head. "You know exactly what you need. Show me."

Oh…wow. I've definitely never done *this* in front of another person. I've done it plenty. I prefer using a vibrator. It's faster. But can I get myself off with my fingers? Of course.

With Alex Olsen watching, though?

I look up into his eyes. He's watching me with a heat I've never seen before. His cheeks are flushed, too. He's breathing faster. His wide, hard chest rises and falls quickly. His abs and shoulders are flexed. He's holding himself tight.

Because he's turned on.

On a deep, chemical, intuitive level, I know that Alex Olsen is holding himself back from *taking me*. His animal instinct is to just fuck me. But he's holding back, making this extra good, extra hot. Extra memorable.

I swallow hard, then flatten my hand against my stomach before sliding it lower, between my legs.

His nostrils flare as his eyes lock on my hand.

I run my middle finger over my clit, giving a soft moan of relief. Yes, I can't deny that I need that. I slide lower, dipping my finger just inside. I'm so wet. My eyes go to the front of Alex's jeans.

"I did get you wet." I can't believe those words just came out of my mouth.

He looks down at the darker spot on the fly of his jeans. "Jesus." His gaze finds mine. "That's hot as fuck."

I bite my bottom lip.

"Make yourself come, Wildflower."

I slide my finger deeper into my pussy, then drag it out and circle my clit, faster and faster.

Rather than being weird with him watching, it makes it all even hotter. I love watching his face as he watches my finger. The way this is turning him on only serves to make my body tighten faster. I'm moving quickly toward my climax. I press harder and moan again. "I'm getting close."

He reaches up and tugs on one of my nipples, and I feel my pussy ripple.

"Oh yes. God."

He suddenly kneels, getting even closer to the action. "That's it. Take care of this pretty pussy."

He pinches my nipple again, and as I start moving even faster, I feel him teasing at my entrance with one finger.

"Do you need something to fill you up?" he asks. "Do you need something to squeeze? Something to strangle with this tight, beautiful cunt?"

Jesus. I'm so damned close. "Yes. You. Please." I pant the words out.

"Oh, you don't get my cock yet," he says. "I have so much more I need from you first. Like two orgasms. But you can have this."

He slides his finger into me. My pussy immediately clenches around it.

"That's right. That's so good. Fuck, you're tight."

I don't say anything. I just press harder on my clit as Alex thrusts his finger in and out.

"Good girl. Keep going. Work that needy clit." Then he adds a second finger.

"Oh! Alex! Yes!"

"I want this pussy nice and sweet and ready. Come on, give it to me."

I come just like that. I let it all go. The tension that has been winding tight suddenly snaps, and I'm gasping and crying out and clenching around Alex's thick fingers that keep fucking into me as my orgasm sweeps through me.

"Oh, fuck, yes. So damned pretty. So. Fucking. Beautiful." He pulls his fingers out as the ripples fade and he lifts them to his mouth as he again looms over me with a hand braced by my hip. He sucks them clean, then says roughly, "Good fucking girl."

My pussy clenches again.

Yeah, *none* of the men I've dated or even considered dating would have done or said any of that to me.

I take a deep, satisfied breath and blow it out. "More."

He gives me a wicked grin. "You have no idea."

His hot gaze tracks over my entire naked body. Then he climbs up beside me. I roll toward him.

"Do you—"

But he grabs me by the waist and hauls me over his body. "Put that messy pussy on my mouth."

I squeak. That's all I can do as he easily drags me up his body as if I weigh nothing.

"I'm too sensitive," I try to protest. I do want to do this, but my clit is still tingling from the orgasm, and I'm still breathing too fast.

His hand gives my ass a quick slap. "I told you, I own you tonight. This pussy is mine right now. Give it to me."

Oh, fuck. Why is that hot? That is *not* hot. The ass slap, the 'own you' thing, all of it.

But a second later, I'm settling myself over his mouth and grabbing the headboard for support. And thirty seconds later, I'm moaning his name and grinding onto that mouth. And three minutes later, I'm convinced there should be an entire religion built around this man's mouth.

"Alex! Oh, my God! I'm coming!"

He squeezes my ass and won't let me move a centimeter away from the lips, tongue, and teeth that push me over the cliff again.

Now he *has to* give me a break.

He pulls me down his body until our mouths are even, and he kisses me. He smells like me, tastes like me, and when he holds the back of my head and plunders my mouth with his tongue, it's clear that he intends for me to realize that.

He grasps my waist and shifts me further down his body.

"Ride my cock, Wildflower," he says, his voice is low and rough. "Need to feel this perfect pussy around me now."

What am I supposed to say to that? "Yes." I push myself up to straddle his thighs. "This position first?"

"I want to see you take me deep. I want to see your pretty tits bouncing. And this way, you control the pace. In any other position, I'm going to fuck you so hard you'll feel me for a month."

I want that.

It's probably not the right reaction to *want* to be sore. But I can't deny my body's reaction to his words.

"Okay."

He lifts his hips, lifting me too. He undoes his button and zipper, then reaches into his jeans pocket and withdraws his wallet. He digs out a condom before tossing the wallet onto the bedside table. He lifts again, pushing his jeans and boxers down. I shift, helping pull them down his legs. He toes off his shoes, and I hear them hit the floor, but I'm suddenly focused on the fact that he's now naked.

Gloriously naked.

He's seriously spectacular.

And huge. He's very huge. So huge that the feeling him for a month seems very realistic.

And this will be the best time I've ever had.

We haven't even done it yet, and I know this is going to be the best time.

That is possibly cause for concern. It will never get better than right now with this man. I already know that.

How fair is that to my future whoever? To future *me*?

Still… I'm not stopping this. Not for anything.

He rolls the condom on, then reaches for me. Those big hands on my hips make me hot and needy all over again.

"Come here," he says gruffly.

He doesn't mean me on his cock. He pulls me into a deep, hot kiss. It's leisurely. It's definitely lusty, but he takes his time. His fingers are in my hair, our bodies are pressed together from chest to thigh, our heartbeats are pounding. And he takes long minutes just kissing me, letting me just *feel* him.

Finally, he rests his forehead against mine. "Fuck me, Nora."

Nora. Not Wildflower. Why does that make this feel so serious?

I shrug that off and push myself up, bracing my hands on his chest, then slide back.

His cock nudges my entrance, and heat floods through me.

"Take me slow and deep, Wildflower," he says, gripping my hips. "Let's make you come again so when I flip you over, you can take me fucking you hard and deep."

Oh, yeah, that's good. That's what I need.

"You're a big talker," I tell him.

"Yes. I am." He presses up against me, and *big* is all I can think. "Let me in."

I reach back and take his cock in hand. I squeeze.

His breath hisses out between his teeth.

Then I shift, position him, and sink down over his cock, my gaze locked on the spot where his length is disappearing as he fills me up.

I moan as he slides deep.

God. That's…so damned good.

His hands squeeze my hips hard. "Jesus. Christ. Nora."

I look up quickly. "What?"

"Stop squeezing me so fucking hard. I'm not going to last."

"I'm not squeezing." I squeeze my pelvic muscles to prove it.

He swears. "You're." He sucks in a breath as he's finally fully inside. "Tight as fuck."

I smile and squeeze again.

He swats my ass.

I laugh. "Doesn't it feel good?"

"You want to be flipped over and just railed?"

I suck in a breath. "I…" I press my lips together.

He gives me a knowing smile. "Naughty girl."

I grin. "It's just that I'm pretty sure that would be amazing."

He swats me again. "Ride me. Come hard on my cock again, and I'll happily make this gorgeous pussy sorer than it's ever been."

I lift and lower on his cock. We both moan. So I do it again. And again.

Alex makes me do my share of the work. He encourages me, though, with lots of dirty words and with his hands on my breasts and nipples, on my ass, on my clit, and then sitting up and resting a big, hot, possessive hand on the front of my throat as my climax starts building.

"Goddammit, Wildflower, how am I supposed to ever survive without this pussy?" he growls in my ear as I ride him faster, grinding my clit against him on every down thrust.

"I…I…" I can't form words.

"I'm going to jack off every damned night thinking of you," he promises. His other hand presses against my lower back, making the thrusts even harder. "How am I supposed to kick this addiction?"

The idea of him thinking of me after this, of his hand around his cock and remembering all of this, winds my orgasm tight.

"I need you to come. I want to feel—"

I come before he completes the sentence.

"God, Alex! Yes! *Yes!*"

I sag against him, my arms around his neck, resting my face against his throat.

But he doesn't let me rest. He tips me back, pulls out, rolls me to my stomach, then pulls my hips back. "Hands and knees."

I shift back, my arms shaky but willing to give him anything.

He strokes his big hand over my ass, then parts my ass cheeks. "Fuck. I'm fucking never getting over you." He lowers his head, and I feel his tongue against my still tingling pussy.

"*Alex*." I'm *so* sensitive. I've come three times. I really don't think I can come again.

He licks a few times, as if he simply needs to lap up as much as he can. Then he positions himself.

"Hold on, Nora," he says gruffly.

I grip the duvet and press back.

He enters me with one long, hard thrust.

I cry out. I'm sore, but it feels amazing at the same time.

He stretches me, going deeper than anyone ever has. He pulls out and thrusts again, hard. And fast.

Hard and fast become the only words I can think of for the next few minutes.

Our bodies slap together. He only says single words at a time, and they're dirty and gruff.

My entire world has narrowed to this man and our bodies.

I feel him grip my hips hard, and suddenly he roars my name as he stiffens.

"Nora!"

He comes hard, filling the condom, gripping my body tightly against his.

Then he just stays like that, breathing hard, holding me firmly.

Finally, what seems like five minutes later, he says, "Jesus Christ, Nora."

He lets go of me, and I sag onto the mattress. But I smile and roll to my back. "What?"

He pulls the condom off and ties the top before dropping it to the floor. Then he stretches out next to me. He runs a hand up my side to my throat.

"Sweet women who smell like flowers and who plan weddings for turtles should *not* have magical pussies."

I stare at him.

Then suddenly I'm giggling. "Who told you about the turtle wedding?"

He grins. "I know *so* much about you. Everyone here loves to talk about you."

"I'm not sure that's good." I did plan a wedding for turtles, but there's a lot more to that story. Like the owner of one of the turtles having a terminal illness, and it making her really happy.

"Well, it definitely did *not* prepare me for how fantastic fucking you would be," he says.

I laugh again. "You thought it would be bad?"

"I thought it would be great," he assures me. "But I thought it would be…"

I lift a brow.

"Not the end of my world as I knew it."

I really like this.

"Sorry," I say.

He shakes his head, tracing his finger over my collarbone. "I don't think you are."

I'm not actually. The idea of Alex in his fancy Portland apartment, in his huge fancy shower after a hockey game, jerking off and thinking of me because he can't get over tonight is *amazing*.

Ridiculous. But amazing.

That's maybe not nice of me.

"I'll let you have a few more 'hits' of your new addiction," I say.

He runs his hand down, over my breast to my ass, and pulls me in. "Oh, will you?"

"For sure."

He starts to nuzzle my neck, but I decide to tease a little more. He's a good time.

"But…" I say.

"But?"

"I need to refuel."

He lifts his head quickly. "Do you have more banana pudding?" he asks hopefully.

I laugh. "I don't."

"Dammit."

"But I have bananas."

"Okay." But he's disappointed.

I have definitely messed up this guy's habits and expectations. I like it.

I get up and go to my closet to grab my robe.

Alex props up and watches me unabashedly.

"How long does banana pudding take to make?"

"A while." I turn back as I tie the robe around me. I take in the way he looks in my bed, muscles bunched, chest bare. "And I have to confess. The one I make isn't classic banana pudding."

His eyes widen. "There are different recipes?"

"Yep. There's the usual one, and then there are lots of variations. I use rum, coconut, and some different spices in mine. And it takes a few hours to set up."

He sits all the way up, seemingly oblivious to the fact he's totally naked. "Do other people in town make different varieties?"

"Yeah. We actually had a banana pudding taste-off a couple of years ago." I grin. "I won."

He swings his legs over the side of the bed. "One, never make the pudding for anyone else ever again."

I laugh. "What? People love my banana pudding."

He strides over to me, crowding close. "Your banana pudding is now all mine. You can make a different one for everyone else."

Wow, that's possessive. And makes me stupidly melty. Especially now that I know he doesn't like banana *things*.

"I'll think about it," I say.

"And two, how long does *regular* banana pudding take?"

I laugh. "The pudding has to set up, so it still takes a couple of hours."

"Dammit."

I pick up his boxers and hand them to him. "But I might have some pudding cups that we can make a mock-banana pudding out of. But you have to promise not to tell anyone I did that."

"That sounds…"

"Terrible?" I supply.

He sighs. "Addictive."

I grin.

Poor hot, rich, pro hockey player who has particular tastes and people who cater to them all the time.

But I just can't quite bring myself to be sorry that I'm "ruining" some of his preconceived notions about banana things. And hockey. And small-town Louisiana. And plans in general.

Who knows what else I might make him rethink?

CHAPTER 23
ALEX

IT'S four thirty in the morning when I roll over and kiss Nora's bare shoulder. She makes a sweet little mumbling sound, but doesn't open her eyes. I'm glad. I don't want to wake her, but I can't spend the night here. Walking into my apartment means walking through the coffee shop where the entire town gathers, starting around six a.m. I need to get there before that.

I dress quietly and slip out her back door, annoyed that I'm not able to lock it behind me.

We are going to have to discuss keys and things.

Something I've never done with a woman before.

Then again, I've never had to worry about my landlord greeting me when I slip sheepishly into my apartment across town after debauching his granddaughter all night.

It's not until I pull my truck in behind Perks and Rec that I realize I don't have a key to this building either. Bruce never gave me one. I suppose he assumed I would be coming and going during business hours. Or maybe my comings and goings didn't occur to him at all.

Until this moment, they didn't occur to me either.

Fuck.

I get out and try the back door anyway. After all, Nora doesn't lock her door and Bruce helped raise her. Maybe they're just not a door-locking family.

But no such luck. Bruce at least locks up his business. Which I approve of. Especially since I am sleeping upstairs.

I sigh and look around. I can go back to Nora's, I suppose, but then I'll have the same problem of explaining where I've been when I come back at six.

There are only two other places in this town where I can be let in at this hour. And not judged.

Beckett's place, or my sister's.

I don't really feel like putting up with Beckett at this hour. There is no doubt in my mind that he's a morning person. A *perky* morning person.

So fifteen minutes later, after a short jog, I'm knocking on my sister's front door.

It takes her, understandably, several minutes to answer.

This is not the first time I've shown up at Astrid's in the middle of the night.

It is probably the first time I've done it completely sober, though.

"What the fuck are you doing?" she asks, swinging the door wide open for me to come in.

"I was at Nora's, and I am locked out of Perks and Rec," I say.

Astrid doesn't need any more explanation than that. She nods. "I appreciate your commitment to this fake dating scheme."

Right.

Nothing about things with Nora feels fake, and that should be concerning.

Instead of dwelling on that, I look around my sister's house.

We're in the "foyer", the small square of linoleum just inside the front door. Two steps ahead and I'll be in the living room.

And I can't stop staring at it.

This place has to be what shows up in the dictionary as an example of a ranch-style house. In nineteen seventy-one.

The suite Astrid lived in at college was smaller than this,

square footage-wise, and with fewer rooms, so this is the second smallest place she's ever lived.

But that's only the beginning of the…staring.

"What the *hell* is with that wallpaper?"

She grins widely. "Isn't it horrible?"

Yes, yes, it is. It's yellow. And orange. And *brown*. There is a lot of brown in this room. The wallpaper pattern looks like multiple halved avocados. But the avocados are orange. On top of yellow. With brown pits.

The orange matches the sofa, though. The yellow goes with the weird round chair. And the brown complements the one wall that's covered in wood paneling that extends all the way around the built-in bookcase that has a gigantic TV right in the middle.

Oh, and I can't forget the mustard yellow draperies at the windows.

"Is the rest of the house…like this?"

"Wait until you see *both* green bathrooms," she says, almost excited.

"And the wood paneling," I say. "Does it…continue?"

"It's *everywhere*," she confirms.

Jesus. "You are married to a billionaire," I say to her. "You're worth millions yourself. And this is what you bought?"

"Declan will hate it, don't you think?" she asks with a wicked smile.

This is nothing like the penthouse Declan O'Grady lives in.

I wonder if Declan has ever even seen this shade of yellow.

"I think that is pretty likely," I agree.

She sighs happily. She's wearing a loose, soft-looking matching pajama set, her hair is tumbling around her shoulders, and she has no makeup on. With her small frame and without her expensive makeup and clothes, she could pass for ten years younger than she is.

"What is up with you and Declan?" I ask her.

She rolls her eyes. "You're really going to knock on my door before five in the morning and ask me to talk about my husband?"

"That actually wasn't my intention, but now that we're on the subject," I say.

"We are not on the subject."

"Why did you marry him if you dislike him so much?"

Her eyebrows arch. "Who says I dislike him?"

"Every action you take, and things you say about him."

She waves her hand. "Come on, it's a marriage of convenience. We got married because our grandfathers wanted us to. It's not like we were crazy about each other and can't live without one another."

I study her for a long moment. I'm close with both of my sisters, and I feel like I know them well, but they know me better than I know them. There is more to this whole story with her and Declan, but I can't tell what it is. Does she feel more for him than she's letting on? Is she happy?

Of course, I know that they got married because our grandfathers made a deal long, long ago. I also know that everyone in both families, including Declan and Astrid, expected that their siblings—in our case, our older sister and, in Declan's, his younger brother—would actually be the ones to get married to combine the two family bloodlines and appease the patriarchs. I was there when Declan burst into his younger brother's wedding and declared that there was only one option left: him and Astrid marrying.

But Astrid went along with it. She tried to argue for maybe two minutes, then she agreed and said the vows. She packed her stuff, got on Declan's plane, and flew to Portland with him.

So what's going on now?

"Want some tea?" she asks.

"Caffeine?" I ask.

"Nope. But I've got one that works great for energy and inflammation and good fortune." She winks at me.

She knows I think a lot of her tea, herbs, essential oils, and yoga practices are a little woo-woo. She got into a lot of natural healing and alternative medicine after her injury and surgery. She constantly tells me that I need to try it, and I did get desperate enough to have her show me some meditation and how to use some oils after I'd been doing rehab on my knee for three months with much less progress than I'd expected.

But here I am, still not fully healed.

"Sure. Who doesn't need good fortune?" I ask.

"That's the spirit."

I follow her into the kitchen. If the living room is orange and yellow, and the bathrooms are green, what's the kitchen look like?

Oh. My. God.

The appliances are the same avocado green I'm imagining in the bathrooms, but the countertops are orange, while the backsplash and tile floor are a combination of brown and orange, and the cabinets are a dark brown.

"Astrid, I feel like this is a cry for help."

She laughs as she fills her tea kettle. "I know, right?"

"Did you say Declan is never coming to Louisiana? So why would you care if he'd hate this? Is he ever going to even see it?"

She frowns. And doesn't answer at first.

She pushes buttons on the kettle's handle to start the water heating and reaches for cups. Once she has tea scooped into two infusers, she carries the mugs to the table.

"He probably won't," she agrees. "It just amuses me to think about him here. He's so…fastidious."

That's one word for it. Declan O'Grady likes things a certain way, that's for sure.

One of those "certain ways" is expensive. And monochromatic. At least from what I've seen of his office, two of the sports cars I've seen, and the few times I've been to his penthouse.

"I think it's good for him to learn that not everything can be *his* way."

Hmm. I don't know that that is a lesson Declan is ready, or even able, to learn.

"Are you okay?" I ask.

The kettle whistles, and she retrieves it. She pours water into both of our mugs, then answers. "I'm good. Things are going well here."

"But are *you* doing well?" I ask.

"Sure." She shrugs. "I'm still doing all of my usual stuff. I'm just doing it from here."

Her 'usual stuff' includes maintaining a vibrant, positive online community, where she coaches and writes an inspirational column that followers can subscribe to. She's also on nearly every social media platform, is writing a new book, and is probably getting constant calls for speaking engagements.

"What about Miles?" I ask.

Miles Stafford is Astrid's best friend. He started as her physical therapist after her injury, but they grew close and have been inseparable for the last few years. Astrid has now been away from him longer than she has been since they met.

"I miss him *terribly*," she says. "But he's coming for a visit soon. He's going to come see you all play."

"Good." I like Miles.

He's a great guy, and I know that most people who follow Astrid "ship" her and Miles. They all wish they were a romantic couple and a lot of people in Portland who follow local celebrities refuse to believe they're not. They are seen out and about the city together all the time, and neither has dated anyone seriously or publicly in years.

But they would tell me if their relationship was more than friendship, and it's simply not. They're more like siblings. And now that Astrid is married to Portland's most eligible bachelor, I assume those rumors have died down.

"But I'm really happy for *you*," she says, removing her tea infuser and adding two spoonfuls of sugar to her cup.

I remove my infuser as well and get up for cream. I'm happy for me, too.

I think.

Nora is amazing.

I'd gone over last night to try to regain some feeling of control, some feeling of I-know-what-I'm-doing-dammit, *some* area of my life where things would go as I expected them to.

And Nora had blown that out of the water, too.

Nothing about last night was as I'd expected. None of that was usual.

I am *more* addicted. I don't feel in control at all. I feel like I'm a snowball rolling down a mountain, only gaining momentum and speed and losing the ability to slow or stop. And when I crash at the bottom it will be a huge mess. And the chances of wiping out a bunch of…stuff…is very real.

But what stuff?

Oh, just life as I knew it before coming to Rebel.

"Thanks. But Nora and I are temporary, you know. Just until April." I return to the table.

Astrid gives me a wide-eyed WTF look. "I was talking about the hockey stuff, but do you want to talk about you and Nora?"

I do not. Because I'm pretty sure I'm falling in love with her, and I'm equally sure my sister will realize that and make me admit it. And what good will that fucking do?

"Nope."

"Okay." She rolls her eyes as she takes a sip of tea.

"What are you happy for *me* about with the hockey?" I ask.

"All of it. You were great last night," she says. "Seriously great. And we're up *four hundred tickets* this morning. Well, last night when I checked. So, thank you."

Well, holy shit. Okay, that *is* good.

"I was kind of pissy about all of it," I admit.

She laughs. "Yeah, that was pretty obvious."

"Other people could tell?"

"So much, Alex."

I sigh. "I'll work on it." If I can keep working out my "frustrations" with Nora the way I did last night, I'm already less annoyed by the upcoming games and scrimmages.

Way less annoyed.

Nora makes everything better.

More chaotic. And better.

How is that possible? What has happened to my life?

But Astrid shrugs. "Your pissiness made it more fun and funny."

Nora said the same thing. "Do you think so?"

"Yeah. It's like the players are all a bunch of different characters out there. Beckett is the enthusiastic golden retriever who's having the time of his life. Lawson is the intense, uncomfortable one who's trying his damnedest and looking awkward, but hot at the same time, somehow. Wes is the one who acts like he's actually playing serious hockey even when it's ridiculous. It's like he pulls off this sarcastic thing while he's doing it. Ingrid is like a superhero ninja or something. She's hilarious and fun to watch. Teddy is a goofball, but in a different way from Beckett. He's quieter and more subtle, which makes his humor different funny. And then there's you, the total grump who thinks it's all silly and beneath you."

She shakes her head, but she's grinning. "It's like each one of you appeals to a different person watching. There's someone for each person in the audience to relate to. Some people will show up and think it's the best time ever, and they'll think Beckett and Teddy are great. Some people won't totally get it, and they'll probably relate more to Lawson or Wes. And then there will be people who are outright appalled that we're doing this to hockey. You'll be their favorite."

I think about all of that. It's an interesting theory, and it just might work.

"But did everyone have a good time?" I finally ask.

"Absolutely. I was watching the crowd intently. And yes. But if I had any questions about it, I just had to get on social media. Oh, and our team email. Everyone is really excited."

I'm surprised to feel a surge of pride hearing that.

"And don't worry, Miles is keeping track of everything and passing it on to Declan. Or passing it on to Iris to pass on to Declan."

Iris is Declan's assistant-slash-bodyguard-slash-best friend. But I frown. "How is any of this helping me with what I'm trying to prove to Declan?"

"You're here to learn about running a hockey organization, so Declan will hire you, right? I'd say you're learning a ton of new, behind-the-scenes stuff."

I snort. "How exactly does learning the lyrics to "I Gotta Feelin'" or how to skate on a rink with forty wiffle balls bouncing around and not killing myself actually prove anything to Declan?"

"You're learning about public relations, what fans respond to, ticket sales, what all has to go into a hockey game from start to finish."

"I'm not doing any of that. That's you, Nora, and Sutton."

"Well, you're definitely tuned into it because of Nora. But you are *doing it*. Just because you don't like it, doesn't mean you're not learning from it." She sips then sets her cup down. "And look at all you're learning about player relations."

"Pulling Beckett and Lawson off of each other?" I chuckle. "Not sure I'm learning anything there except to keep them far apart."

"I'm talking about *you*."

"What do you mean?"

"You're learning what all goes into keeping a player happy. Accommodations, communication, how important community relations are, practice facilities, coaching—"

"We don't have a coach."

"Exactly."

She laughs at the confused look on my face.

"You've only ever played for the Grays, and you were automatically the star and treated as such. People bent over backward to hold your hand and make you happy. Now you're here and you're seeing a different side to all of that."

I definitely wasn't automatically the star here.

"You think Declan will care about all of that?"

"If you can explain it to him. What you've learned. Why it's important. How you can take this experience and use it for the Grays."

I nod. "I think I can do that. This has definitely been…different."

Astrid sips again. "Of course, you won't have Nora there, making you a lot more tolerant and humble than you usually are."

I narrow my eyes. "You don't think I'm humble?"

She snorts.

I grin and sip my tea, deciding not to comment on Nora not being in Portland. Because that really makes Portland a lot less appealing suddenly, and Jesus, it's only been a few days and we're talking about *Portland*. My city. My goal.

"You're really doing a great job selling this fake boyfriend thing too, by the way. Everyone's completely buying it. It's almost like it's not fake at all," my sister comments, in a tone that's casual-and-totally-not-casual.

"Yeah, and you're doing a great job letting the husband, who is only a convenience, influence pretty much every decision you make," I say.

I sip.

She sips.

"We should talk about something else," she says.

"Agreed." My feelings for Nora are going to be way too apparent to my sister, and if I say them out loud, I'll have to deal with what the fuck to do with them when this is all over.

"Have you talked to Mom and Dad lately?" she asks.

We discuss our family until it's late enough for me to jog back to Perks and Rec and pretend I'd slipped out the front door for an early run right after Bruce unlocked it at five forty-five and went back to the kitchen.

He and the earliest of the early birds all seem to buy that reason for me coming in at six thirteen. No one seems to suspect that it has anything to do with Bruce's granddaughter, who looks and seems far too sweet to impact a man's life like a category five hurricane.

I go straight to the back of the cafe to where the washing machine is. I have a basket of laundry waiting there, and I shrug out of my now sweaty shirt and toss it in with the rest. I'll come down and start that up as soon as I shower…and grab the sheet with the directions from Ruth. I've only done one load before this and needed her step-by-step handwritten note. I pull a tank from the basket and shrug into it before heading back out front.

But on my way past the counter toward my staircase, I catch Leo Landry's eye, and he winks and points at his left shoulder.

I smile, but don't understand.

Until I'm in my bathroom in front of the mirror.

Nora left a bite mark on my left shoulder.

I shake my head. *Real subtle, Wildflower.*

But fuck, that's hot. She claimed me. Marked me.

And I want to go straight back over there and leave a few bite marks of my own on *my* girl.

I'm in *so* fucking much trouble.

CHAPTER 24
NORA

I TRY to school my features as I approach the Parks and Recreation office. I don't think I'm going to be able to hide what happened between Alex and me last night from my friends, but I can't just walk around all day with a goofy, I-have-never-been-this-well-fucked grin on my face. Can I?

But I feel that grin the second I step inside the office and realize Andi is here as well. They'll be so happy for me…

"Oh my God, Nora!" Sutton says the instant she sees me.

But that's not a celebratory or a you-go-girl exclamation. She looks panicked.

I stop in front of her desk and look between the two of them. "What's going on?"

Sutton looks worried, but Andi looks amused.

"My dad is texting and calling, asking if he can get tickets to the first game," Sutton says.

Of course, I remember Sutton and Beckett's dad. They grew up here, not moving to Minnesota until Sutton and Beckett were eighteen. Their dad lives in Texas now.

I nod. "I'm sure we can arrange that."

"Ask her why her dad is so excited about it suddenly," Andi says, lifting her to-go cup from Perks and Rec.

"What happened?" I ask.

"Astrid was on a podcast this morning. She got into a big argument with the host," Sutton says.

I frown. "What? What podcast?"

"*Sam The Sportsman*," Sutton says.

The way she says it, I can tell she doesn't know who this is, but my heart skips a beat. "You're kidding. He's huge. He covers way more than hockey, and he's got a nationwide audience. Maybe worldwide. Astrid was on his podcast?"

"Kind of. She called in. They were talking about us. And she called in and got into a fight with him," Sutton says.

Andi chuckles. "It was professional. But it's pretty entertaining." She leans over and turns her phone on Sutton's desk so that I can see the screen. Then she presses play on the image that's filling the screen.

"We have a very interesting caller for you all right now from what I understand," a man's voice says. "Everyone, welcome Astrid Olsen to the program."

"No way," another man's voice replies. "*The* Astrid Olsen?"

Andi hits the pause button. "That's some hockey player named Crew McDaniel, or something. I think he's a pro."

I gasp. "Crew *McNeill*?"

"Yeah, that's it," Andi says.

"He's like the second-best center in the league, behind Alex," I tell them. "I mean, now he's probably the best since Alex is out. He plays for the Chicago Racketeers. He's amazing."

"Well, he does mention that he and Alex are friends," Andi says. "That's how they started talking about this. The podcast guy saw some clips online of the scrimmage, and Crew said it's great to see Alex playing again, but that he's never seen this side of him."

There are already clips from last night online and getting attention? I brace myself. "Push play."

I cannot believe one of the biggest podcasters and one of the most prominent professional hockey players are talking about our hockey team. Except that I can. Because they're actually talking about Alex. He's big, his injury and leaving the pros was big, and having him on our team is big.

This kind of attention is what we wanted.

"Astrid? You're on the air."

"Hey, Sam, hey, Crew," Astrid's voice comes across the line.

"Astrid," Crew says. "It's been a long time."

"It has. Congratulations on your year without having to compete with Alex."

Crew chuckles. "You know I don't see it that way. But thanks."

"Well, Alex is keeping busy down here in Louisiana. But I heard you guys talking some shit about it, so I thought I'd call in and clear up some possible confusion."

"Nah, it wasn't shit," Sam says. "We're just *interested* in the fact that a huge pro hockey star is now playing beer league hockey," Sam says.

"See, that's the problem, Sam, you're misinformed and you're just talking instead of trying to find out the facts. It's not a beer league. I should know. It's mine."

He chuckles. "Yeah, I heard that too. I mean, it's not like a big shot like you can get away with starting her own hockey league without drawing attention."

"I don't mind drawing attention," Astrid says.

"We know." Sam laughs. "You've been doing it beautifully for years, even *before* you married Declan O'Grady. So was giving you your own hockey league to play with a wedding gift from your new hubby?"

"It definitely was not," Astrid says, her slightly flirtatious tone now cooler. "*I've* got a *fun* hockey league. Hockey with heart. Declan wouldn't know what that was if it bit him in his very fine ass."

I lift my eyes and meet Andi's amused gaze, then Sutton's wide-eyed stare.

I lean over and hit pause. "Did she just call Declan's ass very fine on a huge sports podcast?"

"She did," Andi says. "But I suppose if anyone's going to, it should be her? I mean, there are all those rumors about whether they're really married, right? That sounds…kind of married?"

"First, there are?" I ask. "And second, does it?"

"You haven't seen that?" Andi asks.

Sutton is nodding. "It's all over social media. People were wondering why they were suddenly married when *no one* had any idea they were even dating. And now that Astrid's in Louisiana and Declan's still in Oregon, people are really wondering if the marriage is real or just some gossip or a PR stunt or something."

I frown. That's…not good. But it's none of my business. "That can't affect the team here, can it?"

"I'd say, if anything, more people will come because they're almost like reality-TV stars. People will come to get a glimpse of someone even sort-of famous," Andi says.

I nod. Maybe that makes sense. I look at each of my friends. "So…do we think they're really married?"

"Legally? Yes," Sutton says. "I searched the public records, and they have a marriage license."

I laugh. "Okay. But are they in love?"

"Hard to tell," Andi says. "I mean, he *does* have a fine ass. That's more just a statement of fact."

I can't do anything but nod. Declan O'Grady is *very* attractive. If a woman is into dark, broody, totally intimidating, powerful men.

Which I'm not.

But I get it.

I lean over and push play on the podcast again.

"So you're playing 'fun hockey'," Sam says.

"Hockey with heart," Astrid interjects.

"Right. Okay," Sam says. "But there's singing and dancing,

Astrid. So it's not *hockey*. What is this? A mid-life crisis? And if so, is it yours or your brother's?"

"Well, see, Sam, right there's the problem. Some of you don't appreciate sports unless they're all polished and glamorous, right? It has to be flashy and pretty to catch and keep your attention. And I get it. Your attention spans are short, and it's all just one big dick-measuring contest at the end of the day. Well, *I* wanted to go somewhere to hang out with people who just really love the game. So I came to Rebel, Louisiana."

"Oh, I see, that's what this is? The love of the game?" Sam asks.

"Yes," Astrid says. "The players and fans are all here for the same reason. To have a really good fucking time. To hang out together, to watch some hockey, to have some laughs. But then both teams leave the ice and go hang out at the bar together. The fans dress up and cheer their team on, but then they leave the arena and go staff the bake sale together, or hang out at book club. This is just a bunch of really great guys getting together, having a hell of a good time, and helping the fans feel a part of it. Because we all love hockey and want to show that we can do that, and just that, and not let money and egos get in the way.

"I want all of these players to remember why they picked up that hockey stick the very first time. Before they got caught up in the competition, in the glitz, in the idea that everything always has to be bigger and better and faster. And yes, that's what I want for my brother. This past year has been tough on him. I want to give him some joy in hockey back."

I don't hear exactly what Sam and Crew say in response.

I'm totally caught up in what Astrid said about Alex.

I already really liked Astrid Olsen O'Grady—wait, did she take Declan's last name? I need to look that up—but I like her *so much* right now.

I want Alex to *love* hockey.

Not the life hockey has given him. Not the safe bubble he's in because of hockey. Not this sense of self that he thinks only comes from being Alex Olsen, number fourteen for the Portland Grays. Just hockey. The game. And how he feels when he's on the ice. And how he feels on the ice *here* in Rebel. And how he makes other people feel because of how much *they* like hockey.

"I'm thinking this is right up your alley, McNeill," Astrid is saying when I focus again. "If you ever get tired of Chicago, come down and give me a visit."

"I do love the spotlight, and I'm not gonna lie, I have a pretty great singing voice," McNeill says.

"Well, we might just have to make you prove that. I've been thinking that we need to have some All-Star guests come down and join our shenanigans."

Crew chuckles. "Your brother has my number."

"I'm going to let you go," Astrid says. "Stop talking shit about my hockey league, Sam," she says. "If you want to know what it's really about, call me and we'll do a real interview. Or better yet, come down here and see it for yourself."

"I might just have to do that. Do you have a fancy box I can sit in?"

"Hell no. You're going to sit down with the fans and under-stand what this is really about. And you're also going to meet some of the best people you've ever met and have some of the best food you've ever tasted."

"Sounds like an invitation I can't pass up."

"Exactly."

"And thanks for listening, Astrid. I didn't know you were a fan."

"Well, now you do, so watch yourself."

She disconnects, and the two guys chuckle for a moment, then Sam says, "And okay, I'll apologize on air. I have to say that Astrid Olsen is impressive, and it seems that everything she does, she does well and with a lot of heart. I should've assumed that this would be the same."

"Agreed," Crew says. "And honestly, Alex is the same. I love seeing him still playing and able to get out there and laugh. His injury was a blow to the entire league. He was really a big part of the pro hockey world. I'm happy for him that he's found a way to still have hockey be a part of his life."

"Okay, everyone, if you're interested in some hockey with heart just look up Rebel, Louisiana, and the Rebel Revelers and Rascals," Sam says.

I reach over and hit the stop button. I stare at the phone for a moment. Then I look up at Andi, then Sutton.

"Holy shit." That's all I can say.

Sutton nods her head quickly. "I know, right?"

"This is huge for us!" I exclaim.

"It is."

I turn as Astrid strides into the office. She looks impeccable as always, in a dove-gray pantsuit with purple heels and a purple silk scarf around her neck.

"That was kick ass," Andi tells her.

"Oh my God, how did you even know they were talking about us?" Sutton asks.

"I was expecting to make that call, but not until after our first game," Astrid says. "Sam has his finger on the pulse of all professional sports and players, even ones like Alex. Sam is popular and for the most part I like his show, but I knew that he would have some shit to say about our hockey league and Alex. So once I found out that our videos were going viral from the scrimmage, I tuned in. I'm glad Crew was there. That was just lucky."

"So this is really big," I say. "We're going to get a lot of attention from this."

Astrid looks at me and gives me the biggest smile I've seen from her yet. "We already are. And…change of plans."

"Which plans?" I ask.

"Remember how I said I wanted to sell three thousand season tickets?"

"Yes. Do you want more?" I am optimistic, for sure, but I don't want her to get too excited.

"Less," she says.

"Wait. *Less* than three thousand?" I ask with a frown.

"Yes. Because I have been getting calls and emails from people begging me to make more single tickets available. They're saying that either they can't afford season tickets or they simply can't take the time to come to all those games, but that they really want to come to as many as they can. I started thinking about it, and that makes perfect sense. Let's get more people in for single games. That's more people going back to their communities and jobs and talking about what a fantastic time they had here in Rebel, right? The ripple effect is even bigger and wider that way."

I'm nodding. "Sure. But even if we sell three thousand season tickets, we still have two thousand seats."

Now her grin is even brighter. "We've already sold three thousand four hundred and twenty-eight tickets for the first game."

I feel my mouth drop open.

Sutton gasps audibly.

"And I'm going to comp several hundred. We need to bring some hockey clubs down from New Orleans. Get some kids in here. They're going to eat this stuff up. Plus, they all have phones. Which means a lot more videos and social media posts."

I don't know what to say. My mind is spinning. "How have we sold that many tickets?"

"Orders have been pouring in since last night. But since the podcast, we've had tons more from all over," Astrid says. "I told you this was going to be big."

I'm torn between laughing and crying. "Oh my God."

"And just think what will happen if Alex does something public," Andi says. "Or...Declan." She gives Astrid a sly look. "You publicly teased your husband—a big shot in the hockey world—about not understanding hockey with heart."

Astrid's smile fades. "I wasn't teasing."

"Well, what if he says something publicly about *you*? Pokes you back? Or defends himself? Or...decides to show up and see what this is all about himself?" Andi looks positively giddy. "God, that would be juicy. You guys having some kind of little feud about the real meaning of hockey. If he shows up here, social media would explode. Everyone would want to see the two of you together."

"A lot of people *already* want to see the two of you together," Sutton says. "You're like the biggest mystery celebrity couple ever!"

"We're not celebrities," Astrid says with a frown. "Outside of sports, people don't know who we are, and even outside of gymnastics and hockey, we're barely recognized."

"Everyone knows who you are!" Sutton protests. "You were on the cover of like every magazine! You've done commercials. Your online following is huge!"

Astrid waves that away. "No one cares about me and Declan bickering."

"So you *are* bickering," Andi says, her eyes dancing.

"Do I need to have you all sign NDAs?" Astrid asks. She looks serious.

Andi and Sutton both straighten. "No," Sutton says quickly.

"Of course not," Andi says, sincerely.

"Thank you," Astrid says. "Then...just between us...yes, Declan and I are bickering. When we talk at all."

I really want to know more. *Really.* I wonder what I can get out of Alex? Maybe if I do that thing…

"Oh my God," Sutton sighs. But her tone is not exuberant, like the rest of us.

I look at her. "What's wrong?"

"Do you have any idea how much more food we're going to have to order for the crawfish boil?"

I start laughing. I look at Astrid. "Good thing our owner is so supportive."

"Oh, let me show you the new ideas I have for merch!" Astrid says, pulling her phone out.

And I sigh *happily.*

Yes, our owner is spending money on her teams like her husband does on his. But the money is going for crawfish, ingredients for our signature cocktail at the arena—our twist on the Swamp Water cocktail, of course—and things like stuffed otters and Rougarou. We're spending on our fans. On the people of Rebel.

And yes, a part of me would love to know what Declan O'Grady thinks of this.

But I really want to know what Alex thinks of it.

CHAPTER 25

ALEX

"CAN I go with you to deliver all of the stuff in Rebel?" I ask Beckett.

I am staring down at one of the items we picked up in New Orleans.

We have a new stove in the back of his truck. Twenty pounds of potatoes. Miscellaneous items from a pharmacy. Two dozen beignets. A bunch of two-by-fours and some metal bracket thingies that I would never have been able to identify on my own. And a kitten.

I am holding the little orange fluff ball in both hands as it sleeps on our way back to Rebel.

He would honestly fit in only one of my hands, but I have both cupped around him because I'm afraid of dropping him.

Beckett looks over. "Sure. You really want to?"

"I'm fascinated by what you do."

He laughs. "I pick shit up and drop it off. I'm really just filling a gap."

"Well, I've never done anything like that." I look over. "Or…anything."

He grins. "Except be awesome at hockey."

I shrug. "But, end of day, does that *help* anyone?"

"Come on. Sure. You make people happy. You give money away. You're a role model."

I think about that. There's that happy thing again. "But you know the people in Rebel really well," I say. "Picking stuff up for them like this that kind of gives you a glimpse into their life, right?"

"For sure."

"Are they thrilled to have a big-shot hockey player show up at their house on a random Tuesday?" I ask, trying to imagine delivering a bag of acetaminophen, foot cream, and mascara to someone in Portland.

He laughs. "They're thrilled to get the things they need without having to wait for the post office to bring it." He looks at the kitten. "Or go without the things the post office won't bring."

"But having a hockey player as a delivery man is pretty wild."

He shakes his head. "Not really."

"None of these people follow hockey? None of them came to the scrimmage last night?"

"Oh, they were almost all there," he says. "Except for Miss Betty. She likes baseball. And she tells me that all the time."

I chuckle, but quiet quickly when the kitten stirs. "Did the others not enjoy it?" I'm surprised to feel a stab of disappointment.

"Oh no, they had a great time. They all came and told me afterward. But today I am Beckett, the guy who helps them out with deliveries and stuff." He looks over. "The hockey thing's only part of it. It's really interesting. They like it. They're supportive. But it's only part of what I do and how they know me. When I show up today, they'll ask me about the roads, if I've caught up with *Only Murders In the Building*—I have not, by the way, and Cam will be disappointed—, if I have been taking my vitamin C, and if I want any leftovers from last night. By the way, the answer to that is always yes when Kate asks, and no when Tom and Nancy ask."

I laugh as I think about all of that. This is all a very foreign concept to me. I wonder what it would feel like to have people interested in me beyond hockey. I suppose the way it does when people at the coffee shop want personal facts about me, but times ten, or fifty, or one hundred.

"By the way, if you want to keep helping me out with deliveries, I can use you. Either to come along with me like this for the big stuff, or I can send you out on your own. I have enough business and could expand."

I look down at the kitten. I can think of a lot worse ways to spend my time. "I have been a little bored. I'm still trying to figure out a good routine. But yeah, I'll think about that."

It would easily be the best way to get to know the people in Rebel. But should I mention to Beckett that I'm only here temporarily? I don't want him or the people in Rebel to get too dependent on me.

His phone buzzes in the holder he has attached to his dashboard. It's a message from Sutton. He frowns, and pushes the button to have it read out loud.

"Dad's calling for tickets. You guys are huge. *Sam The Sportsman*."

Beckett and I look at one another.

"*Sam The Sportsman*?" he says. "The podcast? What does that mean? Do you think the podcast mentioned us?"

I pull my phone out and go to my podcast app. I start to scroll to find the latest podcast episode of Sam's show. I listen to him a lot and have been a guest a couple of times.

"Does your dad come to a lot of games?" I ask. My parents haven't been to one of my games in person in years. My grandfather used to come a lot before he died, though. I miss having him there.

"Uh. No."

Something in Beckett's tone makes me look over. "Are you and your dad close?"

"Not really. This is probably his way of reaching out." He

looks at me again. "We're not like estranged. We talk and stuff. But there's tension."

"Oh, sorry to hear that. You're from here, right? Is he still in Rebel?"

"Well, we grew up here. Sutton and I. We lived here till we were eighteen. We moved the summer after we graduated."

"You mean, your whole family moved?"

"Yeah. To Minnesota?"

"Because you were going to college?"

"No."

He's quiet for a long moment, and I notice how his grip tightens on the wheel.

"I mean, yes, Sutton and I went to college in Minnesota, but that's not why our parents moved there." He pauses. "Our mom ended up getting pregnant when we were fourteen."

"Oh, wow." That had to be…interesting.

"Yeah, it was, obviously, a total surprise. But it was cool. We were all really close, Sutton and I loved having a little sister. Everything was good."

Trepidation trickles down my spine at the way he says 'was'.

"None of them live here now, though?" I ask.

He clears his throat "No. Mara died."

Shock tightens my chest. I look over. "Damn. I'm really sorry."

He nods, staring at the road in front of us. "She got cancer. When she was four. Brain cancer. We all ended up moving up to Minnesota so that she could go through treatments at Mayo Clinic."

Oh, fuck. That's horrible. I can't imagine one of my sisters being sick like that. Astrid's injury and her surgeries and rehab were bad enough. But at least we all knew she'd survive and get better. I clear my throat. "And you started playing hockey up there?"

He nods. "Yeah. I'd played here growing up, but Louisiana isn't a hockey state like Minnesota. I wasn't on anyone's radar. I walked on at a small college. Sutton had always danced and skated, too, and she was able to do both more intensely. We both had a couple of decent years. But our entire family's life revolved around Mara and her treatments. She was doing well, so things felt good."

I stay quiet when he pauses, letting him tell the story his way.

"But then the cancer came back in our sophomore year. She was dying. Sutton and I both dropped out. I quit the team. I had to be there for my family."

So that's how his career got derailed.

Scrapping for a position on a small school's team was hard enough, but he'd gotten attention. People noticed him. He had promise. But suddenly quitting took away all those opportunities.

"I'm really sorry, Beck," I say.

He nods. "Me too. She was so little. It was so bad at the end. Our family just...broke up. Our mom lost her mind. Our parents divorced. Our mom had an affair with Mara's oncologist. His marriage ended. They ended up getting married. And had two more kids."

I stare at him. "Fuck, man."

He nods. "Yeah. She wanted another baby within months of Mara's death, and my dad couldn't handle that. He moved to Texas. Mom stayed in Minneapolis. And Sutton and I just needed a break. I'd already fucked up my hockey career by dropping out of college, so we decided to come back home. At least to a place that felt like home. A place where we knew a lot of people, and I guess the place that had been happy and normal." He takes a deep breath. "The FPHL team was here and I tried out, made it, and it felt like kismet."

We're quiet for the last few miles.

I have *never* experienced anything like what Beckett and Sutton have been through. My injury felt catastrophic, and it certainly turned my life upside down, but...it's nothing compared to what their family went through.

We pull up at the kitten's new home first.

He's going to be a surprise for a nine-year-old's birthday. He'll be all moved in by the time she and her sister get home from school.

I suddenly really want to see her reaction. That is going to be awesome.

I want to stop by in six months and see how much he's grown. Fuck, I want to deliver kittens all over town.

And Beckett is exactly right. As we make the rest of the deliveries, not one person comments on the scrimmage or says anything about hockey at all.

They thank us for our help, tell us a little about what they needed their deliveries for—April and Mark, for instance, have a huge family reunion coming up, and are going to make some incredible potato salad—and put in orders for other things next week.

When we're finished, I'm tired. Not physically, but mentally. Or emotionally? I don't interact with people like this on any kind of regular basis.

But I feel good.

"Thanks for asking me to help out today," I tell Beckett when he drops me off at Perks and Rec.

"You bet. Thank *you*."

"I think I'm in," I tell him. "For doing more of this." I won't make any long-term promises, and I'll be honest with him about my plans to go back to Portland, but why not help out while I'm here? Why not get to know people? The idea of staying to myself, hanging out alone, just killing time feels cold and…impossible. How am I going to keep myself from getting involved with these people? They're too hard to resist.

He grins. "Awesome. We can go over a plan tomorrow at breakfast."

"Sounds good. See you at practice."

"You got it."

I head into the coffee shop, realizing I'm starving.

"Hey, Alex!"

"Hi, Alex!"

"Alex!"

I'm met by a chorus of greetings. I stop and really take it in. That happened last night, too. I was distracted by my frustrations about the scrimmage and about finding Nora, but now it comes back to me.

"Hey, everybody," I say, with a smile, as I start for the counter.

My gaze lands on the mason jars next to the register.

I stop and stare.

Warmth spreads through my chest.

Was it the scrimmage that made the difference? Nora? Working with Beckett today?

Does it matter?

No.

The sign asks, "What do you like better?" and the options are: Warm chocolate chip cookies or Alex Olsen.

The Alex Olsen jar is overflowing with dollar bills.

CHAPTER 26
NORA

I'M TOTALLY nonchalant the next morning at Perks and Rec.

Okay, I'm *trying* to be totally nonchalant.

But last night I got a text from Alex that said, *Going to work with Josh so I can't come over.*

We didn't have plans for him to come over that I knew of.

But his next text had been, *I know we didn't have specific plans for me to come over, but just assume that I'm going to be at your house every night that I can.*

I'd laughed and also probably swooned a little.

I don't really know what swooning feels like because I've never swooned for any man before, but that's got to be what that aww-melty-I-fucking-can't-resist-this-man feeling is.

Anyway, I'd texted back to ask what 'going to work with Josh' meant but hadn't gotten a reply until I'd looked at my phone this morning.

His reply had come in at two a.m., and it had been just a series of emojis. A fire truck, a flame, a grinning face, a head exploding emoji—which I hope means his mind was blown by something and not that he actually saw someone's head explode—and a face with stars in the eyes.

Now I'm sitting at the counter, picking at my pancakes at seven a.m., and wondering if I can sneak up to his apartment without Bruce noticing because I really want to know more about why and how Alex had gone to work with Josh.

And maybe kiss Alex in a way that the public shouldn't see.

"What are you doing here?"

I look over as Ruth climbs up on the stool next to me.

"Having breakfast. Why is that weird?" I ask. Very *not* nonchalantly.

She grins. "Because it's super early and you never get pancakes during the week. You only get yogurt or smoothies," she says, setting her school backpack on the stool next to her.

Thea drops Ruth off here for breakfast every morning on her way to her physical therapy clinic, and Ruth either walks with her friends from here or Harley comes over and gives them a ride.

"I get pancakes sometimes." I take a bite. "I love pancakes."

"But they take too long on a weekday. You only get them on the weekends."

Bruce comes through the door from the kitchen with Ruth's breakfast. "She's been here for half an hour already," he tells her, setting down her omelet and toast.

"You were here at six thirty?" she asks, jumping off her stool to go behind the counter to pour a glass of juice.

"So? I come in early sometimes," I say.

Bruce is writing on two sticky notes. "But only when you have a really good reason."

"Maybe I do."

"I'm sure you do," he agrees. "But he's not up there."

"Where is..." I stop myself. "Who?" I ask. But it's obviously too late.

Bruce actually grins as he leans over the counter and affixes the sticky notes to the stands for the day's straw poll.

What's more fun? Early morning fishing. Watching the Revelers and Rascals play hockey?

I lift wide eyes to my step-grandfather. "It's not even a question about Alex today?"

He points at the note about the hockey teams. "I'd say that's about him, at least partly."

I smile. "Yes, it is." He's definitely a part of the teams, and how fun it is to watch them.

"He left with Quinn about ten minutes before you came in," he says.

I'm not going to keep pretending that I don't know what he's talking about. "He left with *Quinn*? What for?"

"He's going to work with her for a bit," Bruce says, lifting a shoulder. "She's doing some landscaping over at the Carpenters' place."

"He texted me at two a.m.!" I exclaim. "He was out working with Josh."

"I know," Bruce says.

"They were at a fire seven miles west of Bad," Gerald Collins calls out.

"I thought it was north of Bad," Matthew Winters says.

"It was north of Autre," Lisa Higgins says.

I shake my head. The location of the *fire* that my sheltered, grumpy hockey player went to with Josh last night doesn't really matter. "That means he hardly got any sleep!" I exclaim.

Bruce shrugs. "You know Quinn likes to go out early."

She does, and getting the manual outdoor work done before it gets oppressively hot makes sense most of the year, and I know Quinn likes to keep her schedule the same, even though this time of year the temps are much more bearable during the day.

"Why is he going to work with all of these people anyway?" I ask, bewildered.

"I'm not sure, but people love it." Ruth holds out her phone.

I focus on the screen. It's Alex's social media account on one of the major platforms. The photo makes my stomach flip. He's so damned good-looking. And that grin... I actually feel my body tingle a little just looking at how happy he looks.

He's also holding a kitten.

Oh. My. God.

The smile. The big hands cupped around that sweet, tiny fluffy baby. Just seeing him in a different, "regular" setting, not a hockey stick in sight. It all combines to make me feel a little hot in the clothes I'm wearing. Like I need to take a few of them off.

Yeah, I think this feeling is definitely swooning.

Ruth swipes to another photo. In this one, he's sitting in a fire truck with a fire hat on, looking like a little boy who got to see a real fire truck for the first time. In the next photo, he's standing next to Josh, who is in his firefighter's uniform and has soot on his face. Alex has his arm around Josh's shoulders, and they're both grinning.

I take the phone so I can read the caption.

This guy goes to work every day ready to run into burning buildings. I go to work every day ready to slap a puck around on the ice. We are not the same.

I smile at the use of words I said to him that first day.

But I also feel my throat tighten. He's clearly impressed by and appreciative of Josh off the ice.

I know he went to work with Beckett, helping with deliveries yesterday. Last night I heard a few people in the Rec talking about having him show up with Beckett, and Sutton told me that he'd told Beckett he wanted to do it again.

And now he's hanging out with Quinn.

He's getting to know his teammates. Even the players on the Rascals.

The latest photo is of him and Quinn both pushing wheelbarrows of bricks.

This woman doesn't need a weight room. I have a feeling I'm going to be sore tomorrow!

Ruth takes the phone back and swipes again. "Here's what he's doing." She shows me the screen.

Take Alex To Work.

I laugh. "What?"

"He's going to work with everyone who's on the hockey teams," Ruth says with a grin. She swipes to a new screen and hands the phone over.

This is just a photo of Alex in jeans, a Rebel Revelers T-shirt, and a grin.

My heart flips over in my chest.

I'm a hockey player. That's all I've ever been. And I've always been surrounded by hockey players. Guys who were lucky enough to play professional hockey. And trust me, luck plays a huge part in making the pros. But I got lucky again. I now get to play hockey in Rebel, Louisiana, for a whole new league. And I'm playing with a bunch of people who do a hell of a lot more than just hockey. These people <u>really</u> love this game. How do I know? They have to make time for it. They have to squeeze it in between work, kids, taking care of their houses, cars, families, and communities. They all have a lot more going on than just slapping a puck around the ice. But they still make it happen because they love it that much.

They know what I do for a living. Now I want to know what they do. It's Take Alex To Work! I'm going to hang out with these awesome people and really see what their lives are like off the ice. I have a feeling I have a lot to learn.

My eyes are stinging by the time I'm done.

"Oh my God." I look up at Ruth. "This post has a hundred and five thousand likes."

She nods. "He's got a huge following. You should read the comments. People love this."

I scan through.

First responders deserve all of our respect! Good for you!

This is hilarious! The rich, cocky pro athlete hauling lumber! Don't get a splinter, pretty boy!

Awesome! Our blue-collar workers rock!

Where is this new team????

You're in Louisiana?! How did I not know that!

How can we get tickets???!!!

Women in hockey! Yes, please! More of this!

Love it when rich, privileged people realize that regular people exist.

Why don't you just share some of your money with these teammates so they don't have to work backbreaking jobs?

Maybe they love their jobs?! I love mine. Yes, it's hard work, but I love it and I wouldn't change it.

I'm a firefighter. Thanks for the shout-out from one of my favorite players.

And they go on and on.

"This is really good," I say softly.

"It is. It's good for Alex, too," Ruth says. "He seems to really be enjoying it, and it's good for him to get to know the other players, right?"

"Of course." My mind is spinning.

Alex has always only ever seen himself as a hockey player. His family, his country, hell, the sports world, even some clothing companies, and a sports drink company have only ever seen him as a hockey player. Interviewers have asked him about his favorite things, his habits, have photographed his apartment, but even then he hasn't told them his *actual* favorite movie. He wears clothes other people send him. He abides by a schedule other people set for him.

Is it possible that the first time the world around him has been...more? The first time the people around him have cared about *him* as a person so it's the first time he's really let himself be more?

I realize that yes, that's possible.

I pull my phone out and immediately follow him on all the social media platforms.

Then I text him. *I know you're probably going to need a nap this afternoon, but later I HAVE to see you.*

I'm surprised, and pleased, to get a reply within a minute.

Ditto.

That's followed by another message a second later.

But I have to help Beckett with some deliveries. And then practice.

I grin. Alex is busy. In Rebel. And not entirely with hockey.

Nora: *I'll wait up for you.* *winky face*

Alex: *If you don't, I know my way to your bedroom.*

Goosebumps break out over my skin, and I contemplate pretending I've already gone to bed.

CHAPTER 27
ALEX

I KNOCK but then let myself into Nora's house because, of course, the door isn't locked. We really do need to talk about that.

She rounds the corner from the kitchen as I shut the door behind me, immediately kicking off my shoes, then heading straight for her.

"I'm sorry I'm even later than I expected. I got to talking to Teddy about going to work with him later this week."

She gives me a beautiful, soft smile. "I don't mind, Alex."

"Well, I kind of do." I don't stop until I'm standing nearly on top of her. "I wanted to see you all day."

"Same."

I lift my hand and cup the side of her face, pushing my fingers into her silky hair and loving the way she presses her cheek into my palm. But I frown, heart suddenly pounding as I think about what she said. She wanted to see me all day? That doesn't sound like Nora. "Are you okay? Did something happen? Fuck, I'm sorry I haven't been around. Is everything—"

She squeezes my wrist. "Everything is great. Really great. I love what you've been doing."

I pause. "You do? What do you mean?"

"I love that you've been going to work with everyone and

posting about it. Your posts are amazing and the comments are…awesome."

I'm having a great time, but it's blowing up quickly, and I haven't talked to Nora about it at all. "You've seen the social media posts?"

"Yes. I'm following you everywhere now."

That pleases me more than I would have expected. I grin. "Today was especially good. I mean, the kitten got *a lot* of likes, but people are so into these women doing jobs like this and playing hockey, they're all over my comments. They want to meet Ingrid next and she said she's in. I don't even know what she does."

"She's a cosmetologist and tattoo artist."

I pause. "She's a tattoo artist?" That's very cool. And actually seems fitting for Ingrid now that I think about it.

Nora nods. "She's really talented. And does amazing piercings too. And, of course, can do anything with hair. She's also incredible with nails."

"She'll be so fun to go to work with," I say with a grin. Then I study Nora's face. "Maybe you should let us tattoo you the day I'm there."

Her grin is sly. "Hmm…I could maybe be convinced of that."

Oh fuck, I like that. I like the idea of Nora getting a tattoo. Something small and sweet and in a place where I'm the only one who will ever see it. A sun. Or an otter. No…a wildflower.

I wonder if I can talk her into three tattoos.

"And Teddy is so excited to talk about LGBTQ rep in hockey when I go to work with him. And I want to encourage people to start looking at leagues closer to them, the smaller leagues. I'd love it if people really discovered local hockey, you know? Maybe start something if they don't have one."

Nora nods as she steps back. "I love that. Those are amazing ideas." She unzips the light gray hoodie she's wearing.

"And after the kitten posts blew up, I was thinking I could also maybe do something with animal rescues? Like cats and dogs.

After I go to work with all the players on our teams, I was thinking I could just keep doing that… going to work at different jobs I know nothing about. Which is basically every job except hockey." I stop and shrug. "That's maybe dumb. I might be the only person who has never really thought about all of that."

I watch as she toes off the slippers she's wearing, kicking them toward the door. "I'm sure you're not. We all tend to take some things for granted, like the people around us doing jobs we depend on. I think it's great to focus on the jobs that make communities work."

"You do? I mean, it's just a small thing I can do, but my followers seem into it so far."

Nora laughs as she pulls on the drawstring holding up the loose cotton lounge pants she's wearing. "Some small thing? You have one point five million followers, Alex."

I grin. Then she pulls a condom out of her pocket and drops her pants.

Now she's in only a fitted V-neck baby blue T-shirt and a tiny pair of pale blue panties.

"Wildflower?"

"Yeah?"

"What are you doing?"

"Taking my clothes off."

"I hope you realize that if you keep that up, you're going to end up with a very big, wound-up, obsessed-with-you hockey player between those pretty thighs. And he's not going to be leaving for hours."

She pulls her lip between her teeth and then slips her T-shirt over her head.

Her gorgeous bare tits bounce softly as she tosses her shirt and drops her arms. "You are so hot right now. I want you so much."

"You do?" I've just been rambling.

"Of course. I do anyway, but this? You, passionate and happy? Dammit, Alex, I just need to be naked and against you."

Fuck, that does something to me.

I haven't felt this excited about anything in a long time. Even hockey. Hockey has been a grind for a while. Trying to rehab, trying to get back, knowing I'm letting my team and the fans down, accepting the end of my career with the Grays. Now I'm here and…I'm lighter and more optimistic and yes, happier, than I have been in a very long time.

I give her a grin. "It's almost like I started my own club."

She moans. "That's some pretty potent dirty talk."

I laugh. "You are chaos and sunshine, and fuck, you make me so damned happy, Wildflower."

Her gaze softens. "That means a lot to me. And you have no idea how hot you are when you're *happy*, Alex. I mean, I love seeing you getting to know your teammates, seeing what they do, talking about them online, publicly building them up, and getting your fans involved with the Revelers and Rascals, but it's how happy *you* are, that makes me just…hot."

That hits me low. I'm immediately ready to put her up against the nearest firm surface. But I need a fucking shower. "I—"

She steps forward. Then drops to her knees.

I'm just stunned enough that her hands get my jeans unbuttoned before I haul her to her feet. "No," I say firmly.

"I want to. Let me." She strokes her hand up and down my hard cock. "Let me have you in my mouth."

Jesus, my knees almost buckle.

"Oh, Wildflower, you're going to have it." I haul her over my shoulder and start for the stairs.

"Now, Alex!"

"After I shower," I tell her, my hand on her ass as I carry her to the bathroom. "Or *in* the shower. We can discuss."

"You haven't showered?"

How did she not notice? "I wanted to get over here right away."

"But you had to know I would want to get naked with you!" she says as I set her down on the bathroom counter.

I like that she's so needy now that we've been naked together.

"Okay, greedy girl. You'll get what you need. But that's exactly why I figured I could shower here. With you. And not waste my time at the arena or stopping at home." I strip my shirt over my head. "I just didn't realize you'd be so riled up and horny."

She wiggles on the counter. "You've been grinning and happy and being amazing *all day*. I've been basically fangirling over you online, remembering all the things you did to me last night, and you didn't expect me to want to climb you when you walked through my door?"

I laugh. I can't help it. I'm just so fucking *happy*. I've had a great couple of days with the other hockey players. My social media accounts have awakened. And this incredible, gorgeous, big-hearted woman is willing to get naked with me. How could things be any better?

Nora starts shifting side to side, slipping her panties over her hips and down her legs, and dropping them on the floor. She's also still got that condom gripped in her hand.

I lean back, taking in the sight. "You're so fucking pretty."

"I'm also so ready for you."

She reaches for me, but I step back quickly. I can't get up close until I shower off.

"So ready, huh? You've been thinking about all the things you want me to do to you?"

She nods.

"Like what?" I would love to hear this sweet woman, who is made of sunshine and sugar, tell me some very filthy things.

"I'd really like to feel your tongue on my clit again," she says without batting an eye.

It might kill me to hear these things, but I *need* more.

"That can definitely be arranged. What else?"

"I love your hands and your big fingers, anywhere actually, but especially deep inside me."

"Also definitely on the agenda." I step back, pull the shower door open, then lean to turn on the water. "Will you be a good girl and sit here and wait while I take a quick shower?"

She bites her bottom lip and shakes her head.

I huff out a laugh. "I need to get some of the stink off. I intend to be very up close with you, and I know you'll appreciate it."

"Why can't I get in there with you?"

I face her again, unzipping my pants. "You can. Give me five minutes."

"I don't know if I can wait five more minutes. You've been going around this town, charming everyone all day. You've been online making my town and all the people here, and this new hockey league look amazing." She reaches up and cups my face between her hands. "I love seeing you like this. Involved. Interacting. Smiling."

"Don't you understand that you are a huge part of that?" I ask, shoving my pants and underwear to the floor and kicking them away.

"I hope so. I want that to be true."

I lean in and capture her lips in a sweet kiss, not letting it get too deep. Not yet. "You're the reason for all of it, Wildflower. You make everything good."

"Alex," she says softly, her eyes filled with emotion.

I back away from her, keeping my eyes on her as I step inside the shower. I reach for the soap, but the sweet sunshine sitting on the bathroom counter suddenly turns into a naughty devil. She props one heel on the counter, giving me a gorgeous view of her bare pussy, then slides a hand along her upper thigh.

I groan. "Nora, be good."

"Oh, I think you think I'm *very* good," she says as she circles her clit with her middle finger.

I scrub the bar of soap that smells like Nora over my body, ducking my head under the shower spray, letting the hot water run down, rinsing off.

When I look over again, she has two fingers sliding in and out of the pussy I know I will never get over.

I throw the door open. "Mine," I growl. I grab her wrist and pull her fingers to my mouth. I suck on them slowly, making sure to get every bit of her on my tongue.

Her pupils dilate, and her mouth falls open. Her nipples are hard, and she wiggles on the counter. I reach up and tweak one nipple, then slide my hand between her legs and push my middle finger into her tight, hot cunt.

I pull her fingers from my mouth as she moans.

"*Mine*," I repeat.

I'm dripping all over the bathroom floor, but neither of us seems to care. I pump my finger in and out. "You do feel ready for me, though."

She nods her head quickly.

"Good thing. Because you blew it."

Before she can say anything, I scoop her up off the counter. She gasps and laughs, wrapping her legs around me as I press her against my slippery skin. I step back into the shower and move her underneath the shower spray.

She tips her head so the water will run down her back. I gather her hair in one fist, keeping her head angled so that I can kiss up the column of her throat, then nip her jaw before growling in her ear, "Now you're just going to get fucked against the shower wall instead of having my very talented tongue between your legs."

She whimpers. "I'm sorry. Please put your tongue between my legs."

"If you had been good and just sat there like I asked, then I would've happily eaten you out and—" I add, licking along her jaw before nipping her earlobe. "Let you suck on your very favorite cock. But you had to play with my pussy. Now I need to remind you of who gets to make it feel good."

I feel her thighs tighten around me. But she still says, "That's very possessive of a body part that actually belongs to someone else."

I shift my hips, and my cock slides through her wetness, the firm length pressing against her clit. "I claimed it. No one else will ever love it as much as I do. Or make it feel the way I do." I shift back and forward again, sliding over that sweet nub and making her moan. "Not even you and your fingers or all the toys in the world." I shift again, eliciting another sweet moan. "Right, Wildflower?"

"Alex," she says breathlessly.

"Say I'm right. Tell me that this pussy will never be fully satisfied in any other way."

Her eyes open, and her gaze locks on mine. I feel the impact deep in my gut.

"You're right," she says.

Fuck. I am never getting over this woman.

In that moment, I just accept my fate.

"Condom," I say shortly.

She still has it grasped tightly in one hand, and she opens her fist, but I can't let go of her ass or she'll slide to the floor. Sensing the situation, she holds it up while I tear it open, and together we roll the condom down my achingly hard length.

"Just remember," I say, sliding a hand between her lower back and the shower wall to provide cushion as I press her against the tiles. "You could be spread out on the bed, nice and comfortable, but instead you're going to feel every thrust—" I slide deep and we both moan. "As I fuck—" I slide out. "You." Thrust. "Deep." Thrust. "And." Thrust. "Hard."

"Oh, *God*," she moans, fingers digging into my shoulders and thighs clenching around me.

"One fast dirty one, Wildflower," I say through gritted teeth. "Then I'll take you slow and deep."

Her pussy grips me, and I thrust again, pressing her into my hand against the wall.

"I *love* how you make me feel, Alex," she says, panting the words.

And I love *that*. I pick up the pace, dragging in and out of that hot silk, knowing that I'm the luckiest son of a bitch in the world.

"Oh, *yes!*" She comes, her sweet pussy clamping down, ripping my orgasm out of me as I shout her name.

"Fuck, Nora!"

I crush my mouth to hers, and she opens, her fingers sliding into my hair, holding me close.

We kiss hungrily, as if we didn't both just come hard and fast, as I shut off the water and carry her into the bedroom. I rip back the duvet and then tip us both onto the sheets, still buried deep.

With her beneath me, wrapped around me, I kiss her for what seems like hours. I can't get enough of her. I want to melt into her and never leave.

Finally, her strokes up and down my back slow, our kisses become lazier, and I lower myself to the mattress beside her, rolling so I can pull off the condom, tie the end, and drop it into the wastebasket by her bed. Then I pull the duvet over our cooling bodies, and Nora snuggles in close.

I kiss the top of her head and take a deep breath.

"Just so you know, Wildflower, I've never been happier," I tell her.

I hear her little intake of air and feel the way she presses even closer to me. "God, you really do know how to talk dirty to me, Alex Olsen."

CHAPTER 28
ALEX

THE NEXT MORNING, I'm knocking on Astrid's door again just after four-thirty a.m.

She opens the door. "Is this going to be a regular thing?"

"Bruce mentioned getting me a key when I was out late at the fire with Josh," I say. "I'll remind him of it today."

She steps back, letting me in, and we head toward the kitchen.

"I guess I don't mind. It's nice to have time to talk to you," she says. Then she yawns. "Though later in the day would be nice." She starts preparing our cups of tea. "I absolutely love what you're doing, by the way. Ticket sales keep growing, but that's not the only reason."

"Can you be more specific?" I ask with a smile.

"The take Alex to work stuff," she says. "Brilliant. Your social media hasn't been this active in months."

I nod but shift in my chair. My sisters are both incredibly impressive women, and I have always wanted and worked for their approval. "You really like it?"

"Absolutely. Not only is it getting you back in front of your fans, but it's highlighting what you're doing here in Louisiana. It's perfect."

"It's really about the other people. And I wonder if it's a little silly. Most people probably already know what firefighters and landscapers do."

She turns back to me with a thoughtful look. "Well, first, I don't think anyone ever knows completely what someone else does at work. It's great to see all the details and behind the scenes. And even if we do know what they do, it's fantastic to highlight it, and remind people how important the people around them are and that the jobs they do really matter."

Nora said something similar.

"But it's not just about those people or the jobs they're doing," she says.

The kettle whistles, and she pours water into two mugs before bringing them to the table.

"What do you mean?"

"It's about you."

I frown. "I'm just a hockey player who is willing to admit that he has been a little selfish and self-absorbed and hasn't really ever connected with people doing regular jobs."

She sets her mug down without taking a sip and nods. "Exactly."

"What?" I'm not following.

"That's what's so enchanting about it. Here you are, a rich, very successful, and talented professional athlete, and you're willing to not only admit that you've been incredibly privileged and cut off from the real world, but now you're not just trying to learn new things or highlight these people you've met, you're actually really into it." She smiles. "*You're* the draw here, Alex. Your genuine enthusiasm for being on these job sites and talking to these people is what is so charming."

"Come on," I scoff. "Beckett is filling a really important gap in the community. The kitten was cute all on his own. Quinn is a woman not only playing in a male-dominated sport, but also working in a male-dominated field for a female boss. Josh is a fucking hero. Period."

"Yes, of course, all of that is true. But it's your platform. How do you not see this? The people who are following you and following *this* because of you. And now you're using that platform to be vulnerable and funny and self-deprecating. You're letting them see what's happened since you got hurt and had to leave the pros. But you're not sitting around wallowing, you're not talking down about the lesser league, you're not making fun of small-town Louisiana. You're building it all up. You have never talked about your professional-athlete friends and teammates the way you're talking about these people."

I frown. "I didn't need to talk about them. They have their own following."

"Right. You're giving the small-town delivery guy, the landscaper, the teacher, the firefighter, the youth counselor all a spotlight they'd never have otherwise. It's fantastic."

I want all this to be true. "It's not like what you did after your injury. I mean, you became a fucking inspirational speaker. People follow you because you make them feel better about their lives."

Her eyebrows shoot up. "You haven't been reading the comments online, have you?"

"About me? No, not for several hours."

She grabs her phone. "It's not exactly the same, but you're using who you are and your position to talk to people, and to connect them with each other." She scrolls for a little bit on her screen, then stops and turns the phone toward me. "Look at these comments. Yes, they're impressed by Quinn, Josh, and Beckett. But look at this one. This guy is thanking you for getting his teenage son to ask him about *his* job. This one is saying that you put all the guys on his roofing crew in a better mood on the job today. This one says his little girl asked if she can go to work with him next week." She looks up. "People's jobs are a huge part of their lives, and you're making people feel good about their work. That's making their lives happier, too. You're doing that, Alex."

"I am?" I read through the comments, and sure enough, there are people thanking me.

"You do a job that is very public and that people get to come and watch. Hell, people *pay* to come and watch you work. It just feels great to have someone like you turn around and look at them and really see them."

"Wow, so this could be a good thing," I say. "I mean, I don't want to make money off of it or anything, but I do want to learn about how this works—how these towns and communities come together and help each other. As long as I'm doing that, sharing that seems like a good thing, right?"

Astrid grins at me. "It's a very good thing. And I love seeing you enjoying it too. That's what really matters. That's when using your platform means the most. When it's something you care about."

I smile. "Thanks."

"You're doing great. I'm proud of you."

My chest feels warm. "I appreciate that."

"And you'll host Sam at the crawfish boil before the game on Friday, right?"

"Sam?"

"From *Sam The Sportsman*. He wants to interview you. I told him yes, if he comes to Rebel and hangs out at the crawfish boil and goes to the game." She grins. "I want to give him the whole experience."

"You're accepting interview requests for me?"

"I'm your boss so…yes." She lifts her cup.

I've talked to Sam before. It's fine. "Okay, I'll do it. But I'm going to talk about the other players. And I want to pull Beckett or Ingrid in with me. They're from here. They can talk about the crawfish and tell him all about the swamp werewolves and stuff."

Astrid frowns and sips, then shakes her head. "I hear you. But I need you to be a hockey player for this. You're the big name. His listeners want to hear you."

I sigh. "But I want to do more."

"Like what exactly?"

"I'm not sure. Something."

She laughs. "You'll figure it out. You're using your platform to make people look at hockey differently, and it's making *you* look at it differently. Something will come from that. Something for you and for the fans."

"Does that matter?"

"What do you mean?"

"You are the queen of making things matter after they change."

She smiles softly. "Aw. Well, yes. I mean… loving hockey is the foundation, and you're focusing people on that by focusing on these regular people who are playing and watching hockey here versus the glitz and glamor of the pros. And I think it's helping you look at hockey differently, too."

I think she might be right. "Thanks."

"But you'll do the thing with Sam? And be the big shot hockey player he wants to interview."

I chuckle. "Yeah. Okay. I'll hang out with Sam."

"Thank you."

I pull my phone out, realizing that I haven't looked at it since I showed up at Nora's hours ago. I want to check in on a couple of other platforms, too.

But I frown when I see my screen.

I tap to open my text messages, then look up at my sister. "I have five missed calls and eight texts sitting here from your husband."

Astrid frowns. She sits forward. "What? What about?"

"Something with the Grays," I say, skimming the texts. Mostly they just say *call me, call me immediately, I need to talk to you,* and *team emergency.*

My stomach is in a knot as I press the voicemail button.

Astrid listens to the first message with me.

Her eyes get wider and wider and my heart sinks further and further.

The ones that follow are simply, "Call me", "Call me back, goddamit", "Fucking call me".

My sister sums it all up perfectly when she finally sits back in her chair and says, "Well… shit."

CHAPTER 29
NORA

ALEX: *Need to see you.*

I smile the stupid, goofy, falling-in-love smile that I'm sure has been on my face on and off all day when I read Alex's text.

I need to see him too. I need to kiss him. At least.

Nora: *On my way to the park for otter club, actually. You're invited!*

Alex: *damn. I can't resist that. Can we talk there?*

Nora: *Of course. Otherwise, you can have me all to yourself tonight.*

I'm, of course, hoping that he wants me all to himself tonight anyway.

We obviously can't make out heavily at the park, but I can definitely get a kiss. Or three. The town thinks we're dating anyway, and just because this is all starting to feel a lot more real is no reason to hold back now. I wanted to kiss him before, and now that we've slept together, I can barely think about anything else.

Alex: *See you soon.*

Okay, he can't wait until tonight to see me either. That makes me feel warm and melty.

"Heading to the park if you need me," I say to Sutton as I pass her desk. All of my supplies for otter club are already in the wagon out front.

"Sounds good. Let me know if you need anything," she says.

"Alex is stopping by," I tell her with a smile. "He can be my assistant if I need anything."

She gives me a wink. "Oh, I'm sure he can provide all kinds of things you need. Just don't get too distracted. Someone needs to keep things organized."

I laugh with her. Otter club is arguably one of our more chaotic clubs. I doubt very much if anyone participating or observing would think there was anything organized about it.

Even though I walk the three blocks from City Hall to the park, pulling my wagon of supplies, I still get there before Alex. But plenty of people are already gathered.

"Hi, Nora," Greg and Donna greet.

"Hi, you two. Here you go," I say, handing over one of the small, bright yellow canvas tote bags from the cart.

They take it and head across the park to a bench.

"Hi, Nora, how are you?" Marilyn Walker asks as I hand her a bag.

"I'm great. How are you? Is your ankle feeling better?"

She picks up her foot and rotates it. "A little better every day." She heads off for one of the picnic tables, where she'll be joined shortly by a couple of her friends after they pick up their bags.

I hand out five more bags before I notice Alex striding across the grass. I give him a little wave, which he returns. He stops several feet away, just observing. I continue handing out the tote bags to the people who formed the short line in front of me, greeting each of them and exchanging small talk before they disperse throughout the park.

Finally, it's just Alex and me. There are three bags left. I grab the handle of the wagon and start for a bench under one of the trees near the stream. "Come on, we can sit over here," I tell him.

He falls into step next to me, taking the handle of the wagon from me and linking his fingers with my free hand as we walk. It's silly, but my stomach flips over at the casual way he touches me.

We settle onto a bench, and I hand over one of the tote bags. He looks inside, then gives me the quizzical glance that I'm expecting.

"What is this about?"

I laugh and pull an item out of my bag. It's a mini screwdriver. I also have a small bunch of dried flowers, and a biodegradable plastic bag with sardines inside. Alex withdraws a mini flashlight, a used-up toilet paper tube, and a small package of dry cat food from his bag.

"All you have to do is set the bag on the ground, kind of over to the side where it looks like it belongs to you, but you're not really paying attention to it." I do exactly that with my bag, setting it on the end of the bench, then crossing my legs and angling my body away from the bag.

He sets his on the ground just under the bench, then turns to me.

"This is otter club?"

I grin and nod. "Wait for it." I point to the bench where Greg and Donna are sitting. An otter is already approaching the yellow bag sitting next to their bench.

The otter rummages inside the bag, finds an item, pulls it out, then scampers off toward the bank of the stream where its den is located.

"What is this?" Alex says with a chuckle.

"Our otters are pickpockets," I tell him, watching for his reaction.

His grin grows, and he meets my gaze. "Really?"

"Really. They used to steal things out of bags, purses, backpacks, whatever they could get into. Anything that got set down for too long. Even lunch bags. So, besides warning everyone not to bring bags that are easily opened to the park, and certainly not to leave them unattended, we've trained the otters that these yellow bags are fair game. Each bag has a few little items in it—some things they can mess with, some just junk that they'll play with and then will biodegrade, and some food. But the otters can take whatever they want. They take the stuff back to their dens and hoard it."

I laugh at the look on Alex's face. It's a mix of bewilderment and delight.

"And they can actually tell the difference between these bags and just regular duffel bags or purses?"

"Well, if you bring a bag to the park and leave it somewhere and walk off, you're going to get something stolen," I say. "But over time we've trained the otters that the yellow bags are for them."

"And these same otters have just stayed here?"

"Well, there are new ones, of course, from time to time. But the ones that have been around teach the new ones. They especially like shiny things, and seemingly things with switches and buttons. Like the little flashlight."

Out of the corner of my eye, I see an otter start to approach us.

"Do we need to stay really still?" Alex asks quietly.

I shake my head and laugh, looking over at the animal. "They're pretty used to all of us being around. They don't get spooked easily."

We watch as the otter opens the bag and reaches inside. He first pulls out the screwdriver and seems very interested, but then replaces it and takes out the fish instead. He scampers off as I laugh.

"They do most often go for food. But not always."

"Do you find stuff scattered around?" Alex asks.

I nod. "For sure. And floating in the stream, since a lot of their burrows are right along the banks. We just gather it up and then use it again some other time."

He sighs, and the sound is almost sad. I look up at him. "Are you okay?"

He looks at me for a long moment. "I have become very fond of this little town. And I have a feeling there's a lot more to learn about it."

I nod. "All of the holidays are a big deal here. Just wait for

Halloween. And *Christmas*. We do an annual Christmas competition in town called Merry Mayhem. It's three days long and involves an obstacle course, a relay race, and several other little contests. It's a ton of fun."

He blows out a breath. "I need to tell you something."

My smile immediately dies. His tone of voice and expression both tell me that I'm not going to like whatever this is. I turn on the bench to face him, pulling one leg up and tucking it under the other.

"What happened?"

"Declan called me last night. While I was with you. Several times. I only had a chance to talk to him this morning."

I reach out and rest my hand on his arm. His muscles bunch under my touch. "What's going on?"

"One of the assistant coaches for the Grays was arrested last night."

I can feel my eyes go wide. "*Arrested*?"

"Yeah. By the FBI."

"Oh…wow."

"He was involved in a huge sports gambling ring. There are people from a lot of sports involved. It's kind of shaking up professional sports."

I nod. "I can imagine. I'm sure Declan's pretty pissed."

"Very. And worried about the team."

"Understandable."

"Their opening game is on Thursday."

And I instantly know what's happening. "And he offered you the job," I say, without adding a question mark.

Alex rubs his palms up and down his thighs. "Yes. Not only am I able to step in immediately, but he thinks it will help calm the players and the fans. And it will give the press something else to talk about. I know the playbook, all the players, the other coaches. It would be a very easy transition."

My heart is kicking against my ribs so hard it hurts. My head feels a little dizzy. My stomach is in a knot. But still I say, "That makes sense." Because it does. Of course, Declan needs Alex to come back. "When do you need to leave?" I ask, happy that my voice wavers only slightly.

He looks genuinely torn up as he meets my gaze. "This afternoon."

I feel like he just reached into my chest, grabbed my heart, and squeezed.

I try to take a deep breath, but can't force air into my lungs because my chest is too tight.

"Oh," is all I can manage.

"I'm so fucking sorry, Wildflower," he says, his shoulders slumping. "We were supposed to have more time."

He's going to miss the Revelers' first game, too. Opening night is Friday.

I don't know what to say or do. I want to tell him that I'm falling for him. But that isn't fair. And what good would that do anyway?

"This is what you wanted," I tell him. "It's what you were hoping for. It's good that it's happening even sooner, isn't it?"

He drags in a deep breath. "It doesn't feel good."

"It's still sinking in," I tell him. "As soon as you're back in Portland, it will all feel… perfect."

I stumble slightly over that word. I don't think Portland is perfect for him. He was alone there. Oh, the city loved him, he had teammates, everyone knew who he was. But I don't think anyone *knew* him. He was a hockey player there. But there's so much more to him. And I think even Alex is just now figuring that out.

Still, I force a smile. "You'll get right back to your usual routines. It will feel natural in no time." I clear my throat. "I mean, that's home."

I hate the way my voice breaks a little bit on that last word.

He frowns. "Yeah. That makes sense."

"How much time do you have?" I ask. There's only one thing that I really want to do right now.

"Declan is sending his plane for me," Alex says, giving me a sheepish smile. That quickly fades. "I just have a few hours. Enough time to pack up some things—Astrid is going to send everything that I don't need right away—and say goodbye to some people. I want to tell the team myself if I can."

I nod. I like that he wants to see everyone in person and explain. But I need him for about an hour.

"I think you should do that," I say. "But can we go to my house for a little bit?"

His eyes search my face. I don't want him to wonder what I'm talking about, so I shift, sliding into his lap and straddling his thighs. I take his face in my hands and kiss him.

He groans, his hands going to my hips, fingers digging in as if he's trying to hold onto me.

I kiss him deeply, then lift my head. "I need you. One more time."

He swallows hard and nods. "I'm yours."

I almost sob at that. Oh, how I wish that were true.

"Let's go," I say, sliding off his lap and standing.

He looks around. "Is the club over?"

It's not, but I'm going to do something that I have never ever done before.

I'm going to leave one of my clubs early.

NEITHER OF US wants to rush. I might have expected him to throw the door open, carry me through it, and press me up against the wall. Or bend me over the couch. Or even spread me out on the table, not even bothering to go to the bedroom.

All of those images make my body heat and my pulse thump. But Alex doesn't do any of that. He doesn't seem in a hurry at all.

I push the door open, and we both step inside, taking off our shoes, then he links our fingers together and leads me up the staircase toward the bedroom.

Next to the bed, we stop and he cups my face, dragging his thumb over my lower lip.

"I feel like I've been here so much longer than I have. So much has happened."

I know exactly what he means. "It also feels like you just got here yesterday."

He nods. "Maybe it will never feel like it's long enough."

Okay, I can *not* let him say things like that. It's already breaking my heart that he's leaving. And not in the same way as the other guys who've left. This was always the plan for one thing. But I can also sense his hesitation. I think part of it is that he feels that he's disappointing me. I also think he might have some reasons he'd like to stay.

That makes this harder than saying goodbye to the others. They wanted to go.

I know once Alex is in Portland, he'll be happy. That's his turf. Coaching for the Grays will be second nature. He'll be able to walk into coffee shops all over the city and be welcomed. There will definitely not be straw polls declaring that Brussels sprouts are better than Alex Olsen.

Still, I like that he's not racing out of town.

"I was going to wear one of your Revelers jerseys, but I can't buy a Grays jersey with your number on it now," I say. "What do people do when they have a crush on one of the coaches?"

He makes a little growling noise back in his throat. "I'm going to send you one of my old jerseys. As long as it has my last name on it, you can definitely wear it."

Dammit, I can't let him talk about that stuff either. That sounds intimate, possessive. Almost girlfriend-like.

That will be over when he gets to Portland, too.

I don't know that there's anything safe to talk about. We can't talk about him leaving, or I might end up crying. If we talk about his time here in Rebel, it will make saying goodbye harder. If we talk about anything sweet or funny, I might do something stupid and tell him that I'm falling in love with him.

So instead, I kiss him.

He happily, greedily, dives into a kiss with me.

His hand slides up into my hair, cupping the back of my head, his fingers tightening in the strands so that he can angle my head the way he wants it as his tongue strokes in along mine.

I wrap my arms around his neck and arch my body into his, needing to be closer.

He tears his mouth away and looks down at me. "Why are we standing up with clothes on when we could be lying down naked?"

"That is a very good question," I say as I start tugging at the T-shirt he's wearing.

He strips my Parks and Rec polo over my head, unhooking my bra and tossing it to the side before stopping to help yank his shirt over his head.

Our hands bump as we each reach for the other's pants.

I laugh and take a step back. "You do yours, I'll do mine."

"Hurry up," he tells me, his eyes hot as I unbutton, unzip, and push everything down my legs.

He does the same, and a moment later, we tumble onto the mattress together.

"I need to taste you," he tells me, braced on his forearms above me. Our noses are nearly touching. "I need to kiss every inch of you, then I want to fuck you deep and slow with you spread wide open for me, taking everything I can give you. That's how I want to think about you when I'm not here."

I swallow. "You can have whatever you want," I tell him honestly.

He starts at my lips, kissing me deeply again, slowly, almost leisurely. Then he kisses his way down my neck over both collarbones, down between my breasts, before he pauses on each, taking several minutes to tease each nipple.

My hands are tangled in his hair, and I'm breathing hard. "I thought you wanted time to say goodbye to everybody else."

"Everybody else who?" he asks against my left breast.

"The team, the other players."

"I have no idea what you're talking about," he says." The only thing that exists for me right now is you and this sweet body that I am forever addicted to. "

"I just don't want you to regret—"

He lifts his head. "Wildflower."

"Yeah?" My nipples are tingling, and my pussy is aching.

"This is where I want to be. Where I *need* to be. Everyone, *everything*, else can wait."

God, I should *not* let him talk. It's killing me slowly. I bob my head up and down. "Okay. I just don't—"

He growls again. "Clearly, I need to work a little harder on getting you out of your head. I don't want you to be thinking about anyone or anything else but me and my magical mouth."

I grin. "I promise you're doing a great job."

"Well, there's a difference between great and mind-blowing."

His hot mouth travels down the center of my torso, and he settles between my thighs, and I don't think about a single other thing for the next forty-five minutes.

After, we lie together, completely spent, for nearly twenty minutes without saying anything. My head is tucked under his chin, he has one hand on my ass, the other is stroking up and down my back. I have one leg draped over his, my hand on his stomach. We're pressed together, touching everywhere we can.

I know that when he gets up and leaves, even if he makes other stops in town before heading to the airport, this is goodbye for us.

Finally, he speaks. "Would you come to Portland? To visit me?"

Oh, God.

I wasn't expecting him to invite me to Portland. It's not the same as being asked to move there with him, of course, but I've given no thought to this at all. Of course, he wasn't supposed to be going to Portland so soon either. And I suppose that I thought by April... I don't know what I thought would happen by April. I wasn't thinking that far ahead. He just got here.

So how can I have feelings like this for him? It's too fast. It's been a whirlwind. He's only just started to settle in. And who knows if his good feelings about Rebel even would've lasted?

"I don't know, maybe," I say very noncommittally. "I am really busy. We have so many holidays coming up. And there's always... stuff."

That sounds completely pathetic.

He's quiet for a long moment, then nods. "Yeah, of course. I get it."

Thing is, I know he does get it. He understands my town, my family. Me.

He just got here, but he's had a full dose of what my life is like.

"I should get going," he says. "I really do want to say goodbye to some people, and I have to get on that plane."

He does. I know that. Of course he does.

"Good luck," I tell him as he sits up, disentangling our body parts. I swallow, hoping to keep my voice from sounding scratchy. "I hope Portland is everything that you want it to be." I mean that with all my heart. I want Alex to be happy.

I start to sit up, but he puts his hand against my chest. "Will you stay? Just here in bed like this? This is how I would love to remember you."

That sucks the air out of my lungs. He wants to remember me. That definitely sounds like I'm not going to see him again. But I still nod. "Okay."

He looks like he wants to say something else, but instead he bends and kisses me. Then he pushes up and gets dressed.

He stops in my bedroom doorway and looks back. "This was...amazing," he says. "And I don't mean just now. Not *just* just now. All of this. You. Rebel."

I know what he means. I give him a smile. "I'm glad." I swallow. "Take care of yourself, Alex. Please."

He just nods, then turns and leaves.

CHAPTER 30
ALEX

I DID NOT EXPECT the goodbye with Nora to go that way, but I regret nothing. All it means is that I am going to see all my teammates at Perks and Rec together, instead of stopping by to see each one individually.

But hell, that might be easier. Telling them goodbye as a group might be less emotional than one-on-one. Of course, I mean emotional for me. I don't expect any of them to be too broken up about it. I am definitely the one who's gotten attached. And as surprised as I am by how quickly that happened, I won't deny it.

I am going to miss these people.

I feel like I'm just getting to the point where I feel like I get it. That I might understand how I can fit here.

And that maybe ending up in small-town Louisiana playing bonkers hockey is not at all the worst thing that could have happened to me.

I walk through the door, now anticipating not only the tinkling bell but also the entire establishment turning to look at me.

This time, however, there is a chorus of, "Alex!" as the door shuts behind me.

I smile. "Hi, everyone."

"Come here, we have something for you," Patty says. She is standing near the coffee bar, waving me over with a huge grin.

I see that Beckett is sitting at the counter, as are Sutton and Andi. Everly, Ruth, and Thea are at one of the tables near the bakery case. Lawson is here with all the rest of the players.

I texted them all on my way to Nora's. I knew I would be there for a while and figured that would give them all a chance to get to the coffee shop if they wanted to. I'd had no expectations, but I feel my throat tighten when I realize that even Zeke and Josh came over from Autre.

But I hadn't told Bruce or Patty or anyone else in here that we were going to be meeting up.

As I draw closer to the coffee bar, I see six glass bowls sitting in a row.

"You have to try mine first," Patty says. "It's the classic. If all you've had is Nora's, you haven't even had the basic one to compare the rest to."

Of course, when someone says something about 'having Nora's' all I can think about are all the very inappropriate-for-the-coffee-shop things that I've had of Nora's that I very much enjoyed and want a lot more of.

There's a pain in my chest as I think about the fact that not only did I say goodbye to her today, but she also essentially told me that she won't be coming to Portland.

Of course, she won't. Her life is in this town. If she came to visit, what would that accomplish? Sure, we'd have some great sex and enjoy every second together, but it can't turn into anything. It wouldn't last. It would never go beyond long-distance fuck buddies.

And after a while, that would wear on us. We would both want more, and it would hurt to know that we couldn't have it.

"Alex?" Patty says. "Here." I focus and realize that she's holding out a small bowl to me. There's a spoon stuck in the bowl, and suddenly everything clicks.

What have I had of Nora's that isn't the classic?

This is banana pudding.

"What's going on?" I ask, accepting the bowl.

Sure enough, the bowl is full of pudding with sliced bananas, whipped cream, and crumbled vanilla cookies.

"It's a banana pudding buffet," Muriel says with a grin.

"This is all banana pudding?" I ask, eyeing the six bowls.

"Sure. There's all kinds," Muriel says. "And since you've come around, we decided that you should get to taste all of the best ones. So a bunch of people made you their recipes."

I look at Andi. She just shrugs. Then I look at Sutton.

She laughs. "I had nothing to do with this. Neither did Nora. This is all these ladies. I mean, Nora might've mentioned to me that you really liked her banana pudding, and I might have said something about that..."

"You didn't just make all of these just now, did you?" I ask, looking around.

Is this some kind of going-away party? Could they have found out? Did Astrid say something?

"Of course not. Banana pudding has to sit at least overnight," Patty says. "We planned to do this today before we found out that you were leaving."

So they do know about that.

"Who told you?" I asked, looking at Sutton.

"When Nora left the otter club early, people got concerned. They called me. She wasn't answering her phone, though, so, since everyone saw you leave with her, I called Astrid."

That all makes sense.

I look at my teammates. "Sorry. I wanted to tell you all."

"We get it," Beckett says. "You have to go. We all heard the news about the coach. It makes sense Declan would call you."

Yeah, Nora said that too.

And my brain knows that's true. And a piece of my heart is happy. This is what I wanted. This was the goal all along.

So why do I feel so fucking sad?

"Well, I am really glad you all have impeccable timing," I tell Patty. "If I'd missed this, I would've been really upset."

She smiles. "Now, don't eat too much of it, you have to taste each of the six."

I pretend to sigh heavily. "Well, if I have to, I have to."

I GET to my penthouse in Portland just before six p.m. West Coast time. I have just a few minutes before I need to get on the video call with Sam for his podcast.

I'd sent him a text earlier in the day telling him that there was a change of plans, and that we didn't need to talk about the Rebel Revelers anymore.

Sam had insisted he still wanted to talk.

I've been expecting that. The news of Coach Leon's arrest had shocked the hockey world, not just the Grays, and of course, a sports podcaster like Sam would want to talk it out. The fact that he had a past player and the guy who was going to be stepping into the coach's position made the interview all the juicier.

I run a hand through my hair, gulp down a glass of water, and check my reflection in the mirror.

I look pretty good.

That's what traveling by private plane instead of commercial will do for you.

I shake my head.

I had been dreading the flight even on a private plane. Astrid had even arranged for the plane to pick me up on the airstrip outside of Rebel, and the ride out there had felt heavier with each mile.

What the fuck is my problem?

I sigh and look around my apartment.

It is so *quiet* here. No muffled laughter and conversation drifting through the floorboards. No kitchen sounds coming up the steps. And it does not smell like cinnamon and coffee. There are also zero flowers on any of the upholstery. But instead of making things look better, I'm just struck by how lacking in color and how uninteresting my apartment is. Sure, it's sleek and modern. Expensive. And no one's died here. But the pieces have no history. There's no story behind any of them. There's no character.

Is it possible to buy a candle that will make the place smell like cinnamon rolls and coffee in the morning? Or hell, I could just get a coffee pot. I don't drink the stuff, but I could brew it to get the scent. Seems wasteful, but maybe I could give the coffee to my doorman.

The alarm on my phone chirps, and I realize I need to log in to the video call.

I settle into the extremely comfortable, buttery leather office chair at my desk, which faces a window overlooking downtown Portland.

The view is spectacular. And is just about as different from the view out my window in Rebel as I could possibly get.

Before I log in for the call, I fire off a quick text.

Alex: *do you think Bruce would let me have the lamp from the bedside table in the apartment?*

It's only a minute before Ruth replies. *He says he'll sell it to you. And he's not paying to ship it.*

I grin. *Astrid can send it with my other stuff. Ask him if a thousand is enough.*

Ruth: *wide-eyed emoji. That lamp is like fifty years old, and there's probably a dozen like it at the flea market.*

I laugh for the first time since leaving Perks and Rec earlier. *I want that one. It's sentimental.*

Ruth: *He says twelve hundred.*

Of course he did.

Alex: *I'll send it electronically right now.* I grin even as I hit send. There is no way Bruce has any money transfer apps.

Ruth: **laugh cry emoji* He wants cash.*

Jesus, I don't remember the last time I actually walked into a bank. But that will be hilarious. *That'll take me a day or so.*

Ruth: *No lamp before he sees the money.*

Exactly what I would have expected.

I want to keep texting with Ruth. Instead, I sigh and click on the link to connect to the video call with Sam.

"Hey, Alex!" Sam greets as the call connects.

"Hey, Sam."

"Thanks for agreeing to do the interview anyway. I know things have taken a turn."

"You could say that," I say. I lean in, resting my elbows on the desk. "And before we go any further, I just want to say one thing."

"Shoot."

"I will do this interview, and I will also promise you an exclusive with me after the first Grays game. On one condition."

"I'm listening."

"You still go to Rebel to the first hockey game on Friday. You still highlight the new league."

His eyebrows arch. "Really? That's important to you?"

"It's nonnegotiable. I won't do any more interviews with you at all if you don't show up in Rebel in two days."

Sam shrugs. "I've already got all of the travel plans made. Why not?"

I settle back into my chair. "Okay then, let's do this thing."

CHAPTER 31
NORA

I LAID in bed for about twenty minutes after Alex left, but I'm not really a napper or someone who lies around, so I eventually got up and showered. Then I checked my phone.

There was a group text from my girls.

Sutton: *hey, heard about Alex leaving. Are you okay?*

Thea: *what's going on?*

Sutton: *Alex got called to go back to Portland to coach.*

Thea: *oh shit. Nora, where are you?*

Andi: *I have a text from Alex that he wants everyone to meet down at Perks and Rec.*

Sutton: *I think he's going to say a mass goodbye.*

Thea: *oh I have that text too.*

Everly: *I plan to be there. Nora, will you be there?*

These were all sent before Alex and I even got to my house. He must've sent that group text when he realized he wasn't going to be able to say individual goodbyes.

Nora: *we said our goodbye. I can't do it again.*

Sutton: **hug emoji* I'll let you know when the coast is clear. We want to see you.*

Andi: *we can bring stuff to you. Stuff equals liquor and chocolate, btw.*

I smile. I have the best girlfriends.

Nora: *no. I'll come to the Rec. I want everyone to see that I'm okay. I don't want everyone to hate him again because he left.*

Thea: *but are you okay?*

Nora: *not really. But I'm happy for him.*

I realize that's true. I want Alex to feel like he belongs somewhere, and if that is coaching for the Grays in the city that has been his only home for the last several years, then that's what I want for him.

It's ridiculous to think that he would have gotten attached to Rebel in the short time he's been here. I'm glad he was starting to feel happier here and developing relationships, but maybe it's better that he left before any of that got deeper.

I turn on my computer in my home office, planning to get some work done before I head down to Perks and Rec.

We have our first game in just a few days. It's not like I don't have plenty to do. I am throwing a crawfish boil for thousands of people, for one thing. I also want to be sure that we have plenty of merchandise on hand. I expect people will be excited to buy T-shirts, stuffed Rougarou and otter toys, and other team merchandise after experiencing this first bonkers hockey game.

I actually manage to get caught up in my work for a couple of hours and when Sutton's text dings on my phone, I'm surprised how quickly the time went.

My stomach dips as I reach for my phone.

That ding means Alex's goodbye is over. And he's gone.

Fuck.

That hurts.

He was here for such a short time. I've lived here all my life. Going back to things as usual, back to my typical routines, living my life without him here should be easy.

But I haven't even stepped a foot out my door and the town feels different knowing he's gone.

Dammit.

I need to reassure the whole town that I am not heartbroken

and that we should all be happy for Alex. I will also need to convince them all, including the players, that Revelers hockey will still be successful even without Alex Olsen.

I feel more confident about that now that I've seen how the videos from the scrimmage spread online and how much fun everyone had.

Still, not having his star power on the roster is definitely a loss.

And I just don't care.

I want Alex to be happy. If the Revelers and the Rascals have a slower build now, we'll just have to deal with it. All we need is people to come see the teams play. People will love it once they experience it.

I'll go to my cousin Dane and beg him to keep the arena if I have to.

We'll campaign extra hard for Harley.

We'll run commercials. We'll take out ads. We'll do a bachelor/bachelorette auction with the players. We can do a calendar. Or maybe we should have them each dance and lip-sync in online videos, and have people vote for their favorites.

I'm still brainstorming ideas to spread the word and get our players out there when I walk into Perks and Rec.

"Nora!"

"Hi, sweetheart!"

"Oh, honey, how are you?"

The place is busier than I expected.

I paste on a smile. "Hi, everyone!" I make my way to the bar and gratefully take the stool between Andi and Everly.

Andi rubs a comforting hand up and down my back, and Everly pushes her half-empty martini glass to me.

The liquid inside is purple. And sparkly.

I look at her with a question, then at my cousin behind the bar.

Violet grins. "I made up a couple of cocktails. That's the Rougarou. Andi's trying the Rascal."

Andi's martini glass is full of something green and sparkly.

Violet continues. "I figure even though you're going to have drinks and food at the arena, people might stop down here before or after a game, and we should have some themed stuff going on here, too. And don't worry, the glitter is edible."

I pick up the martini glass and sip. It's really good. And I don't even care what's in it. I drain the rest of the glass.

All three of the women look at me with raised eyebrows.

"But you're totally okay, right?" Everly asks.

"I am," I nod, glancing around the bar. Everyone here needs not to hate Alex. "I'm so happy for Alex. This is what he wanted all along. Obviously, it happened way sooner than expected, but he'll be a great coach."

"Are you going to fly out there for his game and then back for the first Revelers and Rascals game?" A voice calls. I know that voice. "Or are you going to stay here and go to Portland next week?"

I turn to find Muriel and Patty sitting at one of the tables just a few feet away. The sisters often come in for dinner, despite being among the best cooks in town. They don't like cooking for just one or two, and even more, they like being in the middle of the best spot for gossip and news.

"Oh, I'm not going to Portland," I say, even as my stomach knots.

Muriel frowns. "Why the hell not?"

I reach for Andi's drink, which she surrenders easily. I take a sip of the green sparkly liquid. It's very good too. I give Violet a thumbs up, then say to Muriel, "Alex and I weren't dating for very long. It wasn't that serious. He's gone back to his life in Portland, and obviously, my life is here."

Muriel makes a very unladylike snorting noise as she stabs a sausage, and Patty chuckles.

"What?" I ask, aware that the entire bar is listening.

"It doesn't matter how long you were together. He obviously makes you insanely happy," Muriel says. "You have to go to Portland."

"Well, he could come back here," Patty says. "He was very happy here, too."

I think he really was, and her words make my chest ache. "He was. And he did make me happy, of course," I say, not worried about the admission. It's true. "But this job is exactly what he wants. And it's in Portland. I live here. And long distance is really hard, especially when we're both so busy."

Muriel frowns. "But your life doesn't have to be here."

I straighten. "What? Yes, it does. How can I arrange clubs, festivals, and activities for Rebel if I'm not *in* Rebel?" My heart is pounding, and I'm not sure why.

"But you don't have to do *that* for your life, do you? You could do that somewhere else. Ow!" Muriel frowns at Patty and leans to rub her shin. "Why'd you kick me? I'm just saying she can do clubs and festivals somewhere else."

"But doing them for *Rebel* is what I want to do," I say.

"Why?" Muriel asks. Then she glowers at her sister. "I swear to God, Patty, if you kick me again, I'll dump my grits in your lap."

"Stop being rude. You know that Nora does those things for Rebel, because of…" She trails off, looking a little chagrined. "You know why doing them in Rebel is important."

They know why my job is so important to me? I suppose it wouldn't be hard to figure out. I'm giving back. I'm making my hometown a happier, more connected place. Because I love them. That's obvious. Isn't it? I frown. Something here feels off.

"I do those things for Rebel because of what?" I ask.

Patty looks around. "We shouldn't have butted in."

I almost laugh out loud. It's not as if that has ever stopped anyone before, especially these two.

"She means that we know you do all these things for us because you feel grateful for how everyone has always helped you and your family out, and how you consider us family and that you're taking care of us," Muriel says. She scoops a bite of grits into her mouth.

Well…

She's not wrong.

I do feel grateful. I do consider the things I do helpful to the community.

"Is that so bad?" I ask, my stomach twisting and my heart pounding in my ears.

"Of course not," Patty says.

"It is if it keeps you stuck here," Muriel says at the same time.

They frown at each other.

"I don't feel stuck here," I protest.

Muriel points her fork at me. "Bullshit."

My eyes widen. I look at my friends. No one is jumping in to tell Muriel she's wrong.

I look back at the older woman. "I don't. I love it here."

"But you feel like you can't leave. You think we need you."

I feel a sharp pang as my heart clenches. "You…don't?" I ask.

She shakes her head, either unaware that she's hurting me, or not caring. "Of course not." But then she says, "We don't love you because of the things you do for us, Nora. We love the things you do for us, because we love you."

I stare at her.

The words seem to hang in the air.

No one says anything for several ticks.

Then Patty says, "She's right. We love all of you, because of you. What you do for our community is, we hope, your expression of how you feel about us. Not payback."

I press my lips together and nod. I swallow. "Of course it's because of how I feel about you. I love setting up activities and things that bring us all together and make Rebel more friendly and happy."

Muriel nods. "Good. But you can love us and be loved by us in Portland. You feel like you have to *stay* here because you think you have to pay us back." She looks up from her plate. "And you don't."

I feel a weird twist of emotions go from my chest to my stomach.

"We want you to be happy just like you want us to be happy," Muriel says. "If you're here when we know that you'd be happy with that boy in Portland, we won't be as happy either."

I feel a stinging at the back of my eyes. Finally, I say something I've never said out loud, not even to my friends, and certainly not to my family. But right now, in this moment, I'm going to say it to the whole bar.

"If I leave, you'll be mad at me."

Muriel stops with her fork just in front of her mouth. She looks at me, then sets it down. Patty frowns. I feel my friends shift, leaning in closer to me.

"What are you talking about?" Muriel asks.

I feel Andi's hand on my back again, and I hear Violet set another glass on the bar. I hope it's more of the purple stuff.

But I have more to say first. "I believe you love me. And I'm glad that it's not because of the stuff I do. It's just because of *me*. But...you were mad at my mom when she left. You were mad at Hunter when he left. And my other boyfriends. You were mad at Sean Patrick when he left. We're *still* mad at Sean Patrick even though he came back." I take a breath, then let it out in a long whoosh. "We get mad when people leave us. And look how we treat people we're mad at."

I don't have to point out the straw polls and the protests at the arena or the rollercoaster of ticket sales, all directly due to Alex and the town's feelings about him from one minute to the next.

I also don't add that coming home to Rebel to visit, knowing the town was mad at me, or even just really disappointed, would kill me.

Muriel and Patty exchange a look. Muriel nods at Patty.

Patty looks at me. "Yes. We were mad at your mom. And all of those guys."

I know she knows I mean the whole town, at least our part of the town, when I said 'we', and I know that's what she means now.

I nod.

"But, there were *so* many reasons for that, sweetheart," she says. "Mostly that they hurt you. Especially in your mom's case."

"But they all left to go do something else, something bigger, something they loved."

The ladies nod, but then Muriel says, "Each case was different. But the truth is, we are not going to be mad at *you* if you leave with Alex."

I don't know if I believe her.

Maybe she and Patty won't, but Muriel and Patty march to their own drummers anyway. My friends and family won't be mad. Maybe. I don't know how Bruce and Harley will feel, actually. I owe them so much. And my friends? They might not get angry, but how can I go through a week, not to mention my *life*, without seeing them every day?

"Besides, Alex is different from all of those guys," Muriel says. "We wouldn't have encouraged you to go with any of them. They weren't worth it."

"You think he is?" I ask, my heart squeezing as I think about him. How am I going to not see *him* every day? Dammit, how did that grumpy, spoiled hockey player get so under my skin so quickly?

"I do," Patty says with a smile.

"And obviously you do too," Muriel says.

"How do you know?" I ask.

"You left garden club *and* otter club for him."

I did.

I'd thought leaving otter club early was a first, but that's not true.

I did leave garden club early the day I picked him up from the airport. Of course, that was before I really knew him. I left garden club early for the hockey player.

But I left otter club early for the man.

CHAPTER 32
NORA

I SLEEP like crap that night and awaken the next morning way before my alarm.

I give up and get out of bed and into the shower.

My friends hadn't wanted me to come home alone last night, but I'd finally convinced them I was fine to be alone, and they'd settled for each texting me three times before I went to bed.

At least it kept me from texting Alex.

Well, it kept me from *sending* any texts to Alex.

I wrote four, but deleted them without sending.

I really wanted to call him.

But what would I say?

I couldn't stop thinking about what Muriel and Patty said, but I also couldn't shake the feeling that Rebel wouldn't forgive me for leaving.

Most of all, though, I couldn't stop missing Alex.

I decided to have an impromptu activity today to remind myself why I love my job and this town so much.

I sat at my computer for two hours putting together a pre-game party in the parking lot of the arena. Everyone can come and learn the lyrics to the songs the team might sing and dance to on Friday, along with basic dance steps and arm movements they can do in the stands. I'm also going to have a sneak peek at merchandise, and they can sample both the alcoholic and non-alcoholic versions of the Swamp Water, the Rougarou Bites, a sweet snack mix, and the savory snack mix we're calling Rascal Kibble.

It will get everyone ready for the fun on Friday. And it will take my mind off of...everything else.

I finally head into Perks and Rec for much-needed food and caffeine.

"'Morning, Nora!"

"Hi, Nora!"

"Good to see you, Nora!"

"Good morning, everyone," I return with a smile.

At least, I try to smile.

I move behind the counter to start making a latte. Bruce emerges through the swinging doors, laden with plates.

He simply asks, "Yogurt or pancakes?" Which is his way of asking how bad I'm feeling this morning.

"Pancakes. Bacon. No potatoes." In other words, pretty bad, but not quite stuffed French toast bad.

He doesn't seem surprised by *that*.

I'm hoping Andi and Everly will be in soon, but I'm on my own at the counter for now. I stupidly start scrolling through social media, checking the hockey accounts I follow. It's work, I tell myself, but I'm lying. I'm searching for Alex's name.

And it's there.

Already.

They're reporting on his return to Portland, praising Declan's smart move, and the replies indicate the fans are excited.

I'm glad.

For him.

For me...

I start to type in *Parks and Recreation department Portland*.

The door opens, and I look over out of habit. Then I straighten when I realize who just walked in.

Astrid Olsen is crossing the shop toward me.

Have I ever seen Astrid in Perks and Rec? Maybe. But not regularly.

"Mornin', Astrid," Bruce greets as he brings out more plates from the kitchen and steps past the counter.

"Good morning, Bruce."

She takes the seat next to me, and I can't help but let my gaze run over her from head to toe. I have only ever seen her in pantsuits or skirts. She always looks like a kick ass corporate boss lady.

Right now, she's in soft-looking pale blue capri pants, an oversized rose colored sweatshirt that falls off one shoulder, and sandals that lace around her ankles. She's got multiple ankle bracelets and toe rings on. And I note the tattoo at the base of her right pinky toe. Her toenails are also painted a bright blue color.

Her usually loose, wavy hair is now in one braid that lays over one shoulder and she has no makeup on.

Not only does she look nothing like the pseudo-famous sports star and billionaire owner of our hockey team, but she'd also likely get carded at the door of most bars in New Orleans looking like this.

She notices the way I'm studying her. She grins. "Yoga, meditation, tea ritual all before I pretend to like offices and heels."

"You *don't* like offices and heels?"

She wrinkles her nose. "No. I prefer to be barefoot and outside."

"So what's with the pantsuits and, you know, the office?"

"I own a small corporation now," she says with a shrug. "And I'm kind of in the middle of a… sociological experiment. If you *look* a certain way, and based on that, people expect you to *act* a certain way, are they more or less frustrated when you *don't* do things the way they want you to?"

I study her face. "By 'people' do you mean your husband?" I ask. For some reason. It's none of my business, and I'm not sure why that's my guess anyway. I suppose little hints I've picked up, like when she noted to Alex that Declan would hate her office at the arena, and she seemed delighted by that prospect.

She looks surprised for a moment, but then she nods. "Yes, actually."

"And do you want him to be more or less frustrated with how you act compared to what he expects?" I ask.

"So do you have everything?" Bruce asks as he comes back to the counter.

"I do," she says, seemingly grateful to be interrupted.

Dammit.

I like Astrid so much, and I do consider her a friend, but we're not as close as I am with Andi, Sutton, and Everly. I could force any of them to tell me what's going on. I'm not quite there with Astrid.

But we'll get there. I have no doubt. You don't live in Rebel, Louisiana, long before you just give in to having people up in all your business. Resistance is futile.

She pulls a long envelope out of her bag and hands it to Bruce. "Tickets, and other general info. A car will pick you up at the airport and take you to my place."

"Your place?" Bruce asks.

"I've lived in Portland for a few years. I kept the apartment. It's been thoroughly cleaned, and there's a master bedroom and a guest room. I had them stock the kitchen. Make yourself at home. The car will also take you from the apartment to the arena. I was going to put you in the owner's box, and I can still change that, but I assumed you'd want to be down with the fans and closer to the ice."

"Of course," Bruce agrees. "This is wonderful. Thank you."

"Any time."

I'm looking back and forth between them as if I'm watching a tennis match. "What's going on?"

"Harley, Leo, Ruth, and I are going to the Grays game tomorrow night."

My heart skips at the mention of the Grays.

"*What*? But…why?"

"Alex needs some friends there for support."

"But…" I look at Astrid "He's back in the city where he's lived for years. That city loves him. And he's got all of his teammates and the other coaches," I point out.

Bruce nods. "Like I said, he needs some *friends* there."

I study my grandfather. He just looks back at me, his expression calm and confident.

"I thought you didn't like him."

"I changed my mind."

"You still gave him a hard time."

"I had to be sure he could grow up and fit in here. If he can't take a little heat, then he's not the one."

"And he passed?"

"More than."

I feel my throat tighten. Alex won Bruce over. That's no small thing.

"We have another ticket," Bruce says casually. "If you want to come along."

"But you'll have to stay somewhere else," Astrid interjects. "There are only two beds at my place, and the couch sucks to sleep on." She gives me a smile. "I'm sure we can find you a place, though."

"I…"

I want to *so* much. But will that just make this pain worse? Is saying goodbye over and over again just torturing us both?

"Before you answer, you should also know, we're going to leave you there," Bruce says.

I open my mouth, then shut it, then frown. "*What*?"

"You're going to stay in Portland with Alex," Bruce says.

I feel my eyes fill with tears. I start shaking my head. "I…can't."

"You can," he says. His tone is firm but gentle.

"But…Rebel…"

He points to the front of the register

There are two mason jars there. One has a sticky note on it that says YES. The other says NO. The sign behind them says *Should Nora go to Portland to be with Alex?*

The YES jar is overflowing. There isn't even a single dollar in the NO jar.

I look up at my grandfather.

"You've spent so much time and energy making us all happy," he says, his voice gentle. "That's all we want for you, honey. We love you. Enough to let you go so you can be the happiest you can possibly be."

"You think that's in Portland?" I ask softly.

"I think it's with Alex," he corrects.

"And…" I look at the jars again. "I can come home and visit, and everyone will be happy to see me?"

"Thrilled," he says, nodding, his voice sounding a little scratchy. He clears his throat. "That's not to say we won't be doing straw polls and judging things like his proposal and what you two name your cats."

I laugh even as emotions clog my throat.

"So that's five for the flight later today?" Astrid asks with a smile.

I sniff and nod. "Yeah."

The coffee shop erupts with cheers and applause.

I turn to face everyone, laughing even as a tear tracks down my cheek. I swipe it away. God, I love these crazy, nosy people.

Astrid leans over and gives me a one-armed hug. "Thank you," she says.

I look at her. "For what?"

"For falling for my brother. Not the hockey player. The guy."

And another tear tracks down my cheek as I hug her back. "He made it impossible not to."

CHAPTER 33
ALEX

I AM SO FUCKED.

Everyone in Portland that I have seen is thrilled I'm back.

Practice yesterday went great. Everyone wanted to talk about Coach Leon, of course, and our head coach let everybody get their questions and gossip out of the way before we hit the ice. More information has come out in the news, so the story is less of a mystery. It sounds like Coach Leon will be doing time.

According to the local news and sports shows, Portland fans are happy I'm back.

Declan called me into his office and told me the same. He also told me he was impressed with what we'd done so far with the Revelers. I don't even ask how he knows about the behind-the-scenes in Louisiana. I doubt it's from Astrid directly, but Astrid tells her friend Miles everything, and it wouldn't surprise me if Miles tells Iris, who tells Declan. Or Miles might tell Declan directly. Or hell, Declan might hack into Astrid's computers and phones. He's got the money to pay the best hackers. Of course, he'd better sleep with one eye open if my sister ever finds out.

So, I'm back in my city, involved with hockey, and working for my team again. Everyone here likes me. Things are going exactly according to my plans.

But I'm fucked.

Because I miss Rebel, Louisiana.

I'm going to miss the Revelers' first game, and I am actually sad about that.

Ruth and I have agreed that she'll call me during the game and let me watch via video call on her phone, but I've been on my sister's ass about getting a live stream going by tomorrow night.

She told me she's on top of it, then sent me three middle-finger emojis.

I have also typed and deleted eight or nine messages to Nora.

A couple were flirty, a couple were casual, a couple were very emotional.

I don't know what to say to her.

Or, more accurately, I have *a lot* to say to her. But I don't think I should say any of it.

She's going to stay in Rebel. Of course she is. There's no way I could take that girl out of that town. They need her, but even more than that, she's happy there. At home. And I know she appreciates that, but she doesn't even know how great she's got it.

Portland would never feel like home, not the way Rebel is. Portland would love her, but not the way Rebel loves her.

"Nervous about tonight?" Brantley Wilkins slaps me on the back as he walks past me in the locker room.

"Just a lot on my mind."

I rarely got nervous before games anyway, but tonight feels completely different. I'm not the one on the ice. I won't be taking the shots or the hits. I'll be sitting on the bench.

It only took me one practice to realize this isn't what I want.

I'd probably be okay at coaching. I know the game inside and out. I'm someone others listen to. I can recognize when someone needs to make an adjustment and I can help them do that. But well, some guys just know that coaching is in their blood, and I don't think it's in mine. It's a killer to just stand on the side and watch other people play the game.

I want to be in on the action.

Even if the action occasionally includes wiffle balls, lip syncing, and high kicks.

I'm so *fucked*.

I'm going to have to walk into Declan's office after the game tonight and tell him that I'm quitting. Because I'm going back to Rebel.

I woke up this morning and knew exactly what I was going to do today. I knew what to wear, I knew what I was going to eat, and I had a car pick me up and take me where I needed to go. There were no mason jars anywhere, claiming that Brussels sprouts or raisins are better than I am.

And it all felt wrong.

"Wilkins," I say from where I'm leaning against the wall, waiting to go out to the bench.

"Yeah?" Then he chuckles. "I don't know what to call you. I mean, obviously I should call you coach, but that feels weird."

I nod. It feels weird to me too. "Call me what you always have." There's no sense in them getting used to calling me 'coach'.

"Okay, Olsen, what's up?" he asks.

"What's your favorite movie?"

This obviously surprises him. "Huh, I don't know. I really like *Ferris Bueller's Day Off*."

Solid choice, I guess. It's a fun one.

"Why, what's yours?" he asks.

A month ago, I would've told him *The Dark Knight*, but today I say, "*Monsters, Inc.*"

He chuckles as do the other guys listening in.

"Isn't that a cartoon?" Max Carson asks.

I nod. "Yep."

"Yeah, with the big green monster, right?"

"The big monster is blue. The little round one is green."

He laughs and nods. "Right. You like that one best of all? Of all movies?"

"I do. Makes me smile. It's got a good message too."

Ivan Kozlov pipes up. "Watched it with my nephew," he says. "It's good."

"Yeah? Did you get the message?" Max asks.

"That we shouldn't be so afraid. You just picture the things that scare you as cartoon monsters. Then you're not so afraid anymore."

I think that over. Okay, I guess that could be one interpretation.

Wilkins nods and then looks at me. "I like that. Thanks, Coach."

I laugh. I had absolutely zero to do with any of that.

"Let's go!" Coach Blake yells, and everyone heads for the door.

I bring up the rear, finding my place with the other assistants in the bench area. I'm able to lose myself in the game for several minutes, but I find myself scanning the crowd during a media timeout.

I freeze as my gaze finds a small group of fans directly across from our bench.

I feel like all of the air has been sucked out of my lungs.

Bruce, Harley, Leo, and Ruth are sitting right next to the ice, wearing Revelers jerseys, and holding up signs that say, "Go, Alex!" and "Rebel, Louisiana, says hi!" with a huge face of Rougie the mascot.

My heart squeezes hard in my chest, and I am hit by a wave of nostalgia unlike any I've had before.

Then Ruth lowers her sign, and I see who's sitting right next to her. My favorite person in the world. Chaos and sunshine in one little package. And she's wearing her bright yellow overalls over her jersey.

The love of my life, Nora Delaune, came to Portland after all.

The shock wears off quickly. They all came for me. And everything about that feels right.

I pull my phone out and text a member of the PR team. *Need a huge favor.*

Her name is Sydney and she replies after only a few seconds. *Will the fans love it?*

Alex: *So fucking much. Promise.*

Sydney: *I'll be right down.*

I tell her my plan and she lights up. "That's *so* good, Alex," she gushes. "Yes, I can definitely set that up."

"Great. Thanks."

She rushes off to get everything ready for the first intermission.

I pull my phone out again and text the next person who I need to get up to speed.

Alex: *Thanks for the chance, but I quit.*

Declan: *Dammit, Alex.*

I just grin.

Then I notice movement across the ice. Sydney is talking to Nora. Nora asks her something. Sydney nods. Nora shakes her head. Sydney nods again, then motions for Nora to follow her. Ruth, Bruce, Leo, and Harley start encouraging her and finally Nora gets to her feet.

She glances in my direction, and I pretend to be watching the game.

I probably should be doing that anyway. I am coaching right now, after all.

But nothing else matters. Nora is here, and we are not doing a long-distance relationship.

We're also not not doing a relationship.

Finally, it's intermission and the team files into the locker room. We're up by two, and everyone is playing well, so it's going to be relatively low-key in there.

"Hey, Coach," I say to our head coach. "I have something I need to take care of."

He nods. "Fine."

I head back out, but take one of the tunnels saved for arena staff. I lurk at the end, watching Sydney's intermission event. She's out at center ice with two women.

"Hey, Grays fans! We're so happy to be back in this arena with our Grays on the ice, aren't we?" Sydney asks into the mic she's holding.

The fans cheer loudly.

"Well, we've got a super fun contest for this first intermission! I want you to all help me welcome two Grays fans. This is Becky!"

The fans cheer as the blonde in a Grays' jersey with our goalie's name and number on it waves.

"And this is Nora!"

Nora, in her yellow overalls, also waves as the fans cheer. She looks out of place with her purple, gold, and green jersey, though.

"Okay, ladies, so I haven't told you what you're going to be doing, right?" Sydney asks.

They both shake their heads.

"Well, let me tell you the *prize* you're playing for first!" she says with a laugh. "The winner gets a movie night date with none other than one of the Grays' favorite players-now-coach *Alex Olsen!*"

The crowd goes wild. The cheering and screaming is loud and long.

But I don't look at anyone but Nora.

Her eyes are wide, and her whole body is suddenly tense.

I grin.

She doesn't like the idea of another woman winning a date with me. I'd bet a thousand dollars on it.

"I know!" Sydney says to the crowd. "And it's a movie night date in an undisclosed location!"

More cheering.

Nora is now glancing around.

I'd also bet she's looking for me. And I'd bet that images of the park in Rebel are going through her mind.

"And all you have to do to win is be the best at lip syncing and dancing to the song we give you!" Sydney says. She laughs. "We're going to let the fans decide who does it best, so be sure to bring your best performance."

I burst out laughing at the look on Nora's face now. They have the three women up on the jumbotron, and she looks part horrified and part I'm-going-to-kill-him, with maybe a dash of okay-that's-pretty-funny.

I'm completely in love with her.

She's absolutely going to win.

Sydney's been instructed to claim Nora's the winner even if Bruce, Harley, Leo, and Ruth are the only people who cheer for her.

But am I going to make her lip sync and dance on the ice in front of an arena full of hockey fans first?

Oh, I most definitely am.

"You ready, ladies?" Sydney asks.

"Totally!" Becky says.

"I am," Nora says. Much less enthusiastically.

Becky goes first. She lip-syncs the first two verses of "Girls Just Want to Have Fun." She does *very* well and gets loud applause.

But when the jumbotron focuses in on Nora's face, her expression is pure determination.

I love it.

She is *not* going to let another woman win time with me.

Okay, Wildflower, bring it.

I also chose her song. I prop a shoulder against the wall, tuck my hands into my pockets, and settle in to watch.

As Sydney talks to the crowd and hypes up the second contestant, Nora scans the area and, just as Sydney hands her the microphone, she finds me.

Our eyes lock. I grin. Her eyes narrow.

And she starts to lip sync without looking at the lyrics they're scrolling on the screen for her.

Elvis's "Can't Help Falling in Love" never sounded so good.

She does just one verse.

I start walking toward her before she's even finished.

I'm only a step away when she tosses the mic to Syndey and jumps into my arms.

I catch her, just like I did at the airport. This time, though, I'm not holding a bag. And I'm ready.

I crush her against my chest. "I love you, Wildflower," I say against her ear.

"I love you too," she says against my throat. "So much. I'm here. I'm staying. I left Rebel."

I'm vaguely aware that the arena is losing its mind and Sydney is saying something about how she supposes this means Nora wins, but all I can really focus on is what Nora just said.

I reach up and cup the back of her head, tugging gently on her hair. She tips her head back.

"What did you say?"

"I left Rebel. I want to be with you. I'm moving to Portland."

"You…don't leave home."

"Because I never had a good enough reason before. Now I do."

I feel my heart squeezing so tight I almost can't breathe. "No," I say simply.

Her brows go up. "What?"

"No. I love you, and I want to be with you, but not here. *We* are going back to Rebel."

She shakes her head. "No, really. I'm good. I'm good here."

"As much as that thrills me, you don't belong here. And I don't belong here anymore either. Because we belong in Rebel, Wildflower. We belong at home."

She sucks in a breath, and her eyes fill with tears. "Home?"

I squeeze her. "Yeah. Home. I love you so much. And Rebel needs you. I need you. And… I need Rebel."

Her big brown eyes are even bigger than usual. "Really?"

"Of course, really. I'm an ex-hockey player turned coach here. In Rebel, I'm Alex. A guy who loves bananas and *Monsters, Inc.* and that crazy town, and their amazing Parks and Rec director, and who also happens to slap a puck around the ice sometimes."

She slides down my body, but stands, smiling up at me so brightly I have to blink twice. "You'd rather play hockey in Rebel than coach in the pros? Really?"

I laugh. "I still don't know that we should call that *hockey*."

She grins. "Okay, fine. Bonkers hockey."

I nod. "Yes. I'd rather play bonkers hockey."

She laughs, her eyes shining with tears. But she shakes her head. "Thank you for that. I love that. But what you're doing here is important. This is *big*, Alex. Declan needs you. The Grays need you. Portland needs you. I'll move here. It's okay. We can be together here."

I'm frowning as I cup her face and look directly into her eyes. I need to be sure she hears this clearly.

"Nora, this is just hockey. What *you* do is important. Far more important than me coaching here. Anyone can do this job."

She tries to shake her head, but I'm holding her too firmly. I smile. "Okay, not *anyone*, but a lot of people. Declan will find someone else. But no one else can do what you do, the way you do it. You make *people* better, Nora. You make *hearts* better. Jesus, that's the most important thing. And I want that too. I want to be with you *in Rebel*. Please." I lower my head until my mouth is just above hers. "I want a front row seat for all the things you do. I want to come to movie night, I want to help set up for all your festivals, and I want to pick wildflowers with you. *Please* let me live in Rebel with you."

It takes a second, but it finally sinks in, and she laughs as a tear slips down her cheek. "You're actually begging to come back to Rebel?"

"I am," I say sincerely. "I *need* more Otter Club, Nora."

She laughs again and hugs me tightly, pressing her face to my neck.

"And…" I say.

She pulls back and looks up expectantly. "And?"

"I think we can call *this* love now, right?"

She nods quickly. "Definitely."

Then I dip her back and kiss her right there at center ice.

CHAPTER 34
NORA

WE SPENT the night in Portland, and Alex introduced me to his extra-large, very luxurious shower. Also his extra large, very luxurious bed. But he was anxious to get back to Rebel so we boarded Declan's plane late morning and we're back in Louisiana in plenty of time for Alex to get ready for the Revelers first game.

We had thought about trying to keep his return a surprise for everyone, making a big dramatic moment out of him skating on the ice, but it is impossible to keep secrets in Rebel, so instead, Alex and Beckett showed Sam the Sportsman around town and accompanied him to his first crawfish boil. Which he loved, by the way.

Everything was a rousing success.

It turned out that I don't actually have to be physically present in Rebel every hour of the day for fun and frivolity to reign. My friends made sure that every single detail was triple checked, and not only was there enough crawfish for everyone, but Sutton had even taught everyone the lyrics and basic choreography so they could sing and dance in the stands along with the teams.

It was some of the most fun I had ever had, and I spent most of the evening in tears.

Happy tears.

"That's Declan O'Grady, right?" Andi asks, her attention on the owner's box.

"Yep," I confirm.

"Who are those people with him?"

"The woman is Iris Lee, she's his…assistant, I guess? Friend. Bodyguard."

"Bodyguard?" Everly asks, brows up. "Wow."

I shrug. "Yeah. And the guy is Miles Stafford. He's Astrid's best friend and physical therapist."

"Oh yeah, I read about him," Everly said. "So they just hopped on the plane with you."

"Well, it's Declan's plane," I point out with a laugh.

"Right."

"They're very nice. I mean Iris and Miles are. Declan is…"

"Fucking hot," Everly says.

"Rich as fuck," Andi adds.

I nod. "Yes. Those. Also intimidating. And quiet."

"He's not sitting with Astrid," Andi points out.

"I think it's that Astrid isn't sitting with him," I say, glancing at our gorgeous owner, who's sitting on the other side of Ruth and Thea, in the first row with us, straight across from the benches.

"Alex is aware that if he gets another penalty, he's going to have to lip-synch all by himself, right?" Everly asks.

"Uh…probably," I say, my eyes on the man who seems to actually be having the time of his life.

I'm not at all sure he knows what happens on his next penalty. It's possible that Alex has just said fuck it and given up on trying to keep track of the rules and regulations of bonkers hockey.

It would be a definite moment of growth, of course, but he may have just decided to roll with it and do whatever they tell him when it's time. He's already smiling, laughing, and dancing with energy, which is a huge change.

That doesn't mean he's dancing *well*. He's just doing it energetically.

"It seems to me like he's *trying* to get another penalty," Sutton says. She looks at me. "Maybe he *wants* to lip-synch by himself."

I laugh. "There is no way Alex Olsen wants to lip-sync solo. I promise you."

Alex skates up to Zeke Landry and throws an elbow. Zeke jerks back, almost comically, then falls to the ice.

"That was the fakest thing I have ever seen," Ruth says.

"I thought you guys choreographed fights," Everly says to Sutton.

"We have. And they're way better than that. That is so obvious. I don't think Alex even touched him."

It doesn't seem to matter. The referee skates up, blows his whistle, and indicates that Alex just received a second penalty.

"Well, you know what that means, fans," I say into the microphone. "Time for another vote. Should Alex go sit on the bench and wear the giant crown that says Penalty King for four minutes, or are we gonna let him lip-synch for one minute and come back into the game?"

People immediately start voting on their phones, and within seconds, it's obvious that everyone wants to see the big grumpy center at center ice, lip-syncing.

"Looks like someone needs to get that man a microphone," I say.

Even though it's lip-syncing, we have a giant plastic microphone for the guys to use.

Instead, however, I see Rougie, our mascot, skate out with what looks like a real microphone. That's confirmed when Alex switches it on.

"Oh my God, he's actually going to sing," Andi says.

I'm frowning. "Why would he do that?"

As far as I know, Alex hates lip syncing, but obviously, he would hate singing even more.

Still, I do my part. "Okay, everyone, there's a multiple-choice in the app. Pick which song you'd like to see Alex perform."

But when I look down, no one is voting.

I frown and look up quickly. "Is the app not working?" I ask Sutton.

She grins and points.

Alex is at center ice in the middle of the spotlight. The music starts.

And he starts to sing. No lip syncing, and it's not one of the choices in the app.

It's Elvis's "Can't Help Falling in Love.

And he sings it perfectly. Beautifully. Like beautifully enough that I'm hot and tingly and my panties are wet by the time he's done.

Because his eyes never leave me the entire time.

It was one thing for us to goof around and then for him to kiss me at center ice in Portland. There are kiss cams and all kinds of things that happen in professional hockey arenas. It was funny, and most of the people in the stands really had no idea who I was. They probably thought the whole thing was a PR stunt or something.

Here, that is not the case. Everyone knows who I am. Everyone knows who Alex is.

And they just found out today that he has given up a professional coaching job to stay with all of us in Rebel.

It looks like he's adding an exclamation point to the end of that announcement.

And Alex Olsen doesn't use exclamation points.

When he's finished, the crowd literally goes wild.

There's cheering, applause, clapping, and stomping.

And I am madly, deeply in love.

"Oh my God," Andi says. "You know that people are going to be asking him to run for mayor after Harley's next terms up."

I laugh. "He just moved here. A week ago, people were voting for Brussels sprouts instead of him."

She nods. "That's my point. The guy turned the entire town around in their opinion of him so fast. I wonder if there's anything he can't do."

With his penalty taken care of, the other players have returned to the ice, and play has started up again.

But whistles are blowing shrilly.

Players and referees are all crowded together at one end of the ice, and when they part, we see that they are pulling Beckett and Lawson off of one another.

Sutton sighs. "There might be one thing he can't do—make my brother and Lawson get along."

Everly looks at Sutton with one brow up. "Well, that's the trouble with bad boys."

Sutton shakes her head. "What do you mean?"

"You just can't totally take the bad out of them... nor would you want to. No matter what your brother says."

I take in Everly's sly grin, then study Sutton.

She doesn't say anything. Her gaze is locked on the ice. And I don't think she's raptly fascinated by her brother.

I find Alex where he's standing between Beckett and Lawson, looking frustrated.

Now *there's* the Alex Olsen I know and love.

Oh, who am I kidding? I love all versions of Alex Olsen.

Beckett lunges toward Lawson again, and Alex throws up his hand, bracing it against Beckett's chest. He says something to him, then something to Lawson.

"Should we think about putting them on separate teams?" I ask Astrid.

She looks at me with wide eyes. "Absolutely not. This drama is part of the fun."

I chuckle and shake my head. "I wish I knew what the problem was."

"I, uh..."

We all look over at Sutton. Her cheeks are pink when she finally meets my eyes.

"So, it's kind of a long, embarrassing story but..."

"But *what*?" Everly asks when Sutton pauses.

Sutton grimaces. "I'm pretty sure this is my fault."

We all turn to face her as one unit.

"What is?" I ask.

"I mean… they definitely already didn't get along," Sutton says. "But…things between Beckett and Lawson are worse now." She sighs. "And I think it's because of me."

"Go on," Andi says.

Sutton looks from me to Andi to Everly to Thea to Astrid, then back to me. "I can't look at you when I say this." She covers her eyes with one hand. "I, um…might have written down something that…um…indicated that I kind-of, maybe, was thinking that… Lawson would be…um…a good person to, uh, ask to…um… teach me about sex."

She rushes through those last four words, but even with the hockey game noise, we hear what she says clearly enough.

I feel my eyes widen. I *see* everyone else's eyes widen.

Then she drops her hand, takes a breath, and says, "And Beckett read it."

My mouth drops open.

Andi's too.

Thea gasps.

Ruth is, thankfully, engrossed in the game.

Everly grins and pats Sutton on the back. "Oh, yeah, this is definitely your fault."

I turn and look back at the ice.

I'm going to have to fill Alex in. He should know why he has to pull Lawson and Beckett apart constantly.

And why it might get worse.

He's definitely going to grumble and roll his eyes when he hears this.

But I feel my grin slowly spread as the time ticks down to the first intermission and I see Rougie and Rascal, the mascots getting ready to skate onto the ice with giant inflatable hockey sticks, remember that the Zamboni is decorated like a Mardi Gras float, scan the crowd and see people eating purple, green, and yellow popcorn, and drinking cups of Swamp Water.

The seats are filled with people who I usually see at club meetings and town festivities. I find the section where Harley, Leo, Wilson, Brewser, and Bruce are sitting. They're clearly having a wonderful time. Leo is holding the WELCOME ALEX OLSEN sign that they had been carrying at the airport when they'd gone to pick Alex up, but they crossed out the LCOME and turned it into LOVE so the sign now reads WELOVE ALEX OLSEN. I love them so much.

Muriel and Patty are sitting three rows up behind the players' benches. Patty is dressed in the Rascals' colors of green, black, and silver. Muriel is in Revelers' purple, gold, and green. She also recycled a sign. The protest sign that once said "Go Home Alex Olsen" now reads, "Welcome Home, Alex Olsen!"

My eyes well up, *again*, with happy tears.

It's all wonderful, fun, and happy.

And yes, bonkers.

In other words, it's perfect.

❦

Thank you so much for reading **Just Don't Call It Love**! *I hope you loved Nora and Alex's story!*

Want more? I've got a **bonus epilogue** for you right here!
geni.us/Call-It-Love-EPILOGUE
(be sure you get those capital letters and dashes in there!)

And there's so much more to come from Rebel!
Next up its Astrid and Declan's book!
My ~~Hockey~~ Husband Problem!

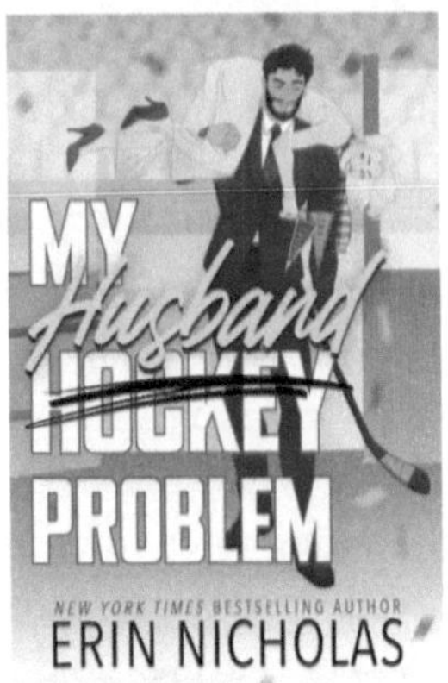

Be sure you're signed up for emails from me right here for first looks and release news!

bit.ly/Keep-In-Touch-Erin

(be sure you get those capital letters and dashes in there!)

And join my **Super Fan page on Facebook** for daily chitchat, behind-the-scenes peeks, first looks, and fun with other Erin Nicholas and Rebel Revelers fans! Just search for Erin Nicholas Super Fans to find the group!

PLAYER ROSTER & CAST OF CHARACTERS

The Revelers

Alex Olsen- Center #14
Beckett Moore- Right Wing #11
Ingrid Archer- Left Wing
Lawson Landry- Defenseman #4
Teddy Rochester- Defenseman
Wes Franklin- Goalie

The Rascals
Quinn Trahan- Center
Zeke Landry- Right Wing
Unnamed (so far)- Left Wing
Josh (JD) Evans- Defenseman
Unnamed (so far)- Defenseman
Hudson Duval- Goalie

The rest of the cast!

Astrid Olsen (O'Grady)- Revelers and Rascals team owner. Alex's younger sister. Married to Declan O'Grady.

Declan O'Grady- Billionaire. Astrid's husband. Owner of Alex's pro team, the Portland Grays.

Harley Delaune- Nora's grandfather. Mayor of Rebel.

Bruce Delaune- Nora's grandfather. Married to Harley.

Leo Landry- one of Harley's best friends and his brother-in-law. Married to Harley's sister, Ellie. Lives in Autre, Louisiana.

William "Wilson" Bienvenu- One of Harley's best friends. Retired lawyer.

Thurman "Brewser" Lafitte- One of Harley's best friends. Retired doctor.

Anderson (Andi) Fleury- one of Nora's besties. Artist. Beckett's crush.

Sutton Moore- One of Nora's besties. Beckett's sister. Dancer, team choreographer. Parks and Rec dept assistant.

Everly Levette- One of Nora's besties. Landscaper.

Dane Delaune- Nora's cousin. Local billionaire. Owns most of the town, including the hockey arena.

Thea Chabert- Nora's cousin. PT. Ruth's mom. Married to Josh.

Ruth Chabert- Thea's daughter. Nora's cousin.

IF YOU LOVE REBEL, LOUISIANA

Want to know more about Alex's family and the royals of Cara?

The Royals Gone Rogue are all available now!

Reluctantly Royal (Torin O'Grady and Abigail Landry)

Reluctantly Rogue (Jonah and Linnea)

Rags to Royals (Cian and Scarlett)

Recklessly Rogue (Henry and Ruby)

If you love Rebel, you're going to love Autre just as much!

Check out the Boys of the Bayou and the Boys of the Bayou Gone Wild!
All available now!

Boys of the Bayou

My Best Friend's Mardi Gras Wedding (Josh & Tori)

Sweet Home Louisiana (Owen & Maddie)

Beauty and the Bayou (Sawyer & Juliet)

Crazy Rich Cajuns (Bennett & Kennedy)

Must Love Alligators (Chase & Bailey)

Four Weddings and a Swamp Boat Tour (Mitch & Paige)

Boys of the Bayou Gone Wild

Otterly Irresistible (Charlie& Griffin)

Heavy Petting (Fletcher & Jordan)

Flipping Love You (Zeke & Jill)

Sealed With a Kiss (Donovan & Naomi)

Head Over Hooves (Drew & Rory)

Say It Like You Mane It (Zander & Caroline)

Kiss My Giraffe (Knox & Fiona)

Better Safe Than Safari (Colin & Hayden)

And much more—

including my printable booklist— at

ErinNicholas.com

ACKNOWLEDGMENTS

A huge thank you to Becky, Jenn, Lindsey, and Heather for that very first brainstorming call about bonkers hockey! You helped fan that spark into a flame and it never went out! I hope it turned out as fun as you imagined it!

And to the whole Buzzing About Romance crew! You were there for alpha, beta, cover questions, taglines...everything! Thank you!

Also a hug, a cookie and teary thank you to Becky, the other Erin, and the other Lindsey ;) for always saying the right things the way I need to hear them. I couldn't do this without you!

Jen, Becky, Lindsey, and Amanda, thank you for the best beta reads! And to Fedora, Cindy, and Jenn who always make me look good!

As always, to my family—my mom who is my most loyal and enthusiastic reader (I never believe it's good until I get your text!), my husband who is my biggest fan in general (even that one chicken dish that I seriously need to just stop making), my kids who are my biggest cheerleaders (your pep talks are the BEST xoxo), and my sister who always says yes to research trips, outings, and "hey would you..." (and my accountant who has never said no to any of those write offs...yet), I love you all SO much! None of this would mean anything without you!

And to all of my bayou world fans... thank you for taking another trip with me! I _love_ how much you love these people and stories in this world. You have no idea. It means everything to me! You are *otterly* the best!

ABOUT ERIN

Lover of coffee, cats, cookies, and other c-words (also tacos) **Erin Nicholas is the NYT and USA Today bestselling author** of over sixty romances.

If you want to have a latte, and chat about all things New Orleans, anything Schitt's Creek, or socializing stray cats, she's your girl. And, of course, if you love rom coms with swoony heroes who fall hard, amazing found families, and quirky small towns. She lives in the middle of the US with her husband and too many cats (his opinion, not hers).

Find her and all her books at
www.ErinNicholas.com

And find her on Facebook, BookBub, Goodreads, and Instagram!

Digital ISBN:978-1-967534-08-1

Print ISBN: 978-1-967534-18-0

Editor: Lindsey Faber

Cover design: Qamber Designs

Cover Photography: Wander Aguiar